THE OLD

FACTORY

THE OLD FACTORY

By William Bury Westall
(1834 – 1903)

REWORD PUBLISHERS

2000

REWORD PUBLISHERS
3 Syddal Crescent
Bramhall
Cheshire SK7 1HS

First published 1885
by
Cassell & Co. Ltd

This edition
Edited by
Roy Westall

ISBN 0 9536743 2 0

Printed and bound by
PROPRINT
Stibbington
Cambs.

**THIS BOOK IS DECICATED
TO
ALL THE LANCASHIRE
WESTALLS**

ABOUT REWORD PUBLISHERS

Reword Publishers was founded in 1999 to promote a wider interest in local history. We publish books on local history, historical novels, and reprints of books originally published prior to the twentieth century.

Other books recently published by Reword Publishers include:

STOCKPORT – A Pictorial History (ISBN 0 9536743 0 4)

CIRCUMCISION BY APPOINTMENT - A view of life in and around Manchester during the Eighteenth Century.
(ISBN 0 9536743 1 2)

If you are interested in purchasing any of our other books or becoming one of our authors, then please write to us at the address above.

ABOUT THE AUTHOR

William Bury Westall was born in Oswaldtwistle, Lancashire in 1834, the son of a cotton mill owner ('The Old Mill' in the novel). Following the death of his father John in 1851, the family firm continued under the guidance of the author's two brothers, whilst William, preferring the life of a writer and traveller, devoted himself to journalism.

Moving to Geneva in 1874, William Bury Westall became the foreign correspondent for both the "The Times' and the 'Daily News', and later editor of the 'Swiss Times', of which he became part proprietor. His first book 'Tales and Traditions of Saxony and Lusatia, appeared in 1877, but his earliest success in fiction, 'The Old Factory, described as a story of Lancashire life with strong local colouring, was issued in 1885.

The author became a British Consul in Russia and went through the Crimean and Armenian Civil Wars as a war correspondent. It was during this time that he became aquainted with Russian revolutionaries, particularly with Prince Kropotkin and with Sergei Mikhailowitch Ktravohinski (alias S. Stepniak). He persuaded the latter to settle in London, and collaborated with him in translations of contemporary Russian literature, and of Stepniak's book on the aims of reform, 'Russia under the Czars' (1885). Westall was long a prolific writer of novels, (which have been compared with those of Jules Verne and Robert Louis Stevenson), drawing freely on his experiences alike in Lancashire and on the continent and further afield. He extended his travels to North and South America and to the West Indies, but finally returned to England, making his residence in Worthing.

He died at Heathfield, Sussex, on 9 Sept. 1903, shortly after completing his last novel.

BELOW Dating from 1748, Stanhill Hall in Oswaldtwistle was the home of William Bury Westall. It became Brandwood Hall in his novel.

ABOVE Following the death of his father, John Westall, in 1851, William Bury Westall and his brother Jonathan took over the running of White Ash Mill in Oswaldtwistle. White Ash Mill, 'The Old Factory' was put up for sale in 1862 at a time when they were employing 930 hands, operating 9600 mule spindles, 2800 throstle spindles and 464 power looms. The photograph, taken in 1989, shows the weir on White Ash Lane, all that remains of the old factory.

Facing Stanhill Hall is Stanhill Post Office, the birthplace of James Hargreaves (1720 –1778). It was here that he invented the Spinning Jenny that was to revolutionise the cotton industry.

The Westall's are descended from a family of ardent Baptists (dippers in the story – as they believed in full immersion during baptism).

Joseph Harbottle, seen here on the left, was Baptist minister at Little Moor End, now known as New Lane Baptist Chapel, in Oswaltwistle between 1849 and 1862. William Bury Westall would have known him and probably used him as the character Mr. Hartwell in his novel.

THE OLD FACTORY

CHAPTER 1

A MANUFACTURER OF THE OLD SCHOOL.

On a certain winter's evening, in the first half of the present Century, a man and a boy were seated in the principal room of a dwelling, described in the rate book of the township in which it was situated as "Moorwell Mansion House."

Before them was a table littered with shirts, collars, stockings, and other articles of apparel.

The room, though sufficiently comfortable, was far from being richly furnished. In a recess opposite the single window, with its white cotton blinds and dimity curtains, stood a massive old-fashioned mahogany side-board. At one side of the hearth was placed a painted rocking-chair; at the other a large easy-chair with a printed cover. The remaining chairs, of which there were some half-dozen, as well as the solitary sofa, were upholstered in black horsehair. A common and much-worn carpet concealed the floor. The parlour was lighted by a pair of candles, in long brass sticks, which appeared to require frequent snuffing, and a coal fire blazed brightly in a high hob-ended grate.

The only works of art visible on the walls were engravings of the "Cottar's Saturday Night" and "Sunday Morning," a coloured print of the baptism by immersion of a crowd of negro neophytes in a river of Madagascar, and a portrait of the first Sir Robert Peel.

The man's occupation at this particular moment was writing names on the collars, shirts, and pocket-handkerchiefs which were handed to him from time to time by the boy - a task that, to judge by his intent look, and the protruded tongue which followed automatically the movements of his pen, was attended with no little difficulty, and seemed to demand considerable concentration of mind. When he had finished a name he would hand the article inscribed to the boy, who thereupon rubbed it industriously on an Italian iron to fix the ink.

The writer was broad-shouldered, deep-chested, and long-limbed; and though his hair was scanty and his mutton-chop whiskers showed a good deal of grey, he was still in the prime of life. His eyes were light blue, his teeth white and strong; his nose was aquiline, his complexion healthy and high-coloured, and, albeit his square jaws and compressed lips denoted much decision of character, the general expression of his countenance was one of geniality and good nature-rusticity, some people considered it-but those who in their dealings with him presumed on this supposed simplicity were apt to be rather painfully undeceived. As for dress, he wore an old black swallow-tailed coat a broad, black stock, a blue plush waistcoat, and plaid trousers, all considerably the worse for wear. This man, by name Adam Blackthorne, was the owner of the Old Factory.

The boy ironing the linen, as the cast of his features abundantly testified, notwithstanding that his nose turned up instead of turning down and his hair was long and dark, was his son. The lad's name, which was being so extensively recorded, was Francis Adam Blackthorne. It was the result of a compromise between his parents. The mother had been desirous of bestowing on her firstborn son her husband's patronymic, just as it was; but he, having a horror of being called old, and above all, Old Adam," bad insisted on the introduction of another name, and in the end it had been agreed that, while the child's legal appellation should be Francis Adam, his every-day name was to be Frank, and as Frank he was ever afterwards known.

The litter of linen on the table was due to the fact that Frank, now in his twelfth year, was going next day to Bigwater's boarding-school at Yewdale, and as this would be the first time he had ever left home, except for an occasional trip to Blackpool, there was naturally some excitement in the family and a good deal of packing up.

"Is that the last, Frank?" asked Adam, as he penned, for about the fiftieth time that evening, the name of his son and heir.

"One more shirt, father, that's all; here it is."

"Well, it is a dree job. I'm not sorry it is nearly done. You'll be well set up with clothes; you will that. I hope you '11 work hard and make the most of your opportunities. I never had such a chance, nor never a Blackthorne before thee. All th' schooling ever I got was two years at old Nanny Raddle's at Four Lane Ends, and a twelvemonth, barring hay-time and seed-time, with Mr. Priestley at Brookside. I've had to work, and work hard, ever sin' I was eleven years old. And it'll cost a bonny penny, too, one way and another. Look at all these clothes. And then th' school bill will be coming in, and I make no doubt it'll be a big 'un. Thirty pounds a year, Mr. Bigwater says his terms are, and ten to one there'll be three or four pounds more for extras. And th' times are most terrible bad; I never knew 'em worse. We haven't sold a piece for going in three months, and we have a matter of twenty thousand or more piled up, here and in Manchester. Ten thousand pounds they're worth, if they're worth a penny. That's a loss of five hundred pounds a year, reckoning no more than five per cent - ten pounds a week as clean gone as if it were thrown down th' brook -and unless a trades-man can do better with his brass than five per cent., he mut as well stop i' bed."

"Are we going to run short time, father?"

"Why, what makes you ask? Has somebody been saying so?" asked Adam, sharply.

"It was only Jack o' Jonathans. He was saying in th' watch-house last night as some of th' mills at Redburn are going on short time, and we might happen be doing th' same."

"I wish Jack o' Jonathans would mind his own business. No, we are not going on short time. I lose by every piece as I make, I know, but then if I don't make a good deal I shall be ruined. Either full time or none - that's my motto. Go on as hard as you can or shut up altogether; there's nowt else for it. We work twelve hours a day now, and I'd run thirteen if th' law would let us, and I ask no man on th' ground to work harder than I do myself. But them o' this generation doesn't know what work is; they're getting lazy - that's what they are."

"Shall I have to learn Latin, father?" interrupted Frank, who was thinking more about Bigwater's school than the economical advantages of long time.

"No; what's the use of Latin? Learn as much French as you like, and arithmetic and grammar, and to write a good hand. That's all I want and I don't care how soon you are ready to come and help me in th' factory. You should learn a good deal in three or four years - quite enough for a business man, and more would do you more harm than good. Do you know what Mr. George Bowles said? - and he should know; for he went to Oxford and cost his father a mint o' money for his education."

"No; what did he say?"

"He said as learning Latin and Greek, and drinking wine after dinner, never did make a tradesman and never would."

"But I have heard you say many a time that the Bowleses made all their money by manufacturing and calico printing."

"And so they did; but Mr. George made nowt. He could spend fast enough, but he never earned nor gained a shilling in his life. It was his father and his uncles; they made all th' brass, and they were only plain men, plainly educated. If th' old folks had brought him up as they were brought up themselves, he might have been carrying th' business on yet, and that would ha' been a vast sight better than idling i' London one half o' the year and sporting t'other, would not it? But here comes mother, and I'll be hanged if she is not bringing some more things to mark. I shall know thy name soon, lad."

Adam Blackthorne's wife was a few years younger than himself, and looked younger than she was; for her black hair was unstreaked by grey, and though the bloom of youth had vanished from her cheek; they were still rosy with the hue of health, and her soft brown eyes were little less bright than when they had fired Adam's heart twenty years before. A single glance at her face was sufficient to show where Frank had got his nez *retroussé,* but her nose, far from turning up impudently or offensively, was delicately curved, and her nostrils were so fine and thin, her lips so shapely and her teeth so white, that people who thought that beauty is, or ought to be, inseparable from gentle birth sometimes said that Rachel Blackthorne had the look of a noble lady. Her hands; though well formed, were large and strong, and had the appearance of being used rather for work than kept for show. Her dress, which was of almost Quaker-like simplicity, consisted of a plain net cap, a merino gown, and a black apron.

To-night her generally cheerful countenance wore a somewhat melancholy air; for the approaching departure of her boy was a sore trouble to her; but she had been trained in a stern school - taught from her youth upward that too much love for the creature was a sin -and she struggled hard, and with almost success, to repress all outward manifestation of her feelings.

"It's only two more shirts;" she said, deprecatingly, in answer to her husband's remark. "I don't know how often they wash at Bigwater's, and I should not like any one to say that I sent Frank off to school ill provided"

"Ill provided?" echoed Adam. "Why, it seems to me as I've marked linen enough to-night to last him a year o' Sundays; and never a washing day among 'em. I don't know how you'll get it all into his trunk. Come along, Frank, let's polish 'em off."

Just as the last shirt had been "polished off" and placed in Frank's trunk, which stood on two chairs in one corner of the room, a servant entered.
"If you please, master, Yorkshire Joe's in the kitchen," she said.

"Tell him to come forrud," answered Adam.

Yorkshire Joe came 'forrud,' accordingly. He was a middle-sized, muscular, wirily-built red-haired, brown-faced fellow of about thirty, with a look and dress half-labourer, half-groom. Joe, in fact, was both these and many things besides - the best and most profitable servant Adam Blackthorne possessed. He looked after the horse and gig and had charge of one of the cart horses as well; took care of the poultry and pigs, and the factory gas, oiled the main shafting, and went twice a week to Redburn for provender, grains, and change for the work-people's wages. He was also a first-rate hedger and ditcher and rough waller; could do a bit of slating and thatching; had once built, almost unaided, a very passable house, and yet thought himself well paid with fifteen shillings a week.

"Well, Joe," said his master, "have you got all ready for to-morrow?"

"Ay, I think I have. I've bedded th' mare down and shoo's finished her feed. Shoo'll be i' good fettle for th' jorna' to-morrow. I washed th' gig this afternoon, and th' harness I cleaned o' Saturday."

"And how about the gas?"

"The gasometer is nearly full. I think there's welly (nearly) enough to last to-morrow o'er. Tommy Upsteps 'ull charge th' retorts and keep th' fires up till I get back."

"That's right. And now how much brass will you want, think you?"

"I cannot justly say; this'll be my fost jorna' to Yewdale. There's a matter o' four bars this side Haslingden - how many there is at t'other side I donut know. And then I'se have to bait both going and coming and put up an hour or so at th' far end. One way and another, I dassay it'll cost welly twelve shillings."

"God bless me, Joe, that's a lot o' brass! You want to ruin me, I think. Here's half-a-sovereign - you must be careful and make it do. Take some proven (provender) with you, and then you'll only have to pay for a feed or two of hay. What time will you start, do you think?"

"As soon as Frank's getten his breakfast and I can have his boxes. How would half-past six do?"

"Can you be ready then, Rachel?" asked Adam, turning to his wife.

"Yes. You can come for his boxes at six, Joe, and Frank shall be ready half an hour later at the latest."

"That's aw, I think - isn't it?"

"Ay, that's all, Joe; you may lock up and go home. Take care of yourself to-morrow, and see as you get back sober."

"Sober! How can I do owt else? I shall not have above threepence, or, maybe, sixpence left o' this hoaf sovereign after I've paid th' bars and baits, and getten & bit o' cheese and bread for myself - and how's a chap' to get sprung, much less drunk, out o' that, will you tell me? Good neet to you aw."

Yorkshire Joe, notwithstanding his many high qualities was unhappily not quite perfect. Being human, he had his faults, chief whereof was a weakness for beer; but his favourite tipple was buttered gin, in which, nevertheless, by reason of its comparative costliness, he could only rarely indulge. "A chap may sup a shilling's worth of buttered gin in no time," he was wont to say, "and then he's no more than sharp fresh." On the whole, therefore, Joe found' it expedient to stick to ale, which he liked, however, to take occasionally fettled - hot with a dash of rum in it, nutmegged, and well sugared. Fortunately for him he had an excellent wife, who looked well after him; and being conscious of his besetting vice, he invariably gave up all his wage to her, all save a single shilling, that he kept for "spending brass" - if he could be said to keep that which, in the course of two or three hours thereafter, invariably went to swell the Saturday night receipts of the landlord of The Blazing ,Stump, or him of The Coach and Horses. It was only on such extraordinary occasions as the general day of his club (Joe was an Ancient Druid), or the funeral of a friend, that he greatly exceeded in his own neighbourhood. But when he went on a journey and fell into strange company, especially if be had a few loose shillings in his pocket, or if anybody offered to stand treat (he was never known to refuse treat), his fate was sealed; and he was apt in these circumstances to come home very drunk indeed - holding on to the cart tail', or fast asleep among his "proven" sacks - to the great disgust of his master, who, once when he found him in this state, ducked him with his own hands in the cold-water lodge, by way of sobering him, a lesson that he did not soon forget, and the remembrance of which kept him steady the greater part of a year.

Seeing that Joe was often trusted with money, especially on his Friday trips to Redburn, when he took bank-notes and brought hack change for wages - it was remarkable that no serious mishap had ever befallen him. But he was very shrewd, and even in his cups quite able to take care of himself.

CHAPTER II

A VISITOR

"Now," said Adam Blackthorne, as Joe closed the door behind him, "I'm going to have a pipe; and Rachel, ring the bell, I'll take a glass of home-brewed with it."

Then, suiting the action to the word, he reached from a shelf behind his arm-chair a long pipe of the sort known as "churchwarden," filled it with "returns" from an iron tobacco-box, and proceeded to smoke with much serenity and satisfaction, while his wife and son completed the packing of the latter's boxes. This had gone on for some time, and Adam had nearly finished his pipe and glass of home-brewed ale, when the parlour door again opened, and the same servant who had appeared before announced another visitor.

"If you please, master," she said, "a man wants to see you in the kitchen."

"Who is he, Jane?"

"A man that used to work at the factory. I believe it is him as they call Little Fourteen, sir," added the girl with a smile. "He says he wants his wage."

At the mention of this name Adam Blackthorne's face underwent a most portentous change; his eyes seemed to take another colour, his brows contracted, and his expression of geniality turned into one of almost ferocity.

"I'll wage him!" he exclaimed, springing from his chair.

Mrs. Blackthorne, when she heard this exclamation, and noticed the change that had come over her husband's countenance, seemed greatly alarmed. She laid her hand on his arm.

"Don't lose your temper," she said. "Adam, don't."

"You need not be afraid, Rachel; I will keep as quiet as I can. I promised never to strike anybody again, and you know I have always kept my word. But I cannot put up with this sort of thing any longer. I shall give this fellow a lesson."

And shaking off his wife's hand he strode across the narrow lobby into the kitchen. It was not large, yet quite in proportion to the size of the house, and well filled with furniture and etceteras. There were a big range and a bright fire, a mantelpiece adorned with burnished utensils of copper and tin; sundry hams and a large bread cratch crowded with oatcake hung from the ceiling; one of the walls was taken up with plated dish covers, and another with a plate rack, underneath which stood a long dresser.

Two servant girls sat sewing near the fire, and Little Fourteen occupied a chair at the end of the dresser. As Adam entered he stood up. There was nothing in the man's appearance to show how he had come by his by-name; for, though lanky, he was rather over than under middle height. It had indeed been bestowed upon him many years before at a time when he was very short for his age, and gave slight promise of growing any longer; and nicknames in Lancashire, once conferred, generally cling to a man during his life and not rarely live after him. Hence Little Fourteen had almost forgotten the sound of his own surname; had probably not heard it since he was married some eight or ten years before. Even his wife called him "Fourteen" as often as she called him "Jim." Though he rose when Adam came into the kitchen, he did not uncover, factory operatives at that time not being much given to over-respectfulness of bearing in the presence of their "betters."

Little Fourteen wore a "slink" (black oilskin) cap, while a red woollen comforter was folded many times round his neck and partially covered his lantern jaws, black with a stubble of several days' growth. His fustian jacket and trousers were dark and shiny, and he gave forth an odour compounded in about equal proportions of rum, sperm oil, and stale tobacco.

"Well, what does thou want?" said Adam, eyeing him sternly.

"I've come for my wage, mayster; they would not give it to my wife when she went to th' factory last pay day, so I've come to ax yo'!"

"Thou knows quite well why they did not give her thy wage; thou knows thou left without notice, and them as leaves without notice forfeits all wages due to 'em at th' time of their leaving. Thou knows as thou went away in the middle of a week without a word and left thy wheels standing."

"That's true, mayster; that's true; I cannot deny it. But th' work were that there dead bad, mayster, I wor fair sick on it. I never see sich work in o' my life, and I've been in a wheelhouse ever sin' I wor eight year old. Th' ends kept breaking that fast as I fair thought it wor snowing i' th' hoile. So I put on my jacket and went and geet a shop at Rawnsley's."

"Thou knows, Fourteen, as that's nowt at all to do with it. We give and take a month's notice, and th' rules are hung up in every room, so as everybody can read 'em; and if the work was a bit bad, what then? We cannot always keep it good; it isn't always good at Rawnsley's, I'll he bound."

"I have never read your rules, mayster - 'cause why? I never larnt to read. But I've heard 'em read, and I've heard 'em talked about, and folk says as they are not fair between mon and mon. You give and take a month's notice! We mun allus give a month's sushow (in any case); hut th' rules says as if hands spoils their work, uses bad language, comes late of a morning, goes off without leave, doesn't do as they're toud, and so on, we can he bagged (discharged) bout notice. Dun yo' think as that's fair, mayster?"

"Why isn't it fair? We cannot keep folks as spoils their work, can we?"

"Why should we be forced to stop with a mayster, then, as spoils his work and doesn't give a mon a chance of addling (earning) a living. If I make bad work, yo' bag me; but if yo' give me bad stuff to spin, I'm forced to go on with it for a month, or loise five or six days' wage, and happen be persecuted and sent to prison into th' bargain. Dun yo' call that reyt Mayster Blackthorne?"

"No more of this nonsense," said Adam, fiercely, to whom these arguments sounded like rank treason. "Thou has forfeited thy wage, I tell thee, and thou'll never get a penny of it while thy heart beats. Come, now, be off"
"I'se not stir out of here, mayster," said Little Fourteen (who had evidently been drinking), sitting down in his chair again, and thrusting his hands doggedly into his breeches pockets - "I'se not stir out of here till yo' give me my wage, fifteen shilling and sixpence-hopenny."

"Will thou go quietly now?" repeated Adam, whose eyes by this time were literally blazing with anger; "if thou doesn't it will be worse for thee."

"Not till 1 get my wage."

"Well, then, I'll put thee out and clap thee in a place where thou'll not be quite so comfortable as sitting in that chair, or by th' fireside at The Blazing Stump."

Then, without more ado, Adam tore Little Fourteen from his chair, and seizing him by his coat collar and the waistband of his trousers, lifted him from his feet.

The spinner, who was little more than a child in the powerful grasp of his late master, feeling that open fight was out of the question, tried to save himself by making a desperate clutch at the pot-rail, when down it came with a run, amid a chorus of screams from poor Mrs. Blackthorne and her maids; and an avalanche of crockery fell crashing on the stone floor of the kitchen.

"Open th' door, Jane," shouted Adam, without heeding the ruin of his wife's crockery. But Jane, who seemed half-frightened out of her senses, stood stock-still, and made no attempt to obey the order.

"Open th' door, Frank, or--"

Frank, who seemed also to be somewhat scared, yet had not lost all his presence of mind, ran forward and did as his father bade him.

"Now, go and open th' yard door"

This order was also promptly obeyed.

Little Fourteen struggled hard to flee himself from Adam's grasp. But it was no use; he was partly carried, partly dragged, through the kitchen door, and down a long paved yard, bordered by poplar trees, into a narrow black road, on the farther side of which ran a brook some two or three feet deep.

"Don't throw me in, mayster! Don't throw me in!" screamed Little Fourteen.

But this appeal had no effect on Adam, and shaking himself free from the man's grasp, he half pushed, halt dropped him into the water.

"There," he said, "that's thy wage, and it's all as thou'll ever get."

As Little Fourteen scrambled out of the brook his teeth chattered with cold, and he muttered curses loud and deep. "Yo'll catch it for this, Blackthorne!" he shouted after Adam as the latter went back towards the house. "I'll have law on yo' for this, yo' owd tyrant, or we'll two yo' some neet and give yo' a good hiding."

Then, fearing that Adam might perchance return and throw him into the brook a second time, Little Fourteen ran down the road as fast as his legs would carry him, in the direction of The Blazing Stump.

CHAPTER III.

A SCHOOL OF THE OLD SORT.

The parting between Mrs. Blackthorne and her boy was a trial to both of them, especially to her; for she was passionately, almost weakly, fond of her children, and Frank had never in his life before been away from her more than a day and a night. She would fain have kept him at home a little longer, but her husband had decided that he must go to Bigwater's after Christmas, and when once Adam Blackthorne had made up his mind, it was not easy to turn him from his purpose. As for Frank, he had only himself to blame for this resolution of his father's. For two or three years he had been a day scholar at Dr. Leatherlad's Fern Grove Academy, whither, but for an unlucky chance that befell him, he might have continued to go two or three years longer.

Dr. Leatherlad was a decidedly clever man, and by no means a bad teacher, but having many irons in the fire (being at the same time pedagogue, popular preacher, public lecturer, and literary character), he had to leave his scholars and masters pretty much to their own devices; and the qualifications of the latter being on a par with their pay, which was as low as the Doctor could make it, the progress of the boys, as well as the discipline of the school, naturally left much to be desired. Fortunately for him, however, the parents of his pupils seemed insensible or indifferent to these deficiencies, and as Fern Grove Academy was the only respectable establishment of the sort in the neighbourhood, it flourished exceedingly, and made Dr. Leatherlad a very comfortable income. As for the boys, the school was exactly to their liking; they could learn almost as little as they liked, play truant when it pleased them, and if they came late in a morning it was the easiest thing in the world by creeping into the school unobserved to escape punishment. There were no weekly or monthly reports to parents, no study plans, no examinations; nor had anybody ever yet taken it upon him to express a doubt as to the efficiency of the instruction given at the Academy. Save for one drawback, indeed, Fern Grove would have been a perfect elysium for idle boys and incompetent ushers. Now and again - three or four times 'n the course of the half-year, perhaps - Dr. Leatherlad, wakening up as from a dream, would take it into his head to look into things for himself and test the progress of his scholars; and on these occasions there was the very deuce to pay. Descending suddenly from his rostrum in the bay window, he would go to the first boy that happened to catch his eye and inquire what he was doing. Perhaps the poor wretch would he learning his multiplication table.

"Very good," would say the Doctor, calmly; "then you know how much twelve times twelve make?"

"Yes, sir; please, sir, a hundred and fourteen."

"Ah! a hundred and fourteen!"

"If you please, sir, I have not got as far as that yet, sir."

"How far have you got then - do you know five times?"

"Yes, sir, I know five times."

"Five times five, then?"

"Fifteen."

Four times four?"

"Twenty-four."

"Go to my desk, sir, and remain there until I come."

"What are you doing, Collins? Ah! the pence table. Come, now, a hundred pence."

"If you please, sir, a hundred pence are six and eightpence."

"Indeed! And eighty pence?"

"Three and fourpence."

"That will do. Go to my desk."

"And what are you about Smith? A Latin exercise? How do you construe *Poeta nascitur non fit?*"

"A poet - a poet - a poet - (then desperately) a poet had a fit."

"A poet had a fit indeed! I'll make you have a fit you won't soon forget my boy. Join Collins and Jones at my 'desk this instant."

And so Leatherlad passed at hazard from one boy to another, and as hardly one could answer satisfactorily there would soon he fifteen or twenty trembling victims gathered before his awful throne. Then he would mount his rostrum, and drawing forth his cane, carefully pitch-lapped at both ends, proceed to deal out execution amongst all who had been tried in the balance and found wanting. He might with equal justice have flogged the whole school, for there was hardly a boy in it who could have stood the most cursory examination; yet strong as he was, twenty were about as many as he could comfortably cane at one time; and he flogged with so much energy and effect that a rumour ran in the school that before becoming schoolmaster and clergyman the Doctor had graduated in a blacksmith's shop.

For a week or two after a display of this sort the Academy was the scene of unwonted diligence - these, indeed, were the only times anything was learned - but as the recollection of it faded away, old habits gradually resumed their sway, and boys and ushers became as idle as before.

All that Frank ever learnt at the Academy was to write badly, spell indifferently, and struggle with much difficulty through a sum of long division. He played truant sometimes, and would probably have played it oftener had he not found it on the whole rather duller work than being at school. On the other hand, he took his time about going in the morning, and at whatever hour he left home he rarely reached Fern Grove before ten o'clock. These derelictions were, of course, unknown to his parents. The father was too much absorbed in his business to be very mindful of his son's bringing up - for anything that appeared to the contrary his duty in relation thereto was comprised in the punctual payment of Dr. Leatherlad's quarterly bills - and his mother, poor soul! thought Franky was getting on very nicely. He had acquired a fair knowledge of sacred history (in which, seeing that the Bible was the only reading book in use in the lower classes at Fern Grove, there was nothing very remarkable), a circumstance that in her opinion was the strongest possible proof of the efficiency of the

Leatherlad system, and sufficient to have covered a multitude of sins, had she discerned any.

At length, however, an incident befell that called Adam Blackthorne's attention to his son's shortcomings, and suggested to him the expediency of placing the lad where he would be more sharply looked after than at Fern Grove Academy.

One morning, shortly before the opening of our story, happening to pass through the farmyard, which was behind the house, he found Frank loitering about with no intention, seemingly, of doing anything else.

"What are you doing here, Frank? Why have you not gone to school?"

"I'm waiting to see the pig killed."

"To see the pig killed?

"Yes, and I'm going to help Yorkshire Joe to scald and scrape it. Look here (showing an old iron candle-stick which he intended to use as a scraper); I shall not be very late for school, you know. Joe and old Shep have gone to fetch the pig, and they say it won't take above half an hour to kill and scrape him; and I do so like to scrape a pig."

"Be off to school this minute, you young vagabond; why you'll be an hour late as it is," replied his father, sternly, though in reality he was a good deal amused, and laughed heartily to himself when Frank had disappeared.

Half an hour later Adam was in his counting-house, looking over his invoice book. The window opposite where he sat commanded rather an extensive view, including a footpath daily traversed by Frank on his way to school. This footpath ran by the foot of a high wall, on the other side of which was a large plantation. Adam, happening, by the merest chance, to cast his eyes in this direction, saw his son, satchel on back, crawling lazily along. Then the lad stopped, and threw a few stones over the plantation wall; next he took off his cap, and after, as it seemed, putting a stone inside, threw it also over the wall; whereupon he turned round, and walked briskly back towards the Old Factory.

"What dodge is he up to now? said Adam to himself, greatly astounded by this extraordinary proceeding.

He soon found out.

In little more than ten minutes Frank, looking greatly distressed, appeared in the counting-house.

"Well," said Adam, "what is it?"

"Oh, father, my cap has blown over into Stimson's plantation. What must I do?"

"It's a lie; I saw you throw it over myself;" exclaimed Blackthorne, senior, at the same time throwing the ruler which he held in his hand at Frank's head.

Frank dodged, and the ruler flew harmlessly through the window. Then he ran down the steps, (the counting-house was on the first floor) two at a time, and did not stop until he had reached the bottom.

"Come here, will you?" shouted his father.

"If you'll promise not to lick me, I will," answered Frank, eyeing his father with a scared look.

"I'll be--" began Adam, furiously. Then, seeming suddenly to change his mind, he added, "I promise; I will not lick you."

"Nor pull my ears?" put in Frank, suspiciously.

"Nor pull your ears, nor lay a finger on you. Now go and fetch Tommy Twirler; tell him I want him first thing."

"May I go to the pig-killing, after?"

"We'll see about that when you come back. Fetch Tommy Twirler, I say."

And Frank, thinking his father's wrath was appeased, and that he was free from school for that forenoon at least, went in high spirits on his errand.

Tommy Twirler was one of the most trusted of Adam Blackthorne's men, and had served him faithfully for many years, though from the nature of his functions he enjoyed little popularity with his fellow-workpeople. He may be described as the quarter-master general of the Old Factory, inasmuch as it fell to his lot to "quarter," or fine, laggards who came late to their work. He acted, too, as cutlooker, and in that capacity had to make abatements from the wages of weavers who spoiled their work - duties which he performed with such rigid impartiality that nobody except his master had ever a good word for him. His proper name was Ramsbottom; the by-name, Twirler, had been given to him because he had once been a twister-in, or twirler of threads, and perhaps because people thought it sounded better than his own not very savoury surname. This, Tommy took as a matter of course. If he had a nickname, so had other folks; and, as he remarked, he was no worse for it; but when people conferred upon him a second post-baptismal designation, and that so queer a one as "Owd Poo' Bell," he felt really hurt, and his naturally woebegone countenance assumed thenceforth a yet deeper shade of sadness.

He came by the name in this way. One of his duties was to ring the factory bell. Every morning at a quarter past five he mounted to the top room (the highest storey), and summoned the diligent to work. At other times, after the breakfast half-hour and the dinner hour, he did this duty by deputy. There was generally somebody in the top room who was glad to ring in his stead, for Tommy, though little liked, was an important personage at the Old Factory. On these occasions, therefore, he only gave the order, and he gave it always in the same words. Looking up to the room in question, he would shout at the top of his voice, "Poo' that bell?"

Twice every day he uttered this formula, precisely at the same minute and exactly in the same voice. For a long time it never occurred to anybody to see anything particularly droll in this proceeding; but one fine Sunday afternoon, when Tommy chanced to be taking a walk with his family, he met a group of merry factory lasses, whom no sooner had he passed than he heard a sound of laughter, and one of them (he could not tell which - he only wished he could) called out "Poo' that bell!"

A little farther on he encountered a number of small boys, and again he heard the ominous words. He tried to take no notice, and the next day, instead of giving his order in the accustomed form, he shouted, "Ring the bell." But it was no use; his fate was fixed. From that time forth the hands began to speak of him as "Owd Poo' Bell," and the name stuck to him for life.

"Tommy," said his master, when in obedience to his summons the incorruptible servant presented himself at the' counting-house, "I want you to take Frank to Leatherlad's school and see as he goes in. He has thrown his cap into Stimson's plantation, so he'll be like to go without, but as you come back you can try to get it for him ; he'll tell you where it is."

At these words Frank's face assumed an expression of such extreme dismay, that if his mother could have seen her darling she would hardly have known him. Conscious, however, that any appearance of opposition on his part would have been both useless and injudicious, he remained silent.

"You may go," said Adam; but when they were halfway down the steps he called Tommy back.

"Here," he continued, "give this bit of a note to Dr. Leatherlad, but don't say anything to Frank."

"Vary weel" answered Tommy, putting the bit of a note in his pocket. "Owt else?"

"No, that's all."

Owd Poo' Bell was no laggard, and Frank did the walk to school in less time than he had ever done it in his life before.

At the entrance to Fern Grove, which had been built for a country house, and was surrounded, as Dr. Leatherlad's advertisements put it by five acres of its own grounds, Frank made an effort to get rid of his companion.
"You may go now, Tommy," he said; "I can go into the school by myself. You can stand here and watch me if you like."

But Tommy was not the man to leave his work half done.

"Nay, I'll see you in, and let's look sharp, for I want to get back to my work," was all the reply he vouchsafed to this insidious proposal.

It was past eleven o'clock when they entered the school. Frank slipped quietly into his seat, hoping thereby to escape Leatherlad's observation, but Tommy marched right up the middle of the room to the master's rostrum. The appearance of a man in clogs, fustian trousers, and a dusty jacket was so unusual in the Academy that every eye was directed towards him, and the Doctor, looking up from a sermon in the composition of which he had been engaged, regarded the intruder with an interrogative look.

"I've 'browt Frank to schoo'," said Tommy, in a voice almost as loud as if he were ordering the poo'ing of the bell; "and here's a bit of a note fro' th' mayster. Would yo' give me a receipt, if yo' please?"

"A receipt! What for?"

"Just a line to say as Frank's come safe to hand; summut as I can show to th' mayster."

The Doctor smiled, wrote on a piece of paper that Frank Blackthorne had arrived at school at 11.15am.; and handed it to Tommy, who thereupon, without another word, took his departure, fully satisfied that he had carried out his instructions to the letter.

The note he had given to Leatherlad ran thus: "I am sorry to say that Frank attempted to play truant this morning, and told a lie into the bargain. I leave you to deal with him as you like, but I suggest a sound flogging."

As the Doctor read he looked as black as thunder; for the fault of all others which he professed to hold in especial abhorrence was lying. Seeing, however, that he obtained so much money, practically under false pretences, by undertaking for a certain consideration to give a sound classical and commercial education, and then turning his scholars over to incompetent teachers and letting the school take care of itself, he might have regarded moral lapses in others with more charity than he was wont to do. But our most inveterate vices are probably those of which we are the least conscious; and it is perhaps in the nature of things that teachers and preachers should be more inconsistent than other men.

"Blackthorne, come hither!" shouted the Doctor in stentorian accents, at the same time rising from his seat and making a vicious cut in the air with his pitch-lapped cane.

Though Frank had no positive knowledge of the contents of the letter which he had seen Tommy Twirler hand to Leatherlad, he guessed its purport, and knew that his father had been too sharp for him. He had kept his promise to the ear but broken it to the hope; and the lad felt that he had made a mistake, for the difference between a cuffing from his father and a caning from the Doctor was the difference between whips and scorpions.

"So you tried to play truant this morning, and then attempted to conceal one sin by perpetrating a greater! To the constructive falsehood you committed by pretending to come to the Academy, and not coming, you added a positive, flagrant, unblushing lie. Is it so?"

Frank was silent.

"Is it so, I ask, Blackthorne?"

"If you please, sir," pleaded the lad in a quavering voice.

"Answer me, yes or no, this moment, sir; did you tell a lie or not?"

"I did, sir, but I did not -"

"You did, but you did not; what nonsense is this? Actually you dare to tell another lie. How can you do a thing and not do a thing, lie and not lie, at the same time?"

"If you please, Dr. Leatherlad, I did not mean, that is, I meant -"

"Silence!" thundered the Doctor. "Dare to answer me again, and I'll (making another cut in the air) - I'll flay you alive, sir. You know what is the portion of liars after death, Blackthorne - you have read it in your Bible; you have doubtless heard it at home and at the place of worship which you attend; you have been taught it here; and now I am about to let you feel, in the most sensitive part of your person, what is their portion in the Academy over which I have the honour to preside."

As the pedagogue finished this harangue, he descended from his dais, seized the trembling Frank by the coat, and, after fixing his head firmly between his legs (Leatherlad's, not Frank's), showered on him blows as hail, leaving no single spot within the swing of his cane untouched, albeit giving preference to the places where the victim's trousers seemed to be most tightly stretched.

Page 17

Poor Frank did his best to howl, hut his face being buried beneath his tormentor's coat tails, his cries were necessarily of the feeblest, and freeing himself from the grip of those herculean legs was out of the question. When the Doctor was tired, and not before, he desisted and sent Frank - sobbing and writhing - to his seat; and the lad for the rest of the day felt as if he had slept all night on a bed of nettles; or as the pig, which was the innocent cause of his flogging, would probably have felt had he been scalded and scraped before execution instead of after it.

When, on the occasion of his next weekly tubbing, the weals and wounds on Frank's back were laid bare to Mrs. Blackthorne's horrified gaze, she wept with pity for her boy's sufferings. The next time she met Dr. Leatherlad she cut him dead; and when he called upon her to explain, she positively refused to see him. Even her husband, who was anything but soft-hearted, admitted that the lad had been too severely punished, and the incident confirmed him in the intention he had already formed to send Frank to a boarding-school after Christmas. The selection of a school offered little difficulty. Adam Blackthorne was a decided Dissenter and a cordial hater of the Church of England and all her works. No child of his should go to a prelatical school, whether taught by a Church parson or conducted by a layman on Church principles.

Respectable dissenting boarding-schools being few and far between, choice in the matter was necessarily limited. As Adam had heard a good account of Bigwater's school at Yewdale, and knew a young cotton broker that had been educated there who promised to be an excellent man of business, and Mrs. Blackthorne had ascertained that Bigwater, though he whipped his scholars now and then, was by no means a severe man, it was unanimously resolved that Frank should go to Yewdale.

Bigwater was forthwith written to, and being a man of energy, who never on principle lost a chance of securing a new boy, he answered the communication in person, when it was arranged that Frank should begin his boarding-school life at the end of the January following, at which time, in the academic English of Bigwater's circular to the parents of his pupils, "the duties of the establishment would be resumed after the Christmas vacations."

But man proposes and God disposes, and an unforeseen event somewhat marred the due carrying out of this arrangement. Two or three days before the time fixed for Frank's departure he fell ill of the measles, and though the attack was of the mildest and did not confine him to the house for more than a week, it was not considered prudent to let him go to school before the end of February.

Frank was delighted. A week's coddling and nursing by his mother, followed by an unhoped-for holiday of three weeks, compensated him in some measure for his sufferings at the hands of Dr. Leatherlad, and would shorten by a whole month the period of his exile. He turned his respite to good account - helped to scrape and scald two pigs (Adam Blackthorne sold a good deal of butcher-meat to his work-people); went sliding on the quarry pond, broke through the ice, and narrowly escaped a watery grave; fell down in the shippen and utterly ruined a new pair of trousers; got his foot trodden on by Punch, the old cart horse; and threw his ball through the drawing-room window. Altogether, though his mother was sorry to part with her boy, it was a great relief to her when his holidays were over.

CHAPTER IV.

GOING TO BIGWATER'S

It was only just coming light when Frank and Yorkshire Joe set out for Yewdale. There had been a slight fall of snow during the night The morning was chilly and depressing. The lad, saddened by the parting with his Mother and his little sister Mabel - the parting with his father did not trouble him much - had lost all his wonted volubility, and Joe being also in a silent mood, they reached the wild and bleak district of Waterhead before either of them had uttered a word.

Around them stretched a vast expanse of undulating moorland, white with snow - except here and there in the hollows, where a piece of black bog had swallowed it as it fell, and the higher ground, where the wind had blown it away. It was a treeless country of stone walls, poor pastures, and rush-grown meadows. Desolate-looking farmhouses dotted the hillsides, and from time to time the travellers passed groups of gray and forlorn-seeming cottages, their broken windows stuffed with rags and pasted up with paper. White-faced women and sad visaged children would occasionally appear at a door, held ajar to keep out the biting blast. In every one of these cottages was heard the clickity-clack, clickity-clack of the hand loom; and gaunt and silent men went to and fro, bending beneath the weight of heavy loads of cotton warps and calico pieces.

Frank was the first to speak.

"My word, Joe, it is cold up here," he said, wrapping his cloak tightly around him. "Let us go a bit faster until we get to a warmer place."

"We will, soon as ever we reach a bit of better ground. Th' mare's a long journa' afore her, and we mustn't owerdrive her, yo' know. It is gradely cowd, and this is a cowd shop, but there's mony a one as is cowder than us just now, Mister Frank."

"Yes, I know, in Russia. Mr. Basel was telling us one night how cold it is there. His father served in the Moscow campaign under Napoleon."

"I don't know nowt about Rooshia, or how cowd it is i' them mak' a' countries," answered Joe, gravely; "but they say as th' folks i' them there cottage houses is fair deeing a' cowd and hunger; and I reckon a chap cannot much more than dee either here or in Rooshia. It cannot be much waur than that, go wheer yo' will."

"But why don't they go and work at a factory, as folks do in our part?"

"Because there's none for 'em to work at. There isn't so very mony factories i' th' country, though mony a one thinks as there up o' th' increase. But that'll be no better for hand loom weyvers. It's just these steam looms as is a ruinating on 'em. When they've plenty to do they cannot addle (earn) aboon fifteen or eighteenpence a day, and just now there's hundreds on 'em as isn't addling aboon twopence-hopenny - work's that scarce. There is mony a one says as there'll be queer doings soon if there isn't a change. They wor' sayin' so only t'other neet at Th' Brown Cow. But it worn't allus so. I mind th' time when hand loom weyvers war welly as weel off as quality - addling their sixty shillings and four pounds a fortneet and lakeing and drinking two days a week at that. And gradely prodigal they wor - supped tay and coffee every day, and had both traycle and milk to their porridge. And some on 'em, when they wor' a bit sharp fresh, and had just drawn their wage, would eat their bread wi' bank notes 'stead a' butter. Mony a one says it wor all along a' their prodigalness as steam looms coom up. Suzhaw (anyhow) they're ill enough off and there'll be rough work afoor long; see if they willn't"

"What sort of rough work, Joe?"

"Why, brunning factories, breyking looms, and happen killing maysters, to be sure. They're terribly set on again them as has started steam looms. They've bornt one factory down at Bowton Moor o' ready, and they welly killed a mayster one neet last week not far fro' here. Yo're father should be careful when he goes out after dark, specially when he's coming back fro' Manchester, and has brass in his pockets. There's all sorts a' queer kracters about jest now, and mayster isn't weel liked. I quite expect summat 'll be happening to him one a' these neets."

"But you always meet him at The Hare and Hound; you know, Joe' when he comes home by coach," said Frank, rather alarmed by this startling suggestion.

"Nearly allus. Bet it's a dark, lonely road fro' Th' Hare and Hounds to th' Owd Factory, and there should be more than one to meet him, and I've towld him so. But he will not hear on it, nor let me bring the gun, nor a pistol nother; and then he sometimes takes th' gig, and other some rides a' hossback. I don't think it's gradely safe, and I nobbut hope no harm 'll happen nayther to him nor th' factory. They sayen as he's hard; but wages as he pays keeps many a poor mon's pot boiling; and it would not mend things to throw two or three hundred more folk out of work."

"How soon shall we bait, Joe?" interrupted Frank, who was growing rather weary of Joe's jeremiads.

"I worn't thinking of baiting at all, Mister Frank, till we getten to Yewdale. I'll gie th' mare some meal an' water when we're about hoaf way - and that'll be soon - and let her have a good rest at th' far end, and bait as I come back. Roads is i' good trim now; we mun make th' most an 'em afore they soften, and it'll maybe snow agean to'rd afternoon. I mun get yo' theer, and get back mysen as soon as I con. Yo're father 'll flight if I'm late. Two hours after this conversation they reached their destination.

Yewdale, an ancient place with a famous church and the ruins of a Norman castle, had once been the appanage of a noble family whose many-gabled and moated mansion, embowered in venerable trees, was still to be seen on the Yorkshire road. But the situation rendered it eminently suitable for the development of industrial enterprise, and it was being rapidly converted into a manufacturing town. The hills about were rich in minerals, water was abundant, and an excellent canal system placed Yewdale in easy, if not rapid, water communication with Liverpool on the west and Leeds on the east. Tall chimneys were springing up here and there, the erstwhile laughing river was beginning to look sour and dark with the refuse of dye-stuffs that were daily poured into it, and the dismal, unwholesome cottages which people in those days thought quite good enough for factory operatives were springing up everywhere.

Bigwater's school, as his boys called it, or, as he himself liked to describe it, "The Yewdale Academy for Young Gentlemen," was a long, slab-sided brick building in the outskirts of the town. The house was at one end, the school at the other. The front faced the street. In the rear were open spaces, used as playgrounds; a large garden, offices, a barn, and a shippen - for Bigwater kept cows and produced his own milk and butter.

The way to the schoolroom door and the boys' entrance to the house lay across this open space, and thither our travellers, directed by a passer by, drove at a good round pace. Like the proverbial Irish postboy, Joe had reserved a trot for the avenue.

Their arrival created quite a commotion. Groups of curious faces appeared at the school-room window; the house door was opened by a smart serving maid, over whose shoulder furtively peered a stout, florid-faced lady in cap and curl-papers. Then the school-room door opened, and the great Bigwater himself bustled on the scene - a portly gentleman of forty, with a clean-shaven, pleasant face and a pompous manner, black-stocked almost up to the ears, and wearing the inevitable swallow-tailed coat of the period.

"Ah! Frank Blackthorne, I presume. How do you do, Frank? I hope your father and mother are quite well? A fine mare you have got there, John - "

"If you please, sir, his name is Joe," interrupted Frank.

"Joe? Thank you. I have not a stable, Joe; but you will find excellent accommodation round the corner at The Rainbow, and if you will come here after you've put up your horse you shall have some refreshment, for I'm sure you will be hungry. It is the boys' dinner in half an hour, Frank. I suppose you would like to join them? Maria, will you and Nancy take Master Blackthorne's trunk into the box-room, and show him his bed - the one next the window in the big garret? Stay, I'll send one of the boys to take you round, tell you the ways of the place, and bring you in to dinner. And now I must go back to my class; they are making a terrible uproar, I hear."

CHAPTER V.

BIGWATER'S YOUNG GENTLEMEN.

In a few minutes Frank was joined by a boy with dishevelled hair, a round, pasty, and not over-clean face, and very inky fingers, who was apparently a little older than himself.

"Are you the new boy?" asked the new-comer.

"I suppose I am; I have only just come," answered Frank.

"Well, I'm an old boy; I've been here three years, and Bigwater's sent me to show you round and put you up to a thing or two; and doosed glad I am, for

I have not learnt a word of my lesson. What's your name? Mine's Tom Gunter."

"Frank Blackthorne."

"What a rum name! Blackthorne, buttermilk, and barleycorn; tag-rag, bob-tail; pig foot toe-nail."

"It's no rummer than yours," exclaimed Frank, indignantly. "Grunter! That's a pig's name; they're always grunting, pigs are."

"Come now, don't call names. I did not say *Grunter;* I said *Gunter.*"

"You began it. Why did you say Blackthorne was a rum name? I'm sure it is not."

"Don't get into a passion; I did not mean to vex you. I suppose you've some money? New boys always have."

"Yes, I've six shillings; but I must be careful of it. My father said it must last me all the half year."

"I had ten," said Gunter, gloomily; "and it all went the first week. You'll be very lucky if your six bob is not all gone in a month. Let us run down the street and buy some brandy snaps at Thorpe's; they're awfully good."

"What were you doing, to spend your money so soon?" asked Frank, as they returned from buying the brandy snaps.

"One of the fellows had played me a shabby trick, and I wanted to serve him out; so I bought four shillings' worth of oranges and four shillings' worth of nuts, and gave some to every fellow but him. The other two shillings I spent on brandy snaps," continued Gunter, as he gobbled up all that remained of Frank's purchase.

"Then you'll have to do without money all the rest of the half year?"

"I suppose I shall," sighed Gunter, "except for my weekly allowance. That's twopence; Bigwater pays it every Saturday. Could you lend a fellow fourpence, Blackthorne? I'd give it you back at a penny a week, the first penny next Saturday."

Frank, not without some misgiving, handed Gunter a fourpenny piece.

"My eye!" exclaimed the latter, "that's the dinner bell; let's hurry up. Bigwater doesn't like fellows going in after grace."

They found the greater part of the boys, some forty in all, already assembled in the dining-room - a large apartment, with an uncarpeted stone floor, and unpapered walls. Three tables were provided for the accommodation of the diners, among whom, seated at the head and foot of the first table, were the four tutors. On a fourth table, at which stood Mr. Bigwater and Miss Bigwater - the latter a maiden lady of a certain age - were placed a vast array of plates; and two huge and smoking dishes.'

"Sit down here next to me," whispered Gunter to Frank.

"Gregson!" shouted Bigwater in a stentorian voice.

Then a small boy, sitting over against Frank, whom the call seemed very much to surprise, after a moment's' hesitation, bent dawn his head and spoke with breathless rapidity as follows:-

"Gosholyname be blessed and praised for these an-all-other-mercies bestowed 'pon us time-to-time. Amen."

This done, two youths rose from their seats, and going to the side table received and handed round the plates, as they were filled by Mr. And Miss Bigwater from the dishes near them.

"Stickthrottle! exclaimed Gunter in great disgust as it came to his turn to be served.

"Why, this is pudding," said Frank, curiously eyeing the yellow-looking mixture which one of the boy-servers had just pushed under his nose. "Don't you ever have flesh-meat?"

"'Oh yes! but we always get pudding first - to make us eat less meat, I suppose - and this pudding is that sticky inside, and that stiff out that it's really something awful to struggle through such a dollop of it as this."

"Why don't you leave it then?"

"I dare say - and get no meat! Unless we send up clean plates old Big won't give us any second course. They deal out no fresh plates here, you know; so here goes.

The "stickthrottle" eaten, each boy was served with roast meat. The bread was *ad libitum,* and the meal, though somewhat rough, was sufficient and none went hungry away.

When Frank went out he found Yorkshire Joe waiting for him.

"I mun go now, Frank," he said; "th' mare has had' a good feed, and I've had my dinner in th' kitchen, and Mr. Bigwater's gan me a shilling."

"And here's sixpence for you, Joe, to drink my health when you get home. Come, Gunter, let's go to The Rainbow and see him off"

Joe went away in excellent spirits, and with thoughts of buttered gin.

"It's a half holiday this afternoon," observed Gunter, as they returned to the school, "and there's going to be a fight in the playground between Bobby Fountain and Bill Thomson."

"What are they going to fight about?"

"To see which is the better man, to be sure. Come on; I would not miss it for a shilling's worth of brandy snaps."

They were just in time.

A ring had been formed at the end of the playground farthest from the entrance. In the centre of it stood two of the biggest boys in the school, glaring and squaring at each other. Neither seemed much disposed to strike the first blow. But after considerable dodging, one of them, throwing hesitation to the winds, rushed furiously at his antagonist, and dealt him a tremendous kick on the shins, the crack whereof was heard all over the playground. The other returned the blow with interest and a fierce "up and down" fight in Lancashire fashion, followed. They plied both fists and feet. They seized each other by the hair; they pummelled each other's faces and rolled together in the mud. The one who happened to be uppermost never hesitated, when he had the chance, to kick the other while he was down.

The excitement of the onlookers was intense. They vociferated as if they were possessed. "Now, Fountain!" "Now, Thomson!" "Pitch into him, Bobby!" "Go it Bill!" "That was a hot 'Un!" "Give him one on his nob!" "Catch bold of his topping!" "Never say die!" they screeched, making as fearful an uproar as if Yewdale Academy had been turned into a pandemonium, and its impish tenants were holding high festival.

At the very moment when the noise was at its height it became suddenly hushed. The combatants, who were struggling on the ground, separated and jumped to their feet. The onlookers rapidly dispersed.

This miracle bad been wrought by the single word "Nix!" uttered by a small boy.

Two minutes later, "Nix," in the person of 'Mr. Bigwater, entered the playground.

"What's all this noise? What have you been doing? A fight, I presume, from the terrible commotion you made, and the general appearance of things. Who has been fighting?" he demanded of the small boy who had given the alarm.

"If you please, sir, it was somebody, sir'" quavered the little fellow hesitatingly. Then, as if struck by a sudden thought, "If you please, sir, I think there was two of them; but I'm too little, sir, and I could not see, but I think there was two."

"The truth is, I suppose, you dare not tell. Never mind; I'll find out."

"Nix" walked round the playground, looking sharply about. He spied a boy walking abstractedly to and fro, his head bent down, and seemingly deep in the study of "Lindley Murray." There were several patches of wet mud on his trousers.

"You are very studious to-day, Thomson: what book have you got?"

"If you please, sir, it's my grammar lesson for tomorrow."

In answering he was obliged to raise his head.

"Ah!" exclaimed Bigwater, "you are one of them; who's the other?"

Thomson's nose, never small, had become portentously large; one of his eyes was almost swollen up, and there were traces of blood on his cheek.

"Fountain's the other, sir," answered the lad promptly, for he saw it was useless to attempt any further concealment.

"Fountain, come hither," shouted Bigwater. Fountain came. His face was even in a worse condition than Thomson's.

"Ah, you have given it to each other pretty well, I think. A good caning would not have hurt you half as much; and seeing what a severe castigation you have both received, I shall refrain from inflicting on you much further punishment. Still, I must mark my sense of the misconduct and brutality of which you have been guilty. I suppose you both know Dr. Watts's hymn, 'Let dogs delight to bark and bite'?"

"Yes, sir," answered the culprits simultaneously.

"Very well. Then you will write it out each of you five times, and repeat it aloud to-morrow morning before the whole school after prayers, and write out also the 17th chapter of Proverbs."

Then with sternly compressed lips, from the effect of which a merry twinkle in his eye somewhat detracted, Bigwater quitted the playground, leaving Fountain and Thomson gazing blankly in each other's face. They would rather have pummelled each other another hour than recite "Let dogs delight to bark and bite" in presence of the whole school. They would never hear the last of it, and lads have no less keen a sense of the ridiculous; and even a greater dread of ridicule, than their elders.

By this time Frank had got separated from Gunter, and he entered into conversation with the small boy who had called out "Nix."

"What does 'Nix' mean?" he asked.

"Why, don't you know? Old Big, to be sure. It means any of the masters too; so when you hear 'Nix' you've got to look out."

"Does Big cane much?"

"Not much, except when he gets into a wax; then he lays on. But that is not often; he is not half a bad sort, old Big isn't. I wish all the masters were as good."

"Do you know Gunter?"

"Of course I do; I know every fellow in the school. He's always eating brandy snaps when he can get 'em, and borrowing money from new boys."

Frank pulled a long face.

"Has he borrowed any from you?"

"Yes, fourpence; but he said he'd pay me back at the rate of a penny a week, beginning on Saturday."

"Out of his allowance, didn't he say? Oh, my eye, you were green. Why that allowance is bespoke by lots of fellows. You'll have to look uncommon sharp if you get your fourpence again. Don't tell him I told you; if you do he'll wallop me."

"If he does I'll wallop him; and if he does not give me my fourpence back, I'll wallop him too," answered Frank indignantly.

Can you?"

"I think I could; at any rate, I mean to try if he either touches you or does not keep his word to me."

"Perhaps you might; I don't think he's so very plucky at the bottom. Anyhow, don't seem afraid of him, or you'll never get your money back."

At five o'clock night had fallen, and all the boys had gathered in the school-room. Most of them were seated on a long form with their backs to the desk, which ran up the middle of the floor. One youth sat near the door, holding on his knee a big brass bell.

"What's that fellow doing with the bell?" asked Frank of Gunter.

"Nursing it."

"What on earth for?"

"To have the first take of bread and butter. The crusts are all on the top, you know, and the first taker gets the most of them. The fellow who rings the bell is entitled to the first take.

Just then one of the masters came in with an immense tray, on which were heaped up at least a hundred very thick slices of bread, covered with exceedingly thin layers of butter.

The bell-nurser, after ringing the bell, helped himself to a handful of crusts, and the master, beginning at the top of the form, allowed every boy to help himself in turn.

"Where's the tea?" demanded Frank.

The lads who beard him laughed.

"There's no tea here, nor yet coffee," said one of them.

"What do you drink, then?"

"Water. There's plenty at the pump, isn't there, Gunter?"

Then there was another laugh; for Gunter hated water in any shape, and never washed even his hands, save on compulsion.

"But you are not limited to bread and butter, you know. You can have, almost at a moment's notice, red herrings, black puddings, sausages, or polonies."

The speaker was a tall youth who stood with his back to the fire. He had an incipient moustache, a hooked nose, a single eye, "and a little one at that," and his name was Cliffe.

"But how do you get 'em?" asked Frank. "I think I'd like a red herring."

"Easy enough. By sending down to Barnish's. Herrings two for three-halfpence, one a penny; and sausages, polonies, and black puddings you can have on equally moderate terms. Awkward price, though, two for three-halfpence, unless you buy two, by far the cheapest way. Now, I'll tell you what I'll do, Blackthorne. We'll have a couple of red 'uns between us; and I'll toss you up whether you pay for them or I do. That's a chance for you, now; for I've such awful bad luck that I always lose when I toss."

"Very well," said Frank, who had a great weakness for fish. "I will."

Cliffe fumbled in his pockets. "Very strange," he ejaculated, withdrawing his hands empty. "I must have left my purse in my other breeches pocket. However, no matter. Has any fellow a coin?"

No answer.

"I am not particular. A penny will do - or a halfpenny-has nobody got a halfpenny?"

Still no answer.

"Upon my word, we're a penniless lot. But you have doubtless a coin or two, Blackthorne. Tip Us one here, and I'll toss. If I lose, as I'm sure to do, I'll pay up when I find my purse."

The lads who heard this grinned; and the small boy whose acquaintance Frank had made in the playground fairly chuckled.

"Silence, you little whelp, or I'll choke you," exclaimed Cliffe fiercely. "I never saw such a fool as you are, Carter; you are always giggling, just like a girl."

Meanwhile Frank had handed him a penny.

"Here goes," said Cliffe, poising the copper dexterously on the forefinger and thumb of his right hand. "What do you say, Blackthorn - head or tail?"

"Tail."

"By Jingo, it's heads. First time I've won a toss this half; I swear it is. Better luck next time, Blackthorne," he added encouragingly, for Frank looked rather glum.

He was thinking of his father's exhortations to economy, and that, at the rate he was going on, his six shillings, instead of lasting him the half year, would be gone in a week - or rather his five, for it had already sunk to that sum.

"If you'll give Carter a halfpenny more he'll run to Barnish's and fetch the herrings. Choose good ones, Carter - plump, and with plenty of belly in 'em - and you shall have the roes for your trouble, if there are any.

Carter trotted off, and in five minutes he was back with the fish.

"Do you eat 'em raw?" asked Frank, who, fond as he was of fish, did not quite feel like eating uncooked red herring.

"Lord bless you, no," laughed Cliffe. "Here, Carter, cook 'em for us."

On this Carter took a piece of dirty string from his pocket, tied the two ends of it to the herrings' tails, and held them before the fire, which was hot and bright. In a few minutes they were pronounced "done," and Frank and Cliffe, with the help of their pocket-knives and using their bread and butter as plates, made a hearty meal - "bagging" the boys called it.

"The next time we toss it shall be for a black pudding?" observed Cliffe interrogatively.

Frank assented, but with a mental reservation that it would be a precious long time before he tossed with Mr. Cliffe again.

"This is not the only repast old Big gives us, you know," said the latter. "The day winds up with a magnificent supper; beats the bagging into fits."

"Hot meat and that, I suppose?" said Frank with a sigh; for he felt that after all the herring and bread and butter he had eaten he would not have much room for supper.

"Not quite. Dry bread and blue milk."

"Only that!"

"But such milk! You have no idea. In winter it's warmed, in summer it's sour, but it's that strong that not everybody can take it. It's been known to make new fellows drunk before now. Yes, old Big's very generous about supper, I must say, only somehow I don't often take advantage of his kindness. Dry bread and blue milk's a good deal too rich for me; my stomach won't stand it; and my mother said I'd to be very careful of myself, and not to have as many black draughts in my bill as I had last half. Old Big always makes you swallow a black draught when you are seedy, and they cost tenpence apiece, besides being bad to take. I chucked the last out of the window, and then he said, when I told him afterwards that I felt better, says he, 'Ah, black draught's a capital medicine. I knew it would set you to rights.'"

"Well for you he didn't catch you," said Gunter "When he caught Pudson throwing away his black draught, he sent for two more, and made him take both at one swallow."

"Serve him right; the beggar was shamming."

"Anyhow, he's never been ill since - shamming or not."

"I should think not. Who would be ill if he knew he'd have to take two black draughts? I'd rather have a caning any time; but some fellows would take a dose every day if they could miss school, and have a long sleep every morning."

"What's a black draught?" asked Frank, to whom this conversation was an enigma.

"Oh, golly, just fancy! Here's a fellow who does not know what a black draught is. You'll know soon enough. How old are you, Blackthorne?"

"Eleven."

"Well, some morning, when you complain of a head-ache, or look rather yellow about the gills, old Big will say, 'You are not looking very well to-day, Blackthorne. Here you, Carter, just step down to Dr. Killjoy's, and ask him to be good enough to send a black draught for a boy of eleven - or stay, Blackthorne's tall for his age - twelve years old.' And when you get it I wish you joy of it - that's all. You have no appetite that day, and be sick all the next. I think that is why old Big is so fond of physicking us; it saves his larder."

At half-past eight the bell rang for prayers. The boys occupied one side of the school-room, sitting with their backs to the desks, while Mr. Bigwater's family and domestics occupied the other; and as he had nearly a dozen children, the two sides were almost equally well filled.

Then Bigwater mounted a rostrum, not very unlike a pulpit, and, after reading a chapter in the Bible, delivered a long extempore prayer. After this the boys all went up to bed.

"Come along," said Gunter; "I'll show you the way. You're to sleep in the big garret, Miss Bigwater says."

The garret was a large, low chamber, with a single window and an uncarpeted but scrupulously clean floor, literally covered with wooden beds; there being no fewer than twelve of them, ranged in two rows, with their heads against the wall and their feet pointing to the centre of the room. Than these there was no furniture – neither chair, table, nor mirror.

"This is your bed," said Gunter, showing him one near the window. "It's all right; see, Miss Big has laid out your night things. Look sharp and get undressed. Old Cuckoo never lets us have the candle long."

Most of the boys - some sixteen in all, for several of them were "doubled up " - were already between the blankets, and Frank hastened to follow their example. He was only just undressed when the individual elegantly denominated by Gunter "Old Cuckoo," who was, in fact, one of the masters, stumped into the garret with a great clatter - for he wore heavy Wellington boots, and carried two rickety candlesticks, which he had brought from the other garrets, in one hand, and a bunch of keys in the other - took up the candle, a halfpenny dip, from the floor, and with a curt "Good-night, boys," clattered out again, bolting the door behind him.

"It's an awful shame to make fellows go to bed at this time of day," said a voice from the darkness. It cannot be much after half-past eight. We might all be children. What shall we do? By Jove, if it were not so confoundedly cold we'd have a pillow match."

"Let's have a tale."

"No, a song," suggested another; "I vote for a song."

"And me - and me - and me," shouted a chorus of voices from the darkness.

"That's all very fine," put in the first voice, "but who'll sing?"

"Gunter. Come, Gunter old fellow, tip us a stave."

"No, thank you; I don't feel like singing to-night. Ask Blackett, there; he can sing better than I can."

"Blackett will sing afterwards. Won't you, Blackett?"

"If Gunter sings I will."

"There, now, Gunter, be a decent fellow."

"Let a fellow alone, can't you? I'm doosed sleepy; I can hardly keep my eyes open."

"Come, now, Gunter; I'll tell you what I'll do; if you'll sing 'Gaily the Troubadour' and 'The Old English Gentleman,' I'll be a halfpenny towards half a pound of brandy snaps for you."

"And so will I - and so will I," exclaimed two other voices.

"Agreed!" shouted Gunter, "but no encores."

"Yes, one encore; at least one," answered the three subscribers.

"No."

"Then devil a halfpenny you'll get of mine," said one.

"Nor of mine," said the other two.

"Well, I'll stand one encore then, but no more. Is it a bargain?"

"Agreed; it's a bargain."

After this knotty point was settled, Gunter, in a very fair voice, sang, "Gaily the Troubadour" and "The Old English Gentleman," both of which were loudly applauded, and the latter enthusiastically encored.

Then Blackett, in a piping treble voice, gave "Will you Marry me, my Pretty Maid?" "The Girl I left behind me," and "Home, sweet Home."

Meanwhile, Frank was thinking rather sadly of those he had left behind. He had never in his life felt so much alone as in that room full of boisterous boys, his destined companions, probably, for years. He thought of his mother - who, he knew, was at this moment either praying or weeping for him - and his little sister Mabel, with her bright blue eyes and red, round cheeks; and of his father, albeit his love for him was somewhat tempered by fear. From them his thoughts wandered to Yorkshire Joe (how he wished he could have gone back with him!), to Tommy Twirler, Shep, and all the people at Moorwell and the Old Factory; and as little Blackett warbled the last verse of "Home, sweet Home," he buried his head in the bedclothes and quietly cried himself to sleep.

CHAPTER VI.

AT THE TINKER AND BUDGET.

Yorkshire Joe went on his homeward way rejoicing. He felt himself rich, or, in his own language, "gradely set up." What with Bigwater's shilling, Frank's sixpence, and the saving he had made by giving the mare meal and water instead of a regular bait, and getting his dinner at Bigwater's instead of The Rainbow, he was at least three shillings to the good. Three shillings! And Joe pulled the horse into a walk that he might the more fully give his mind to the contemplation of the good fortune which had befallen him, and all the possibilities it opened up.

He would have Welsh rarebit for his bagging - that was one point settled - and wash it down with a pint of fettled ale; and then - why, then he would have one glass, perhaps two, of buttered gin, just to pass the time while Frisky ate her feed, which he had resolved should be an eightpenny one, in addition to fourpenny-worth of hay. After that he would drive comfortably home, whither he hoped to arrive just at the edge of dark – say between five and six o'clock.

'As he came along in the morning he had noticed, shortly after leaving Waterhead Moor, a quiet little inn with the sign of a Tinker and Budget. There he resolved he would feed his horse and refresh himself. It was about half-way on the road home, and its general appearance, he thought, suggested a happy combination of good spirits, comfort, and low charges.

Three o'clock had only just gone when he drove up to the inn door - rather soon for bagging, as he said to himself; but the day was cold and his appetite good, so that he felt quite in trim for the Welsh rarebit and etceteras, early as it was.

They had not much of a stable, the woman said who came to answer his summons.

"It was nobbut vary seldom as 'osses and gigs coom to Th' Tinker and Budget - to tell th' truth they had no stable at all; but he could happen mak shift i' th' shippen, just behind th' house there."

So Joe was compelled to put Frisky in the shippen and the gig in the barn, a tumble-down old building with a rickety door. However, he managed to make the mare pretty comfortable; and after feeding and watering her, he went into the inn, full of gleeful anticipations of Welsh rarebits, fettled ale, and buttered gin. Joe was not disappointed with what he found there - a large kitchen, with a clean sanded floor, a bright fire, comfortable settle, and a couple of big arm-chairs, in one of which was seated the woman who had come to the door - a stout middle-aged, motherly-looking body - darning a stocking.

"Draw up to th' fire," she said; "it's a gradely cowd day; as cowd a one, welly, as we've had this winter. Con I get yo' owt?"

"Con yo' mak a Welsh rabbit?"

"Con I? That I con, and a gradely good 'un, too. We'n some rare good cheese i' th' house just now."

"And fettle some ale?"

"Ay, and fettle some ale; nobody better."

"Well, I'll have Welsh rabbit and fettled ale for a start; and then, if th' mare hasn't finished her feed, I'll happen have a glass o' buttered gin, just to keep the cowd out."

"Ay, ay, they wanten summut this weather - them as con get it - to keep thersells warm," said the landlady as she cut the cheese. "But there's mony a one about here as connot get porridge, much less a drop o' drink. The times is just fearfu'; folks has clean gan o'er supping, and they mon be ill off when they dun that. We're fair selling nowt at all. My mayster's gone to-day to Haslingden to pay th' beer bill, and it's that little as he's fair shamed o' facing up at th' brewery. It's o' along o' these steam looms i' my opinion. I wish they were all smashed, and them as browt 'em into th' country had their heads knocked off - that is what I wish."

"Hush, miss us, yo' shouldn't talk i' that way - it's not safe."

"What for? Yo're not a factory mayster, nor yet a factory mayster's servant, I expect?" exclaimed the landlady, turning sharply round.

"Not I," said Joe, with ready cunning. "I drive for Th' King's Arms at Orrington. I'm of ' th' same mind as yo' are, but it is not allus safe to say what yo' thinkin, somebody mut be listening."

"Listening! Why, there is nobody here to listen but wer two selves. But yo're happen reet. It is not a thing to he much talked about. But it will be talked about, mark my words if it is not. There's too much clemming going on for quietness. But willn't yo come up to the table? Th' rabbit 'll be ready in a minute or two."

When Joe had eaten his "rabbit" and drunk his pint of fettled ale he went to see how Frisky was faring. She seemed very comfortable, and was munching away heartily at her feed; so, after adjusting her rug, and giving her an armful of hay, he returned to the house and ordered a glass of buttered gin.

"I've no gin up," said the landlady. "I'll go down into th' cellar and fotch some."

"See yo' now," was her exclamation when she came back - a' jug in one hand and a candle in the other - "there is some rare stuff here - look!"

And popping a pudgy finger into the jug, she held it near the candle. A light-blue flame flickered for an instant round the finger and vanished.

"Rare stuff, isn't it?" she repeated complacently; "see how it blazes. And yo' shall hev it as it comes out o the cellar for once, though it wouldn't do to let every-body have it i' that way; it couldn't be afforded."

"Bout (without) being bobbed, yo' mean?" said Joe, with a grin.

The landlady gave a responsive leer.

"Now," she continued, "yo' can mix for yourself. Here is hot wayter, and butter and sugar."

Then Joe proceeded to concoct the villainous drink which he liked so well. It was simply gin and hot water, well sweetened, and with a lump of butter in it - a mixture that, coming on the top of Welsh rarebit and fettled ale, would have floored most men, but which had only the effect of making Joe feel intensely happy; so happy, indeed, that after the first glass was finished he helped himself to a second, and the second naturally led to a third.

When he had arrived at this stage, and his sense of happiness was beginning to merge into one of overpowering sleepiness, the house door opened and gave admission to two men.

They were clad in fustian. One was a big fellow, with a rather heavy countenance, and a heavy pack on his back; the other was small, sharp-looking, almost diabolically dark complexioned, and had a club foot.

"He looks devilish like Owd Nick," muttered Joe to himself, "you does. He's as black as a Jew, and that game leg of his looks most terrible queer. By gum, it happen is him. They say as he's going about a good deal just now. But it's allus best to speak a man like him fair. I'll ax him to hev a glass o' buttered gin."

"A cowd day," he remarked in his civilest manner to the new-comers.

"Bith mon, I'm not cowd," laughed the big fellow; "and yo' wouldn't be, neither, if ye' had carried these warps as I hev, all th' way fro' Manchester."

"Well, I did feel it rather cowd," said his companion, "but then I've had no warps to carry."

"Have a sup o' gin and hot water; buttered - it'll warm yo' - it has done me," said Joe, with a half hiccup.

"Thank yo'; I'll take a drop o' gin, but no butter, if it is all the same to you. You're a stranger i' these parts, I think?" remarked the little man, eyeing Joe keenly.

"Ay," answered the latter, "I don't belong to this country. I come fro' Orrington (Moorwell he was going to say; but remembering the story he had told the landlady, he checked himself in time). I'm a driver fro' The King's Arms, and I've just been taking a rider-out (commercial traveller) to Yewdale."

"Oh," said the other, sipping his gin; "and are you thinking of going there to-neet?"

"I'm thinking o' doing nowt else; if I don't I'se catch it. Con onybody tell me what time it's gettin?"

"A bit after six o'clock," said the dark-complexioned little man, pulling from his fob an enormous pinchbeck watch.

"Yo' don't say so!" exclaimed Joe, looking greatly surprised, as indeed he was. "I mun be pikeing off, and sharp too. Why, I said I'd be at huom afoor six o'clock."

"Afoor six o'clock to-morrow morning, maybe," answered a little man, with a sardonic laugh, "but not to-neet; it's nearly half-past six now."

"What's th' shot missus? I'm going," said Joe, swallowing the last of his buttered gin; for he would have thought it a sin to leave the least drop of it undrunk.

After paying the reckoning, which left him with only sixpence in his pocket, he asked for a lantern, and went to the barn with a view to immediate departure.

As he opened the inn door he heard the Satanic-looking little man ask the landlady how soon she expected the others.

"Towards nine o'clock," answered the landlady.

When Joe stepped into the fresh air he felt so queer that he began to suspect he was in a condition which he mentally characterised as "welly sharp fresh;" that is, very nearly drunk; and he had some difficulty in finding the shippen door; for.the night was dark, and there were several awkward corners to be doubled.

The mare was tying down.

"Shoo looks vary comfortable," said Joe, raising the lantern with one hand, and swaying to and fro, as he tried to steady himself against the wall with the other. "I think it would do me good to lie down a bit, too. A bit of a nap would set me up. Bith mon, I will; I'll lie me down hoaf an hour. Just hoaf an hour," he repeated, as, after making an extempore bed of hay, he threw himself on the shippen floor, not far from Frisky. "Hoaf an hour, just hoaf an hour," he murmured again, and the next moment he was buried in happy oblivion and hay.

When he came to himself his first impression, as he afterwards said, was that he had been sleeping in a field "with th' gate wide open," he felt so terribly cold; and he was about to spring to his feet when he heard the sound of voices in the barn, from which the shippen was only separated by a partition some three feet high. One of them he recognised as that of the little swarthy man with the club foot, in whom he had seen so striking a likeness to our ghostly foe. The discussion seemed to be a heated one, and a name was frequently mentioned that sobered Joe in a moment, and made him as vigilant and observant as an Indian brave on the war-path.

"I tell you," the voice was saying, "we must begin with this Adam Blackthorne. He is th' hardest and most tyrannical master in th' country-side. He was one of th' first to bring steam looms into these parts - him as has made a fortune out of hand loom weavers - and he uses his hands like slaves. A delegate as has just come fro' Orrington heard this afternoon as he threw a spinner in th' brook last night, just because he asked for his wage as had been wrongly kept back from him; and it is not the first time that he has done th' like. 'Live and let live,' that's my motto, and this man Blackthorne does not seem disposed to let anybody live but himself. He takes bread out of poor folks' mouths, and if they complain he ill-uses 'em. He must be made an example of. These cursed looms of his must be smashed; and if that is not enough, his factory burnt down. I'm only a delegate and stranger i' these parts, as yo' know. It's for you as lives hereabouts, if you're agreed, to say as how th' job shall be carried out; but if I may say what I think - the sooner the better."

"I don't see as there's much use i' smashing looms," said another; "they'll nobbut buy fresh 'uns, and then it'll be as bad as ever - happen waur. We should smash them as makes 'em, and likewise them as runs em - them's my principles. Smash owd Blackthorne and a two or three moor o' th' same sort, and then we shall be doing some good.

"Ay, that's it," exclaimed several voices together, "let's knock his owd heyd off."

"That might come afterwards," said the stranger, who, being a delegate, spoke as one having authority; "but let us try loom-breaking first, and if that does not do, why then we'll try summut else."

"If so be as Blackthorne comes near me when we getten there," growled another, "I'll give him summut as'll mak his heyd warch (head ache). I've getten a big hommer, and I'se use it. It's as easy to crack a skull as to break a loom."

"I don't think he'll come near you, Grindleton; he's too much sense for that. Now, what are our plans? Con we be ready by Sunday night? I think that will be as good a time as any."

"Ay con we," said Grindleton; "me and two or three moor can give th' lads warning between now and then. We could meet here, or between here and Orrington, about th' edge o' dark, so as to reach th' Owd Factory toward eleven o'clock."

"How many can we muster?"

"About a thousand, I reckon; and two or three hundred moor will join us on th' road."

"Twelve or thirteen hundred, then, all told?"

"Somewheer about."

"Quite enough for the purpose, I expect. We are not likely to meet with opposition," said the delegate, "if we are all true, and the secret is well kept. Nobody must say a word as to where we are going. Only tell th' lads of th' place of meeting and th' time, and to bring hammers and crowbars with 'em."

"And when shall we meet again, Dearden?" asked an another.

"Grindleton and me will fix that to-morrow, and let you know one by one; it'll be safest, I think; walls have ears, sometimes. Now let's go into Th' Tinker and Budget and wet wer whistles."

"My God, what's that ?"

It was Frisky's head showing dimly above the partition as she rose to her feet. But the apparition was so sudden and startling that the conspirators made a general skedaddle towards the barn door.

Dearden and Grindleton alone kept their ground. "Come back, you fools!" shouted the former; "it's only a horse."

"Oh, it's nobbut a hoss, is it?" said one of the fugitives. "I thowt it were th' Owd Lad. I know I wor gradely ill flayed. But they said as the barn wor empty, didn't they?"

"Whose hoss is it, I wonder?" said Grindleton, taking a lantern and going towards the partition. "Hullo! here's a mon asleep i' th' boose (stall); hang me if there isn't."

This announcement created. a great sensation. The conspirators gathered round Grindleton and stared at Yorkshire Joe, who, to all seeming, was fast asleep, half-buried in a bottle of hay. The man called Dearden was the first to speak.

"Why," he said, "it's the fellow as was drinking buttered gin i' Th' Tinker and Budget when we went in. And very kindly he was taking his liquor too; and this is his hoss. Why, Yarker's wife said he'd gone."

"Happen he wor too drunk to go."

"That's it, I expect, and he has just fallen down in that hay and slept ever since. He cannot have heard what we have been saying?"

"If I thought he had," put in Grindleton, savagely, "I'd throttle him. He mut hang every devil on us, or leastways send us to Botany Bay."

"It would happen be th' safest course to stick a knife into his ribs," said Dearden, thoughtfully. "Dead men tell no tales."

Or cut his windpipe," suggested another.

"No," said Dearden, after a pause. " No, he has every appearance of being asleep. See (turning the light of the lantern full on Joe's face); and when a mon has been drinking fettled ale and buttered gin he generally does sleep sound. To put him out of th' way might bring us into trouble. You see he has a horse and gig with him; they'd be missed and inquired after, and soon, too. No, we'd best let him alone. Come, let's be going. Me and Grindleton's stopping here till Saturday, so you'll know where to find us if we are wanted."

When Joe heard the barn door close behind the plotters he heaved a deep sigh of relief, yet he neither opened his eyes nor changed his position, for he was by no means sure they might not come back. He had lain thus perhaps half an hour, when he beard the sound of approaching footsteps. Then the door opened, and he felt himself roughly shaken by the shoulders.

"Waken up!" shouted a voice, which he recognised as that of the little dark man. "Waken up, mon, are yo' going to sleep here all neet?"

"He's gradely fast asleep; I never see nobody faster," said Grindleton. "Poo' his toppin, Dearden."

Dearden gave a tremendous tug at Joe's red head, whereupon the latter opened a pair of surprised eyes and inquired what was up.

"What's up? Why, Mrs. Yarker, thats th' landlady, wants to know if you're going to stop here all neet."

"Why, what time is it?

"After ten o'clock."

"Ten o'clock !" exclaimed Joe, jumping up with great alacrity, "and me as should ha' been huom by six, and if I don't get through th' bars afore twelve I shall have 'em to pay o'er again; and all my brass is done. I mun be off i' three minutes, that I mun. I nobbut thowt o' sleeping hoaf an hour, an' I've slept four."

"Come, Grindleton, let's give him a lift. Where is your gig, old chap?"

"In that shed at th' end o' th' barn. Come hup, Frisky!"

"Shall we go and get it out for you?"

"Thank yo' kindly, I wish yo' would."

"He's heard nowt," said Dearden to Grindleton, as they went towards the shed, "that's certain."

"Not him, no moor than if he'd been a corpse."

"That's th' little un an' th' big un," Joe was saying to himself: "him as talked o' sticking a knife into my ribs and him as wanted to throttle me. If ever I meet either on 'em by hissell, I'll give him what for, that I will. Come hup, Frisky! - come, owd lass, we mun put th' best foot foremost this time. I want to get out o' this hoyle, I do that. Come hup, 1 say!"

CHAPTER VII

YORKSHIRE JOE TO THE RESCUE.

Meanwhile, Joe's prolonged absence was causing great uneasiness, and even anxiety, at Moorwell. Adam Blackthorne had confidently counted on his being back not later than six o'clock. When seven o'clock came, and Joe did not appear, he knitted his brows; at eight he was furious.

"He's fuddling in some public-house, the fool!" said Adam to his wife, as he gloomily smoked his pipe before the parlour fire, "and the mare, ten to one, getting her death of cold outside."

"It is that lad I'm thinking about," observed Mrs. Blackthorne, with a wistful look, suspending her knitting to listen for the sound of Frisky's hoofs in the avenue. "Perhaps some ill has befallen him. I thought I heard something then; did you?"

"No; besides, Rock would hear them before we could, and his bark will tell us. Don't worrit yourself about Frank, Rachel. He's safe and sound at the far end long since. Joe generally does his errands right enough: I will give him that credit; it is coming home that he gets into mischief. I thought I had put it out of his power to get any drink as would do him any harm. He had not a shilling more with him than he needed to pay his way."

"A man can get a good deal of drink for a shilling."

"Not much; at any rate, not so much as to make a man like Joe so drunk that he could not drive straight home. I'm only afraid of some harm happening to the mare or the gig."

"Would anybody rob him, do you think? There are many loose characters about, they say."

"What could they rob him of? If he was bringing money, I should, maybe, have some misgivings. It is all drink: you'll see if it isn't; somebody's been treating him: that is what it is. I'll give him a bit of my mind when he does come, confound him! It is getting on to halfpast eight; he cannot be long now."

But when another hour passed and yet another, and there was still no sign of Joe, Adam lost all patience.

"I'll go and look for him," he said abruptly, rising from his chair; "and if he's as drunk as I expect to find him, I'll throw him into the nearest ditch and leave him there."

"Don't you think it's dangerous, Adam, going out alone at this time of night?"

"No; why should it be dangerous, Rachel? I shall not go far. Ring the bell: I'll have my boots and cloak."

"I cannot tell why, Adam, but I am always uneasy when you are out after dark. There are many people out of work, and you are not very popular, you know."

"That's likely enough, but it's long after bedtime, and nobody will expect one to be out at this hour. I shall, ten to one, not meet a soul. However, I'll take my ash stick: that with a bit of lead in the knob."

"And let Rock go with you, won't you?"

"Then you'll have nobody to give you warning when the gig comes."

"Never mind that; I have sharp ears."

"Very well, then, I'll take him - though I don't think it's necessary - just to please you, Rachel."

"That is very good of you, Adam. Don't be any longer than you can help."

"You may be sure of that."

Adam, after whistling for Rock, walked rapidly down the avenue, which was bounded on one side by a row of trees and shrubs and the factory wall, and on the other by a wide grass plot, until he reached a pair of iron gates, flanked by a smaller one. Opening this with a latch-key, he stepped into a narrow cinder-covered lane, bordered by tall hedgerows. Everything was perfectly still, not a sound could be heard, and the darkness and quietness of the cottages by the roadside indicated that all their occupants were in bed.

There was no moon, but the sky was starlit, and where the road was level Adam could easily see a score of yards or so before him.

He had walked very nearly half an hour - covering, perhaps, two miles of ground - in the direction in which he expected to find Joe, without meeting anybody, when a sound of revelry struck his ear, and as he entered a straight part of the lane he saw a light gleaming from the window of a solitary house.

"They're keeping it up late at The Blazing Stump," he muttered to himself. "I wonder if Joe's stopping there. As like as not. I'll just peep in if I don't see the gig outside, for he has mayhap put it into the shed behind."

When he reached the house, a small roadside tavern, he stepped up to the window of the principal room, where the drinkers were generally gathered, and looked inside. As far as he could see, there were at least a dozen, nearly all miners apparently, but Joe was not amongst them. The only face he recognised was that of Little Fourteen, who was hammering the table with a glass, by way of expressing his satisfaction, while a half-tipsy collier was attempting with very indifferent success to sing.

"What a drunken little rascal it is!" thought Adam. "I've heard of him being here before; he's always fuddling somewhere. Glad none of my chaps are among 'em. Where can Joe be, I wonder? It is eleven o'clock by this time."

At this moment Little Fourteen suddenly ceased his hammering, and uttering a name which brought the singing to an abrupt conclusion, pointed his pipe towards the window.

"That's owd Blackthorne's face!" he shouted, "him as pitched me i' th' bruck last neet. What the blazes is he doing theere?"

On this Adam, though he had not quite made out what Little Fourteen said, thought it was time to be going, and whistling the mastiff to heel, resumed his walk, now more lonely than ever, for he was on the edge of the moor, and the houses were few and far between.

But his journey was not destined to be quite so uneventful as he had expected. He had hardly left the inn half an hour when he heard behind him the sound of clogs coming on at a run. Then he knew that he was being followed. Colliers in their cups are always ready for mischief, provided it be sufficiently brutal. Little Fourteen had recognised him, and he would have little difficulty in persuading his half-drunken companions to give his late master the good "hiding" with which he had threatened him the night before. But Adam knew that with colliers bemused with beer "hiding" a man may mean kicking him into a state of insensibility, and he nerved himself for a struggle which might not improbably end in his death, for Little Fourteen and his friends were not likely to leave much life in him.

"If Joe would only come!"

He tried running, but finding that he was not as light of foot as he used to be, he quickly came to the conclusion that his wisest course was not to exhaust himself by a probably useless attempt to distance his pursuers, but rather to preserve his strength for the struggle which it was very unlikely he would be able to avoid. Then he had the idea of trying to escape by the fields - an expedient, however, which was abandoned almost as soon as it was conceived. The lane was bounded by a steep bank on one side and a high wall on the other, both difficult to climb, and before he could get over either of them the comers might be up with him. The country, moreover, was bare of trees. There was no cover anywhere about in which a man could conceal himself, and to leave the road would be to lose all possibility of help from Joe or any chance wayfarer. The best thing possible in the circumstances he did - walked as fast as he could without actually running, not forgetting to cast an occasional glance over his shoulder.

The clogs came nearer. They rang loud and clear on the hard road and in the frosty air.

Adam Blackthorne quickened his pace - he almost ran. Still the clogs gained on him, and as he glanced behind he could see the forms of four men running in the middle of the lane.

Adam continued to walk at his utmost speed - and he was one of the fastest walkers in the country side - for he felt that the gain of a few minutes might save him from being cruelly hurt, if not from something still worse; and only when his pursuers had almost overtaken him, and it was no longer safe to have them at his back, did he turn round and face them.

Then was seen the advantage of the course he had pursued. The four colliers (for colliers they were - Little Fourteen evidently keeping himself in the background) were so breathless that they could hardly speak, while he himself was fresh and cool.

"What do you want?" he asked sternly, as he rapidly drew off his cloak and threw it round his left arm. "Why do you follow me in this fashion?"

"To give thee a good hiding, thou owd tyrant. We'll stop thee throwing poor folks into th' bruck because they asken for their bit o' wage. Come on, Bill, let's run him in and punch his heyd off"

But to this call Bill did not seem very eager to respond. Adam Blackthorne standing there at bay, with a firm grip of his ashen cudgel and the mastiff crouching by his side, looked decidedly dangerous. At least one of his assailants would be pretty sure to get his crown cracked, and Bill meant to keep his skull whole as long as he could.

"Noa; thee go fost Sam; thou's getten a stick, and us'll follow up; or shall us wait till t'others comes?"

There were others coming, then.

"Nay, we should never hear th' last on't if we let owd Blackthorne baffle four on us."

Then they put their heads together and whispered.

"Now, then," said one of them, who appeared to have taken the lead, "us two th' fost, and yo' two second. Come on, let's crash him down!"

On this, the two foremost colliers, both of whom had sticks, rushed straight at Adam and the dog, the intention of the others being evidently to pass Adam on either side and attack him from behind, while their companions were engaging him in front.

"At 'em, Rock!" shouted his master.

The next moment one of the leading colliers was lying on his back in the lane, fighting desperately to keep the mastiff from his throat and before the second could raise his cudgel, Adam struck him down with his leaded stick. He was only just in time; for the other two were at his elbows, and in a few seconds more they would have had him on the ground. As he stepped backward, however, they gave way and got out of the range of his stick.

"Call yer dog off; mayster - call yer dog off!" screamed the fellow who had been borne down by Rock, "or else he'll kill me. He's bitten me all o'er, and now he's trying to get at my windpipe. For God's sake call him off, mayster!"

"Here, Rock! Here!" shouted Adam, and the mastiff came growling to his side.

" By gum!" said the fellow, as he scrambled to his feet, "I thowt I wor killed; and there's Sam o' Betty's welly killed too. How thy heyd did crack, owd hoss! Get up, mon."

But Sam did not seem at all disposed to get up; the crack on his skull had evidently settled hint for some time to come.

"Never mind," said another, " we have not done with him yet. Have we, Bill? There's a lot more coming and then we'll warm his jacket for him. Bith mon, I believe I can hear 'em now. Harken!"

A faint sound of clogs was audible in the distance, and almost at the same moment Adam thought he could distinguish in the opposite direction the ring of a horse's hoofs on the frozen road.

This was enough for him. Whistling to Rock, he turned quickly round and set off at a run. Two of his late assailants were *hors de combat,* and he did not think the other two would now dare to molest him. Neither did they, albeit they followed sufficiently near to keep him in sight.

The ring of the horse's hoofs became every moment more distinct, but so did the sound of running clogs.

"There's a dozen of 'em, if there is one," said Adam to himself; "and if they overtake me before Joe comes I'm done for. They'll kill me this time."

Nearer came the clogs, louder rang the hoofs.

Adam, as he glanced back over his shoulder, fancied he could see a dusky cloud looming through the darkness and Rock growled and barked by turn.

But when a trotting horse and a running man are approaching each other the intervening ground is quickly covered, and the same moment that he heard the shouts of his pursuers lie caught sight of Joe and Frisky coming at a great pace. He knew it was Frisky, because he recognised her trot.

"Joe!" he shouted, raising his arms as he ran down the lane. "Stop! It's me!"

"What, you, mayster!" exclaimed Joe, pulling sharply up.

"Ay, is it. Now, look here. Has the mare any go left in her?"

"Shoo's quite fresh; we've had a long rest."

"'Gad, I think you have. There is a lot of colliers after me; don't you hear 'em yon, shouting? They want to kill me, I think. Now, as soon as we come up to 'em, put the mare into a gallop and drive right through 'em. If we run over one or two, so much the better. And have you your pistol?"

"Ay, it's here, i' my topcoat pocket."

"Give me hold of it. Here they are! Give her a cut with the whip, and let her go."

The colliers were too much taken by surprise to offer any resistance. As Frisky galloped past they scattered on each side of the road, and in two minutes the gig was out of sight.

"Pull her into a trot Joe," said his master; "the danger is past. But it was a tight shave. And now, tell me how it is you are so late? If I had not come out to look for you, I should not have been so near getting maimed or killed as I have been."

Adam was too glad at his escape, and too pleased to find Joe sober, to reproach him overmuch.

"It's weel as I am late," answered the latter; " for if I hadn't been, I shouldn't have heerd what I have heerd."

And then he told what had happened to him at the Tinker and Budget.

"Well, Joe," said Adam, when he had finished, "I never thought I should have had to say I was pleased you got drunk and overstayed your time; but I am this bout. Now, not a word of this to a soul, Joe: not even to your wife."

"You may be sure o' that. I mut as weel send th' bellman round as tell her. Do you mean to send for th' sowdgers?"

"I cannot tell what I shall do yet. I want you to go to Mr. Basel to-morrow morning early, and ask, with my compliments, if he'll be so kind as to come and breakfast with me. I want to see him on particular business."

"I'll go at seven o'clock."

"That'll do. And now we are at home. The sooner you get the mare bedded down and go to bed yourself the better or else, after all that buttered gin, you'll not be fit for your work to-morrow."

"It was a good thought of yours, Rachel," said Adam, kissing his wife, whom he found waiting up for him, "to make me take Rock with me. If it had not been for him I hardly think I should have got home tonight."

"Why, what has been the matter, Adam?" returned Mrs. Blackthorne, with a look of mingled pleasure and concern, for, though according to his lights a kind husband, he was not much given to kissing.

Then he told her what had befallen him, but he did not deem it expedient to tell her what Yorkshire Joe had heard at The Tinker and Budget.

CHAPTER V111

A COUNCIL OF WAR.

Though it was considerably after midnight when Adam retired to rest, and his thoughts kept him awake the greater part of the night, he was at the factory next morning before the engine started, shortly after half-past five. His first proceeding was to cast a glance at the boilers, and when he saw that the steam was not being got up fast enough, he spoke a few sharp words to the fireman, seized a shovel, and threw additional coal into one of the furnaces, while the stoker replenished the other. He next went round the mill, passing rapidly from room to room, saw that the gas was lighted and the overlookers at their posts, and then, returning to the watch-house (lodge), superintended the operation of fining the laggards, giving the most dilatory of them a sound rating into the bargain. As he passed through the repairing shop he caught two workmen, who had not yet stripped off their jackets, indulging in a little gossip, and one of them was laughing rather loudly.

"Take your hands out of your master's pockets," he exclaimed almost savagely. "I don't pay you to laugh and talk, but to work; and when you do aught else you are robbing me."

No wonder that Adam Blackthorne was unpopular, and small wonder that he was prosperous.

When he had seen the hands in, as the phrase is, and all seemed to be going on smoothly, he turned into his office, and worked at the books until it was time to go to breakfast; for though he was a much occupied man and had a large business, he kept his own accounts.

Shortly before eight o'clock he went to his porridge, for, albeit there was always a cup of tea for him when he chose to take it, porridge and milk constituted the principal dish of his first meal. This was followed by a beefsteak or ham and eggs - as often as not washed down with a glass of his wife's home-brewed ale. But on this particular morning, Mr. Basel being expected to breakfast, coffee had been substituted for tea, and for porridge brewis, which those of my readers who are so unfortunate as never to have tasted this once favourite north-country dish may be pleased to learn is a toothsome stew, whereof oatcake forms one of the principal ingredients.

"If you please, mayster, here's Mr. Basel," announced Jane, two minutes after Adam entered the house.

"Good morning, Madame Blackthorne; good-morning, my dear sir. I am much obliged for your kindly invitation, though it was so early. My wife sends you kindly greetings."

The speaker was a tall, spare, somewhat ungainly-looking man, about the same age as Adam Blackthorne, with very little hair on his head, and none at all on his face. He had a broad, intellectual forehead, dark and rather dreamy eyes, sallow complexion, and the general cast of his countenance was frank and prepossessing.

"I am sorry to trouble you, though," answered Adam; "and if the business I want to consult you about had been less pressing I would not have asked you to come. I did not want to be closeted with you and Yorkshire Joe at your office, for fear of exciting suspicion, and we shall have to ask Joe some questions."

"You are very mysterious. What does it all mean? Has it some connection with your exploits of last night?"

"What exploits? Have you heard already?"

"Only that you and Joe killed six colliers, wounded ten, and put a few scores to flight."

"Who the mischief has been talking such dratted nonsense as that?"

"Everybody by this time, I expect. It was from one of my white-room men I first heard the story - Bob o' Betty's they call him, a fellow with a remarkable knack of picking up the latest news. He asked me soon after six this morning if I had heard the buzz about Mr. Blackthorne, and when I said I had not, he narrated a long legend, of which I have told you the gist."

"Well, it was bad enough, but not quite so bad as that."

Whereupon Adam told his guest what had happened to him the night before, following up his narration with an account of Yorkshire Joe's adventures at The Tinker and Budget.

Mr. Basel looked grave.

"This is very serious," he observed. "We must not have your looms broken if we can help it, Mr. Blackthorne. Do you think, if they were, the Government would make you compensation?"

"The county would, I suppose."

"But only for the actual damage; you would get nothing for loss of profit and the disorganisation of your business."

"Not a penny?"

"And I should get nothing for any inconvenience or loss I might be put to in procuring elsewhere the cloth you are weaving for me."

"Not a farthing?"

"It therefore comes to this, my dear sir, that we must not let these foolish people destroy your machinery."

"That's just what I've been thinking myself."

"What do you propose to do?"

"Get the soldiers here, and shoot 'em down as they come up."

Mr. Basel shook his head.

"Did you ever see the effect of fusilade?" he asked.

"No, I can't say as I ever did."

"Well I have, and I should be very sorry to see another. When I was a young man, I chanced to be in a town in Alsace at the time of the passage of a number of allied troops, who were following up the French after the campaign of Leipsic, and shortly before the abdication of Napoleon and the fall of Paris. How it happened nobody could tell, but just as the troops were entering the main street of the town a couple of shots were discharged from a window, probably by some mad or intoxicated French soldiers, one of which killed a mounted officer. The commander, suspecting treachery - for the authorities of the place had told him there would be no resistance - ordered his men to fire, and in an instant the street was strewed with the bleeding bodies of men, women, and even children - the survivors scattered in dismay, and the soldiers were left alone in presence of their victims. I witnessed the incident from the window of the inn in which I was staying, and it made an impression upon me I shall never forget - the flash of silence that followed the discharge of musketry, and the disappearance of the crowd, who seemed to have vanished underground; a silence broken the next moment by the cries and groans of the wounded the hoarse command of the officers to re-load, and the rattle of the ramrods as the men pushed home their cartridges. And when I think of the misery wrought by that one volley - for further murder was stopped by the arrival of a general, who came galloping up from the rear - the motherless children, the bereaved mothers, the widowed fathers, the wasted lives, the cruel wounds - and, remember that all this did not represent a millionth part, probably, of the misery caused by the wars of this century alone - I detest war, gunpowder, and glory with an intensity that words cannot express; and, except in the very last extremity, I would deprecate destroying life even to protect property. Don't have these poor, misguided devils shot down, I entreat you, dear Mr. Blackthorne. If you do, you will repent it for as long as you live, and your children after you."

"Oh don't, Adam!" pleaded Mrs. Blackthorne, with feeling. "I would rather lose all we have than that anybody's death should be at our door."

"Who wants anybody's death to be at our door?" answered Adam, who appeared rather nettled. "And I don't see neither as war, and gunpowder, and glory, as Basel talks so much about, has aught to do with it. When I said as I'd get the soldiers to shoot the loom-breakers down, I never meant as I'd shoot them without warning. That would be murder, maybe; but if they were told, fair and plump, that if they tried to get into the factory yard and break th' looms they'd be fired on, and they did not heed, then their deaths, if any of 'em were killed, would be on their own heads, not at my door. I should be no more answerable for what had happened after that than if they went and jumped into the big lodge and got drowned. Are we to let folks ride rough shod over us, and do as they like? What are law and government worth if they cannot protect us, and what belongs to us, from violence?"

"The Bible tells us to return good for evil, and love them that hate us, you know, Adam," interposed his wife, gently.

"We don't live in them times, Rachel," said Adam rather impatiently. "There were no loom-breakers in Judea, I reckon; and all as I have to say is that I don't mean to let my machinery be smashed, and my business ruined, if I can help it."

"Neither do I want you to do," said Basel. "I am quite of your opinion that we must make the law respected, and provide for the protection of life and property at any cost. But this is a peculiar case. These poor devils of loom-breakers are ignorant, hungry, and ill-advised. As I understand, they neither want to steal anything nor hurt anybody. They suffer, and, looking on machinery as the root of all evil, they seek to destroy it. In this they will fail and they ought to fail; but it would be a mistake to treat them as thieves and murderers. It is quite possible that some of them may have to be shot or bayoneted, or ridden down by dragoons before the end comes; but leave the responsibility of that to others, and let us try some less extreme remedy."

"With all my heart. Let us hear what it is. But won't you come up to the table, and have a plate of brewis?"

"You are very friendly; I will. Of all your English dishes which I have tasted, brewis is the one that likes me best, and your good wife makes it to perfection. As to a way of preventing those foolish people from breaking your looms without hurting them much I am not yet quite sure. Nevertheless, I have an idea which, with the aid of a pipe when we have finished our breakfast, may possibly develop into something. Will you allow us to indulge in a little tobacco when we have done eating, Madame Blackthorne?"

"What's the use of asking, Mr. Basel?" answers the hostess, with a smile. "I never object to smoking and I don't suppose it would be any use if I did. Adam could not live without his pipe, I think. Yes, smoke by all means; if it gives you pleasure it gives me pleasure too."

"You are very friendly, madame. Tobacco, I find, is a great breeder of ideas; smoke has helped me out of many a difficulty, perhaps it will help us out of this."

When the breakfast was over the two men each took a seat near the corner of the fire and proceeded to charge their pipes, while Mrs. Blackthorne went into the kitchen to attend to her household duties.

Send one of the lasses for Yorkshire Joe," said Adam as she left the room. "We had better have him in, Basel, don't you think? I should like you to have his tale from his own lips."

"Perhaps it would be as well, though I make no doubt the facts are exactly as you have stated them."

Joe was called in and catechised accordingly; but, as Mr. Basel had anticipated, he was unable to add anything of importance to the information they already possessed. On the other hand, he fully confirmed the story he had told the previous night, indignantly repudiating a suggestion of his master's that he had, maybe, dreamt it all.

"I think you may go now, Joe," said the latter, when the cross-examination was finished. "You look rather queer about the eyes; don't you feel well?"

"Oh, ay! I'm root enough; nobbut a bit unfine, that's all."

"I'm not surprised you are unfine," observed Mr. Basel. "My only wonder is that any creature with a stomach could survive such a fearful debauch as you had last night, Joe - Welsh rarebit, fettled ale, and buttered gin. I daresay, now, you feel as if a glass of ale would do you no harm?"

"I do that" answered Joe eagerly; "it would mak' a new mon on me. I'm that dry as I fair darn't spit for fear of setting summut o' fire."

"I think he deserves one," said Basel, with a significant look at Blackthorne.

"You are always for spoiling Joe," laughed the other. "Tell the misses as I say you may have a glass of home-brewed Joe."

Whereupon the Yorkshireman incontinently vanished.

Then Adam Blackthorne and his guest drew near the fire, and, each lighting a long pipe, began to smoke. They smoked in silence, Basel slowly, with his head bent on one side, as if absorbed in thought, Adam intermittently, sometimes almost letting his pipe go out then puffing away furiously until his head was wrapped in a white cloud. This went on for full twenty minutes, and perhaps might have gone on for twenty minutes longer, had not Adam, weary of waiting for the oracle's deliverance, broken the spell.

"Well," he said, "how is it to be?"

"I think I see my way now. We must frighten them."

Oh, that's it, is it?" answered the other, with just a touch of scorn in his voice; "but how?"

"Scare them so that they will never meddle with us more. Yes, I think we can do it."

"How?" asked Adam again.

"Don't be impatient. It can be done, as you shall see by-and-bye. But tell me, are there any soldiers at Redburn?"

"A company, I believe. But I thought we were not to have any soldiers. Besides, the Redburn folks won't want to part with any; they're a terribly frightened lot and they want to have 'em at hand in case of aught happening in the town."

"I only require half-a-dozen for a few hours, and the loan of a dozen uniforms, muskets, and a few blank cartridges. I'll provide the artillery; for we are going to have both infantry and artillery. Cavalry we shall have to do without this time.

"Why, what a queer chap you are, Basel! It's hardly half an hour since you were all against shooting these loom-breakers, and now -"

"And I'm not going to shoot any of them. Wait till you know what my plan is. I'll tell you all about before the day is over. But I should like to have these soldiers. Still if we cannot get them we must just make shift without."

"Well, then, we'll go over to Redburn this afternoon, and see what the borough-reeve says. I expect he is the chap we shall have to apply to."

"Good. I'll go with you - what time?"

"Say two o'clock. I'll drive round and pick you up,'

"It is a thing agreed. And now I must go and look after the shop."

"How is the dyeing going on?"

"Very well; I have a thousand pieces ready to send off that are just perfection - every one a splendid colour, and, what is better still, exactly the same shade - not a badly dyed or finished piece in the lot. There is a profit of full three hundred pounds on the thousand piece; friend Blackthorne."

"That's the best news I've beard to-day. Only go on like that and we shall be both of us rich men one of thee days. Come, I'll go out with you. I must see what they are doing at the factory; unless I look after 'em nobody else will. Sharp two, think on."

"I'll be ready, and as we drive to Redburn I'll unfold my plan for the defence of the Old Factory."

CHAPTER IX.

PREPARING FOR BATTLE.

They found the borough-reeve very hard to deal with. He was an obstinate, narrow-minded old gentleman, terribly afraid of responsibility and full of objections. To all Blackthorne's and Basel's arguments he opposed the plea of invincible ignorance. He refused to know anything; did not know that he had power to send soldiers to the Old Factory; did not know that it was his business to protect the property of His Majesty's subjects - at any rate, when it was outside the borough; not know that the country was in an uneasy state; did not know that hand-loom weavers were starving and desperate, and that more violence was to be feared; did not think six soldiers would do any good; did not believe they could spare any; and, finally, he did not see what he could do - at least, until he had taken counsel with his brother magistrates and consulted the town clerk, and that, he feared, would require a day or two.

This irritated Adam exceedingly, and he was about to reply in a style that would have brought the negotiation to an abrupt close, when Basel quietly interposed. He began by lauding the borough-reeve's caution, and paying a compliment to his well-known impartiality and firmness of character. Having in this way put the old fellow on good terms with himself, he cleverly turned his timidity to account by suggesting that if, by his refusal to consent to a few soldiers being allotted for defence of Mr. Blackthorne's mill, mischief should ensue, he might get into hot water with the Government and the county, which would be called upon to make good any damage his friend might sustain; and he pledged their joint word that if the half-dozen men asked for were placed at their disposal no harm should come to any of them, and that the loom-breakers would be kept effectually at bay. If not, they could not be answerable for the consequences, the responsibility for which must rest with the authorities of Redburn.

These arguments, delivered in a quiet, yet effective manner, had evidently great weight with the borough-reeve. He said he must consult his clerk, and retired for that purpose. On his return he announced that if Mr. Blackthorne would sign a formal requisition for the soldiers, and engage to pay all expenses, he would request the officer in charge of the troops to place six men and a sergeant at his disposal on the following Sunday night.

To this Adam, of course, consented, and then, armed with the order, he and Basel went to the barracks, and had an interview with the officer in command, who readily fell in with their plans, of which he fully approved. He agreed to lend them a dozen old uniforms and twice as many muskets, for which, as well as for the men's arms and accoutrements, a cart was to be sent on Sunday afternoon. It was further arranged, in order not to attract attention, that the detachment should not set out for the Old Factory until after dark.

CHAPTER X.

A MIDNIGHT MEETING.

A hollow in the hills above Orrington. A pale moon looking down on scattered groups of gaunt, ghastly, and travel-stained men - some talking in knots of twos and threes - some sitting on chairs eating their morsels of dry bread - some lying prone on the grass. From time to time they are joined by others, who come singly or in couples, never in crowds.

Every one of these men is armed in some fashion or other. Some have hand-hammers and crowbars; not a few carry on their shoulders big sledge-hammers, and several such as are used by stone-breakers.

Their talk is carried on in whispers; the newcomers are invariably met and questioned, and their faces keenly scrutinised by three or four sledge-hammer men, who seem to be leaders. They appear to have detected one black sheep already, for an unfortunate man is sitting on a stone away from the rest, round which stand three loom-breakers, who fiercely warn him from time to time that "if he offers to stir they will hammer his brains out."

At length, when nearly five hundred men are assembled and the arrivals have become few and far between, a group appears whose advent creates some excitement.

"It's them - it's them!" whispers one man to another, while the three watchers receive the new-comers with much deference.

The individuals of whom this group is composed are five or six in number - our friends of the Moorcock Inn, Dearden and Grindleton, and a few others.

The first-named is mounted on a little nag, probably a of his lameness, and armed with a big double-barrelled horse-pistol. While he is exchanging greetings with the watchers, and asking questions from the people who crowd around him, a man of almost gigantic stature slips with soft and noiseless footsteps past them into a hollow, as it might seem, unperceived by anybody, and places himself in the shadow of a tall tree.

"Well, lads," said Dearden, riding forward, "are we all here?"

." Not far off, I think," answered one of the watchers. We've kept count of all as has come, and there's not many short of five hundred."

"That's quite enough, more than enough, for this night's work; but the more the merrier, you know. Besides, there's safety in numbers; the more of us there is the harder will it be to follow us up and pick us out if trouble comes of it. You all know, I think, what we are met for to-night. But if there's any here as doesn't, it's to smash th' looms at Moorwell Mill - th' Owd Factory they call it hereabouts. Blackthorne is a very hard man with his hands, as you happen know. Not only so, but we've heard as he thinks of starting more steam looms and it's as much if he hasn't given th' order for 'em already. Now, I need not tell you that the more power-looms comes into use the worse will it be for hand-loom weavers. You're clemming now, many of you, and they are not put down you'll be a deal worse before you're better. But I've no occasion to say more on this score. We are all agreed, I think, or we should not be here this night. Isn't it so?"

"Agreed! Agreed! Agreed!" shouted the loom-breakers in chorus.

"I have been sent for from Ashton to lead you on as most on you very likely know. It's a risky job, as I well know, but I'm not one as hesitates at the call of duty. We'll set off in half an hour, for I don't want to get there afore one. I'll go first, with Grindleton and the sledge-hammer men. We'll break th' factory doors in. Them as has walling hammers comes next, and next again them wi' stone-breakers' hammers and hand-hammers. Crowbars and bludgeons will bring up th' rear. Only them as has hammers will go inside to smash th' looms; t'others must stop about th' factory gates to keep guard and give warning of danger, though the secret has been so well kept that danger there is none. Now, if there's any of you that's feared, and does not want to throw in their lot with us, let 'em go home. Cowards are no use, and the help of the unwilling we don't want. I think that's all I want to say; but if there's any here as would like to speak a word, let him speak."

"Yes, I would," said a deep voice, as the tall form of the last comer emerged from the shadow of a tree where he had been hidden into the light which a new-risen moon was just then beginning to cast over the scene. "I would like to speak a few words to my friends and neighbours, some of whom I am sorry to see here."

"Who is he? Who is he?" asked the loom-breakers of each other.

"As many of you cannot see my face, and some of you would not know me if you could, I will begin by saying as my name is Peter Shuttleworth."

"Ay, ay, it's him," exclaimed several voices. "It's Long Peter from Whitworth."

"I heard last night what you were bent on - as you were going to break somebody's looms - and I made up my mind to come here to try and persuade you to give the job up, for I am sure it'll be a bad job, a gradely bad job."

"Come, come, no more of this!" shouted Dearden excitedly. "We know what we are about, and are not going to be turned from our purpose by the croaking of a cursed old coward like you. Stop him, Grindleton; knock him off his perch!"

"Noa, noa!" exclaimed a number of the loom-breakers, whom a hundred or more came forward and stood round Shuttleworth; "we knowen Long Peter. He's a good sort, Peter is, and we'll not have him touched, nayther by Grindleton nor nobody else. Go on, Peter; say thy say out"

"Thank you, lads; I will. This fellow here has called me a coward. There was a time when if he had spoken that word he would never have lived to speak another; but that time has gone. I've suffered too much to be easily made angry. Who he is I don't know, but I think if he had been worth knowing I should have done. As for myself, let me tell you by what right I claim to be heard, and to ask you to listen to me. By trade I'm a block printer, but when I was a young fellow I 'listed and went to the wars. I've been in many a hard fought battle, and was wounded at Waterloo. When peace came I took my discharge, and went back to my old trade, which at that time was doing finely. I got no pension, but that was my own fault; I took my discharge instead. Well, when I was soldiering I had picked up a bit of learning, and after I went back to my old job, which did not long remain prosperous, I began to think for myself and put two and two together, and I soon saw as the country was very ill-governed, and poor folks very badly off, mostly, as I thought, owing to the selfishness and ignorance of the ruling classes. You know as soon as th' war was over they put a tax on corn to keep rents from falling - one of the cruelest deeds, to my thinking, as any Government ever wrought. I really believe, lads, as that law has caused more deaths than all the wars that England has waged this century. Well, I got papers from London; I read 'Cobbett's Register' and Hone's political pamphlets, and I talked to my neighbours, and soon became known as a Reformer and a Radical. The same sort of thing was going on all over the country; Government got frightened, the Habeas Corpus Act was suspended, and lots of folks were arrested and lodged in prison. I had done no wrong, talked no treasonable talk, attended no treasonable meetings; but I was suspected, and my opinions disliked; and after a while I was fetched out of my bed in th' middle of th' night, taken off, and kept in confinement for more than a twelvemonth. When I went away my poor wife was near her downlying; when I came back she and her little one were gone for ever - they had perished from want. But even this did not quench my ardour for reform. I was imprisoned a second time; yet I am a Reformer still, and I am glad to think that our sufferings and our exertions have not been entirely in vain. There is a better spirit abroad than there used to be; the feeling of the upper classes to the lower is more kindly. Noble-hearted men are pleading our cause, and, bad as things are now, I am persuaded that we are on the eve of better times. But – and that is why I am here this night - I never knew good done by violence. You will break this man's looms, you say. How will that benefit you? He will get more, and that without paying for 'em - the county will have to pay. Then some of you will be found out – for among so many there's sure to be traitors – and you'll get transported – happen hanged. Just think, now. How can a few poor hand-<u>loom</u> weavers cope with a whole Government as can dispose of thousands of soldiers and constables, and millions upo' millions o' money? For all Governments are bound to protect property, and this Government of ours – and sorry I am to say it - sets more store on the property of the rich than on the lives of the poor; and when you attack Blackthorne's factory you attack the King's Government. You are as sure to be licked, lads, as if you went with your hammers and crowbars to fight a regiment of soldiers. I've walked eighteen miles to tell to tell you this – I shall have to walk eighteen miles back; and before I set off I had to borrow a shilling to pay my way, for I am as poor as you. Since block printing has come so bad I've started a bit of a day-school – but poor people cannot pay much for schooling nowadays - and it's hard work to make both ends meet. Yet I'd do twice as much to keep you out of mischief. And now, lads, I've nearly said my say out. It's hard for a chap to clem, and, what is waur, to see the wife and children clem - to be willing to work and have nowt to eat. I don't say as it is right; but I do say as loom-breaking and law-breaking cannot do any good, and may do a great deal of harm. New inventions keep coming up, and have done ever sin' Adam delved and Eve span, and will do as long as the world goes round; and them as opposes 'em run their head agen a stone wall. Don't you be guilty of such-like foolishness. Better join with others and try to get Parliament reformed and bad laws repealed; for if the laws were just and the law-makers honest, there would be work and porridge for us all. And now, lads, it is time to be going home, so I'll say 'good-neet' to you all; and them as does not want to get sent to Botany Bay, or maybe worse, will go home too."

The speech made a deep impression, and when Peter descended from his stony rostrum men crowded round and shook him warmly by the hand, and a considerable number of them were so much affected by his homely eloquence that they took his advice and left the ground in a body.

Dearden muttered to Grindleton, "I'm afraid the old fool has spoiled all. I'd like to throttle him."

"It would not be safe to try owt o' that sort on," said Grindleton; "some on 'em thinks a good deal of Long Peter Shuttleworth."

"I must try what a bit of talking to 'em will do then. Look here, lads (raising his voice and facing the most considerable group), you must not let yourselves be daunted by what Peter Shuttleworth says. He is no fool, we all know that, but he is getting old, and has not the spirit he once had. I daresay he talked different in the days of Cobbett, Hunt, and liberty. It's maybe true what he says, that we cannot stop steam looms for good, but we can keep 'em back a bit till the times mend and hand-loom weavers can find summut else to do. And if the country pays for new looms, nobody suffers and we benefit. They cannot make two or three hundred looms in five minutes. As to us being found out and prosecuted, that's all nonsense, if we are all another; and I'm sure we are. Give it up and go back? Not me! Nice we should look going home like whipped hounds with their tails between their legs. How would you face up, do you think? Why, you'd be th' laughing-stock of all the country-side. Me and Grindleton's going, if nobody else goes. Let them as are feared slink off and go home."

CHAPTER XI

OLD FACTORY FIGHT.

DEARDEN touched the right chord. His appeal took so well with the men who remained that nearly the whole of them followed him down the hillside.

After reaching the high road, they marched swiftly and in good order in the direction of Moorwell Mill. Dearden, surrounded by Grindleton and several other of his principal supporters, led the way on his little nag. Having no desire that their presence in the neighbourhood should get noised abroad, and Adam Blackthorne possibly put on his guard, they chose the least frequented road, and every effort was made to preserve silence in the ranks. Nevertheless, so large a body of men could not quite efface themselves, nor avoid making some noise; and it was agreed that if inquiry were made as to their purpose and destination, they should say they were going to Redburn on a shuttle-gathering expedition - shuttle-gathering being an expedient frequently adopted for stopping mills without destroying machinery. For without shuttles there can be no weaving, and when all the shuttles in a district were taken and destroyed, they could not be replaced under several weeks. The loom-breakers, however, were little troubled with requests for information; they looked so formidable that the few people who met them were more intent on getting out of their way than asking questions.

One man only was bold enough to accost them. When they were within three miles of the Old Factory, a horseman emerged so suddenly, and at so fast a trot, from a lane at right angles to the road they were following, that he all but rode over Dearden and scattered his escort far and wide. His horse, apparently young and restive, plunged about in all directions, and before it could be quieted the whole column was brought to a standstill.

As may be supposed, there was a good deal of swearing – Dearden and Grindleton especially distinguishing themselves by the fluency and profanity of their curses – Dearden indeed, threatened to pistol the stranger on the spot if he did not stop the caperings of his steed.

"He is welly flayed (frightened) out of his senses," pleaded the man submissively. "Whoa, whoa, oss! Whoa, young 'un, I say. He's never seen as mony folks altogether in awe his life afore. I wor flayed too, I wor that – whoa oss! but he is quiet now. Yo're enough to slay onybody. What's up, is there a fire or summat?"

"Nothing particular," answered the delegate. "We're only going to Redburn after a few shuttles. And what may you be after at this time at night, master?"

"Me?"

"Aye, you."

"Taking this cowt (colt) to Preston Fair."

"And where do you come from?"

"Chatburn."

"Had we not better keep him with us a bit?" whispered Grindleton to Dearden. "I durned much like th' cut of his jib, as far as I can make him out; and he coes (calls) that a cowt, and anybody may see, dark as it is, as it is a howd oss. Let's tak' him wi' us; it is better to be on the safe side."

"Very well; you and Wiggin seize hold of his bridle, and if he makes any nonsense I'll just shove my pistol in his face. Here, Wiggin!"

But these whisperings had not passed unobserved by the stranger, and just as Grindleton and Wiggin were approaching to lay hands on his bridle, he gave his a sharp pinch behind the saddle, on which the creature lashed out so viciously that the two men were glad to give him a wide berth, while the loom-breakers tumbled over each other in their efforts to get out of the way.

"Whoa, oss! whoa, I say! Whoa, oss! Be quiet Smiler! Whoa, oss!" exclaimed the stranger, an injunction which he emphasized by giving the horse a tremendous cut with his whip, whereupon the animal plunged madly forward, and before the loom-breakers recovered from the confusion into which his pranks had thrown them, he was tearing wildly up the road, far beyond their reach.

Ten minutes afterwards Yorkshire Joe was back at the Old Factory, and deep in conference with his master and Mr. Basel.

The incident rather alarmed Dearden and his counsellors. They feared it might bode some unpleasant surprise, and when they reached the Cinder Lane leading to Moorwell Mill a halt was called, and four men were sent forward as scouts.

After half an hour's absence the scouts returned, and reported that everything was quiet; no lights were visible in the Old Factory; the

Blackthorne household, to all appearance, had gone to bed, and the only persons they had met were a couple of courters and a drunken man. On this, Dearden ordered his men to march quietly up the lane.

The sky meanwhile had become overcast, a few drops of rain were falling, and the moon being hidden by black clouds, the night was very dark.

The road up which the loom-breakers were now walking was bounded on one side by a high wall, and on the other by a tall hedge. Near the factory the wall was replaced by the embankment of a reservoir. As this road led only to the factory - the one which ran into it at right angles being closed at nights by a heavy iron gate – it constituted their sole line of advance and retreat.

When the men arrived before the factory gates there was necessarily a pause. They all strained their ears to listen. Not a sound could be heard - not even the footfall of a watchman or the bark of a dog.

"That's reyt," exclaimed Dearden gleefully; "Nobody's heard us and there is not a soul inside. We'll have th' job done before an hour's over, and be home afore daylight. Now, Grindleson and yo' sledge-hammer men, come forrud and force these gates. But don't use your hammers if you can help it. Try what a good thrutch (push) will do first; clap your shoulders agen 'em, as mony on them can find room; here in the middle. Are you ready? Now, when I say 'Three', thrutch as hard as you con - all together, mind,"

One – two – three."

Before Dearden had well got the "three" out of his mouth, the big heavy doors yielded to the pressure applied to them. So easily and suddenly did they open, indeed, that several of the leading loom-breakers entered the factory yard head-foremost and the first blood was drawn by the mother earth, with which some of their noses came in rarther violent contact.

"Come on, lads," shouted Grindleton, flourishing his hammer; we'll smash every loom i' th' hoyle, and owd Blackthorne, too, if he does not mind what he's doing."

"Now," exclaimed a deep voice from the darkness.

In the same instant the ground seemed to open beneath their feet, and two broad pillars of yellow fire, shooting swiftly skyward, made the factory yard as bright as day, and threw every object it contained into strong relief.

The sight before the rioters, who were pressing into the narrow entrance and rushing impetuously forward, brought them to a sudden standstill.

The light came from two braziers placed on either side of the road. Between these braziers were planted three cannons. Beside each cannon stood a red-coated gunner, match in hand. Behind the artillerymen were ranged, as, it seemed, endless ranks of soldiers, their gleaming bayonets and open gun-barrels pointing towards the conspirators.

Before the latter could recover from their astonishment, the word was given to fire, and, with a report that made the Old Factory tremble to its foundations, the three great guns belched forth three sheets of flame.

A volley of musketry followed, and then the soldiers, lowering their pieces, prepared to charge.

But this was more than the loom-breakers had bargained for, and, in an agony of fear, they turned and fled.

Water!" shouted a voice.

In an instant the reservoir bank was lined with men, at whose head appeared Yorkshire Joe, each carrying hose, from which thick streams of water were poured over the devoted heads of the loom-breakers in the lane below.

Joe, having a keen recollection of the way in which Dearden had proposed to deal with him at The Tinker and Budget, aimed a watery shot sheer into that worthy' face, which sent him clean out of the saddle; and the little nag, frantic with fear, went galloping and kicking among the fugitives with all the effect of a charge cavalry. The rout was now turned into a regular *sauve qui peut;* they went tearing down the lane like people possessed, and half an hour later there could not have been found a single loom-breaker within three or four miles of the Old Factory gates.

The miracle had been wrought by Mr. Basel. It was he who converted three steampipes into great guns, contrived the braziers, and suggested the putting of a number of mill hands into the old uniforms which Adam Blackthorne and himself had procured from the barracks at Redburn. As only blank cartridge had been used, the attacking force, though terribly frightened, had received no great damage, unless by the water with which they were deluged from the lodge bank. This was Yorkshire Joe's idea, and to him had been confided its execution.

The garrison of the Old Factory remained under arms until they were fully assured that the loom-breakers did not mean to come back. It was a somewhat superfluous precaution; but Mr. Basel, who acted as commander on this occasion, or, rather, as chief of the staff to Adam Blackthorne, was cautious to a fault, and he thought that when Dearden and his men discovered the trick that had been played upon them they might possibly rally and return to the attack.

Yorkshire Joe and several others were therefore sent out to see if they had really gone.

In ten minutes Joe came galloping back.

"I cannot see one," he said, "and they've thrown all their hammers away. They've guon for good; I don't believe as we shall ever see th' loom-breakers at th' Owd Factory ageean as long as we live." Joe was right-they never did.

"This will be a famous event in the annals of the Old Factory, friend Blackthorne," observed Mr. Basel. "What shall we call it?"

"Oh, they've fun' a name for it awreddy, if that's what yo' mean," put in Joe.

"Who are 'they,' and what's the name?"

"Some of our chaps there; they've christened it the Owd Factory Feyt."

"Very good," said Basel, pensively, "if that can be a fight in which no blood is shed and no bones broken. But though a bloodless, it has not been a waterless victory, eh, Joe? Don't you think you gave them just a little too much water? Poor fellows! it's a cold night to wear a wet jacket."

"Poor fellows!" exclaimed Adam. "What do they come here for, wanting to smash my machinery? I think they've got off very cheap."

"Perhaps they have," said Basel. "At any rate, a flight and a ducking are better than shooting or imprisonment; and we have done well in getting rid of the loom-breakers with so little trouble to ourselves and so little harm to them. Yet it is sad that the necessity should have arisen - sad that there should be so many men in the country driven by want to desperation, and so ignorant as not to see that in destroying machinery they are doing their best to ruin the trade on which they, and their children after them, must depend for a living. If they could at one swoop smash all the looms in existence, and prevent more being made, there would at least be method in their madness; but to destroy machinery here and there is the wildest insanity. For if they drive weaving out of one district it will only take root in another; and even if they were to succeed in destroying every power-loom in

England, they would simply benefit foreign nations, to their own loss and the loss of the country. They will be wiser some time, perhaps. Meanwhile, we will try to do them good against their will, and the best way is to put down more power-looms so as to find employment for more people. The day will come - see if it does not - when there will be more looms than Weavers. The use of machinery cheapens production, and everything that cheapens production improves trade and promotes the well-being of nations. Eh, friend Blackthorne, what do you say? Am I not right?"

"So right that I mean to square my practice by your theories. I'll build another loom shop and start three hundred more looms: that shall be my answer to their attempts to frighten me. But look here, I must see after getting these soldiers a bit of supper; they've done good service, though they have not hurt anybody, and we must not send them empty away. Will you come with me?"

"I will come, friend Blackthorne; and we celebrate our victory by drinking a pot of beer together, and then we will smoke the calumet of peace."

"Come along, then; I ordered supper to be laid out in the new warehouse, and Joe is coming to say that it is quite ready."

CHAPTER XII.

WHO ADAM BLACKTHORNE WAS.

Adam Blackthorne was the son of a small farmer who held as tenant-at-will about forty acres of rough land at Moor Top, a mile or so distant from the village of Moorside. But farming was not his only resource. In the shop behind the house he had four looms, which found constant occupation for as many members of his family, and he took a cartload of coals every day from a neighbouring pit to Orrington. Without these helps, as he himself said, he would never have been able to find porridge for the six lads and four lasses with whom Providence had blessed him, much less to have had them all taught a bit of reading and writing, and apprentice several of his sons to good trades. They were brought up sternly and frugally; for though Daniel Blackthorne was not much of a chapel-goer, he came of an old dissenting stock, and his notions of family discipline were of Puritanical austerity. When his sons were young they had to work on the land, to milk, to look after the horses, and to weave; and as they grew up they had to swarm. One became a pattern-designer in a print-works; another a colour-mixer; a third emigrated to the United States; a fourth, terribly to the annoyance of his parent; enlisted in the Royal Artillery, and went to the wars; a fifth found a place as a farm bailiff on a nobleman's estate in Wales.

Adam, being the youngest, remained at home the longest and the last. There was work for him about the farm, in fetching warps and weft for the four looms, and in carrying to the manufacturer by whom they were employed the cloth woven by himself and his sisters. But one by one his sisters, all of them notable women, married and went away, except the eldest, who died of consumption. Then the father died, leaving behind him just sufficient property, if carefully realised and put out at interest, to keep his widow for the rest of her life.

Thus Adam at twenty years of age found himself without resources and occupation; for he was deemed too young to carry on the farm, even had the necessary capital been forthcoming. Everything, the looms included, was sold off, and his mother went to live as a lodger with her youngest daughter. He could weave, of course, but for that he required a house and a loom, and he possessed neither.

"Has thee thought what thee'll do, Adam?" asked his mother the day after the sale, as they went together to his sister's house at Orrington.

"Yes, I'll go to-morrow to Manchester and see Mr. Broome; he can, maybe, find me a shop; he's allus seemed kindly disposed towards us."

Mr. Broome was the manufacturer and merchant for whom his sisters and himself had mostly wrought, and Adam had occasionally seen him when he came with his "putter-out" to Orrington and Moorside.

"It's happen the best thing as thou can do," answered the old lady. "Thou'll be setting off i' good time, I reckon. Has thee any brass?"

"I've sixpence; that'll be enough. I'll get Mary to give me a bit o' cheese an' bread to put i' my pocket. It will save having to buy owt but a glass of ale on th' road, an' happen a plate o' beef at th' far end. I'll start soon after four."

"Ay, I daresay sixpence will do, and I am sure Mary will give thee 'as much cheese and bread as thee likes, though John is near - and she says as thou can bide with them a twothry days till thou gets summut to do."

"It'll be again th' grain, mother, if I do. If Mary were left to hersel' she'd make me welcome, I know; but John's never axed me. It's plain to see as he does not want me; and he only takes you as a lodger for eight shillings a week because he thinks as you'll happen leave Mary your bit o' brass. He'd ride a horse to London for the sake of its hide and tallow, John would. I'll trouble him as little as ever I can help, you may be sure. If Mr. Broome doesn't give me a shop I mun try summut else. If I can do nowt better I'll get a place as cowman or carter."

"There'll be no need for that Adam. I'm sure there will not. I think Mr. Broome will find thee a job; he's always spoken well of us, and he had a great respect for thy father. And Tom, as is doing so well at Oaken Clough, addling (earning) his four pounds a week, and William, as the masters at Broadbent think so much on, would not like thee to demean thysel' by turning cowman or carter: it wouldn't be respectable."

"It's all very well for Tom, as is a designer, and for Will, as is a colour-mixer, to talk," said Adam, rather bitterly; "but you see I've learnt nowt but farm-work and weaving, and I mun do what I can get to do."

"Well, go to Mr. Broome afore thou tries owt else. And see now, Adam, as thou doesn't hold thyself too cheap with him. When he axes thee what thou can do, and make th' most on it. Modesty's very nice in a young woman, but a bit of impudence is better befitting a young man as has his way to make in the world."

Adam set off next morning for Manchester. It was more than twenty-three miles thither, and he meant to return the same day, but he did not look upon a fifty-mile walk as anything extraordinary when he had nothing to carry. He had once walked to Manchester with a pack of pieces slung across his shoulders, and returned with a couple of warps on his back.

At a pleasant roadside inn, not far from Bury, he ate half his store of bread and cheese, washing it down with a standing gill of ale, for which he paid a penny; and so effectually did he put the best foot foremost that he passed the Collegiate church before the clock had gone eleven, and he reached Mr. Broome's warehouse in Market Street Lane minutes after that hour.

This gentleman, who was reputed to be very rich, lived, after the custom of his time, in his place of business.

It had never occurred to him that a villa at Alderley Edge or a castle in Wales was necessary for his comfort or his health. On the other hand, factories in those days being few and far between - for the power loom was a thing of the future – the atmosphere was almost pure, rustic lanes and green fields were within easy reach, and Mr. Broome's favourite recreation was fishing in the Irk at Crumpsall, where he caught many a fat perch, and on occasions a fine trout. For the rest, he was quite a merchant of the old school; wore his hair powdered, cultivated a pigtail, and his ordinary dress consisted of a blue coat with brass buttons, a buff waistcoat, kerseymere breeches, and black silk stockings. He had an excellent cellar of port and Madeira, and possessed several dozens of rare old claret, with which he often regaled his friends and customers; and his slightly rubicund face, clean-shaved save for a pair of mutton-chop whiskers, showed that his habits were by no means those of an anchorite.

"Well, what can I do for thee, Adam Blackthorne?" said Mr. Broome, as the young fellow was shown into his private office. "I was sorry to hear of thy father's death. I looked upon him as a worthy, striving man."

Mr. Broome did not belong to the Quaker persuasion; but it was the custom in Lancashire a generation or two ago for people to address their employee's and those whom they looked upon as their inferiors, especially the young, in the second person singular, a custom which in country places probably still lingers.

"Yes, sir," said Adam, "it is a hard job for all of us, and 'specially for me, for now as all's been sold off and th' farm given up there's nowt for me to do, and I'm come to ask you if you thought you could find me a shop."

"Find thee a shop?" said the merchant, reflectively helping himself to a pinch of snuff the while from gold box so ponderous that Adam thought his fortune would be made if he had the money's worth of it in his pocket. "What can thee do?"

"I can milk, and cart, and plough, and weave, an warp, read and write a bit, and cast accounts."

"Quite an Admiral Crichton, I declare. Thee can do more things than I can, Adam. I cannot milk and plough, nor yet warp and weave."

"But you can do lots of things as I cannot, Mr. Broome," answered Adam, wondering who on earth Admiral Crichton could be, and beginning to fear that he was not going to be successful in his quest. "And I'm willing to learn and put my hand to owt as you tell me."

"Very good, very good. I like thy spirit, and I think I can find thee a shop. Thou knows Thomas Burtonshaw?"

"Th' putter-out?"

"Exactly. Well, he's getting rather old, and just a bit shaky on his pin, like some others of us; and I could do with an active young fellow that knows cloth and yarn, to go round with him on his putting-out journeys, an take his place when he cannot go himself, as sometimes happens. Does thee think it is a job that would suite thee?"

"Oh, Mr. Broome," exclaimed Adam, overjoyed, for he had never expected anything half so good, "do you think I'm qualified for it?"

"I do think so, else I would not have proposed it to you. You know what good cloth is, for we've had better pieces from your family than from almost any other," said Mr. Broome, dropping unconsciously into the use of the plural. "You can read and write, and you know something of arithmetic. With a little tuition from Burtonshaw I think you will do admirably. You have only to be steady and attentive. As for wage, I think I could afford you twenty shillings a week. It's rather a responsible post. How would that do for a start? I like to be as liberal as I can with my people."

"Very well, Mr. Broome; very well indeed. I will try to make myself worthy of your confidence. When shall I start?"

"Let me see. This is Friday. Suppose we say Monday morning. Can you come on Monday?"

"Can I? Of course I can. I can walk over on Sunday and look out for lodgings, and be here when the warehouse opens on Monday morning."

"Good, Meanwhile I'll speak to Burtonshaw, 'and tell him what you are to do. I think that's all. No; there's one thing more. I hope you are not a Radical, Adam."

"A Radical!" echoed Adam in surprise.

"Yes, a Radical," repeated the merchant emphatically, "one of those firebrand, infidel fellows that want to root religion out of the land and overturn our glorious Constitution in Church and State; for that I really could not abide."

"No," replied Adam, wondering at this outburst - for albeit his sympathies were Radical, he had no idea of letting his political principles interfere with his worldly advancement - "I am not one of those fellows. I don't understand much about politics."

"So much the better. Don't try to understand 'em; leave politics to your betters, and if some other folks would do the same the country would be the gainer. I have no patience with these subversive doctrines. And now it's nearly noon. I'm sure you will be wanting your dinner after that long walk. Here's half-a-crown for you; go and get a good feed at my expense."

"Thank you kindly, sir," said Adam, pocketing the tip with great satisfaction, as he withdrew from the office. But he had too keen a sense of the value of money to spend two-and-sixpence on a single meal, and in the neighbourhood of Shudehill he found a cook's shop where a plate of boiled beef and potatoes was obtainable for threepence, which, together with a pennyworth of bread, made him a capital dinner.

On his way home he halted at the same inn where he had stayed in the morning, and spent the balance of his sixpence on a second glass of home-brewed, with which he washed down all that remained of his bread and cheese.

When he reached his sister's house late in the evening, the first question his mother asked him was how he had fared?

"First rate," was the reply. "I've got a shop and gained half-a-crown. I'm two shillings better off than when I started."

"I think Adam is fit to turn out," remarked his sister after he had gone to bed, "he'll make his way."

"Oh, he'll make his way," said old Mrs. Blackthorne, "I've no fear about Adam getting on. If ever he gets into trouble it'll be on account of his temper. He's welly as hot as his father was when he wor young, and he cannot abide to be thwarted."

"Maybe," observed her son-in-law, with a sneer; "but he knows which side his bread's buttered on, Adam does, and he'll put up with a good deal afore he'll lose owt"

CHAPTER XIII.

PAUL DOGGET'S ADVICE.

Adam Blackthorne remained in the service of Mr. Broome for several years, and by his assiduity in the discharge of his duties, and his intelligence, so completely won the confidence of his employer that when Thomas Burtonshaw became too shaky on his pins for active work, he succeeded to the old man's place as principal putter-out. The position was important and responsible. His duty consisted in going round the country to give out yarn to weavers to be converted into cloth at their own houses, receiving from them in return the calico they had woven, and paying them their wages. There were certain fixed days when he attended at Redburn, Orrington, Moorside, and elsewhere, on which occasions weavers came from far and near with their cuts (pieces) on their backs, and took away in their wallets the warp and weft which Adam "put out" to them. Hence the term putter-out."

The business was one of considerable labour and anxiety, and required for its efficient performance both tact and resolution. The pieces had to be examined before payment to see that they contained the right number of threads to the inch, and were free from serious faults. The yarn put out had to be accompanied by precise instructions as to the make and quality of calico into which it was to he woven.

Then there was the question of "mooter," a burning one in those days, but the very name of which has almost disappeared from the manufacturing vocabulary of the present generation. Mooter was to the handloom weaver what "cabbage" is to the working tailor. It was impossible to "put out" just as much weft as was required to produce a certain number of pieces. Some spinnings ran out better than others, some weavers were more careful of their material, or less conscientious than their fellows in putting into the calico they made the required number of threads or picks; hence in one way or another it often came to pass that they had yarn over, which the few honest returned and the many dishonest appropriated. This cabbaged yarn, known in the trade as "moote;" was sold secretly to roguish dealers and scampish manufacturers; and the practice led to so many evils that very severe laws, which are still found on the statute book, ware passed for its repression; but it was never entirely put down, and only ceased when rendered impossible by the general substitution of weaving by power for weaving by hand.

Many weavers indeed, if not weavers generally, could never be brought to see that there was anything reprehensible in keeping their mooter. If, by superior care or skill, they succeeded in saving anything out of the weft given them to weave, they were apt to consider that they might rightly dispose of it for their own benefit. This confusion of thought probably explains the etymology of the curious word chosen by a sort of natural selection to designate the custom. It was a much-mooted question whether the surplus weft belonged to master or man, manufacturer or weaver. Hence the object in dispute came in the course of time to be known as "mooter."

Adam in his heart rather held with the weavers in this matter; but Mr. Broome being naturally on the side of the masters, he deemed it expedient to discountenance the practice to the utmost of his power; and so sharply did he look after the weavers to whom he "put out," that he made weft go much further than his predecessor had been wont to do, and reaped the reward of his faithfulness in the approval of his employer and a considerable increase of salary.

As he went his rounds on horseback, and received an allowance for expenses, his own outlay for living was light, and he was thus enabled to lay by the greater part of his wage. Not that Adam was naturally of a very saving disposition, but in the implicit, if not the avowed, opinion of the class to which he belonged extravagance was one of the worst of sins and thrift a sign of grace. A rogue was held in less detestation than a spendthrift, and everything was forgiven to the man who got on. Adam, moreover, had special incentive to exertion in his desire to show his brothers - the colour-mixer and the pattern-designer - that, albeit he had not been taught a trade, he could succeed as well as they; and to falsify the croakings of his brother-in-law, John Dunn, the prosperous grocer at Orrington, who never lost an opportunity of sneering at him. He knew that in order to succeed it was necessary to save, and he did save, waiting meanwhile for an opportunity of turning his economies to good account.

His opportunity came, as such opportunities generally do come, in an unexpected manner. One Saturday afternoon Mr. Broome went fishing to Crumpsall and as he had not returned next morning search was made for him. He was found lying face downwards in a shallow part of the stream dead, where, in the opinion of the doctors, ha had fallen and died in a fit of apoplexy.

This event made a great change in Adam Blackthorne's prospects, for the heir, a nephew in London, having no taste for trade, resolved to liquidate the business as quickly as possible, and gave notice to all his uncle's employee's that their services would not be required after the termination of their engagements.

As Adam knew the ins and outs of his department better than anybody else he was retained to the last, and though he put out no more yarn than was necessary to complete existing contracts, he had to continue his rounds for several weeks after Mr. Broome's death. Time, nevertheless, went on, as time has a way of doing. His engagement was fast running out, and as yet he had neither been offered another place nor heard of a suitable opening.

John Dunn was jubilant. "What will Adam do now, I wonder?" he said. "He will have to live on his savings a while. He had just the length of old Broome's foot. Well for him as he had, for nobody else'll have owt to do with him. Get another place? Not him."

This amiable prediction was fulfilled. Adam did not get another place, but he did much better - he set up for himself.

It came about in this way.

On his last putting-out visit to Redburn he had occasion to see Paul Dogget, the most extensive spinner in the town, which, seeing that it did not contain more than five or six mills, instead of the fifty or sixty whose smoke now darkens the air, is perhaps not saying a great deal.

Paul was a stout broadly-built, florid-complexioned man, with a closely-cropped red head and immensely long red whiskers, equally renowned for his success in business and for his prowess as an eater and drinker. He took his matutinal porridge with beer instead of milk, and could, and often did, drink ten glasses of whisky after factory hours "without turning a hair," and be at his work next morning when the bell rang "as fresh as paint." Once in his hot youth, when still a common workman, he laid a wager, and won it, that he could eat a pound of beef-steaks, fried with a pound of candles and washed down with a gill of rum, at a sitting. On another occasion he undertook to consume for his supper a whole rotten (plum) pudding. But this time he had over-estimated his powers, and was fain to cry for quarter long before his task was completed.

Though Paul was one of the most successful spinners of his day, and died worth "a mint of money," he could neither write nor read. But he could figure, and possessed a marvellous memory. Shortly after he began business on his own account he was under the necessity of coming before his creditors to ask for time. They asked for a statement of affairs.

"I haven't getten any," answered Paul.

"Well, your books, then. Where are your books?"

"I haven't getten any books nawther."

"How on earth do you keep your accounts, then?" demanded the astonished creditor.

"I keep 'em all in my heyd."

It was quite true; they were all in his head, and he gave so clear a verbal statement of his position that he got the reprieve he asked for, and eventually paid all his debts in full - more, probably, from a sense of expediency than of honour; for Paul's neighbours considered him to be somewhat of a rogue, an imputation which he accepted rather as a compliment than a reproach. When he had shown anybody over his mill, which he was very fond of doing, he would turn round and put to his visitor this 'somewhat searching question: "Now, whether would you rather be called a rogue and have this factory, or be called a honest man and be bout (without) it?"

Another characteristic of Dogget's was his love of contrasts. He liked a little house and a big factory, large profits and a small expenditure; and it was only when he had two hundred thousand pounds to the good, and his sons and daughters, who were better - though not very much better - educated than himself, began to grow up around him, that he was persuaded, much against his will, to leave the cottage near the factory gates in which he had lived and prospered for a dwelling more befitting his condition.

When Paul died at a ripe old age, the *Redburn Rooster* gave him a long and laudatory obituary notice, and a marble tablet - which told that he had been a Justice of Peace for the county, lord of the manor of Mallam, and a munificent benefactor of the borough - was erected to his memory in the parish church. His eldest grandson, who married an earl's daughter, is now a country gentleman, a county member, and a shining light of the Conservative Party.

When Adam had finished his business, which related to a yarn contract made by the late Mr. Broome, Dogget, who, to give him his due, was a kindly, good-natured man, inquired about the young man's prospects - what he thought of doing after the old business was finally wound up, and when his services were no longer needed.

"I am looking out for a fresh place," said Adam.

"Looking out for a fresh place! Why don't you start for yourself?"

"I have thought of it, but I don't see my way. I'm short of that stuff as they buy pigs with."

"But you have had a good shop. You must have summut laid by - two hundred pounds perhaps?"

"More than that; nearly three hundred."

"Start for yourself; Adam; start for yourself. I'll sell you as much yarn as you want, and give you double credit to what I give other folks - six months 'stead o' three. You cannot miss doing well. You'll have all Broome's connection i' your fingers. You know what sorts pays best and where weavers is to be fun'. You've nobbut (only) to tak' a place wi' room enough for a winding frame, a warping mill or two, and a warehouse, and you'll never look behind you."

"Are you in earnest about letting me have yarn, Mr. Dogget?"

Of course I am. I want another customer or two. I've watched you, and I think you'll do. That's why I'm willing to give you a lift."

"Would you mind putting it down in writing?" said Adam, rather dubiously.

He had heard that Dogget did not hold verbal engagements to be binding. "That's nowt," he would say when reminded of a promise which it was not convenient to keep, "that's nobbut word o' mouth."

"What! you willn't trust my word?" rejoined Paul with a laugh. "Well, you're happen not far wrong. I think no waur on you for that. I'll get our Mary Anne to write it down, and then I'll put my mark toot"

Mary Anne, a stout, hard-featured lass of twenty, his daughter and book-keeper, was called in, and at her father's request wrote in a sprawling hand, and with many eccentricities of spelling, an undertaking on the part or Paul Dogget to sell Adam Blackthorne such yarn as he might require, to the extent of five hundred pounds, at market price, against his acceptance at four months, to be drawn at sixty days from date of invoice. Then it was signed, "Paul Dogget - his mark, X."

"Now, Adam, that's doing you a gradely good torn," said Paul, as he handed him the document. "I never tries to run off owt as I've put my cross to, and I hope you'll be a good customer to me. It'll make things a deal easier for yon in mony ways. When folk sees as I'm trusting you, they'll trust you too. You'll have quite as much credit as you want. The sooner you start the better it will be - afore Broome's customers gives their orders to anybody else. And be sure to pick th' best on 'em. Bad debts is awkerd at any time; but at starting they're the vary devil."

"I'll lose no time, you may be sure, Mr. Dogget. I know of a place close to Moorside, as I think will suit, and I can get cheap. There's a good warehouse, a winding and warping room, and a bit of a cottage, and the neighbourhood is a good one for weavers. But will you not come round to Th' Lord Nelson, and let us wet our bargain?"

"You've taken th' word out o' my mouth, Adam. It's just what I wor going to say mysel. You stand treat now, and I'll stand treat fost (first) order as you give me. Come on. I'll be back in hoaf an hour, Mary Anne."

But Mary Anne knew better; and in point of fact her father did not return until late in the day, with a more than usually red face, and smelling very strongly of rum. Fortunately for Adam he could really spare no more than half an hour for the wetting of the bargain, and so got off with a couple of glasses. Very little business was done in Lancashire in the early part of the century, and for many years thereafter, without drinking. Masters drank as hard as their men, and a strictly sober manufacturer was almost as great a rarity as one really idle or incompetent. Habits which would now rightly be regarded as intemperate, pernicious to health, and injurious to business, did not seem to militate against their success.

Adam found no difficulty in securing the warehouse Moorside of which he had spoken to Paul Dogget, nor was he long in setting to work.

He bought a winding machine, a couple of warping mills, and a little furniture for the cottage in which he intended to live. One of the warping mills he ran himself besides being his own cut-looker and putter out. He kept his books at night and on Sundays; and when he had need to go to Manchester, went thither on foot, never spending on these occasions more than sixpence or a shilling. His only relaxation was an occasional pipe and a glass at The Brown Cow, and a talk over the affairs of the township and the nation with the neighbours whom he found there, chief among whom were Kit Nudger, the master blacksmith; Bob Badger; the master plasterer and painter; and John o' Bens, the overseer and rate collector. He picked up information at these times which he sometimes found useful, and he generally went home sober; which is more than could be truthfully said of his companions.

"I was right," said Paul Dogget, when he saw how his *protégé* was shaping. Blackthorne 'll do - he's both sharp and careful. I said I'd trust him five hundred pounds. I'll trust him a thousand if he'll let me. He'll make his fortune, mark me if he doesn't."

"Adam 'll break," said John Dunn, "you see if he doesn't and soon too. How can he expect owt else - starting for hissel with two or three hundred pounds? - a thousand would ha' been all little enough."

CHAPTER XIV.

RACHEL ORME.

But the time came when Adam's success was so palpably assured that his sneering brother-in-law was obliged to hold his tongue. He even admitted to his wife that Adam seemed to have getten hold o' th' reyt end o' th' stick at last," and suggested that his sister Betty would make him a very excellent helpmate.

Nor was John Dunn the only one who had conceived the idea of ensuring Adam's happiness by providing him with a wife. The gossips of The Brown Cow had frequent discussions on the subject; for these worthy fellows held single-blessedness to be a state so unnatural that they simply could not imagine anything so monstrous as that a man who could afford to keep a wife should voluntarily remain a bachelor. And there was nothing so clear as that Adam possessed the wherewithal to become a Benedict. True, he had not altered his style of living; he continued to practise the same ferocious economy with which he had begun; complained constantly of the hardness of the times, and refused to admit that he was more than making both ends meet. But this was the fashion of the day, it being considered neither decent nor politic for men to admit that their trade was flourishing and themselves were getting on, thereby inviting competition and encouraging their workpeople to demand higher wages. All Adam's disclaimers, however, could not hide the fact that his business was increasing. He had set up another winding machine, bought two more warping mills, and he "shopped" new weavers almost every week. Then he had engaged Jabez o' Jocks as winding and warping master and cut-looker, all his own time being required for his books, going to market, and putting-out. There was therefore every reason why he should "get wed and be like other folk" - and so the gossips of The Brown Cow often told him. Some of them, having eligible daughters of their own, had a more than abstract interest in the matter, and one day Bob Badger; in a burst of confidence, told him that he was quite welcome to their Madge, a big, bouncing maiden of nine-and-twenty. She was "a gradely useful lass in a house," Bob said, had always been steady, and as she could write a bit - in fact, made out her father's quarterly bills - might be of great use to Adam in his business, and could keep both his books and his house.

But Adam was proof against this and several similar temptations, and when his neighbours asked how soon he was going to be wed, he would laugh and make some joking reply - say that he could not afford to keep a wife, that he preferred to keep his family under his hat, or that he could not find a lass to suit him. Such insensibility to the charms of the sex being absolutely incomprehensible to the people of Moorside, they could only suppose that Adam was courting on the sly, the fortunate damsel, generally considered to be his prettiest winder, being a girl of the name of Mary Kershaw, better known, however, as Mary o' Jocks. But when one Sunday night Mary was seen "linking" (walking arm-in-arm) with Tom Badger in Tinker Lane this theory had to be abandoned; and the gossips began to think that Blackthorne's excuses might, after all, be true, and that he was really too near to indulge himself in the luxury of a wife.

Meanwhile, the object of all these speculations was only dimly conscious of the interest which he excited. He had never seriously contemplated matrimony, his real opinion being that a wife was more of an encumbrance than an advantage; and though not a proud man, he felt that, if he did marry, he might look higher than either Madge Badger or Betty Dunn. So he dismissed the subject from his thoughts.

But one day when he least expected it his fate came.

He had been to Orrington on business, and as people were busy with their hay, the time being June, he took the "pad gate" (the field way) back, though it was a little roundabout; for Adam retained the taste for farming, which rarely leaves a man who has been bred to husbandry, and one of his most cherished ambitions was to have a bit of land of his own. It was always a pleasure to him to see a fine meadow of hay, or a field full of golden corn; and as he passed a group of hay-makers he would ask them questions about the weight and quality of the crop, and perhaps drink a glass of ale with them.

When he was about half-way home a sudden change took place in the aspect of the weather - black rain-clouds gathered overhead, and there was every sign of an approaching storm. Adam's first impulse was to hurry homeward as quickly as he could, but just then his attention was drawn to a group of haymakers in the next field. They were making frantic haste to get in the last load before the rain came on. The hay was nearly all in windrow. The forker, who seemed to be also the carter, was forking as if for bare life, while an old man and two or three women were completing the windrows, and raking after the cart. Among the latter was a young girl, who by the directions she occasionally gave, appeared to be in command of the party. She was tall and shapely, wore a man's straw hat, and her rather short petticoats showed off to advantage a small foot and well-turned ankle. The hat covered so much of the girl's face that Adam could only catch an occasional glimpse of it, yet the little he did see made him extremely wishful to see more, for he felt sure that the brown curls which escaped from the clumsy hat, and fell low on the scarlet bodice could not fail to be matched by a well-favoured countenance.

He never felt his curiosity so piqued by a girl before, and while he was thinking how he might obtain a closer view of the face, which he had made up his mind must be a bonny one, he was startled by a chorus of screams from the women and a howl from one of the men. The forker had let a wheel of the cart run over his foot, and lay writhing among the hay.

To jump over the low wall which fenced the field from the footpath, run to the spot and offer his help, was with Adam the work of a moment. Happily no bones were broken. The ground being soft the forker's foot was only bruised, and possibly, slightly sprained; but it was quite clear that he could do no more forking for that day at least.

"I'm glad it's no worse," said the girl with the man's hat, who was evidently the mistress; "but it's very awkward - the rain just coming on and not another forker in the field. I'm afraid the hay will be all spoiled."

As she spoke she looked at Adam. Her face was even bonnier than he had believed possible - soft brown eyes, pink cheeks, a dimpled chin - and her voice, he thought, was the sweetest he had ever heard.

"Never mind," said Adam, doffing his coat and waistcoat, "I'll fork for you."

"You!" she exclaimed in surprise.

"Yes, I was bred to farming, and, as you will soon see, I haven't forgot how to fork."

Then he set to work with a will, throwing the hay in the cart so fast that it was almost more than the loader could do to keep pace with him. When the loading was finished he helped to rope the hay; and as the first drops of rain came down the cart was on its way to the barn.

"Just in time," said Adam to the scarlet-bodied sylph. "And now, is there anything more I can do for you?"

"No, thank you," she answered in a rather embarrassed manner. "I am - that is, my aunt will be very much obliged to you - it was very kind of you-and you fork so well, a deal better than poor Tim there. But for you I'm sure the hay would have been spoiled."

"Your aunt! Why, I thought Solomon Smalley farmed this land."

"So he did; but he's left, and my aunt has bought this year's hay crop; and as she couldn't leave the shop this afternoon she's sent me to look after the hay-makers."

"Your aunt?" repeated Adam, who seemed rather bewildered.

"Yes, my aunt," answered the girl with a smile that showed a row of beautiful teeth. "Nanny Cooper; do you not know her? I thought everybody hereabouts knew my aunt."

"Know Nanny Cooper! Yes, ever since I was a child; but I did not know she had a niece."

"Oh, I have not been with her long. I don't belong to this country; my name is Rachel Orme."

"And mine is Adam Blackthorne."

Then followed an embarrassing pause. Neither Rachel nor Adam appeared to know what to say next

The lady was the first to break the silence.

"Won't you come to the barn and have a glass of ale," she said, "and wait until the storm is over?"

"Well, I do feel rather dry after that spell of forking. Yes, I'll go with you and have a glass of ale," rejoined Adam, quite forgetting that he had appointed to meet a waste dealer at his warehouse at four o'clock, and that the time was already past.

Never before had he neglected to keep a business appointment. But his thoughts just then were full of Rachel Orme, and he had eyes only for her. He insisted on relieving her of her rake, and eyed her so earnestly that she became almost painfully embarrassed, and was very glad when they reached the barn. Nevertheless, she gave him a glass of ale with her own hand, and as he took it from her their eyes met – to Rachel's great confusion; for she was as modest as she was handsome; and she shortly afterwards disappeared. Adam did not like asking after her, and when he had waited as long as he decently could, and drank more ale than was good for him, with a view to keep up appearances, he took leave of the haymakers and walked slowly homewards.

"Anything new?" he asked Jabez o' Jocks as he entered his warehouse. "Has all gone on right?"

"Ay, middling weel, I think. There's nobody bin but that waste dealer fro' Redburn. He said you towd him to come at four o'clock; and he waited till welly six."

"So I did. Gad, I'd clean forgot. Did he seem vexed?"

"He did that; he went away swearing like mad."

"Never mind, I'll write to him. I say, Jabez."

"Ay, mayster."

"You know Nanny Cooper, don't you?"

"Ay, do I. Everybody about here knows owd Nanny."

"Who's this niece as has come to live with her?"

Jabez grinned. "What! durn't yo' know?"

"No, I never heard of her before to-day."

"You've happen seen her?"

Adam did not answer.

"Yo' would have both heard on her and seen her afore now if yo' had gone regular to th' Dippers' chapel at Orrington. Her name's Rachel Orme; her mother wor sister to Nanny, and as both father and mother's gone dead Nanny 'dopted her - leastways that's what folk says. Nanny's not much gan to talkin' about hersel' and them as belongs to her. Hoo is a real beauty, hoo is that."

"Who? Owd Nanny?"

"No, no; yo' knowin' weel enough who I mean mayster - Rachel Orme. Yo' would never have axed ahout her if yo' hadn't seen her. Everybody as sees that lass wants to know who hoo is."

"Has she been in this country long?"

"Six months, maybe. Hoo'd suit yo', mayster, yon would. They sayin' too, as hoo's a good scholar, and makes hersel' vary useful to her aunt. There's many a young fellow as would like to mak' up to her if they nobbut knew how; but owd Nanny watches her like a cat watching a mouse. They sayin' as Bill Nudger, that's the blacksmith's owdest lad, is after her."

"What! that fellow?" shouted Adam, so abruptly as quite to startle old Jabez. "Why he's just a drunken wastrel."

"Not quite as bad as that, mayster. Bill isn't good enough for Rachel Orme, I know; but getting a sup too mich now and again does not entitle a chap to be called a drunken wastrel."

"Well, he willn't do for Rachel Orme, anyhow, The Nudgers are Church folks, and that would be enough to stop it if there were nowt else."

"That's true; owd Nanny's a fearful strict Dipper. They sayin' as hoo wor never in a church in aw her life, and wouldn't put her heyd into one for no brass."

"Very likely not. But this isn't business, Jabez, Has anyone brought any pieces today? I promised to send five hundred seventy-two reeds to Mole Hill tomorrow. Can we manage it, do you think? Let us count up."

CHAPTER XV.

ADAM BLACKTHORNE BECOMES DEVOUT.

The Sunday morning after his meeting with Rachel Orme, Adam donned his best suit – a Blue coat with brass buttons, yellow waistcoat, and drab breeches - and set off for Orrington Tabernacle.

He felt that he had rather neglected his religious duties of late (as it was more than a year since he had been to meeting, his self-reproaches were probably not undeserved), and he made up his mind to turn over a new leaf. Though rather loose in practice, Adam was strictly orthodox in theory. He had not forgotten his Baptist breeding; and if Sunday had not been so convenient a day for entering up his books and overhauling his machinery, and Orrington had been rather nearer, it is conceivable that he might have gone to chapel oftener than twice a year. As may be supposed, the Tabernacle people looked upon him as carnally minded almost beyond hope of redemption. A man who worked on Sundays, and was occasionally seen in the bar parlour of The Brown Cow on that sacred day, albeit he might call himself a Baptist, was in reality little better than a confirmed backslider. He could hardly be worse, unless he were to descend to the very lowest depth of infamy - "turn Church" and take a pew at St. Saviour's. There were many, indeed, who thought he was already drifting in this direction; for had he not gone to the last Church charity sermon? It was even rumoured that a few days thereafter the new curate had called at Adam's house and left his card, and that Adam had been heard to speak of it as very neighbourly attention.

Great, therefore, was the surprise, and considerable the satisfaction, when the subject of these misgivings appeared at service on this particular Sunday; for Adam was a rising man (worldly speaking), and the pious joy of the Orrington deacons at this sign of grace was probably not diminished by the reflection that the returning prodigal might, if so disposed, render important help to the cause. The welcome accorded to him was warm in the extreme, and he was shown by the senior deacon into the latter's own pew.

The Tabernacle, despite its hideous name, was by no means an unsightly building. Though it had no architectural beauty, it was built of stone, possessed an old-fashioned porch, lozenge-shaped windows, and, contrary to the usual wont of chapels, was covered with ivy and mellowed by age. The neatly-kept yard sloped gently down to the margin of a rippling brook (now, alas! a Stygian stream of filth), between which and the chapel lay the baptistry, surrounded by a thick hedge of hawthorn, and the air was filled with the sweet scent of wallflowers and southernwood.

The interior of the chapel, though rather gloomy in winter and dark weather, was cool and pleasant on a warm June day, and Adam sat down in the deacon's pew after his long walk with an agreeable sense of repose and relief. As the minister had not yet entered the pulpit, he took the opportunity of glancing at his fellow-worshippers; for I am sorry to say he was not quite in so devout a frame of mind as he might have been. His eye wandered searchingly from pew to pew until it was arrested by a figure in the one most remote from that in which he was seated. There his gaze remained fixed until the spell was broken by the giving out of the first hymn.

Yes, she was there - more, lovely, thought Adam, than ever. And so modest-looking, too, and everything about her so becoming - a dress of almost Quaker-like simplicity - hair smoothly braided, the rebellious curls being carefully concealed by the huge bonnet of the period. Her attitude was reverent, and her every gesture bespoke a mind in full harmony with the solemnity of the occasion.

"Yes," he said to himself, "Rachel Orme shall be my wife, or nobody else shall."

But how to approach her, how to set to work, was the question; for even supposing Rachel to be willing (as yet no means certain), what would her old dragon of an aunt say - she who was so strong in the faith - would she not bring against him his worldly life, his neglect of the means of grace, and his general indifference to "better things?"

For Nancy Cooper was a Baptist of the primitive type - strong in Biblical lore, and so active and energetic a supporter of the cause withal that people would sometimes speak of her as "th' leading mon among th' Orrington Dippers." Was it likely that such a woman as this would consent to the marriage of her niece with a backsliding Baptist, so utterly lost to a sense of the fitness of things that he had not been to meeting for a twelve-month? Adam could only come to the conclusion that it was not likely she would; and from all he had heard of Rachel's character and her affection for her aunt, to whom she was under considerable obligations, he did not deem it possible that she would favour the advances of any man without her aunt's sanction. The first thing for him to do, therefore, was to propitiate Nanny, and get into her good graces by regular attendance at the Tabernacle, and generally, by a more faithful performance of his religious duties. This plan would have the contingent advantage of throwing him more into Rachel's company, and might possibly afford him an opportunity, sooner or later, of getting speech of her alone.

In coming to this resolution Adam was guilty of no conscious hypocrisy. He was neither a notorious evil liver nor an unbeliever, and he only proposed to himself a course which in any circumstances it was his duty to follow. His neglect of spiritual things had often caused him twinges of conscience, and (for he accepted literally all the tenets of the sect in which he had been brought up) occasionally sore misgiving. If; therefore, his love for Rachel Orme should be the means of reinforcing his feeble faith, and cause him to listen to the Word more frequently than he had been wont to do, he might look upon it as a blessing specially vouchsafed to him by Providence

Adam pondered these things while Mr. Hartwell, the minister at the Tabernacle, was preaching - a sin, however, for which he might have fairly pleaded the excuse that the sermon was somewhat too profound for the comprehension of unregenerate souls. It concerned such mysteries as predestination, prevenient grace, and the final perseverance of the saints; and though the discourse was evidently *caviare* to the multitude, the rapt attention of the older and more experienced members of the congregation showed that, in the opinion of the elect, it was a theological disquisition of rare merit.

The sermon lasted a full hour by the clock, and Adam, despite his newly-awakened religious zeal, felt thankful when it was over; less, perhaps, from weariness of the flesh -albeit that counted for something - than a longing to have another look at Rachel, who, the better to follow the sermon, had placed herself during its delivery with her back to him and her face to the parson.

After the dismissal of the congregation he lingered about the chapel door in the hope that he might get speech of Rachel and her aunt. He was not disappointed. Nanny, as was her invariable custom on Sundays, wore her black silk dress, and being tall and of good presence, despite her sixty years, as straight as a picking rod, she was decidedly the most imposing member of the congregation. Her face was rather long and full of character, nose large, and the silver-rimmed spectacles with which it was surmounted added to the dignity of her appearance.

"Good-morning, Adam Blackthorne," she said, as she caught sight of our friend in the porch; "I have to thank you for so kindly giving my niece Rachel a helping hand with the hay the other day. It was very neighbourly and thoughtful of you, and I am right glad to see you at chapel. Why don't you come oftener?"

Adam muttered something about living so far away and having no pew.

"So far away! Why, it's nothing for a young man. You are not much farther off than we are, and we come twice every Sunday, and Rachel takes a class in the Sunday school besides. As for a pew, anybody will give you a seat. If you don't like Deacon Dabchick's pew you are quite welcome to come into ours."

"It's very good of you to say so. Next time I come I will go into your pew."

"When will next time be'"

"Next Sunday, maybe."

"See as you do, now. What a capital discourse Mr. Hartwell gave us this morning. I have not enjoyed anything so much for a long time. Don't forget, as we shall expect you next Sunday," she added as she turned to greet another member of the congregation. "Good-day."

Rachel seemed rather shy. All that she had said was, "Good-morning, Mr. Blackthorne," and though she took his proffered hand she did not once look him in the face.

What could be the reason of this? Adam asked himself - was it the presence of her aunt, or had she seen and been displeased with the ardour of his gaze? That was more than he could tell; but he could not help looking upon it as a sign propitious for his hopes that Nanny had shown herself so friendly and invited him to her pew. He was at a loss, indeed, to account for the cordiality of her behaviour; for she had the reputation of regarding recreant Baptists with aversion and scorn. He forgot that there is more joy over one penitent sinner than over ninety and nine just men; and that his appearance at meeting after so long an absence might be considered a sign of incipient grace. At any rate he would come to service on the following Sunday; he would have gone again that same afternoon had he not feared that such a proceeding might rouse the suspicions of the aunt as to his motives, and cause the keen-scented gossips of Moorside to talk. Not that he was particularly thin-skinned, but he did not want his name to be coupled with that of Rachel Orme just yet. Well as he knew the people about him, he never thought it possible that his single visit to the Tabernacle would become a subject of gossip almost as soon as it was known. If he could have heard a little conversation which took place next morning between his housekeeper, Peggy Hothersall, and Jabez o' Jocks, he would probably have seen reason to change his opinion.

Peggy was a little, thin, wizened woman, with a sharp nose and a sharper tongue, who divided her time between winding and keeping Adam's house, for he did not feel that he could afford a servant all to himself. When she had made his bed, "tidied up," and "set the 'kettle on'," in a morning, she would go into the shop and do a bit of winding until it was time to get breakfast ready; and she shared the rest of the day almost equally between the two occupations. If anything, she gave too much of her attention to the winding; and Adam, sometimes with good reason, complained that she neglected her domestic duties - a neglect, however, which was rather his fault than hers, as from reasons of economy he gave her a fixed sum of half-a-crown a week and her food, permitting her to do as much winding "between whiles" as she could, for which she was paid by results. It was thus her interest to do as little for her master and as much for herself as she might. Adam could easily have altered this arrangement, but the alteration would have involved an additional expenditure of at least half-a-crown a week, and, as he said to himself; half-a-crown a week was six pounds ten shillings a year - the interest of one hundred and thirty pounds at five per cent, - far too much to pay in order to avoid a trifling inconvenience. So

Peggy, much to her satisfaction, continued to fill the double position of housekeeper and winder.

On the morning after Adam had been to chapel, the housekeeper went to Jabez 0' Jocks for her set - that is, for the yarn she was to wind.

"Why th' mayster wor at Orrington Chapel, yesterday, Molly 0' Jeff's has been telling me; she seed him there," observed the overlooker.

"Well, if he wor, what then - hasn't he as much reyt to go as onybody else?"

"Oh ay, I wor nobbut thinking -"

"Nobbut thinking - thinking about what?"

"As it's a long time sin' he wor at chapel afoor."

"Welly a year, but what by that? he's allus guon to th' Dippers when he's guon onywhere; he's a sowl to be saved as weel as onybody else, hasn't he?"

"I dare say he has, but it's not dipping, nor his sowl, nor owt o' that soort that he's after now - it's a body!"

"What do yo' mean, Jabez? Yo' talk like a riddle and look as fause (cunning) as an owd tup sheep."

Jabez, who seemed rather pleased with the compliment, gave a ponderous wink; and as he was a widower and Peggy a widow, she began to think he might possibly be meditating a proposal.

Jabez winked again, then he chuckled.

"Drat the chap," exclaimed Peggy, "what does he mean? Have yo' owt to say, because if yo' haven't I'm gooin' to my work?"

No, it isn't his sowl," said Jabez - and his chuckles and winks followed each other in such rapid succession that Peggy felt quite nervous. "Devil a bit he cares about his sowl just now, I'll be bound - it is summut better than his sowl - it's a lass."

"A lass! yo' surely don't mean as th' mayster's gooin' to wed Madge Badger?"

"Not him," replied Jabez, scornfully, "nor yet Betty Dunn. Madge doesn't go to th' Dipper chapel, does hoo?"

"Hoo mut, hoo'd go onywhere if hoo could get a chap."

"No, I don't mean Madge. I mean a different one, fro' her. What thinken yo' o' owd Nanny Cooper's niece, Rachel Orme?"

"Eh, but it ud be a gradely bad job for me if th' mayster wor to get wed to th' likes of her. Hoo wouldn't want an owd woman like me; hoo'd be for getten a bran new servant fro' Redburn. But who says so? it's happen not true."

"Nobody says so. I wor nobbut tellin' you what I thowt. But he seed Rachel i' th' hayfield o' Thursday and spoke to her - that I do know - and he axed a lot o' questions about her when he coom back, and now he goes reyt off to Orrington Chapel - him as doesn't go to a place o' worship in a regular way aboon once a year. There's summut i' th' wind, Peggy, yo' may depend on't. Only durnd say as I said so - what's least said is soonest mended, that's my motty."

"I shall say nowt, yo' may be sure o' that, Jabez; but all the same I do believe you're wrong. As if a mon couldn't speyk to a lass in a hayfield and go to his chapel of a Sunday bout (without) wanting to coort her."

Nevertheless Peggy went to her work with a heavy heart, for she set much store by her situation.

Half an hour later every one of Adam's winders had heard that "th' mayster" was "after" Nanny Cooper's niece; and the same night the "buz" formed an interesting and inexhaustible topic of conversation in the bar parlour of The Brown Cow.

CHAPTER XVI.

JABEZ O' JOCKS DELIVERS JUDGMENT.

In happy oblivion of the keenness with which his movements were being watched, and of the gossip to which his appearance at the Tabernacle had given rise, Adam, as he had resolved, went thither again on the following Sunday morning.

At his own request he was shown into Mrs. Cooper's pew, where he had the pleasure of being near Rachel Orme for the space of nearly two hours. He even walked part of the way home with them, and had the further pleasure of hearing a second sermon from the aunt; for the old lady was well versed in the theology of her sect, and on one memorable occasion she had completely overcome Parson Goodwood, of Christ Church, in an argument on the subject of infant baptism. Adam followed, or seemed to follow, the elucidation of certain knotty points (suggested by Mr. Hartwell's discourse) with so much attention as greatly to please her; but he appeared on divers momentous matters so ignorant that she offered to lend him for his further enlightenment certain books which she had at home.   This offer he gratefully accepted, and said he would call for the books the first time he passed Mrs. Cooper's house.

To this conversation Rachel listened in silence. Neither in chapel nor on the road homewards had Adam been able to catch her eye. Nevertheless he saw; or thought he saw, a faint and slightly amused smile flicker over her winsome face when her aunt offered to place her library at his disposal.

"I'm glad to see that Adam Blackthorne is beginning to take an interest in better things," was Nanny's first remark to her niece after the young man had taken his leave. "He has not been two Sundays together at chapel, I don't know when.   Do you know when, Rachel?"

"Not since I have been with you, I think, aunt."

"Bless me, how forgetful I am getting. Why, you have not been here a year yet - how can you know. Well, he hardly ever used to come at all, and we were beginning to look upon him quite as a lost sheep.   But the Lord put it into his head to come to service last and now he has come again to-day. Who knows? peradventure the Spirit is now at work within him, and it is in the design of Providence to raise him up to be a shining light in the denomination and a strong pillar in the Tabernacle. I do hope as them books may be the means of opening his eyes to the truth. It is a very interesting case; we must do all we can to help on the good work, Above all, let us remember the young man in our prayers Be sure you pray for him to-night, Rachel!"

"Yes, aunt," said Rachel quietly; and I have no doubt she was as good as her word.

Nanny Cooper, as her neighbours generally called her, though none of them ever ventured on so familiar a form of expression in her presence, was the widow of a colour mixer at Mole Hill Paintworks who had been dead many years.   The position he occupied was an important one, and his pay high; but he was a free spender, and after the funeral expenses and his debts were paid Nanny found herself almost destitute, and with two sickly children to support. Being a woman of great energy and resource, however, she neither gave way to useless repinings nor appealed to her friends for help. With the trifle she had left her after satisfying her husband's creditors she opened a small grocery shop, or "badge," near Mole Hill, and as her business increased she added to her stock almost everything her neighbours required. As she was capable and attentive, and sold unsophisticated wares at reasonable prices, she prospered accordingly, and the first use she made of her prosperity was to take a farm and add to her business the sale of milk and fresh butter. At a later period she started a butcher's shop, and as she had a quick eye for capacity, and rewarded liberally faithful service, she had no reason to be dissatisfied with the result of her enterprise. Meanwhile, to her inexpressible grief, she lost both her children, and was left quite alone in the world. Not that she was absolutely without kith and kin, but the few kinsfolk she had were widely scattered, and she rarely saw them or heard from them. In these circumstances it would have been singular if she had not received offers of marriage. She did, in fact, receive many, for, as her neighbours were fond of saying, "Th' man as weds Nanny Cooper has nobbut to go in and hang his hat up" - to houseless bachelors and desolate widowers, doubtless, a most desirable prospect. But she would listen to no matrimonial overtures, and so peremptorily did she refuse them that it gradually came to be understood that she had finally made up her mind never to remarry, and with the lapse of years suitors ceased to trouble her.

Nanny was generally supposed to be well off - how well off nobody save herself and her lawyer, old Torney Bluff of Redburn, was allowed to know. She had bought the house in which she lived and two or three fields behind it, and beyond these and her stock in trade there were no outward and visible signs of her wealth - if wealthy she was.

Rachel Orme was an orphan, the daughter of Nanny's brother Thomas, who had cultivated a small farm with indifferent success, and done a good deal of promiscuous preaching in the neighbourhood of Tarporley, in Cheshire After his death, which occurred about a year before Adam and Rachel's acquaintance, Nanny had adopted the now fatherless and motherless girl, and the two had already become warmly attached to each other. Nobody could know Rachel well without loving her much; and it did not take the girl long to find out that, under a somewhat cold and reserved manner, her aunt concealed a warm heart and a generous nature. The girl had been well brought up, for her father, albeit rather extreme in some of his notions, was a sensible man in many things and a sincere Christian, and by no means devoid of culture.

Though it would not be correct to say that the possibility of her niece marrying had never occurred to Nanny, the possibility seemed altogether too far off to be seriously thought about. In the first place, "the child," as her aunt often called her, was not yet twenty - and in her opinion five-and-twenty was quite soon enough for any young woman to take upon herself the burden of matrimony - indeed, having regard to her own experience, she was disposed to think that marriage at any age was a mistake. Then there was nobody in the neighbourhood good enough for her, not even among the frequenters of the Tabernacle; and as she felt quite sure that "the child" had never thought of such a thing, there was no reason why she should trouble herself about so remote a contingency. One of her principal causes of satisfaction with Rachel was the latter's indifference to the society of young women of her own age; and as for young men she neither noticed nor talked about them, which, considering the quality of the rising generation of Mole Hill and Moorside, was, perhaps, not greatly to be wondered at. She had never thought of Adam Blackthorne as a possible suitor for her niece; for had it not been settled that he was too much taken up with his business to think of marrying, if not actually too penurious to burden himself with the keep of a wife? His visits to the Tabernacle, which soon became frequent and regular, admitted of easy explanation; for she had been taught to believe that every good thought, every aspiration towards a better life, was due to the direct action of the Holy Spirit, and to this cause alone she ascribed what she deemed to be the awakening of the young man's conscience.

Adam called for the books, of course, and had a long conversation with Mrs. Cooper, or rather she gave him a long exposition of her views on regeneration and predestination, and unfolded at great length the difference between the views of General and Particular Baptists; to all of which he listened with exemplary patience, in the hope that he might, perchance, be left alone with Rachel, or otherwise get a word with her.

But no such happy chance befell, and he went home in a very dissatisfied mood, with a monstrous bundle of books under his arm, deeply depressed with the thought that he had promised to read them.

The news that he had been to Nanny Cooper's reached his house before him, and poor Peggy Hothersall was on the tenter-hooks of expectation. She quite counted on being told forthwith that "th' mayster" was going to bring a wife home - long courtships not being the fashion at Moorside - and that her services would not be wanted the month's end. Instead of that, however, Adam threw a big bundle of books and tracks on the table, and gruffly demanded why his supper was not ready.

"Bith mon!" said Peggy to herself; "he's axed her, and hoo willn't have him. It can be nowt else. Why, he's in a gradely tantrum. I've never seen him i' such a tantrum sin' th' work wor bad and th' winders turned out. I mun (must) tell Jabes o' Jocks about this. And them books, too. I wonder what they're about."

The moment her master's back was turned she made a searching investigation of them, but her education having been neglected in early life she did not receive much enlightenment thereby. Her curiosity was all the greater, as never before had she known Adam to bring books home, and he rarely looked at one. His library consisted of Goldsmith's "Animated Nature," which he had bought at a sale for "an old song," an odd volume of "Waverley," a copy of Buchan's "Domestic Medicine," and a Bible; and his reading was chiefly confined to the *Redburn Gazette,* to which he subscribed on joint account with the landlord of The Brown Cow; for, though there was very little of it, the price was sixpence, and Adam thought twice before he spent sixpence.

Early next day Peggy mentioned "th' mayster's" visit to Nanny Cooper to her friend Jabez, and told him of the strange parcel Adam had brought home.

"Books," said Jabes, thoughtfully; "what does he want wi' books? By gum! (with the air of a man struck by a happy thought) they're happen coorting books - what they callin' poetry, yo know, Peggy - summut like hymns, nobbut a deal different."

"Songs, happen."

"No, they willn't be gradely song books. Ten to one they'll be about lads and lasses, moonleet, primroses, kusses, and sich like."

"And dun yo' really think, Jabez, as aw them books as he browt huom last neet is full of sich like balderdash?"

"Ten to one, Peggy; ten to one. But I'll tell yo what. Bring one on 'em here next time yo' go into th' house. Yo' can put it under yor apron; nobody 'll see it. I am a bit of a scholar, yo' know, and I'll tell yo what it's about."

This hint was acted upon, and at a moment when Jabes was not much occupied Peggy laid before him one of Nanny Cooper's books and two or three of the Pamphlets.

The book was a large folio.

"Bith mon," said Jabez, "if this is poetry, or owt else, there's a bonny lot on't. There's been moore than one, or two awther, at th' makin' o' this. Why, it would tak' a man aw his life to read it, let alone to write it. But it isn't poetry. It's Char- Charnock on the Divine Attributes. That's a bit aboon me, but its summut to do wi' relgion, I reckon. It is not a coorting book, that's cock sure. Now, let's look at th' tracts. 'A 'Word to Impenitent Sinners,' 'The Backslider's Doom,' 'A Discussion on Infant Baptism between the Rev. Peter Poundtext of Leeds and Mr. Daniel Dipman, Minister of Salem Chapel, Rodlesworth.'"

"I tell 'yo' what it is, Peggy," said Jabez, with great deliberation, as he took off his spectacles, after spelling out the title of the last tract, "we've bin mista'en; we've been mista'en. Th' mayster's noon courtin'."

"How do yo' know? Have yo' been reading it i' one o' them books?"

"No; but I've learnt it fro' them books. He's what they callin' wakkened; that's what it is. He's gettin' convarted."

"As how?"

"That's what I connot quite mak' out; but I think its sumut i' this way: Dippers thinks terrible ill o' theirsells till they're converted and baptised, and then they believe as all their sins is washed away, and they'll be saved.

"Wor yo' ever converted, Jabez?" asked Peggy, who did not seem to be altogether satisfied with this explanation.

"Me! No; I've no 'casion."

"Why?"

"Cose our folk wor church folks, and I were born on a Sunday, and kesend (christened) afoor I wor eight days old. They sayen as them as is born on a Sunday and kesened o' th' seventh day is sure o' being saved, let happen what will."

But yo' never goin' to church, Jabez."

"I've never bin since I wor wed; but that's nowt to do wi' it. I wor kesend, and that's aw as is wanted – what they callen the one thing needful, yo' know."

"I wish I'd been kesend afore I wor eight days owd then," observed Peggy, who was by no means sure that bad been christened at all "So yo' think as th' mayster is not courtin', Jabez?"

"I'm sure on't," said Jabez, emphasizing his answer with a thwack on "Charnook's Attributes." "No mon could read books like them theer as had a lass on his mind."

This was decisive; and when Peggy joined her fellow-winders she told them that in her opinion there was "nowt at all in the 'buz' about th' mayster being after Rachel Orme. "He was getting "convarted," that was the sole reason why he went so often to the Dippers' chapel; and, as like as not, he would be "dipped" in a week or two.

This story was as quickly noised about as had been the previous one, which to some extent it replaced. As it travelled from mouth to mouth the rumour assumed a more definite shape, and the Sunday but one following the Tabernacle was crowded with people from Moorside, who fully expected to see Adam Blackthorne baptised.

But, so far from being baptised, he was not even at chapel. The fact was that Nanny Cooper, in her zeal for his conversion, had so completely taken possession of him that he was beginning to feel rather disgusted. Whenever he called at the "badge" and farm at Mole Hill he was always warmly welcomed, and - his visits being generally made in the evening - often asked to stop and have a bit of supper. Then the aunt would tackle him on one of her pet theological subjects, ask him how much he had read of "Charnock," and so utterly bother him that he more than once went away half resolving never to return. But that was not the worst. He could never catch Rachel alone; her aunt was nearly always there or thereabouts, and when she was not somebody else was. He became at length so discouraged with these repeated disappointments that he intermitted his attendance at meeting, to Mrs. Cooper's great concern, for she bad begun to regard him as in some sense the captive of her spiritual bow and spear. Hence, when he re-appeared in her pew after a fortnight's absence, her satisfaction was great, and the look and smile with which Rachel, on the impulse of the moment, greeted him, made Adam more determined than ever to tell her of his love, and ask her to be his wife.

CHAPTER XVll

LOVE AND WAR.

All this time Rachel, though she fought hard against the feeling, and refused to admit the truth even to herself, was as much in love with Adam as he with her. His appearance in the hayfield, and the help he had so promptly and kindly given, had favourably impressed her and she more than suspected the motive of his frequent visits to the Tabernacle and her aunt's house at Mole Hill. And then he was physically a fine fellow, a man of thews and sinews, and, though not much of a scholar, he had been, as his conversation showed, well-trained in the school of life, and had acquired, for his age and position, a rather varied experience. He had learned much during his stay at Manchester, where he came in contact with many men of fair education, and in the course of several journeys to London, whither he had been sent on his master's business. Though he generally affected the manners and language of the people among whom he lived, Rachel found him in every way superior any other young man whom she had known, which, seeing that she had known so very few, is perhaps not saying very much.

Her father had been a zealous, if not a fanatical, Particular Baptist. Being fluent of speech and a man of more than average attainments, there was a great demand for his services as occasional preacher from all parts of country; and as he was fully persuaded that it was his duty to speak the Word in season and out of season, he never refused an invitation to preach when it was physically possible for him to accept it. The consequence was that his farm suffered, a circumstance that Thomas Orme little heeded, and his wife's health broke completely down under the weight of care which her husband's religious zeal, and its outcome of frequent absence from home, imposed upon her. In the end she died, and Rachel was left to the care of her father, who, to do him justice, did his best to take the place of the mother and bring up his child in the way he thought she should go. But society she had none; her father would hold no communication with the world - the world, according to his interpretation of scripture, signifying everybody who did not believe in the particular redemption of the elect and the eternal reprobation of the wicked. His only associates were men of his own stamp, who, when they came to the farm, rarely noticed Rachel except to bid her beware of the wrath to come, and warn her against the pomps and vanities of the world. Her father's peculiar religious tenets and political views - for he was as strong a Radical as a Calvinist - would have effectually hindered all friendly intercourse with their neighbours even had he been as solicitous for their society as he was the reverse. They were Church and Tory to a man, and his opinions were so unpopular that it was generally understood he would be turned out of his farm at the expiration of his lease. Hence Rachel had been debarred from the usual pleasures of childhood and the diversions of youth; and only the sweetness of her disposition had prevented the spoiling of her character - the substitution of a permanent religious gloom for the native joyousness of her nature. But though now emancipated from her father's authority, and tenderly and even indulgently treated by her aunt, his influence still lived, and she could not indulge in an innocent pleasure without fearing that she had committed a heinous sin. Her love for Adam Blackthorne in the beginning was a sore trial to her. She almost felt that it was an offence against modesty to think about a young man at all, and she had been taught that too much love for the creature was incompatible with love for the Creator. Did she love Adam too much? was a question she frequently asked herself. It was certainly difficult to draw the line, but she feared she did, and against this love she struggled with all her strength, and prayed much and often. None the less did the love grow, and she had never felt so unhappy as during the time Adam stayed away from chapel and discontinued his visits to Mole Hill. And then the consciousness that she had been unhappy in his absence and happy in his return made her more miserable still. She acknowledged to herself with almost dismay that she derived more pleasure from Adam's presence in the pew than from the minister's presence in the pulpit; and thought so much about him that she was unable to profit by Mr. Hartwell's sermons. Then, to punish herself for so terrible a dereliction of duty, she kept out of Adam's way when he came to see her - for her heart told her that it was for her sake he came, and not for her aunt's theological lectures - took no part in the conversation if she happened to be by, and generally gave him the cold shoulder. Nevertheless, she was occasionally surprised out of her reserve, and by some inadvertent look or gesture betrayed the feelings which she desired to conceal.

This treatment drove Adam nearly wild. He accused her, in his thoughts, of being a prude and a coquette, and resolved that if she did not soon give him an opportunity of learning his fate he would make one.

The opportunity came sooner than he expected, and in a way which he little anticipated.

He was returning one evening by the field road from Orrington, and had almost reached Solomon Smalley's farm, where he had first met Rachel, when he saw two figures before him on the footpath. There being nothing very unusual in this circumstance, he did not at first give any particular heed to their proceedings. But as he neared them it seemed to him that the woman was trying to get out of the man's way, and that the man was detaining her.

This roused his curiosity, and he hurried forward.

Surely he knew that shawl, and that bonnet and the pose of that figure? Yes, it was - it could he none ether than Rachel - and in the man he recognised Bill Nudger.

Then Adam ran, keeping on the grass, so that his approach might not be heard.

Bill had hold of Rachel's hand. She was trying desperately to get away; and begging of him to release her.

"Do let me go - please let me go - you are hurting any hand let me go -"

"Not till yo've gan me a kuss - give me a kuss and I'll let yo' go - that is if yo' willn't stop a bit longer with me - "

"Take that, you villain!" shouted Adam, at the same time giving Bill a kick that fairly lifted him from the ground and sent him rolling into the gutter.

"Oh, Mr. Blackthorne," exclaimed Rachel with a sob, almost in her agitation, throwing herself into his arms. "I'm so thankful you came. That man has followed me nearly all the way from Lotties. I don't know what I should have done if you had not come. He seized my hand and would not let me go. But I'm afraid you've hurt him."

"Never mind him, he hasn't got half as bad as he deserves. Come, dear, I'll see you safe home."

"Yo're not going yet, Blackthorne," shouted Bill Nudger, who by this time had picked himself up and somewhat recovered from the effect of Adam's lusty kick. "I'm as good a man as yo' ony day - better too - for nobody but a coward would come and punch a chap fro' behind, as yo've done me."

"Serves you right for laying your hand on a woman."

"Never mind him, Mr. Blackthorne - come, let us go - do let us go," said Rachel entreatingly, who was beginning to fear that the two men might come to blows - Nudger looked so savage, and Adam's teeth were hard set.

"Nay, he'll not go yet, Mistress Orme; leastways till I've paid him back for that theer punch as he gave me just now."

"Come away - do come," pleaded Rachel, who was growing more and more alarmed.

Adam was rather reluctantly yielding to her request for he would have liked to administer a little more chastisement to Nudger, when the latter, exclaiming, "I'll give it yo' back then," rushed viciously at him.

Adam saw his object barely in time to draw Rachel aside and avoid the tremendous kick which Nudger aimed at him. Before the blacksmith could recover himself, Adam fetched him a blow in the face that nearly brought him to the ground a second time.

Then they stood and glared at each other, Nudger evidently meditating another rush. Adam watched him warily, for he could see that the young fellow, who was a renowned fighter and wrestler, meant mischief. It would have been throwing a chance away in such circumstances to act merely on the defensive and await his opponent's onset, so, like him, he began, in Lancashire phrase, "to dog for the first grip."

After a few minutes spent in this way they rushed together and grappled.

It was a tough struggle. The blacksmith, albeit not taller than Adam, was somewhat heavier, and from the nature of his calling decidedly more muscular. But he had drink in him, and drink is no help to a man either in peace or war. This gave Adam the advantage, and although he received two or three savage kicks that made him wince, he held on to his grip until he felt that Bill's wind was failing him, when, profiting by the raising of the latter's foot to deal him another kick, he knocked his foot from him, and, exerting his utmost strength, threw the blacksmith so heavily that all his remaining breath was forced from his body, and he lay helpless on the ground.

Then Adam knelt beside him, seized his arms, and waited for him to come round.

While this scene was going on, Rachel had been almost petrified with horror. She wanted to run away, yet could not. She tried to turn her head and close her eyes, but there was something in the sight that seemed to fascinate her, and, even against her will, fasten her to the spot. When she saw the two men struggling so fiercely for the mastery - their writhing bodies swaying to and fro - their legs, as it seemed, locked together - the bulky form of the blacksmith trying to bear Adam to the earth – she sank on the ground, and covered her face with her hands. Then she heard a great crash, and, looking up, saw Nudger stretched full length on the grass, and Adam bending over him.

"Oh, Adam," she cried, coming forward in sore dismay, "have you killed him - is he dead?"

"Not he, he's only lost his wind; see, he is coming round."

The blacksmith made an effort to rise. This Adam prevented by kneeling on his chest and placing his hands on his throat. If there was to be a ground fight it was desirable to keep the advantage he had won.

"Are you satisfied," he asked, "or are we to have another tussle?"

"Nay, I cannot say as I am vary weel satisfied," answered Bill faintly, "but I've getten as much as I can carry. You've bested me this bout, Blackthorne. Let me get up."

"Will you go away quietly then?"

"Ay, that I will."

"Honour bright?"

"Honour bright."

"Get up, then, but take care as you don't meddle with this young woman again, or it'll be worse for you."

The blacksmith rose with difficulty - for the fall had shaken him - picked up his hat, wiped the blood from his face, and walked slowly away.

"Let us go, too," said Adam to Rachel, who was very pale and seemed almost ready to faint.

"Are you hurt?" she asked, seeing that Adam limped a little.

"A crack or two on the shins - that's all. The soreness will go off when I've walked a bit."

Then Rachel saw that his stockings were cut and saturated with blood.

"Oh!" she exclaimed in great distress, "you're hurt, you're badly hurt, and it is all for me. If I had not gone to Lotties to see Widow Birket - and aunt did not want me to go - this would never have happened."

"It is nothing, I tell you. My shins will be all right in a day or two. And don't you think, Rachel, I would have done a thousand times as much for you?"

Rachel was silent.

"I want you to give me the right, Rachel, to protect you against fellows like this Bill Nudger. I want you to be my wife. Will you? Ever since I first saw you in Solomon Smalley's hayfield there - looking so bonny - I've fairly doted on you, Rachel. Will you, Rachel?" And he took her hand.

Still she remained silent; but she did not withdraw her hand.

"Will you not speak, Rachel?" he continued, bending over her until his face almost touched hers. "Or maybe you don't care for me."

"I - I've a respect for you, Adam," she said, in a voice almost too low to be heard.

This would have been cold comfort for some lovers, but Adam was so much encouraged thereby that his arm stole round her waist, and before she could make an effort to prevent him his lips were pressed to hers.

This was dreadful. What would her aunt say - what would Mr. Hartwell say - what would everybody say if they knew? What was the use of her pious bringing up - the principles so carefully instilled into her by her father - the sage counsels of her aunt - if she could let herself be kissed by a man in that way, and - worse than all - not feel so much horrified as she ought - feel a sinful pleasure in it even.

"Oh, Adam, do take your arm away; suppose anybody was to see us. And please don't kiss me any more; what would my aunt say?"

"I mean to go home with you and ask her consent."

"Oh, Adam!"

That was all she could say. Her heart was so full that words failed her. She wanted Adam to speak to her aunt, and still she did not. Would not her aunt think her ungrateful and wicked in listening to Adam's offer and letting him see her home? Ought she not to have given him a peremptory refusal - ought she not to give him one now? It was not too late. But she could not; her tongue clove to the roof of her mouth when she tried. She must let things take their course.

So they walked quietly homeward in the deepening twilight - he very happy, and she, despite her misgivings, not very miserable.

CHAPTER XVIII.

MRS. COOPER THINKS SHE HAS BEEN AN OLD FOOL

When the lovers reached Mole Hill, Rachel went in by the house door, while Adam took the way through the shop, where Mrs. Cooper was generally to be found; for though she kept a couple of shopmen she liked to be to the fore herself; and always insisted on knowing what was going on.

"Is that you, Adam Blackthorne?" she said, looking up from her ledger in some surprise; for it was not usual for him to call before shutting-up time, "You are rather early to-night."

"Yes, I have a little order here for some flour and sugar and things, which my housekeeper asked me to give you."

As he gave her the bit of paper on which the order was written, he asked her in an undertone, so that the people in the shop might not hear, if he could have a word with her in private.

"Certainly," she answered; "go into the parlour. I'll come to you in a minute or two."

"What can he want?" was her reflection, as she followed Adam into the parlour, a pleasant little room, with a window looking out into a trimly kept garden; "it's maybe about something in 'Charnock' that he doesn't quite understand - or that passage in Revelations as Mr. Hartwell took for his text last Sunday. But he might have waited till I had added my ledger up."

She found Adam looking out of the window. He fancied he had caught a glimpse of Rachel in the garden.

"Won't you sit down," said Mrs, Cooper, "and have a bit of supper with us? It's nearly closing time, and I don't think as I shall go into the shop any more tonight."

You are very kind, but I'm not sure whether I can or not. I have got something very particular to say. I don't know whether it will surprise you or not,"

"Dear me," she thought, "it's come an last. He's going to ask me to speak to Mr. Hartwell about getting baptized. I knew there was something on his mind, he's looked so serious the last two or three weeks. I'm truly thankful to think as I've been permitted to be instrumental in his conversion."

"No, Adam, it will happen not be so much of a surprise as you think. I've been watching you. I can see as far into a stone wall as anybody else."

"You will not be angry, then?"

"Angry! What is the man thinking of? I'm truly thankful to think as the Lord has brought it about. If you only knew how I've prayed for you; as has Rachel too - many and many a time, both down on our bended knees. She'll be as thankful as I am when she hears."

"I have just told Rachel about it," said Adam, in great surprise at the turn things were taking, and wishing he had spoken before.

"Well, didn't she say she was very thankful?"

"Not exactly. She said she had a respect for me, and I told her I'd speak to you."

"Well, if she did not say it she felt it; you may be sure of that. And now I suppose you'd like me to speak to Mr. Hartwell for you?"

"If you like; but Mr. Hartwell cannot marry us, can he? We shall have to be married at Church you know."

"Marry you, marry you!" screamed Mrs. Cooper, jumping up from her chair and laying her hands on the table, while she looked at Adam full in the face with flaming eyes. "Who's going to be married? What do you mean, Adam Blackthorne? Tell me Mr. Adam Blackthorne - what do you mean?"

I mean," answered Adam – who was very bewildered by this unexpected onslaught – "I mean as I have been asking Rachel to be my wife; and now I have come to ask your consent to our marriage"

"You didn't come here to-night, then, to say as you wanted to be baptized, and to ask me to speak to Mr. Hartwell about you?"

"No I never thought of such a thing. I came to ask you for Rachel."

"What an old fool I've been!" said Mrs. Cooper, sinking back into her chair. I was never so befooled in all my life – never. I see it all plain enough now. And me as has been trying to enlighten you, and praying for you, and lending you good books. You're a hypocrite, Adam Blackthorne - that's what you are - a base hypocrite, to take advantage of a poor lone woman in that way."

"That's a hard saying, Mrs. Cooper," said poor Adam humbly. "I'm sure I didn't mean to be a hypocrite; I think I could make Rachel a good husband, and I could give her a good home; but I'm sure she will not have me without your consent. She has as much affection for you as if you were her own mother."

"And what did she say when you spoke to her?"

"That she had a respect for me."

"Humph! She said so, did she? I suppose that means as she's set her heart on having you. The more fool she. But lasses always are fools. I was one myself once, so I ought to know."

"You will give your consent then?"

"I don't know whether I will or not. How can I give my consent to the marriage of my child with an unbeliever?"

"I'm not an unbeliever, Mrs. Cooper," answered Adam, with some warmth. "You'll be saying as I'm an infidel next."

"You are not a church member, and that is nearly as bad."

"Happen I shall be some time, if you'll only have a bit of patience."

"It's no use pressing me now, Adam. I cannot say anything to-night; I'm too much upset. I must think over it and pray over it. Come on Saturday night, and you shall have your answer."

"Very well," said Adam in a disappointed voice. "And now I think I'll be going."

"Will you not stay and have a bit of supper with us?"

"Nay, I think I'd better be going. You'll be wanting to talk to Rachel, and I should only be in the way. You won't be hard on her, will you, Mrs. Cooper?"

"Hard on her! What can you think, Adam, to ask such a question? Don't I love her as well as I ever loved my own little ones as God in His goodness took away from me long years sin'? And now to lose her so soon! Yes, I'll see what she has to say, and we'll expect you on Saturday night. But don't be too sure, and pray that the Lord may guide us all aright."

Rachel, from her own room, saw Adam go, and then she went down to her aunt. She found her in tears.

"Come here, child," she said in a troubled voice, "and tell me what Adam Blackthorne has been saying to you."

Tears are contagious, and Rachel went and laid her head upon her aunt's bosom and wept too.

"He asked me to be his wife," murmured the girl.

"And you - what did you say?"

"I said I had a respect for him. And - oh, aunt, I know it is very wicked - yet I can't help lov - liking him. But I will do whatever you want. He said he would speak to you."

"And so he did. How long has this been going on?"

"What do you mean by going on? He never spoke to me before to-night."

"I mean how long have you had this liking for him?"

"I cannot exactly tell how long. It seems to me almost since the first time I saw him."

"Dear, dear, and I've been so blind! I think there never was such an old fool. Do you know as my heart's nearly breaking at the thought of losing you, Rachel'?"

"Dear aunt I won't leave you; I'll stay with you all my life. Haven't you been more than a mother to me?"

"Nay, nay, child, that will never do. I must not let my feelings stand in the way of your happiness. You're young, and I'm old; and young folks will be young folks. But I've sore misgivings about this Adam Blackthorne. I'm feared he's a worldly man, and no fit helpmate for a Christian woman. We must think well about it, and lay the case before the Lord in our prayers. He's to come for his answer on Saturday"

"Did he tell you about Bill Nudger?" asked Rachel timidly.

"No. What about Bill Nudger?"

And then Rachel told her aunt how the blacksmith had behaved to her, and of the fight between him and Adam.

"On this Mrs. Cooper seemed much disturbed. "It's very bad," she said, "and very hard as a young woman cannot go out for a walk without being meddled with and exposed to insult. I'm glad Adam came to your help, very glad. He seems to have behaved well, too. But this fighting's a terrible thing, and it's hardly right as Christian folks should be mixed up with it, even as lookers on. I must consult with Mr. Hartwell what's best to be done. Isn't to-morrow his day for calling?"

"Yes, to-morrow's Friday, and he generally calls on Fridays."

"Well, when he comes we'll ask him to take a dish of tea. He has a wise head on his shoulders, and he'll maybe - the Lord leading him - help us to a right conclusion. Get th' best blue chinay out of th' oak cupboard, Rachel, and see as Betty scrubs th' parlour floor and cleans th' windows first thing in th' morning."

CHAPTER XIX.

THE MINISTER'S OPINION.

At about four o'clock on the following afternoon a short, solidly-built, elderly gentleman entered the shop at Mole Hill, and asked one of the shopmen if Mistress Cooper was within. (This gentleman, having a great respect for the purity of his mother tongue, never used such debased words as "missis" and "mister.") He was dressed all in black - black coat, black breeches, black stockings - all save his cravat, a voluminous affair of white muslin, which, reaching almost to his ears and covering the lower part of his chin, matched well with his snow-white hair, and added greatly to the dignity of his appearance. He had a broad, bright face, surmounted by a massive forehead. His beautiful eyes seemed dim, as if with much study, and a smile, half-humorous, half-sympathetic, played about his finely-cut lips. It was a noble countenance, but whether intelligence or benevolence was its predominant expression it would have been hard to determine.

"Ay, that she is," answered Nanny herself, who was just in the act of serving a small boy with some treacle. "Why, didn't you see me, Mr. Hartwell?"

"I'm not sure that I did, Mistress Cooper. As you know, I am, unfortunately, rather near-sighted. At any rate, as I never saw you with your head in a treacle-tub before, I may be pardoned for overlooking you. Albeit I have an excellent memory for faces, I do not readily recognise figures; though, to be sure, Mistress Cooper, yours is one that is not easily forgotten."

You will be having your joke, Mr. Hartwell. Well, I had a figure once, and, though I say it as shouldn't say it, a figure to he proud on too. But them vanities has long gone by. But why didn't you come in at th' front door?"

I always enter the shop way, you know. I think it must be by a sort of instinct. Your good things lead me by the nose, as it were. Truly, this is a place of plenty. What a fine show of hams you have up there!" looking towards the ceiling, which was profusely garnished with the remains of many pigs. "I think I must ask you to send me one. What may be the price?"

"Nothing to you, Mr. Hartwell. I'll send one of the best I have to your house to-morrow."

"You are very kind, Mistress Cooper, but only on condition that you let me pay for it. My people do quite enough for me without making me presents of hams. If you have anything to spare, and are charitably disposed, rather bestow it upon poor Thomas Inskip. He is out of work, his wife and children are sick, and I fear they have hardly enough to eat, though he never complains."

"That I will, Mr. Hartwell. But don't you think a bit of flour and meal, and a quart or two of milk, would do them more good than ham?"

"You are always practical, Mistress Cooper. Not a doubt of it."

"Well, then, I'll send them a score of meal and half a score of flour and some milk. But as you make conditions, you must let me make one too."

"This is only just, I think. What is the condition which you seek to impose?"

"Your acceptance of that ham," pointing to one above her head. "If I may send it to your house - as a present, mind - I'll send the meal and flour and milk to Thomas Inskip's. Is it a bargain?"

"Surely that is taking an unfair advantage, Mistress Cooper. You must really let me pay. I should be uncomfortable else."

"No, no, Mr. Hartwell," laughed Nanny; "I mean to have my way. If Thomas Inskip gets his meal, you must take the ham."

"For the sake of Thomas, then, I consent. Nevertheless -"

"And it is for your own use, you know. It has not to be given away. Is that agreed to?"

"Yes, I agree to that too; nevertheless -"

"No, no! I'll have no neverthelesses. And now come into the house and have a dish of tea. I am sure you must be hungry after your walk."

"I agree to that too, and without any nevertheless. I never refuse an invitation to tea at Mole Hill Farm. Your teas, Mistress Cooper, are things to be remembered for a lifetime, and, as you rightly surmise, I have somewhat of an appetite to-day."

They found Rachel in the parlour, looking as fresh and bright as the roses she had just placed in a vase on the mantelpiece, albeit a little anxious; for she knew the answer Adam was to have on the morrow depended on the advice her aunt was about to receive from Mr. Hartwell.

The table was already laid. On a gorgeous tea tray of antique pattern, which reposed on a snow-white cloth, was arrayed Nanny's blue china - a bequest from her mother, only brought out on rare occasion - garnished with sundry pots of honey, jam, and cream. Then Betty was ordered to bring in the teapot, to which speedily followed a roast fowl, a boiled ham, and plates of muffins, crumpets, toasted oat cake, and thin bread and butter - in quantity sufficient for a company of hunters. Well might Mr. Hartwell say a tea at Mole Hill was something to be remembered.

After the minister had eaten as much as he could, and perhaps a little more than was quite compatible with good digestion - for Nanny took it ill when her guests did not do full justice to her fare - and a suitable thanksgiving had been offered, she installed her guest in a huge arm-chair, and, sending into the shop for a long pipe and an ounce of the best tobacco, invited him to make himself comfortable, drawing his attention at the same time to the fact that there was a decanter of whisky and a jug of hot water at his elbow.

Meanwhile Rachel, after intimating that her presence was required in the dairy, had withdrawn.

"You dispense a munificent hospitality, Mistress Cooper," said the minister as he mixed himself a glass of toddy. "The tea was almost too good, and this whisky is superb."

"Ay, that's whisky as is whisky. It's some as my husband had sent him as a present out o' Scotland by an old shopmate as was doing well at Glasgow, not long afore he died, and that's more than thirty years since. I never take any myself, except when I'm bad in my inside, and that is not often, I'm fain to say. If we were only like whisky, Mr. Hartwell, and got stronger as we got older, what a blessing it would be."

"I'm not very sure about that, Mistress Cooper, if you mean physically stronger. In that case I am afraid some of us would be living too long. We must give place to the young ones, you know, else the world would soon become overcrowded. The desire for very long life, however natural, is, methinks, somewhat selfish. Yet if we cannot, like whisky, grow stronger with age, we may at least grow in godliness, in faith, in wisdom, and, above all, in charity. I mean not merely the charity that bestows alms, but that gift of grace which enables us to feel with our fellow-creatures - to weep with the sorrowful, laugh with the merry, comfort the afflicted, and judge others as leniently - if we judge at all - as we hope God will one day judge us."

"If we could only do likewise, Mr. Hartwell! I do strive, but it's hard for a lone woman getting into years, with a shop to look after, and a farm, and twenty sheep i' th' croft, and a cow calving and wanting gruel, maybe every week, and knowing as if I don't look after things they will go to rack and. ruin, to cultivate all the Christian graces. We are all weak vessels, and I am one of the weakest. But as you was saying, sir, we ought to grow in wisdom as we increase in years - though there's many a one as does not - and make room for them as should come after us. And that is why I want to ask your advice. I'm sorely troubled and perplexed about Rachel, sir."

"Why, what can Rachel have been doing amiss? She is one of my favourites. I have always considered her a most exemplary young woman, and thought she was a great comfort to you. What is the trouble, Mistress Cooper?"

"I'm afraid she and Adam Blackthorne have fallen in love with one another - nay, I may say I am sure."

"Indeed. That accounts for his frequent attendance at chapel of late. I thought there was something. And why should you fear this, Mistress Cooper? Master Blackthorne, from all I have heard, is a very steady young man who is getting on nicely in his business."

"Oh, Mr. Hartwell, I am afraid he is very worldly, and Rachel is a church member; and the Bible says, 'Be ye not unequally yoked with unbelievers.'"

"Truly, and we who take the Scriptures for our guide must reverently follow their leading. Nevertheless, it is as great a mistake to place a wrong construction upon the words of divine truth as to despise them; and I am disposed to think that the command, or rather the exhortation, which you quote will hardly bear the meaning you ascribe to it. The unbelievers of whom St. Paul was speaking were doubtless Pagans, and the Apostle rightly deemed it inexpedient for followers of Christ to yoke themselves with the worshippers of heathen gods. But I am sure that St. Paul, who was not alone a high-couraged but a large-hearted, and, so to speak, a broad-minded man, had never objected to the union of a Christian maiden with a husband of good report who believed in Christ, merely because he had not been baptized and joined himself formally to the Church."

"Well, Adam is not an infidel, I will say that of him. He talks very nicely about better things, only he doesn't see his way to getting baptized."

"Very likely - that is the case with many a one. And, at least, if he should marry your niece he will be brought under favourable influences. The seeds of good that, let us hope, have been sown in his heart may spring up and bear fruit. It may be God's own way of bringing him to a saving knowledge of the truth."

"You think you would let it go on, then?"

"That's my opinion. Always provided, of course, that you are satisfied as to the reality of Master Blackthorne's affection for Rachel, and that he is likely to make her a good husband."

"Oh, he likes her well enough, there is no doubt about that, and, worldly speaking, it will be a very good match for her. You have removed the only doubt from my mind. It is not often I ask advice from anybody, but when I do I always follow it. When Adam comes to-morrow night he'll get the answer as he wants. But it'll be a sore trial to me, Mr. Hartwell."

"I am sure it will, Mistress Cooper, though not, I hope, an affliction; for though the marrying of your niece may cause you a certain sorrow, it will also be an occasion for rejoicing. She will be taking upon herself the chiefest of the duties assigned by Providence to her sex; and it cannot be otherwise than a comfort to you to reflect that when in the course of nature you are called hence, she will, if it please God to make her marriage fruitful - which, let us hope, He may - be a happy wife and mother. And now if you will permit me - having smoked my pipe and finished my toddy - I will step up as far as Master Blackthorne's. He is doubtless undergoing considerable perturbation of spirit; for nothing is harder to endure than suspense, and young lovers are not generally the most patient of mankind. It will be a deed of charity to put him out of his misery. Moreover, an opportunity may be afforded me of giving him useful counsel."

"I am glad to hear you say so. A word from you will go farther than from any of us. Tell him not to be in too great haste to be rich. I don't think he's over fond of money and power now, mind you, he is only over anxious to get on; but it may become his besetting sin later, and that's what I'm afraid of."

"I will remember, Mistress Cooper. And now, before I go, I should like to say good-bye to Rachel."

Rachel, who was not far off, came at her aunt's call. Mr. Hartwell took both her hands in his.

"I am going, my dear," he said, "to see a particular friend of yours - one Adam Blackthorne - charged with a message from your aunt, the purport whereof I think it behoves you to know. I am going to tell him that she gives her consent to your betrothal, and I earnestly pray that you may be blessed in each other's love."

Rachel gave the minister a look eloquent of gratitude. She felt herself at the moment powerless to speak.

"Have you no message to send him?" he continued. "Still silent "(after a pause). "What! may I not give him your love?"

Rachel blushed scarlet, gave her questioner a slight affirmative nod, and then ran hastily from the room.

CHAPTER XX.

MR.. HARTWELL AND ADAM.

Mr. Hartwell, albeit only pastor of a small chapel in an out-of-the-way place, at a time when the ministers of the denomination to which he belonged were not remarkable for culture, and though he had never been to college, was a man of rare learning and catholicity of spirit. His views in many things were far in advance of those of his brethren in the ministry and of his flock. But he was so temperate in his expression of them, so careful not to give offence, and so meek in spirit withal, that even those who thought that some of his opinions lacked soundness paid him the homage of sincere respect. His people at Orrington adored him. He had endeared himself to them by many years of faithful service. None ever sought his counsel or his sympathy in vain, and though his means were scanty he was always a liberal helper of the poor. His time was divided between his pastoral duties and his books, to which he was almost as devoted as a lover to his mistress. Besides being a famous textist he was a great linguist, and could read most of the sacred books of the East in the original tongues. He had been a missionary in India, and people said he knew as much of the religions of Buddha, Brahma and Mahomet as his own.

Mr. Hartwell lived all alone in a cottage near his chapel. A charwoman came every day to do some indispensable dusting and cleaning, but he prepared all his own food and brushed his own shoes. This style of housekeeping, as may be supposed, made him an object of intense compassion to the fair members of his flock, and many were the efforts put forth to persuade him to live in a more conventional fashion, or, as they said, "Like other folks." Yielding in most things, he could not, however, be prevailed upon to alter his domestic arrangements even to the extent of taking a housekeeper. He did very well as he was, he said. He had nobody to consult or to please as to his time of eating or drinking, uprising and downsitting. He could go out when he liked and come in when he liked. He had no need to regulate his movements by considerations of the dinner hour, and he never knew what it was to fear the frowns of a cook. A housekeeper - even a common servant - could hardly fail to be in a measure tyrannical. If she were a virago he would be afraid of her, and life would be a burden to him; if she were amiable, and had about her the grace of godliness, he would be in a perpetual fidget lest he should unwittingly say or do something that might hurt her feelings. Next to his books he valued his liberty, and it was his misfortune to be so constituted, that with a woman under his roof, however kind and well intentioned she might be, he would feel himself more or less in bondage.

Men smiled when they heard the minister argue thus, and women pretended to be indignant; yet all admitted that there might be truth in what he said, and it came to be understood in the end that he was too confirmed an old bachelor even to reform his domestic habits.

Mr. Hartwell found Adam in his office. The latter's first impression on seeing the minister was that he was a bringer of bad news. He thought he had come to break to him Nanny Cooper's refusal of his offer for her niece's hand; and when he learned the real object of the minister's visit, though far from being a demonstrative man, he was deeply moved, and thanked him warmly for his kindness.

"I shall never forget this, Mr. Hartwell," he said. "You have placed me under a great obligation. I know I have been very remiss in my attendance at chapel, and I feel really unworthy of your kindness. But for the future - well, I'll make no promises; it's not in my way - you shall see for yourself. If there is ever anything I can do for you, any little help I can render, you must be sure to let me know."

"I will bear your obliging offer in mind, Master Blackthorne, and whenever an occasion arises for your help, I shall not fail to let you know. And now, in order to complete my mission, I have to perform what I feel to be the only unsatisfactory part of it; for unasked advice is rarely pleasant to the giver, and still more rarely to the receiver. I overcame, as I have told you, Mistress Cooper's objections to you on the ground of your not being a church member; but she fears - and I promised to speak to you on the subject - that you set too much store by the things of this world to the neglect of things heavenly; that you are too intent on laying up treasures on earth, where rust and moth do corrupt, and are in danger thereby of becoming one of those who live to work, instead of working to live. I know not how far this may be true; it is known, indeed, only to your own heart and the Divine Reader of hearts. But, setting all other considerations aside, a too intense devotion to business might militate against your domestic peace and the happiness of her who is about to become your wife. For if I read Rachel aright, she will prefer her home to all things else; riches and high position will have few, if any, charms for her unsophisticated nature and gentle spirit."

"I dare say you are right, Mr. Hartwell," said Adam. "You have formed the same opinion of Rachel as I have, and I like her all the better for it. As for my liking money too well, whatever folks may think, I don't feel as I do. I want to get on, that's true; so does everybody as is worth his salt; and when a man has his own way to make, there is nought for it but to save hard and work hard. But I'm not of a roaming greedy sort like Paul Dogget and Ringdale, and a lot more on 'em. I shall be content with a competency, and when I've scraped enough together to make wife and children comfortable, if it please God to give us any, I mean to give up business and buy a bit of land. I was brought up to farming, and I always liked it better than manufacturing. Fifty acres of my own land, twenty or thirty cows, and a home or two - that's the height of my ambition. Do you think it's too much?"

"On the contrary; I think it's as little as a man of your energy and aptitude can aspire to - too little, almost. If this spirit continues to animate you, I predict for you a contented and useful life. Of happiness I say nothing. It is the lot of few if any of us here below; and when I see Mistress Cooper I shall tell her that her fears are groundless, and that both from a worldly and a religious point of view she may safely entrust the happiness of her niece to your keeping. She, and I am sure Rachel too, would like you to join the church. That is a matter about which I cannot press you. Paul may plant and Apollos water, but it is God that giveth the increase. In His own good time - if it be His will - He will bring you to a saving knowledge of the truth; and when that time comes I shall esteem myself highly blessed if it be my privilege to seal you with the sign of His elect, and baptise you in His name."

And then the minister, refusing a pressing invitation to stay longer, on the ground of the lateness of the hour, bade Adam good-night and bent his steps towards Orrington.

CHAPTER XXI.

WALLOPER HILLOCK

Adam and Rachel did not make a long courtship of it. There was no reason why they should. Though young, she was not "o'er young to marry," and he had long since arrived at years of discretion. They were married, not, as they would have liked, by Mr. Hartwell, but by the rector of Orrington; for the law in those days offered candidates for matrimony only Hobson's choice - they had either to do their marrying at church or not at all. Quakers preferred the latter alternative. For many generations their marriages, conducted after their own fashion, were regarded as illegal - a terrible hardship; yet even this they freely accepted rather than take part in a ceremony which they looked upon as superstitious, and believed to be contrary to the Word of God.

The newly-wedded pair spent the first three days of their honeymoon at Blackpool - then little more than a village, with a few modest hotels and lodging-houses for summer visitors - the remainder at their house, Adam being unable to spare more time from his business.

During their short stay at the seaside Rachel, upon whose gentle nature Adam's fight with Bill Nudger had made a very painful impression, exacted from her husband a promise that he would never strike a man again, save strictly in self-defence. While admiring his courage, and deeply grateful for the protection he had afforded her, she could not help thinking that, if he had begun by remonstrating with the young blacksmith, instead of kicking him, the latter would have apologised and moved quietly away. In this opinion she was probably mistaken, as Adam tried to prove to her; nevertheless, he gave the promise, and, as we have seen in the case of Little Fourteen, he kept it, though probably not exactly in the way contemplated by Rachel. There are probably few men who would not prefer to be given a blow to being dropped into a brook or thrown into a reservoir.

The home to which Adam took his bride was a five-roomed farmhouse, on the brow of an eminence known as Walloper Hillock, some half mile from Moorside. The dwelling faced the road. Behind it were a warehouse, winding and warping rooms, and farm-buildings.

The motive power of Adam's machinery were a daft lad - whose mental weakness nature had in some measure compensated by the gift of abnormal physical strength - and a youth who, having had the misfortune to be born with eyes so immovably fixed in their sockets that he could only see straight before him, was glad to earn a living by turning a handle.

Peggy Hothersall, much to her contentment, was retained on the Blackthorne establishment, Rachel greatly preferring the old woman to a brand-new servant from Redburn; a resolution which her husband warmly applauded, for he rather liked Peggy, and her aunt declared to be proof of her niece's good sense.

"A known ill is better than an unknown ill," said Mrs. Cooper, who looked upon all servants as necessary evils, "and if Peggy is a bit slow and slovenly, it's better than being young and flighty. And there's another thing sure, Rachel, you won't be bothered with no chaps (followers), and that's a deal to be thankful for; and whenever you can spare her for half a day's winding - and you often may, if you manage - it'll be so much gained. With seven pounds a year, as you're giving her, she'll never expect to be paid for her sets, I'm sure."

But Rachel did better than send Peggy into the winding-room. She proposed to her husband to go thither herself whenever she could spare the time, and see that the girls attended to their work, and - a most important point - did not make too much waste. This proposal quite delighted Adam, and he greatly pleased Rachel by telling her one day that he believed the oversight she exercised over his workpeople was equal to a saving of at least one-half their household expenses. In return for so much devotion,

Adam could do no less than go with his wife to chapel on Sundays, although it was rather a long walk. When it rained - and it often did rain in the region of Moorside - they generally borrowed a shandry from old Dorothy Pinchnoggin, the landlady of The Brown Cow; and their attendance at the Tabernacle was so regular that Mistress Cooper soon ceased to have any serious misgivings on the score of Adam's too great worldliness. She regarded chapel-going as the proper and sufficient antidote to carnal-mindedness. Provided you went to service twice on Sundays, you might tie to business as hard as you liked on week days. The only thing wanted to complete her satisfaction was that Adam should join the church; and even this she hoped that time and Rachel's influence, backed up by Mr. Hartwell's preaching might accomplish.

As for Adam himself, he was heard to say in after years that his Walloper Hillock days were the happiest of his life. He had few cares and great prosperity, and his wife and he pulled well together. He would often rise in a morning before four o'clock, walk over to Mole Hill Printworks, sell a thousand pieces of cloth, go round by Marley Mill, purchase the yarn wherewith to make them, and on his return home sit down to his porridge with an appetite begotten of a ten-mile walk, and the pleasant consciousness that he had made a hundred pounds before breakfast. He was wont on these occasions to say that he had "addled"(earned) his porridge.

When, from accumulations of profit, he came to have more capital in his business than he could use with advantage, he bought the house and farm of Walloper Hillock. He was as proud of this estate of fifteen acres as if it had been a great domain, and began to look forward to the time when he should be able to retire from business, albeit he no longer limited his aspirations to a farm of fifty acres. Nothing short of a hundred would content him now; and even then he was not sure that he should like to retire absolutely, though he might take things a little easier, and make a hobby of farming. Perhaps he might have a son, who could step into his shoes. As yet there had been only a little girl, who, to Rachel's great grief and his own, died before she was a year old; but a boy, or even a series of boys, was quite on the cards.

One day Adam came home with great news.

"What do you think, Rachel," he said, "Redgreave has broken, and the Old Factory will have to be sold. I always thought he would. He was fonder of hunting and shooting than minding his business; and then he had no luck. He was always making bad debts. He'd trust chaps with hundreds of pounds as I wouldn't touch with a pikefork."

"It will be bad for his wife and family, and she such a proud woman, too," said Rachel, who was always more concerned about the domestic consequences of commercial disasters, than their business bearings.

"Not so bad. She has a settled fortune, they say - two or three hundred a year. They will not starve with that; and she must put her pride in her pocket for once in a while."

"Poor woman, it will be very hard for her, though - "

"I say, Rachel," interrupted Adam, who was too full of his own plans to give much thought to Mrs. Redgreave and her misfortunes, "what do you suppose I'm thinking about?"

"I cannot tell, Adam. What are you?"

"I'm thinking of buying the Old Factory. That is, if it can be got a bargain."

If Adam had suggested the possibility of his buying Pendle Hill, or Whalley Abbey, his wife could not have appeared more surprised.

"Whatever are you saying?" she exclaimed. "Why, I've heard you tell that it was worth twenty thousand pounds, and where are we to get twenty thousand pounds from?"

"I said it had cost twenty thousand pounds; but there's a slight difference between the cost of a thing and its selling value. And there are peculiar circumstances about the Old Factory. It is not Redgreave's own, though it is in his name, and the real owner - that is, the mortgagee - took possession yesterday. They say the machinery's mortgaged to him, too, and he'll sell it as soon as he can find a customer at a price as will cover his claim. I should not wonder if all the property, and there's a lot of land and cottages beside the factory, might be bought for a matter of ten thousand pounds, or maybe a trifle less."

"But we have not got ten thousand pounds."

"Not quite happen, but not far short. I am worth more than ten thousand, reckoning everything; but I could not mortgage Walloper Hillock and th' Old Factory to their full value; and if I could it would leave me short of working capital, and for outlay on the new machinery as would be wanted. I mustn't stretch my arm further than th' coat-sleeve will reach. If I could see my way to about three thousand pounds, besides what I could easy enough raise on mortgage, I could manage."

"But don't you think we are very well as we are, Adam? Why should we go away from here, where we have been so happy and God has prospered us so wonderfully? We may do worse, and can hardly hope to do better."

"If we could always be sure of doing as well as we are doing now, it would happen the best to stop here. But are we? There's no standing still in business - we must either go backward or forward. These new steam looms seem to be succeeding; and if they do, handloom weaving is done for. How can hands compete with power? I'm not a having man, but I would like to keep what we've got. And this is such a chance. We could do our own spinning - no yarn to buy - and I would fill the bottom room with looms, and give up hand looms altogether, except, maybe, for a few fancies. It's a chance I wouldn't like to miss, though I'm bound to say as I don't quite see my way, yet. Three thousand pounds! three thousand pounds! It isn't much when a chap has it, but it's a deuce of a lot when he is that much short. I'll see Lawyer Bruff to-morrow, but I know what he'll say - he'll say as his clients object to advance more than two-thirds or three-fourths of the value of the property offered as security. However, I can only ask him."

"It will he a great undertaking," sighed Rachel, who, little as she liked the idea of leaving Walloper Hillock, did not urge any further objection to the scheme, for she had great confidence in the business judgment of her husband, and saw the justice of his reasoning. "Will you tell aunt about it, do you think? She's coming up to night, you know."

"Yes, I think so. Why not? She's a shrewd woman and might help us with an idea or two."

When Mrs. Cooper came she heard all about Adam's scheme over a cup of tea (with a drop of rum in it), first from Rachel and then from Adam himself. It interested the old lady greatly; she expressed a hope that he might be able to raise the purchase-money, and strongly recommended him to carry out his idea of seeing Lawyer Bruff. "He has always money passing through his hands," she said, "and who knows that he may not be able to accommodate you."

"Able, I dare say," rejoined Adam, "but will he be willing? That's the main point, I expect, aunt."

"Well, you can't get to know without asking, can you? Go and see him - that is my advice."

CHAPTER XXII.

A FRIEND IN NEED.

Adam acted on Mrs. Cooper's advice - went early next morning to Redburn, and laid his case before Lawyer Bruff. But he did not get much encouragement from that shrewd old gentleman.

"I can procure you on mortgage two-thirds of the value of the property," he observed. "Perhaps as a special favour to me personally I might get it made three-fourths, but I don't think I have a client who is bold enough to go further. Trustees and ladies - and trustees and ladies are our principal clients - are very timid, you know. The money would be as safe in your hands as in a bank, of that I am sure. If I had as much of my own at command you should have it at once; unfortunately I have not, and I cannot impart my confidence to others."

Adam knew what this meant - it meant that there was no chance of help from Lawyer Bruff - for with an advance of only three-fourths he would be unable to carry out his purpose, and he returned home greatly discouraged. He told Rachel that he saw nothing for it but to give the idea up. With time, perhaps, he might succeed in raising the money. Unfortunately, however, there was no time to spare. The matter was urgent; and unless he could act promptly somebody might forestall him, and the chance be lost - and he now looked upon it as good as lost.

But just as he had arrived at this conviction he received a letter from Bruff; saying that if he would call at his office the first time he happened to be at Redburn he thought that the business Adam had proposed to him the other day might perhaps be arranged.

Adam "happened" to be at Redburn the very same day, and went straight to the lawyer's office.

"You have not been long in coming," said Bruff; who, though generally spoken of as the "old lawyer," probably because he had been practising in the town for thirty years or more, was still considerably under sixty. "I suppose the matter is pressing?"

"Of course it's pressing. If I don't make a bid for the property soon somebody else will. How much can you let me have?"

"All you want, I think. On Walloper Hillock fifteen hundred; on the Old Factory seven five - say nine thousand in all - as first mortgages, and then on the equity of the two together from another lender - let me see (referring to a memorandum), three thousand eight hundred - that's nearly thirteen thousand. Will that suit you?"

"To a T. I shall be able to pay ten thousand for the factory - more I shall not give, and I shall try bard to get it for less - and the balance, together with what I have in my present business, will make me easy for working capital, besides allowing me to spend a good round sum in new machinery and repairs; for I make no doubt Redgreave has let the place get into bad order. But who is the bold lender that's going to advance on the equity? I thought your clients were all so timid?"

"There are always exceptions," said the lawyer; with a smile. "It is somebody you happen to know."

"Somebody I know? Nonsense. I know many people who are able to lend on a second mortgage and many who are willing - only the deuce of it is that the able are not willing, and the willing are not able."

"Nevertheless you do know her, Mr. Blackthorne, and well. Her name, for it's a lady, is Nanny Cooper."

"What - my wife's aunt?"

"Yes, your wife's aunt."

"God bless me! and do you mean to say that she's worth all that money?"

"Clearly, or she would not have it to lend."

"And then there's her stock, and her farm, and her land. Why, aunt Nanny must be rich."

"Richer than many folks give her credit for, I suspect," said Bruff dryly.

"But why has the offer come through you? She was up at our house the other night and did not say a word, though she knew 1 was after buying the Old Factory."

"Because she was not quite sure that she could find the money at such short notice, and had to see me first; and perhaps because she wanted to give you a little surprise. But I managed it for her. You see, one of her mortgages *(one* of her mortgages, thought Adam; why, the old body must be as rich as a Jew) falls to be repaid at the end of December; but you cannot wait till then, so I just spoke to my banker, and he'll advance the amount - this three thousand eight hundred - on my undertaking to cover the amount when the mortgage money comes in, and that's at your disposal whenever you want it - of course against your agreement to execute the necessary instruments. Oh (referring to his memorandum), there is one other matter I have to mention. Mrs. Cooper thinks that the fact of this being a second mortgage, and the security, therefore, inferior to a first charge, ought to be taken into consideration in fixing the interest. She is getting five per cent now - could you afford to pay five and a half?"

"Certainly. You may be sure I would not take the money at all unless I could make more out of it than that. But I say, the old lady's just a little keen, isn't she?"

Rather," said Bruff with a grin. "She knows what she's about, Mrs. Cooper does. She insisted on everything being put on a business footing, just as if you were entire strangers. Do you know why she is giving you this lift?"

"To help her niece's husband, I suppose."

"That is one of her motives, I dare say. But it is mainly because you did not ask her. If you had, I don't think you would have got a penny. She has a great objection to being thought rich, and the very suggestion that she had money would have been quite sufficient to prevent her lending you any; and the less you say to her on the subject, the better for your own interest."

"Must I not thank her, then?"

"You should say a good deal in a few words if you do. She is more shy and close about her investments than you have any idea of."

"Well, I think I shall let my wife manage that part of the business. And now I must look Happy Jack up."

"Ah, has Jack got the selling of the property, then? What a foxy old fellow he is. You'll have to keep your weather eye open, Blackthorne."

"I mean to do. If we arrange anything I'll let you know."

"Good, I hold myself at your disposal."

Happy Jack, or Mr. John Brazendale, as he wrote himself on his address cards, was the principal land agent and surveyor in Redburn, and had the reputation of being a very successful, albeit a not very scrupulous man of business. He was of immense girth and tall in stature; and his great fat face was so often wreathed in smiles, and he wore altogether so contented an air, that the name of Happy Jack had been bestowed on him by common consent. He was always wanting to do people good turns - said good turns consisting in selling them lands and houses at as high a price as he could persuade them to give. A Redburner whom he had over-reached in a bargain once said of him - and the saying met with general acceptance - that you might always tell at any given moment what Jack was doing - he was either laughing or lying.

This was the man with whom Adam Blackthorne had to treat for the purchase of the Old Factory. He found him in his little den of an office surrounded by plans and papers, and though he declared he was "most terrible throng," he looked as jovial as if he were out for a holiday, and his reception of Adam was as warm as the welcome of a prodigal son.

"What can I do for you, friend Blackthorne?" he asked, after a cordial hand-shaking, and various inquiries touching the wellbeing of his visitor, his family, and his business. "Ah, the Old Factory. I thought so. You are just the man for it, and it's just the thing for you. A more promising property never came into my hands for sale, and man and boy I have been in the land surveying and agenting business a matter of forty years. Why, in the hands of a man like you - of your energy and ability and with your credit - it would double its value in ten years. You shake your head, but I know it would, and in ten years more you would be one of the richest men in the country-side. Why, this cotton spinning is just coining - absolutely coining. I am too old to learn a new trade, or I declare solemnly I'd buy the place myself."

"Come, now, Mr. Brazendale, I'm not going to be taken in wi' talk like that," said Adam bluntly. "Hasn't th' Old Factory just ruined Redgreave?"

"No, he has ruined himself. However good a trade may be, it wants looking after, and Redgreave left the Old Factory to look after itself; but with you - "

"Oh, never mind me. What is the figure - that is all I want to know."

"Well (sinking his voice), I can do you a good turn. As you are a personal friend and old acquaintance (Adam had not spoken to him three times before in all his life), you shall have the property at the lowest price I am empowered to take. You shall have the entire concern - factory, forty acres of land, water privileges, machinery, cottage houses, mansion house, and all the appurtenances thereto belonging - for fifteen thousand pounds - and by the Lord Harry, it's just giving it you. Shall we say done?"

"I should be done if I did. Nay, I think I'll be going home. I don't know as I have aught more to say."

And he took up his hat as if with the intention of leaving forthwith.

"Sit you down a bit, man. What are you in such a hurry for? I thought you were going to make me an offer."

"What's the use when you ask such a fool of a price as that. Besides you say as fifteen thousand is the lowest as you can take."

"Did I? Well, I meant approximately, of course. Of course I have a little discretion. Come now, what will you give?"

"I don't think I am prepared to give anything, Mr. Brazendale. I only just wanted to know what you were asking. But if I did consider to make an offer, it's not fifteen thousand as I would bid, nor yet ten."

"If that be the case, I think you had better go home. Why the machinery, they tell me, cost nearly ten."

"Ay, when it was new; you must reckon it at th' price of old iron now."

"Well, will you give ten?"

"I cannot make an offer, I tell you. But if you ask me what I think it's really worth, I should say seven or eight at th' outside."

"If that's your idea it's no use talking. I shall be like to let Turner have it; he was here yesterday, and very keen, but I wouldn't open my mouth till I had seen you."

"Ay, let him have it. Do him a good turn," laughed Adam, "instead of me."

Happy Jack joined in the laugh and extended his hand to Adam.

"Well, if we cannot bargain we can, at any rate, be good friends. If you change your mind, you know where to find me, and if you want to make a rapid fortune, just let me advise you not to miss this chance."

There was nothing more to be said. Adam took up his hat again, and this time put it on and went home.

As he was "looking pieces" in his warehouse the following afternoon, his wife sent him word that a gentleman from Redburn wanted to speak to him.

"I thought he would come," muttered Adam to himself.

He was not mistaken. His visitor was Happy Jack.

"I saw the mortgagee and Redgreave's assignee," observed Brazendale, after he had exchanged greetings with Adam, and inquired as solicitously after his health as if he had not seen him twenty hours before; "and I've done my very best for you. They won't hear of your bid of eight thousand; but I might happen get 'em to take ten if you'd authorise me to offer that much."

"You are mistaken, Mr. Brazendale. I did not offer you eight thousand, nor any other sum. What I said was, as I did not consider the property to be worth more than seven or eight."

"It's the same thing, Blackthorne. I know what that meant; a nod is as good as a wink to a blind horse, you know. It meant as you'd be deuced glad to get the Old Factory for eight thousand. You know as well as I do as it would be dirt cheap at ten."

"That may be," said Adam. "But whether it is or not I will not give ten."

"Will you split the difference, then, and say nine; or must I go back to Redburn? I can have plenty of customers at that price; but I've a great respect for you, and want to give you the first chance."

Adam did not much believe either in the customers or the respect; but as he knew that the Old Factory was really a great bargain at nine thousand, he began by offering eight thousand six hundred, and after a long wrangle - in the course of which Happy Jack once or twice forgot to smile - the property became Adam's for eight thousand seven hundred and fifty pounds.

"It's just giving it away," declared the surveyor, after he had closed the transaction with an emphatic "Done with you, then - absolutely making you a present of a fine property, by Jingo. You'll drive over with me to Redburn, I suppose, to sign the contract and put things into ship-shape?"

"I'm ready," answered Adam, "and the brass is ready too."

"Gad, if I'd known that, I'd have been a bit harder. You should not have got the better of me as you have done."

"It would have made no difference if you had, Mr. Brazendale. It's not my way to bid for a thing I'm not able to pay for. You may be sure of that. Have a glass of home-brewed afore we start?"

"With all my heart; for, by Jingo, I'm as dry as a kippered herring. Bargaining's thirsty work, and hard work, too."

Adam had no opportunity until he returned from Redburn of informing his wife that the die was cast, and that in a few weeks they would have to leave their cottage at Walloper Hillock for the grand house at Moorwell, though the grandeur was rather a figment of her admiration; for, albeit dignified by the rustics of the neighbourhood as th' 0 (the hall), in point of size and accommodation it was little more than a large cottage.

Rachel's misgivings as to the change in their fortunes were greatly diminished when she heard of the part her aunt had taken in bringing it about. She was pleased to think that a connection of hers had given such important help to her husband in his new venture. On the other hand, she was hardly able to reconcile her aunt's economies with the protests against worldliness in which the old lady so frequently indulged; and when she thanked her in her husband's name and her own for the help so kindly rendered, she thought she perceived in her aunt's manner a consciousness of her inconsistency."

"Don't say anything about it, Rachel," was all the answer she made. "It's just a bit of money I have saved up little by little, and I thought if it could be useful to Adam he might as well have the use of it as anybody else, though all the security as he can offer is a second mortgage. However, he is welcome, Rachel; he is welcome. I hope it'll be for the glory of God; but don't say anything more about it - neither to me nor nobody else."

CHAPTER XXIII.

THE BLACKTHORNES COME INTO A FORTUNE.

The Old Factory was so named rather from its relative age than its actual antiquity. At the time when Adam Blackthorne became its owner it might almost have been termed a "modern mill." It was called "old" because it was less new than one or two other spinning mills in the same neighbourhood; and, perhaps, because there was something ancient in its appearance and associations. It lay in a valley, and was built on the site of an old corn mill, which had bequeathed to its cotton-spinning successor extensive and valuable water rights. A brook, fed by springs on the moors, flowed through the valley, and a broad sluice conducted a part of its water into a dam above the works for the service of the great water-wheel which, together with a small steam engine, made by Boulton and Watt, furnished the mill with motive power. The part of the factory (which, though only four storeys high and fourteen windows long, was considered a "big concern") not overgrown with ivy was white-washed every spring, and with the gardens on the sunny side, planted by Mr. Redgreave, who had a fancy for that sort of thing, formed a picturesque feature in the landscape, except late in the year, when the whitewash had become smoke-stained and rain-furrowed.

The factory yard was divided from the grounds of Moorwell House (which were out of all proportion to the size of the dwelling) by a high wall covered with fruit trees. Between this wall and a wide grass plot, bordered by a plantation and separated from the road by another high wall, ran the avenue. Before and about the house was a considerable extent of garden, stretching as far as the great dam - or reservoir, as it was becoming the fashion to call it - from which it was hidden by a broad belt of trees. Behind the house were stables, a coach-house, and farm buildings; for the forty acres of land which formed the Moorwell estate were always farmed by the owner.

The house was built of sandstone, gray with age and lichen-covered. It had a turreted porch furnished with oaken settles. A nail-studded door gave access to a miniature hall, on either side of which was a small parlour, known respectively as the sitting-room and drawing-room. Farther on, the hall opened into the front kitchen, and above stairs were five or six not very large bedchambers. The window-panes were lozenge shaped - those in front being set in heavy mullioned frames - and the porch and one side of the house, and a part of the roof, were thickly covered with ivy.

In the back yard was the well from which the place derived its name; for the country thereabouts had once formed part of a wide spreading moor, a fact that explains the frequent occurrence of the word in the local nomenclature.

Here the Blackthornes dwelt many years. The sixth of these years was marked by three of the most important events in their lives - the death of Nanny Cooper, the meeting with Hermann Basel, and the birth of their daughter Mabel.

To the surprise of everybody except Adam Blackthorne, and possibly his wife, the fortune Nanny left behind her amounted to more than twenty thousand pounds, not reckoning the advance she had made to Adam on the equity of the Old Factory. All save one thousand pounds was bequeathed without restriction to her niece - in effect, therefore, to her niece's husband. The thousand was to go towards the building of a Baptist chapel at Moorside, for which she expressed, in her will, a hope that Adam Blackthorne would give the site.

"I knew," said Adam, talking the matter over with Lawyer Bruff, "ever since she lent me that thirty-eight hundred, I knew the old body was worth money, but I really cannot understand how she contrived to save such a lump. Can you?"

"I think I can," answered the other. "She spent next to nothing on her living, and whenever she had a hundred pounds to spare she put it out on mortgage; then she put the interest arising therefrom out on mortgage too; for she did not want it for her living. Now, if you reflect that it is pretty nearly forty years since her husband died, and that during all that time she has been steadily investing her profits as they accrued, and reinvesting her interest as fast as she received it, you may understand how she contrived to leave, for a woman in her position, such a fine fortune. Cast up, for instance, how much a hundred, or two hundred, pounds laid by every year, with compound interest added, would come to at the end of; say, five-and-thirty years. It would roll up like -"

"A snowball," put in Adam. "Why, the first hundred would grow to five or six in that time. I feel a bit sorry though, Mr. Bruff, though we are getting the benefit of her money, as Aunt Nanny did not get a bit more pleasure out of her brass."

"She had all the pleasure it was possible for her to have, Mr. Blackthorne," said the man of law, who could see as much farther than his nose as most men; "she had the satisfaction of accumulating it - a greater satisfaction, you may be sure, than any amount of spending could have afforded her. She had more pleasure in watching the growth of her store year by year, and in feeling that she was a woman of substance, though she did keep the fact so entirely to herself; than she would have had in spending ten thousand a year. Some have one object in making, earning, or spending money, some another; but all have the same motive - their own gratification. You are a money-making man, Mr. Blackthorne. What is your object?"

At this home-question Adam reddened a little, and looked conscious; for he had an object - something very different from the one he had described to Mr. Hartwell a few years before - though he was yet so far from its achievement that he shrank from avowing it even to his lawyer.

"I have no particular object," he replied, "except to make a provision for my children and find work for myself. A man must have something to do, you know."

Then the lawyer hinted that as Nanny Cooper had left her fortune to Mrs. Blackthorne, it might be as well to settle at least a part of it on her and her children.

To this Adam demurred.

"Nay," he said; "I think I can take care of it as well as anybody else, and use it to better advantage, too."

"Business has its vicissitudes, you know, Mr. Blackthorne, and it is well to have a reserve in case of any thing unpleasant happening."

"Oh, I see; you think I shall happen be breaking one of these days. Make yourself easy. I shall do nothing of the sort."

"I hope not, I am sure, Blackthorne. But you know there is nothing certain in this world but death and taxes. I considered it my duty to make the suggestion, and having made it I have done. What do you propose to do with the money, then?"

Leave it where it is for the present; maybe build another factory with it eventually. I know of no better investment."

CHAPTER XXIV.

A NEW ACQUAINTANCE AND A FRESH ENTERPRISE

On a Sunday afternoon, a few weeks after his conversation with Lawyer Bruff, Adam was walking round the milldam to study the effect of a recent enlargement, which had converted it into a small lakelet, when he spied an individual he had never seen before, in the act of filching his water by putting a quantity of it into a large bottle. The singularity of the proceeding roused his curiosity, and he drew near to the man, who, as he perceived, was well dressed, and of gentlemanly appearance.

I am robbing you of your water," said the stranger, with a slightly foreign accent, at the same time raising his hat; "for I presume you are Mr. Blackthorne, and this I ought not to have done without your leave."

"Nay, nay," answered Adam, returning the salute, although, as he had never attempted a similar courtesy before, he did it rather awkwardly. "You are welcome to as much as you like; there is plenty more where it comes from.

But I did not know as our Moorwell water was worth carrying away in a bottle."

"I am taking it to analyse," said the stranger smiling, "not to drink. I am a chemist, and I want to find out its qualities. Unless I am very greatly mistaken it is an excellent water for certain purposes. Very soft, is it not?"

"Ay, you can wash yourself with it almost without soap."

"So I heard. And you have a good supply of it, I suppose?"

"Any quantity, and all the year round, too. The brook's never dry, and it's always clean like that."

"A valuable stream."

"They say so; but I don't get much value out of it, except for running the water-wheel; and with coal at four and sixpence a ton, laid down, a water-wheel does not save much."

"Would you like to turn your water to better account?"

"Of course I would, if I only knew how."

"I can tell you."

"Can you?" said Adam, who was becoming greatly interested in the conversation. "I wish you would tell me then."

"Start turkey-red dyeing."

"A good thing, I dare say; only, unfortunately, I can no more dye turkey-red than I can fly."

"But I can."

"And you -"

"Ach, Gott! I was forgetting you did not know me. My name is Hermann Basel. I am a native of Zurich, in Switzerland, where I received my early education and learned something of chemistry. I served an apprenticeship to the trades of dyeing and calico printing at Mulhausen, in Alsace. Then I came to England, and for several years I was a chemist and colour mixer at Buttercup Printworks. At present I am a partner in the firm of Furguson, Scholes, and Basel, manufacturing chemists at Orrington, of whom you may possibly have heard. But I want to go into dyeing, and turkey-red dyeing is the most money-making business I know of."

"Why don't you go into it then?" asked Adam bluntly.

"For several reasons. I have not money enough to put up the necessary buildings, buy machinery, and conduct such a business to advantage, and I do not know of any suitable site that is available, unless this be available. This is exactly the place. You have an abundant supply of water of the right sort, cheap coal, and plenty of room for extension. You are not too far from Manchester, and you have a canal hard by which places you in direct water communication with Liverpool. Yes, it is exactly the place I would like."

"How much capital would you want for a start, do you think?"

"Fifteen to twenty thousand pounds; and towards that I could find five thousand."

"Well, I have just come into a little money," said Adam hesitatingly, "and if I could see my way - I'll tell you what, Mr. Basel (here his tone became more decided), if you'll just put down a proposal on paper, what you can do and what I should have to do to carry your idea out; how the money would have to be used - so much for plant, so much for working capital - estimated cost of dyeing a thousand pieces, probable profit, and so forth - and give me a week to think it over, I'll see what I can do with you. I have heard before as this turkey-red dyeing is a good trade."

"There's no mistake about that. You shall have full particulars to-morrow."

"That's right. And if you'll come over next Sunday afternoon and have a cup of tea with us, I'll give you an answer."

"You are very friendly. The time will suit me very well. I see you are not so particular as some of your countrymen about not doing business on Sundays."

"Business? We shall do no business - we shall only talk, you know, and talking is allowable, or else what would folks do? But won't you come down to the house and have a glass of something?"

"You are very friendly. The day is warm, and I am thirsty. I will drink a glass of beer, if you have such a thing."

"That we have. I can give you as good a glass of home-brewed - none of your brewery rubbish for me - as you'll find in a day's journey. Come on, we'll wet little Mabel's head with some of it."

"What mean you?" asked Basel, who could not for the life of him imagine what his host was driving at.

"Why, my wife was brought to bed last night of a little lass as we are going to call Mabel, and I'd like us to drink her health. That's what we call wetting a child's head in these parts."

"Very gladly I will drink her health, and also that of the mother, who I hope is doing well?"

"Very well, could not be better."

"That is very pleasant. I also have a little girl who was only born a week ago."

"So much the better," said Adam, "we'll wet her head, too. How many does that make?"

"How many does that make, do you say? As my little girl has one head, and yours, I suppose, has the same number, that makes two heads to wet."

"I don't mean that," answered Adam, laughing heartily at Basel's answer; "I mean how many children have you besides this little girl?"

"Ah! I understand. We have now a boy and a girl. As my partner, Mr. Scholes, was good enough to observe, I have now as many sorts as anybody else."

"You are like us - we have a boy and a girl. And what do you call the little one? I ask with a view to wetting her head, you know. We cannot wet a child's head unless we know its name."

"Valérie we shall call her, after her mother, who is French. The boy, who is now with his grandparents in Alsace, is called Fritz."

"And my boy is called Frank. But here we are at the door. Shall we go inside, or shall we sit here in the porch?"

"With all my heart let us sit here in the porch. It is a very nice place to wet our children's heads in, I think. I hope it will make them happy."

"Happen it will, but children are always happy except when they are ailing."

"I did not mean happy merely as children, but lucky, prosperous, fortunate in their lives."

"Well, I am not altogether sure that wetting their heads will do 'em much good in that way; anyhow, wishing 'em well and drinking their health in a glass of good ale cannot hurt them. But if I go on talking in this way we shall get none. Sit you down here a minute or two, and I'll go and tell one o' th' lasses (servants) to bring a jugful out of the cellar and a couple of glasses."

It was a beautiful afternoon, and the scene on which Hermann Basel looked as he sat in the porch was very pleasant. The sweep before the door which terminated the avenue was bordered by a broad fringe of verdant turf; beds of brilliant flowers, interspersed with laurel trees and box-fenced walks, covered the space between the grass and the reservoir bank, where the shining water was only partially hidden by a row of weeping willows. To the left was a large apple orchard, and on the right the garden was bounded by the ivy-covered end of the Old Factory. On the opposite side of the reservoir was a belt of rich meadow land and green pastures; and the air was filled with the sweet scent of newly-mown hay. Farther on stretched a wide expanse of purple moorland, flecked with grey farmhouses and white cottages with thatched roofs. Southward stretch the broad and beautiful valleys of the Hodder and the Calder, with castle-crowned Clitheroe in the far distance; and the huge form of old Pendle basks in a flood of sunshine. No discordant noises mar the harmony of the hour and the scene; the only audible sounds are the buzzing of bees among the flowers, and the splash of water as it falls down the by-wash of the reservoir into Moorwell Brook.

"How very quiet you are here," observed Basel, as Adam returned, followed by a maiden bearing a tray, on which were arrayed a jug of foaming ale, glasses, pipes, and tobacco. "And what a beautiful garden you have."

"Well, I think we have. It's my wife's doing. I'm too busy to bother with flowers even if I'd a taste for gardening, which I have not. I like to see a nice garden as well as anybody, but I don't care about rooting and pottering among nast. But there is no accounting for likings, as the man said when he kissed his old cow. I contract with a jobbing gardener to keep the place in order for twenty pounds a year. My wife directs him, and works herself too, a good deal when she's able. That's how it's done."

"A cheap gardener, a good wife, a beautiful place, and a flourishing business - you are a much blessed man, Mr. Blackthorne."

"Yes, we have a good deal to be thankful for," replied Adam, as he handed the iron tobacco-box to Basel. "I'm not quite sure about the gardener though. He is not as cheap as he looks - a lazy beggar as wants a deal of looking after. As for business, I've known it better and I have known it worse. At the most you can only call it just middling - we are happen seeing our own back and a trifle besides. You are right about one thing, however - that I will say. I have a good wife. There is no mistake about that; and, what's more, though I married her a poor lass, and never expected a penny with her, she's brought me twenty thousand pounds. If it had not been for that I could not have talked to you about going into turkey-red dyeing."

"Well, if you have not quite all the blessings, Mr. Blackthorne, you are at least a much blessed man - you cannot deny that."

"No, I don't think we shall have much cause to complain if things keep as they are. But will not you fill your glass? We must not forget to wet the little lasses' heads, you know."

"Do you like this country better than your own, Mr Basel?" asked Adam, after the healths of Mabel and Val□rie had been duly drunk.

"For some things, perhaps. It is better for business, I think. But a true-born Switzer, you know, can never love any country as well as his own, and it is always my hope to end my days in the land of my birth"

"You came over here for business purposes, then?"

"It would, perhaps, be more correct to say I came to seek my fortune. I will tell you how it befell if you would like to hear; for the thought has come to me that the acquaintance we have made with each other today is the beginning of a long friendship."

"With all my heart. I like to hear a story, especially when it's about anybody making his fortune."

"I have not made my fortune yet," said Basel, with a smile. "I am trying to do, that's all."

"It is all the same. Trying is the most interesting part, I think. There is not much to tell in a general way after a chap has made his fortune. He is at the top of the tree then, and all that he has to do is to stick where he is."

"Well, my father was a soldier. When quite a young man he entered the Royal Swiss Guard of the French king. He was one of the few survivors of the massacre of August 2nd, 1792, when nearly all his comrades were killed in the Carrousel court of the Tuileries by a Paris mob. He owed his safety to the courage and devotion of a young girl who a few years afterwards became his wife and my mother, and after remaining some time in hiding he got away to Switzerland. At the beginning of the war of 1799 he entered the French service a second time, received the commission of captain, and fought at Marengo. From that time to the fall of the Empire he was almost incessantly fighting and campaigning. He fought at Austerlitz, Aspern, Wagram. He served in Spain, made the campaign of Moscow, commanded a regiment at the battle of Borodino, won his brigade and the Cross of the Legion for his conduct at the passage of the Beresina. After the battle of Dresden he was made general of division. His last fight was the Voelker-schlacht of Leipsic, where he was badly wounded. When he recovered he joined his family at Zurich. Very fortunately, as it happened, for he was a devoted admirer of the Emperor, he was not in fighting condition after the return from Elba, and so missed the battle of Waterloo and kept his pension, which, with a little paternal property he had, made us very comfortable. By us I mean my father and mother and their only children, my brother Fritz and myself. I was destined for the career of arms, Fritz for the law. But man proposes and God disposes. My poor mother died, and my father, who, though an old soldier, is simple-hearted to a fault, allowed himself to be beguiled into marrying a young widow less than half his age, whose only dowry was good looks and a healthy constitution. She produces a baby every year with the regularity of the seasons, and now at sixty-five he has ten small children. This event made a great change in my brother's prospects and mine. We had to take care of ourselves. I abandoned the idea of becoming a soldier, and glad I am that I did. I went to Mulhausen, studied chemistry, and learned the arts of dyeing and calico printing; Fritz went to the United States, and is doing well there as a merchant. As my father with his young and yearly-increasing family had hard work to make both ends meet, we made over to him a little fortune we had inherited from our mother. After I had finished my apprenticeship at Mulhausen I received the offer of a post as chemist in an English calico-printing establishment, which I retained for several years. Then I became manager of the chemical manufacturing concern at Orrington, in which I am now partner and I am here to-day seeking to carry out my long-cherished idea of becoming a turkey-red dyer, which, please God, with your help I hope I shall"

"We will see," said Adam. "I must look over your papers and think well about it before I decide. They are serious steps - taking a partner and going into a new business - almost as serious as getting wed."

A fortnight after this conversation the two men (Adam having meanwhile satisfied himself about Basel's capacity and trustworthiness, and taken the opinion of his brother, the colour mixer, as to the accuracy of the Switzer's estimates and calculations) signed a contract of copartnership. The main conditions of it were that Basel was to contribute five thousand pounds to the capital stock of the enterprise, Adam ten, and, if necessary, three or four thousands more. The profits were to be equally divided, and Basel was to have a liberal salary for his personal services. One stipulation which he made seemed to amuse Adam vastly. It was that the latter's share of the profits should never exceed ten thousand pounds in any one year. That is, if they exceeded twenty thousand the whole of the balance above that amount should fall exclusively to the share of Hermann Basel.

"You may make the limit five if you like, Basel," said Adam, with a slightly sarcastic smile, when this condition was first proposed - "ay, or three. If we make six thousand a year between us I shall be uncommonly well satisfied, and what more you can gain you are quite welcome to."

"That would not be fair to you, Mr. Blackthorne. You don't know what the profits of turkey-red dyeing are, or rather what they can be made with my process, and I do know, for I have been studying and experimenting for a long time. You may think my estimates exaggerated, but wait and see."

"Ay, we shall see," answered Adam with the same incredulous smile; "and when I see myself making ten thousand a year out of this business - or any other, for that matter - I'll believe it."

CHAPTER XXV.

RAISING THE DEVIL

Bigwater's boys had ample leisure, little work, and plenty of play. They were allowed two half holidays a week, occasionally three; and those of them who were not inveterately lazy or hopelessly ill-behaved had always the whole of Monday afternoon at their disposal, with full liberty to ramble whither they listed.

The speciality of the school was caligraphy.

If a lad wrote a good hand, especially if he were in the first class, over which Bigwater presided in person, he had not much trouble about his lessons, and at the worst they were few and easy. Cliffe, the one-eyed youth, who was introduced to the reader in a foregoing chapter, was in the habit of boasting that he had not learnt a lesson for two years. He sat directly opposite Bigwater in class, and, having acquired the art of reading upside down, he would say aloud from the master's book the task which his less fortunate companions had learnt, or were supposed to have learnt, by heart. This advantage, however, did not always avail him, and he sometimes came to desperate grief; but being one of the best writers in the school, much was forgiven him.

For boys who had not the gift of elegant penmanship the writing hour was a time of dire tribulation. The perfect penning of a line was supposed to occupy five minutes; every line had to be shown to the master, and passed by him as "good," until eight accepted lines had been produced. An unfortunate master cutting quills for bare life to supply the incessant demand for pens, and bombarded at the same time with copybooks, was a sight for gods and men. No wonder that the teachers sometimes waxed furious, howled like wild beasts, and danced like maniacs. There was one - Frank Blackthorne's special detestation - who frequently distinguished himself in this way. He was a little man, with high-heeled Wellington boots, big black whiskers, and a diminutive red face. In public his pupils always addressed him as "Mr. Richards;" in private, they universally spoke of him as "Old Blazes." He had the reputation of being the best writer in England. You could not distinguish the copies he set from copperplate, and he was able to flourish a swan, and inscribe the year of the Lord in the middle of its stomach, without once lifting his pen from the paper. And he seemed to expect everybody to write as well as himself. He would sometimes keep poor Frank (whose caligraphy, it must be admitted, was susceptible of improvement) writing away two or three hours at a stretch, until the poor boy's hands were almost as black as his copybook, and his very nose was smeared with ink.

Next to writing, Frank's time in school hours was chiefly devoted to novel reading. After he received the first half-sovereign from his mother, in the seal of a letter, he went shares with Ned Brackly, who was as fond of fiction as Gunter was of brandy snaps, in a three months' subscription to a circulating library in Woolpack Street, kept by an old maiden lady of the name of Hopps, whom Frank one day mortally offended by inadvertently calling Miss Malt. During these three months they read pretty nearly every novel the library contained. They always tossed up for the "first read," but in order to lose no time one would tackle the second volume while the other was at work on the first. In this way they made the acquaintance of "St. Clare of the Isle," "The Mysteries of the Forest," "The Romance of the Pyrenees," "The Recluse of the Lake," "Captain Kidd," "Nick of the Woods," "Jack Sheppard," and sundry other choice productions of a previous generation. Marryat's works were of course immense favourites, as were all books that abounded in incident and adventure. The final test of the quality of a romance was the quantity of fighting matter it contained; and one day, after a prolonged discussion among the most literary of the boys, it was carried *nem. con.* that the best books ever written were "The Last of the Mohicans," "The Scottish Chiefs," and "Thaddeus of Warsaw." Bulwer's "Leila" was also counted a masterpiece.

Frank had always a novel in his desk, and he generally managed to pass a good part of the time set aside for arithmetic and French in its perusal, besides spending a considerable portion of his leisure in the same way. But on Sundays this solace was denied him, Bigwater being as strict on that day as he was lax on others. The morning began with special prayers; immediately after breakfast there was writing of verses on a slate; then chapel. After dinner there was a learning of verses by heart, and, what was worse, repeating them. Then came afternoon service, and the evening often concluded with prayers and a sermon or lecture by Bigwater himself; making three in all, which was, perhaps, about as much as juvenile human nature could bear, and more than it could digest.

Between the afternoon bread and butter, or "bagging," and the bell for prayer; "the young gentlemen," as Miss Bigwater was wont to call them, were allowed to stretch their legs in the playground and garden; but on no account were they suffered to walk in the country - that would have been Sabbath-breaking. On rainy Sundays Bigwater provided them with suitable reading matter in the shape of sundry back numbers of the *Youth's Magazine* and *Baptist Reporter,* and perhaps a few copies of "The Dairyman's Daughter." As may easily be supposed, lads whose mental pabulum during the week had been books "with lots of fighting in them," romances, "Stories of Shipwrecks," and "Lives of Pirates and Sea Robbers," did not take very kindly to this species of literature, and many and various were the dodges resorted to in the intervals between prayers and sermons to while away the tedium of the day of rest.

One Sunday evening, when it was so wet that they could not go out, and so dull that they did not know what to do with themselves, a dozen or more of the fellows, among whom was Frank, were gathered near the fireplace (from habit probably, for there was no fire) at the upper end of the school-room, engaged in an animated conversation - the subject being our ghostly foe.

It had been suggested partly by a story founded on the legend of Faust that some of them had been reading during the previous week, and partly by the numerous references to his Satanic Majesty with which the sermon they had heard that afternoon had abounded. The preacher had depicted the spirit of evil as a real personage, with human attributes and unlimited power of mischief, who literally went about seeking whom he might entrap; and he warned his hearers to be constantly on their guard against his wiles. Nevertheless, although there was probably not a lad in the school who had the faintest doubt of the devil's objective existence, they somehow did not much fear him. In the stories they had read of his dealings with men and women he generally seemed to get the worst of it; and in the last production of the sort that had come under their notice he was represented as a very pleasant-spoken, well-informed gentleman, who could only be distinguished from other gentlemen by his somewhat sardonic smile, a slight deformity in one of his feet, and his readiness to treat for the purchase of your soul - cash down, and no hurry about delivery. Fortunately, however, his contracts were so loosely drawn that his victims, after receiving the consideration agreed upon, and having their fling at his expense for seven years, almost invariably contrived to evade the fulfilment of their part of the bargain. The general opinion among Bigwater's boys, notwithstanding the rather appalling sermon they had just listened to, was that the devil must be rather a poor sort of chap after all. The talk, albeit somewhat discursive, had special reference to raising him. One lad contended that the right thing was to go at midnight into a cellar and repeat a certain terrific invocation contained in the book they had been discussing. Another had heard that the proper way to go to work was to stick a fork in the roof of a cellar, place a big coal underneath it, and, when the fork fell down by its own weight and struck the coal, the devil would incontinently appear.

On this, a lad with a crooked nose and a double squint, by name Ollerhead, who came from a remote part of the West Riding, observed that he had "heard tell" of a better plan than that. You must draw a chalk ring on the floor of a room, in the centre of which had to be placed a Bible, opened at the last chapter of Proverbs. On the Bible a key was to be laid. Then the operator, kneeling on the floor, had to read the last chapter of Proverbs backwards, and by the time he got to the first verse the devil would walk quietly into the room - without thunderclaps, smell of brimstone, or any of the other unpleasant incidents which were generally supposed to herald his approach.

"By Jove," said Cliffe, "let's try it!"

"That's all very fine," put in Frank, "but where?"

Page 139

"Why, in the little room, to be sure. Old Big, and Blazes, and the rest of them, are at tea; they won't trouble us for half an hour or more."

"But who will do the reading and that?"

"I will," answered Cliffe, "I'm not afraid. I question very much if he'll come, for Ollerhead never tried the dodge himself - did you, Ollerhead?"

Ollerhead shook his head.

"And if he does he won't make a row, you know. Come along. Some fellow get a Bible. Who has got a bit of chalk?"

"I have," said Gunter.

"Chuck it here, then."

When it became known that Cliffe was going to raise the devil, all the boys crowded into the "little room," a small class-room, separated from the principal apartment by a short lobby and a heavy door.

With the aid of the bit of chalk and a string, a very pretty circle was made in the middle of the floor. Then the Bible, opened at the last chapter of Proverbs, was placed in the centre of the circle, and everything was ready for a start.

But at this point a difficulty arose. Were the verses to be read in the reverse order merely, or were the words themselves to be read backward? Ollerhead was appealed to, but Ollerhead failed to solve the problem. He had "heard tell" that the chapter should be read backwards - that was all he knew. After a rather noisy discussion, it was resolved that the verses should be read one after the other, beginning with the last; and if this did not answer, the experiment should be tried of reading the words themselves backwards.

So Cliffe went down on his knees, with his latter end towards the door, and set to work. He read very slowly, and when he was halfway through made a long pause, as if he were beginning to feel just a little uneasy touching the probable issue of his undertaking, and would gladly have abandoned it if he could have found a sufficient excuse.

"Go on, Cliffe, go on," shouted several voices. "You are not going to funk it, old fellow, are you?"

"It's all stuff; I don't think Old Nick will come," broke in Frank.

"If he does he'll take Cliffe, for being so wicked," piped little Carter.

"And you for being such a fool," exclaimed Cliffe, savagely. "Of course I'll finish it - who said I wouldn't?"

And he resumed his reading.

They were all so intent on watching him that nobody noticed that the door was slightly ajar, that a hidden hand was pushing it slowly open, and that a pair of big eyes were glancing furtively on the scene.

Cliffe had reached the first verse and the last.

"It's just as I said," interrupted Frank scornfully, "he'll not come, not he."

At these words, and just as Cliffe, with a sigh of relief completed his task, the door burst suddenly open, and before he could rise from his knees a shower of fierce cane strokes fell on his back, shoulders, and the region where his trousers were tightest.

The lad howled with anguish and terror. He thought he was being belaboured by the devil in person. Without looking behind him he bounded frantically to his feet, jumped upon the desk nearest to him, bolted through the open window, and incontinently disappeared.

"What does all this mean?" demanded Bigwater furiously, for it was the dominie, and not the devil, they had raised. "I know it is something atrocious, blasphemous, and wicked, and that you are breaking the Sabbath, or you would not look so guilty. But what is it?"

Nobody answered, and all seemed as scared as if the evil one had actually come at their call.

Then Bigwater turned hotly on Frank.

"I think I heard you say, Blackthorne, that you did not believe Old Nick would come. I presume your remark applied to me."

The schoolmaster, though well aware that he was often described as "Nix," did not altogether relish being so completely identified with his Satanic Majesty as to be called "Old Nick," especially on a Sunday.

Frank indignantly denied the imputation, for he rather liked old Big, who had always been kind to him.

"No, sir, I don't mean you," he said. "I never thought of such a thing."

"To whom then did the expression refer, may I ask?"

"To Old Nick himself sir, to Satan, that Mr. Jones was preaching about this afternoon."

Just then Bigwater caught sight of the Bible, the key, and the magic circle.

"Ah," he exclaimed with the air of a man who makes a discovery, "I see it all now. I understand your consternation and Cliffe's terror at my appearance. He was performing some incantation - trying to raise the devil, I suppose, and it was his expected apparition of which you were speaking, Blackthorne?"

Frank remained silent.

"It is so, then. Well, if you have not raised the devil you have raised me. I really never knew anything more wicked and absurd. I did not think you were capable of such folly -blasphemy, rather - for you have both desecrated the Bible and broken the Sabbath. I shall devise a punishment which shall reach you every one, of which you shall hear something to-morrow morning. Meanwhile, go into the school-room, and I will give you some verses to learn until it is time for prayers."

When Frank went home for his holidays his father one day, by way of testing his progress in arithmetic, set him to work in the counting-house. He first of all gave him some tremendous columns of figures to add up, which Frank, with great labour and after many failures, contrived in the end to do.

"You are very slow," said his father, "but it's happen want of practice; the knack of adding up does not come by nature. Here's something else. I have just been measuring up Sam Sawyer's week's work. You will find all the dimensions on this paper; just reckon up how many cubic feet he has done."

He might as well have told the lad to square the circle.

However, Frank set to work and did his best; but his best was a hopeless muddle, and when he showed the result of his reckoning to Adam, the latter seemed almost as much surprised as if his son had laid a rattlesnake before him.

"God bless me!" he exclaimed. "Why, if I were to pay Sam Sawyer at that rate he would have more than five hundred pounds to draw. It's all wrong, every bit of it. Don't you know how to do cross multiplication, Frank?"

Frank had to confess that he not only could not do cross multiplication but had not even the most remote idea what it was like.

At this moment Sam Sawyer entered the counting-house.

"What do you think,' Sam?" said Adam. "I've got a lad as has been three years at a day school and one at a boarding school, and he cannot do a bit of cross multiplication?"

"I durned see as there's so much use i' sending childer to school," replied Sam, a big brown-faced fellow in corduroy breeches, check shirt - the sleeves of which were rolled up nearly to his armpits - and with a red handkerchief bound round his head, "they are ofter waur for it than better. There's Ned o' my Granny's theere (this was Sam's way of designating his uncle), just look at him. He's a gradely good scholar, there's no denying that, and can do a sum i' cross multiplication and make a bill wi' onybody - but he couldn't set a saw, nor yet saw a straight board, not to save his life. What's consekence? He's a bottom sawyer, and he'll never be nowt else but a bottom sawyer. Now, if he'd ha' spent th' time as he spent at school i' learnin' his trade he'd ten to one ha' bin' a top sawyer at this minute. Look at me - I can naythur read nor write, and I've bin' a top sawyer will be ten year come next Michaelmas; and I'll saw a boke or set a saw wi' ony man, I durned care who he is."

"You are a good workman, Sam, I know, but you would be none the worse if you could do your own reckoning and make out your own bills."

"Happen not, but I'm nuon so easy chetted, though I'm not a scholar. I can tell within a trifle at th' end of a job how much I've addled. I can tell now, to-day, to a shilling or eighteenpence how much I've to draw. I do it i' my heyd."

"It's more than our Frank can, for all he's been learning arithmetic four years. You must turn over a new leaf, my lad, or you'll find yourself in a hobble one of these days."

This incident suggested to Adam's mind grave doubts as to the efficiency of Bigwater's method of instruction, which did not seem, indeed, much superior to Leatherlad's, and he took counsel on the subject with Basel, whom he regarded as a learned man. Basel advised sending Frank to another school.

"But where?" asked Adam; "they all seem bad, like."

"Send him to Dr. Berrs, at Redburn; he is a strict and capable man, and as he takes only a few pupils he can give them all his time. Fritz has been there a year, and he is doing very nicely."

Page 143

But he's a Church parson."

"What matters that? You don't want Frank to learn theology. And he can come home every week if you like. I cannot advise you anything better. It is clear that he will never learn anything at this school of Bigwater's that he would not learn at a common dame's school. It is not so good as a common village school in Switzerland. And when he has been with Dr. Berrs for a few years send him for a short time on the Continent. It will be good for him."

Adam acted on his partner's advice. Frank was sent to Dr. Berrs, who took care that he neither read romances nor raised the devil, and before he went into the mill to help his father he spent two years with Fritz Basel in a continental school.

CHAPTER XXVI.

ADAM BLACKTHORNE BECOMES AMBITIOUS.

At the time of Frank's departure for Yewdale, Adam Blackthorne, albeit he lived carefully and dwelt in a cottage, was a man of considerable substance. Ten years later he was a man of wealth, as wealth in those days was counted.

The turkey-red business exceeded his utmost hopes, and confirmed all his partner's calculations. By the operation of the clause in the contract of copartnership which had occasioned Adam so much amusement, Basel was now making by the dyeworks fifteen thousand a year, and himself ten; and the profits, the former assured him, had by no means reached their maximum. Indirectly, Adam was making even more. As he had a heavier capital in the business than his partner, his annual accruing interest was greater; and the bulk of the cloth he produced being used at the dyeworks, he avoided the expense of sending it to Manchester for sale, saving thereby sundry commissions and minimising his risk. For selling his goods to Hermann Basel and Co. was like selling them to himself.

Unbroken success had increased his self-will almost to arrogance, and it very rarely happened that anybody about him dared to oppose his wishes. On one important occasion, however, he had to give way. It was when he wanted to pull the Old Factory down to make room for a new building.

When Rachel heard of this project she was strangely excited.

"Pull the Old Factory down!" she exclaimed; "never with my consent, Adam, nor I hope, while I live. And I've a right to speak, for it was my Aunt Nanny's money helped you to buy it. Has not the Old Factory made us what we are? Why, the place would not be Moorwell without it. If you pull it down, Adam, I do believe we shall never prosper again."

Adam was moved by this appeal, the more readily as there was a responsive vein of superstition in his own character. He concluded that, everything considered, it was perhaps as well to let the Old Factory alone, and he found another site for his new building.

There were many new buildings at Moorwell now. The Old Factory was quite dwarfed by a huge spinning mill; a great loom-shed covered the field next the reservoir, and the dyeworks, which were ranged alongside the brook for convenience of water and drainage, seemed to grow bigger every year.

These changes were far from approving themselves to Rachel - her ambition being limited to a modest provision for her children, and a quiet, useful life for herself and her husband - and they had so entirely altered the aspect of the place, that when Adam came home one day, and told her that he had bought the Brandwood Hall estate for a hundred thousand pounds, and they would have to flit, she was surprised indeed, yet less grieved than might have been expected. It is true she shed a few tears, but she neither tried to turn him from his purpose, nor made any demur to the flitting. She reflected that Adam was now an important man, and much looked up to in the neighbourhood. He had lately been made a county magistrate, too, and it was clear that Moorwell was no longer a fit residence for a person in his position. She had, moreover, the comfort of knowing that they were not going to quit the old place altogether. The furniture was to remain where it was, in charge of a housekeeper, for Adam and Frank would take at least one meal a day in the house - perhaps occasionally sleep there - Brandwood Hall being nearly five miles off; and Adam having no present intention of retiring from business.

He had got the estate a bargain, as ho got most things a bargain. The former owner, Hugh Brandwood, the last scion of an ancient race, and the last heir-in-tail, was a gambler and a spendthrift. After raising as much money on the estate as he could, he had tried, through our old friend, Lawyer Bruff, to borrow a further sum on the equity. Bruff mentioned the circumstance to Adam, who had often money to invest.

"No," said the latter, "I don't like lending on equities; but I will tell you what I will do. If young Brandwood likes, I'll buy the estate out and out."

As young Brandwood wanted money just then very badly, and Adam, on the strength of Bruff's assurance that the title was all right - he had investigated it on behalf of the first mortgagee - was willing to accommodate him at once, he accepted, though ruefully, the offer, and Adam, who forthwith gave notice to pay off the mortgage, became owner of Brandwood Hall, lord of the manor of Claylands, and patron of the fat living of Clayland-Conyers.

The Brandwood estate was not alone an ancient domain, but rich in mines, minerals, and timber, and a part of it consisted of valuable potential building land. Adam's intention was to develop its resources to the utmost; and he calculated that by judicious outlay and good management, his purchase, even in his own lifetime, might be doubled in value.

Brandwood Hall, if not a baronial mansion, was at least a very large house. It did not belong to any particular style of architecture, and when new, and the place was young, its appearance could hardly have been very attractive; for it was square, slabsided, and unadorned with either porch, turret, or verandah. But time had mellowed the once raw stone to a soft gray, and covered its slab sides with ivy; and the uniformity of its profile was broken by quaint gargoyles and dormer windows. Brandwood Hall was approached by a noble avenue of chestnuts, and lay in a fair setting of greensward and garden; and in a grove of lime-trees, which a former owner had planted to protect the house from the east winds, nestled a numerous colony of rooks.

The offices were extensive. Behind the house there was stabling for twenty horses, and the kennels were large enough for a pack of hounds, for the Brandwoods had always been keen sportsmen and hard riders.

So much for the outside. As for the inside, the house was much bigger than it looked, as all square houses are. Adam Blackthorne said it was big enough to hold a regiment of soldiers; and when Rachel went through the rooms she felt grateful that she had been relieved, by her husband's forethought in getting the contents "thrown in," of the thankless and laborious task of furnishing; although, as she observed, most of the things would want a good deal of doing up, and the carpets were that faded and worn that they would all have to be renewed. But she had sufficient good taste to see that the old furniture was far more suitable and congruous than any she could buy; and with the exception of necessary repairs, and the rubbing and polishing which was so dear to her woman's heart, she left things pretty much as they were. Even the new carpets she felt constrained to order were close imitations of their predecessors.

When he told Bruff that he meant to live at the Hall the old lawyer lifted his gray eyebrows in surprise, and helped himself to a pinch of snuff.

"It will cost you," he said, "five or six thousand a year to keep it up as it ought to be kept up."

"Well, I can do that and lay three times as much by; without reckoning what the estate makes. And 1 mean to keep it up as it should be kept up. I've worked hard and lived carefully all my life, and now I mean to take things a bit easier.

"Why, you'll be quite a country gentleman, Blackthorne. Brandwood Hall's a fine place. What will you do with the kennels? Are you going to keep the harriers?"

"Nay, not quite," laughed Adam, "I'm too old to go a-hunting. Frank may if he likes. Say, he has begun already."

"So I hear, and he rides well to hounds, too, they tell me."

"Oh, young fellows must have their fling, you know. But all the same, I mean him to stick pretty close to business. We are not going to let Brandwood Hall make us forget the Old Factory. It will not do to have our house whiter than our pieces, you know."

"Your house whiter than your pieces! What does that mean?"

"Don't you know? Well, one of Sir Robert Peel's leading men - the first Sir Robert Peel, I mean - left him to set up for himself as bleacher, and he did very well, and built a nice house, and then invited his old master to come and take a bit of dinner with him and look at the place. Sir Robert, who always liked to see those as he had brought up making a bit of figure in the world, accepted the invitation, and drove over to see him - and rare and proud Tomlinson was. Well, he showed him his works and his crofts, and everything; and then he took him round the house and gardens - as he had got a gardener from London to lay out - and after he had seen all, be asked Sir Robert what be thought of it. "Very nice, Tomlinson; it's all very nice," said the old gentleman, "but take care as thou does not make thy house whiter than thy pieces."

"I see, I see," said the lawyer, smiling and taking another pinch of snuff. "A very apt anecdote. A very shrewd old gentleman was the first Sir Robert Peel."

"I mean to have a nice house and that," resumed Adam, "and I can afford one, but it shall not be whiter than my pieces while I live."

It was remarked by Adam's friends at this time that he had fallen into the habit of referring frequently in conversation to the enterprising Lancashire baronet, quoting him as an example, and repeating the sayings that were attributed to him. Sir Robert's marvellous success, indeed, had fired his imagination; he had taken him for his model, and was trying to tread in his footsteps. He had set his heart on founding a family. Brandwood Hall was to be the nucleus of the family estate, and sooner or later he intended to settle it strictly on Frank. But he did not mean the lad to be a mere country gentleman; he hoped to see him some time in Parliament - no very extravagant pretension seeing that Redburn (lately enfranchised by the Reform Bill) was represented by two singularly commonplace cotton spinners, neither of whom, if the truth were known, was as well off as himself. Frank, moreover, was sharp. The four years with Dr. Berrs and the two on the Continent had made a man of him, and who knows, thought Adam, that he may not one of these days have a handle to his name?

Adam as yet had kept his plans entirely to himself. He was not sure that Rachel would approve of them if he told her, or rather, he was sure she would not, and the time had not come for communicating them to Frank. For the success of the larger scheme was in a measure contingent on his co-operation in a relatively smaller, but to his son personally an even more important one, the premature disclosure of which might possibly throw difficulties in the way of its realisation.

The first step towards the object Adam had in view was the purchase of the Brandwood estate and the removal to the Hall. For himself, individually, he would have preferred to remain near the Old Factory and end his days with the busy hum of spindles and the racket of looms ringing in his ears; but he knew that, to gain the ends he aimed at, it was necessary to impose on men's imaginations, or, as he put it to himself, to make a show. Redburn would never look for a candidate in Moorwell House, nor could it be considered as a fit residence for a County magistrate.

Frank by this time was a tall, stalwart young fellow of one-and-twenty. His mother thought him the very image of his father, while his father thought him very like his mother, the fact being that he resembled them both as closely as it is possible for anyone to resemble two persons. He had the figure, the dark hair, and the cast of countenance of the one, the fair skin, the brown eyes, and the winsome look of the other. There was no mistake about his being a Blackthorne, yet a single glance sufficed to show that he was Rachel's child.

He had been three years about the factory, or rather the factories, for Adam was now running two besides the old one, and, much to his father's satisfaction, he had taken kindly to the business and was already a great help to him. He possessed a turn for mechanics and a capacity for organisation, and had suggested and carried out several improvements in one or two of the most important departments; and being naturally more receptive of new ideas than his father, he infused a spirit and vivacity into the enterprise which are often lacking in long-established concerns. He was popular with the hands, too, and took more interest in their comfort and well-being than was customary with employers of the older generation. Frank's notions in this regard, however, found much less favour with Adam than his innovations in more technical matters. The latter held as an article of faith that hands should not be pampered; by which he meant that they should work as long hours for as little wages as they could be made to accept. He was pretty much of Paul Dogget's way of thinking, who once, when a deputation of his workpeople waited on him to ask for more habitable dwellings than the wretched hovels in which they were compelled to live, told them with a curse that he built factories, not houses, for them to live in. Houses were only meant for their occupation from eight o'clock at night to five o'clock in the morning, and anything was good enough for that.

Hence, when Frank wanted to pull down and rebuild a nest of wretched cottages at Lower Fold, constructed in utter defiance of every law of health, and so abounding with vermin that, as one of their unfortunate tenants said, they were not fit for dogs to live in, let alone Christians, Adam, who would have been sorry to house his horses in them, strongly demurred to the proposal, and it was only after his son had enlisted the doctor on his side, and there were rumours of cholera at Redburn, that permission was given for their demolition.

"Frank would quite spoil th' hands," the old man grumbled; "he was too good and familiar with 'em by half and if he didn't mind what he was doing they would be quite past managing.

Perhaps there was a grain of truth in the charge of over-familiarity, for Frank had not only a kindly greeting for the workpeople whom he encountered after factory hours, but if he chanced to meet a pretty girl when nobody was nigh, and he was in a merry humour, he would sometimes give her a chuck under the chin, or pinch her cheek and ask her who her sweetheart was. But of his sons susceptibility to the charms of beauty Adam was as yet happily ignorant.

CHAPTER XXVII.

LYDIA FELL.

About the time the Blackthornes removed from Moorwell to Brandwood, Adam lost his principal bookkeeper, and had need of another. He made this want known among his friends, and one day, being at Redburn market, he was accosted by the eldest grandson of Paul Dogget, who inquired if he was not looking out for a head clerk.

Young, or rather youngest Paul (for he was called after his father, and the grandfather still lived), was the most superfine youth of the cotton-spinning class about Redburn. He had been to the University (where, according to report, he was ignominiously plucked), looked down on Redburn people as coarse and vulgar, and, to show his superiority over the common herd, he always (when he did not sport a rare flower in his button-hole) carried a posy in his hand, people said in order the better to show off a big diamond ring which his Aunt Mary Anne had given him on his birthday. He had long, light hair, a long nose, and a long narrow face; and having a neat, slim figure, and dressing in the height of fashion, his family considered him to be the genteelest youth of the age and destined to bring lustre on the name of Dogget. The Redburn folks could not for the life of them understand how Paul came to have such a dandified grandson, until Happy Jack (who was on the other side in politics) described the youth as a fine thread from a very coarse roving, an explanation which was generally held as sufficiently accounting for the phenomenon.

"My papaw has heard, Mr. Blackthorne," said the young man, with a simpering and supercilious air, "that you are in want of a bookkeeper, and, as he cannot come to the market to-day himself, he desired me to inform you that there is a young man he can recommend for the situation, by name Stephen Fell."

"What does he know about him?" asked Adam bluntly, for if there was one thing that he hated more than another it was affectation, and the word "papa," especially when used by young men, he could not abide.

"Well, I believe he is a good bookkeeper, you know, a worthy young man, and that - and, ah - let me see - yes, there is something else - he has a sister

- and he is very good to her - supports her and that, you know. I believe they were left orphans and destitute, or something of that sort."

"Is that all?"

"Yaas, it's all they told me, or at least all I remember. If you want to know more you had perhaps better call at the mill and see my papaw; he will be there at five o'clock."

So Adam went down to Dogget's mill and had an interview with Dogget the second, old Paul being by this time imbecile and on his last legs. The son was almost as coarse a roving as his father, and the very antithesis of the gilded youth whom Adam had met at the yarn market. He had short legs, an immense protuberance of stomach, a bull neck, a fat face, and out-starting eyes. He was known among his workpeople as "Owd Brosenun," and, being short of breath, his speech was at times rather broken.

From him Adam learnt that Stephen Fell was an excellent bookkeeper, and, as Paul II. believed, honest and trustworthy.

"The worst thing as I know agen him," he gasped, "is as he's a bit of a rowling stone - been to London and America, and two or three more places. But he's getting a bit of sense now, I think, and is disposed to settle down to steady work. We'd take him in here if we'd room; for he's a rare 'un with the pen and he's a head like a book."

"I don't much like rowling-stones," said Adam, "but as you speak so highly of him in other respects, and we are very short-handed in our counting-house just now, we'll give him a trial."

"He'll be glad of the chance, and I think he'll please you. To tell the truth, I'm a bit sorry for the lad. He's been well browt up. Father was a rich farmer, wide of Preston - farmed a bit of his own land, you know - but when he died there was nowt for nobody, and the children had to turn out and work and do th' best as they could. My wife comes out of the same neighbourhood – that is what makes me know."

"And what about the sister your son was mentioning?"

"I believe she's a decent lass, but a bit proud - willn't work at th' factory, you know. Stephen's always been very good to her, and she sews a bit and suchlike. 1 daresay he'd like to put her in a cottage, if you have one to spare."

"I think we could accommodate them as far as that goes. If you'll send him over to-morrow we'll see what we can do."

"I'll send him, sure enough. Th' wife knows where they're living - him and his sister I mean."

"Let him bring his sister if she has nothing better to do," said Adam, as if struck by a sudden thought. "I may happen find her a job as would suit her. Is she up to housework, do you think?"

"I should say so - farmers' daughters generally is - I'll tell my wife to tell her to come," wheezed Dogget, who being from temperament, as well as by reason of his infirmity, a taciturn man, was beginning to find the conversation rather fatiguing.

Adam seeing this, and having got to know all he wanted, took his leave. On his way home he thought over the scheme that had occurred to him while talking to Dogget; and the more he thought over it the better it liked him.

The next afternoon, as the master of Moorwell and his son were in the former's room, looking over some samples of cotton which had just come by canal from Liverpool, they were informed by the lodgekeeper "that a mon fro' Redburn, and a young woman," wanted to see Mr. Blackthorne.

"Show 'em in," said Adam. "It'll be that book-keeper and his sister I was telling you about, Frank. If th' lass looks likely I shall propose that to 'em as I was telling you about."

"All right. There they are in the lobby, I think. You'll soon be able to judge."

Though Paul Dogget II had spoken of Stephen Fell as a lad and Lydia - for that was the sister's name - as a. lass, their ages were probably not less than eight-and-twenty and four-and-twenty respectively; though, as he looked older, and she younger than her years, the difference seemed greater.

Both the Blackthornes were struck with the appearance of the brother and sister as the two entered the office. It could be seen at a glance that they were not of the common type. Frank, who thought he knew a pretty face when he saw it, unhesitatingly pronounced Lydia Fell to be good-looking, albeit his final verdict was that she was more striking than beautiful. She had well-formed features, a good complexion, dark hair, gray eyes, and a sufficiently graceful figure. So far, there was nothing in her appearance to excite attention, for, as everybody knows, comely maidens are by no means rare in the County Palatine; but when you regarded her a second time - and most people did regard her a second time - you saw that her eyebrows and eyelashes were quite white, a freak of nature that gave her at times - especially when her eyes were half closed, as they often were - a strange feline look, as attractive to some as it was repellent to others.

The brother was tall and spare, his face thin and hairless, and in the keenness of his gray eyes, the quick nervousness of his manner, and the fashion of his speech, there was something, as Adam thought, decidedly more American than English. Whatever might be his other qualifications, there could be little doubt that Stephen Fell was quite able to take care of himself.

After some conversation touching his previous experience in business and bookkeeping, Adam mentioned the salary he was prepared to give, or, as he said, what the place was worth. Fell thought the pay rather little for the work, and, remarking that he had his sister as well as himself to keep, asked Mr. Blackthorne if he could not say five or ten shillings a week more. Adam did not think he could, but remarked, on the other hand, that he had a proposition to make, which, if Fell chose to accept it, would be a good deal more than that in his way. He wanted somebody to take charge of Moorwell House, and, if the brother and sister liked, they might live in it rent free. The two Blackthornes would take at least one meal there every day, for which they would pay at a sufficiently liberal rate, to be agreed upon by Mrs. Blackthorne and Miss Fell. A bedroom would be reserved for Mr. Frank's use whenever it was necessary for him to stay all night at Moorwell. Miss Fell would be remunerated for her services by a fixed monthly payment; she could get what help she desired, and she would be free in the intervals of her household duties to sew or do any other work that might suit her.

"For my part, I accept the offer with many thanks," said Stephen, "and I have no doubt my sister will also. What do you say, Lydia?"

"You know, Stephen, if I am with you, I shall be content wherever it is; and if Mr. Blackthorne thinks I am qualified to take care of the house, I will do my best to please him and young Mr. Blackthorne."

As she glanced at Frank her eye caught his, for the young fellow was just then looking at her rather intently. He blushed a little, but she dropped her eyelids, with their long, cat-like lashes, in the most natural manner possible, and without the least appearance of self-consciousness.

"Oh, you'll be able to manage well enough," answered Adam. "We don't want anything out of the way; just plain and substantial, you know. Well, I think we understand each other. When can you come?"

"How would Monday morning do?"

"Very well. Let it be Monday then, and Mrs. Blackthorne shall be here to receive your sister and put her in the way."

In accordance with this arrangement the Fells presented themselves at Moorwell on the following Monday morning; and while Adam was initiating the brother into the business of the office, Rachel was instructing the sister in her new duties. She stayed at the house all day - finding, doubtless, its simplicity and ancient memories a welcome change from the grandeur of Brandwood Hall - and in the evening went home in the carriage with her husband; Frank, as he generally did, going on horseback.

"Well, what do you think of our new housekeeper?" was the first question Adam asked of his wife.

"What do you think of your new bookkeeper?" said Rachel.

"That's like a woman, answering one question by asking another," observed her husband with a smile "Well, so far as I can see, Stephen Fell knows his business. There's hundreds as call themselves book-keepers, but there isn't many as is real good ones. Now, unless I'm mistaken, this Fell's a real good one. But I shall be able to tell better in two or three days"

"Is that all?"

"All! What would you have more?"

"You've told me what like he is as a book-keeper, but you don't say what you think of him as a man."

"That is a question easier asked than answered, Rachel. It's not easy to find out what a chap is in a day, particularly when it's a chap like Stephen Fell. He's no fool - that's one thing sure; and he's seen more o' th' world than most o' the folks in these parts. I fancy he's aspiring, you know, and wants to get on, and will not long be satisfied with his present pay and position. That is happen why he's been a rowling stone, as young Dogget says he has. Impatience to rise is almost as great a hindrance to getting on as laziness. A man as cannot play a waiting game very rarely succeeds. As for this Fell, what I think is as he'll want watching. He's not one as it would do to let get the upper hand, and I expect he'll want to get it. And now I think it is your turn to tell me what you think of th' sister - Lydia, don't they call her?"

Well, I should say, from what I've seen to-day, that she's orderly and industrious, and will make a good house keeper. She is quiet and well-spoken, too, and very respectful. But she is not communicative, nor easy to read. I've been in two minds about her nearly all day, and I am in two minds about her now. Sometimes she looks all that's innocent and single-minded - that's when her eyes are wide open, I think; and then, when they are half-closed, as they always are when she's thinking, she looks deep and designing. Perhaps it's the fault of her white eyelashes. Time will show I suppose."

"I suppose it will. Anyhow she can do us no hurt - unless she poisons us, and she's hardly likely to do that," Adam answered with a laugh.

"I'm not so sure about that," said Rachel gravely. "Frank will be there every day, and sometimes he'll have to stay there all night, you say. And he's only young, and -"

"Anyhow, he's not a fool," interrupted Adam rather warmly; "and he would be to take up with the likes of her. But if ever I see owt o' the sort I'll -"

As he did not complete the sentence, Rachel was left in ignorance of what course her husband would take in the contingency he had named. But the suggestion of such a possibility seemed to have given her food for thought. Nothing further was spoken between them until the carriage entered Brandwood Park and they perceived the subject of their late conversation and present reflections galloping a thorough-bred chestnut mare across the turf towards a flight of hurdles, over which he flew like a bird on the wing.

"Well done?" exclaimed Adam with a gratified smile. "You doesn't look much like a lad as would want to wed a book-keeper's sister, Rachel, one as is not much better than a servant. Our Frank must do better than that."

CHAPTER XXVIII.

TOMMY TWIRLER MAKES A DISCOVERY.

Tommy Twirler, otherwise "Owd Poo' Bell," though older than when he escorted Frank to Leatherlad's school on the memorable occasion when that hopeful youth threw his cap into Stimson's plantation, is still an institution at Moorwell, and, as he was fifteen years before, one of Adam

Blackthorne's most trusted servants. In consideration of his age and long services, he had been relieved of his bell-pulling duties and promoted to the position of general caretaker and weigher of coals. No black diamonds that have not passed under Tommy's Argus eye, and been tried by him on the balance, are allowed to enter Moorwell gates. Against every load found wanting a mark is made, and with many more similarly deficient it will rise up against the colliery proprietor on the day of reckoning. His master says of Tommy that, not alone is he one of the chosen few on the "ground" who have his interest at heart, but that he saves more than his wage in short weights. In the intervals of his coal-weighing Tommy acts as general caretaker. If he sees any waste, idleness, or petty larceny going on, Adam, or Adam's son, is immediately informed thereof. Yet he is no spy, and never wastes his time in observing trivialities or retailing gossip.

Careful as he is of his employer's interest, Tommy takes no less thought of his own. Though until very lately he has never earned more than fifteen shillings a week, he has nearly five hundred pounds laid by, for which Mr. Blackthorne, who acts as his banker, allows him interest at the rate of five per cent. - for these two men, neither of whom trusts anybody else, trust each other implicitly. It is only fair to say, however, that Tommy's wealth is not altogether the fruit of his own economies. His wife, who is hardly less thrifty than himself, makes a nice little sum every week by knitting healds; and his daughter Betty, being a six-loom weaver, earns even more than her father. Tommy is particularly proud of his Betty, who turns out more pieces, with fewer faults, than almost any other weaver at Moorwell; and Adam, though a stern master, treats her and a few other equally diligent workwomen with what a Frenchman would call "distinguished consideration;" for he knows the value of good hands. They were the *elite* of Moorwell, and once or twice every summer, when they wanted to have a jaunt to "th' sawt water" (Lytham or Blackpool), Yorkshire Joe and a couple of carts were told off to convey them thither, cheap trips and railways (except that from Manchester to Liverpool, and one or two others) being not yet. It was rather a slow business as far as speed was concerned - nearly all going and coming. They had hardly taken a dip in the sea, gathered a few mussels, bought a few shrimps, and snatched a hasty meal, when it was time to be off back. But they had rare fun. They were not hurried through the country like so many bales of goods. They had not a single dull moment from first to last; the breakfast at Preston, and the bait and "putting on" (another breakfast) at Kirkham, were scenes of uproarious mirth. Though the carts were springless, and it was only rarely that Yorkshire Joe could get more than three miles an hour out of his horses, the travellers enjoyed themselves in a way of which "trippers" of this generation have no conception. The event, moreover, served them to talk about all winter, which is more than can be said of a journey to the seaside nowadays.

Tommy and his family lived at the lodge of Moorwell House, which was hard by the Old Factory gates. Shortly after the Blackthornes went to Brandwood a loom shed was built on the ground formerly occupied by the avenue. At the back of this shed ran a footpath, which formed a communication between the lodge and the upper part of the garden, and it had been ordered by Adam that Tommy and his family should he free to walk therein whenever it pleased them, and have the privilege of plucking fruit from certain of the trees.

This arrangement the Fells in secret bitterly resented. It seemed to be placing Tommy and his womankind on a level with them; and they thought themselves superior in every way. Hence arose strife and enmity between the two families, heightened, probably, by the sense of distrust which Tommy had from the first conceived for the Fells. Stephen was now an important man in the counting-house; Tommy had often business there, and they rarely met without having words. Then Stephen was known to ridicule Tommy and his ways behind his back; and though the old fellow, being by nature taciturn, never said much, he treasured these things in his heart, and, not feeling disposed to return good for evil, he watched his enemy more vigilantly than he watched anybody else, in the hope of having him one day on the hip; and as he was firmly convinced that the Fells, the sister as well as the brother, were no better than they should be, he had little doubt of success.

Adam, meanwhile, was well satisfied with both. Stephen performed his duties to his entire satisfaction. The books had never been in such order before, and his demeanour and conduct were everything that could be desired. As for Lydia, although Mrs. Blackthorne had not been able to conquer her aversion to the girl's white eyebrows and her occasionally feline expression, she rendered willing testimony to the exemplary manner in which she fulfilled the duties of her situation. The house, and the furniture, and the linen were kept in apple-pie order, the cookery was unexceptionable, and her manner to Mr. and Mrs. Blackthorne, albeit rather reserved, was never wanting in respect.

This was the state of things, the Fells having been at Moorwell six or eight months, when one day about noon, just after the hands had gone to their dinners and all was quiet, Tommy Twirler entered Adam's room and asked if he could have a word with him.

"Certainly, Tommy," said Adam; "either now or any other-time. You are not like some folks - you never speak unless you have something to say. What is it?"

Tommy carefully closed the door.

"There's nobody listening, think yo', is there?"

"Nay, how can there be? I am quite by myself. Frank's off at Liverpool, and Fell and the others have gone to their dinners."

"That's why I come now; I thowt there would be nobody here but yourself."

"It's something important, then, that you've got to tell me," replied Adam, struck by the unusual gravity of Twirler's manner.

"You'll think so when you've yerd, unless I'm far mistaken. It's about these here Fells and yo're Frank."

"The devil it is!" exclaimed Adam, whom this announcement seemed painfully to surprise.

"Here, take this chair, Tommy, and sit down and tell me all about it. What have you heard?"

"Nay, mayster, it's not what I've heard, it's what I've seen. Yo' know yo' told me if ever I seed owt as yo' owt to know - whether in th' factory or out on't - I wor to tell yo'."

"So I did, Tommy; I remember it perfectly."

"And it mak's no difference whether yo're Frank is mixed up in it or not."

"Yea, it does; you should tell me all the sooner in that case."

"That's what I said to mysel'," said Tommy, nodding his head in approval of his own penetration. "For owt as consarns him consarns you - just as owt as consarns our Betty consarns me."

"Just so, Tommy. And now I think, as we quite understand each other, you may tell me what you have heard - seen, that is."

"Well," returned Tommy, taking off a rabbit-skin cap, and smoothing it on his knee as he spoke, "it wor this way: A two thry week sin' our Betty wor walking i' th' garden - it wor a Sunday afternoon - when hoo met Miss Fell, as they callin' her. "Yo' come here very often, I think," says hoo. "No ofter than yo'," says our Betty, "and what's moor," says hoo, "I've as much reyt here as yo' have; and for aw' as yo' wearin' sich fine feathers (hoo'd gotten a new gowd cheen round her neck), I daresay as we're weel off as yo' are - happen better'."

"'No more of your insolence, girl," says Miss Fell, says hoo, "or I'll speak to Mr. Frank, and have you sent about your business."

"'Have me sent about my business, will yo', miss?" says our Betty. "You'll find yoursel' mista'en, I think. Nayther yo' nor yo're brother, nor th' young mayster, nor anybody else on this ground, as long as th' owd mayster lives, will get Betty Twirler bagged. Yo'll loyse yo're shop afore I shall loyse mine, Miss Fell."

"And with that hoo left her, and gradely mad hoo looked, our Betty says."

"I should think that's very likely," observed Adam, with a smile. "But that isn't all?"

"No, that isn't aw' - that's nobbut th' beginning, fost (first) chapter i' Genesis like. Well, when Betty towd me what had come to pass, I says to her, says I: 'Thou may depend on it, Betty, as there's summut up between her and th' young mayster, or hoo'd never ha' said that theer; so just shut thy mouth and keep thy een open, and if thou sees owt, tell me.'

"Well, hoo did see summut, and not long after, nayther. One neet, about a fortnight sin', hoo'd bin up th' loin (lane) after th' factory had loosed, wi' two thry moor lasses, and hoo took into her heyd to come hack through th' garden. It's a bit nearer, yo' know, than th' loin gate. Well, when hoo'd getten into th' padgate (footpath) between th' loom shed and th' garden wall, hoo thought as hoo seed a man and a woman coming toward her, and being a bit feared, hoo slipped behind a big bush as wor hard by. As they come nearer, hoo could see as they were th' young mayster and Miss Fell. He had his arm round her waist, and he wor a-kussing on her to that end as th' lass wor fair shamed, and when they had guon past hoo ran straight home and towd me. That wor aw reyt as far as it went; but still, as I thowt to mysel', I mun have a different tale fro' that afore I speyk to th' mayster. I mun see for mysel'. Well, a day or two after, there wor a bit o' work to be done in th' middle room - a pair o' spur wheels had been striking fire, and Bill o' Owd Jack's and Stuttering Bob were guoin to gear 'em up afresh. It wor a neet job, and th' young mayster said as he'd stop aw neet, and see it through hissel'. I had my thowts when I Yerd o' this, for it wor a simple soort ov a job, one as th' chaps could do quite well by theirsel's. So after the engines stopped I went up to th' middle room, just to see what wor going on. Bill and Bob wor theer wi' their tackle, and a bit after comes th' young mayster. He axed a two thry questions, looked at the wheels, towd me to send for half a gallon o' beer for th' chaps to sup, and then he pikes off. I waited a bit, and then I pikes off too, went huom, put my shoon on (clogs crunches so on gravel), slipped quietly into the garden, and stole up to the front o' th' ho' (hall). There wor a leet i' Frank's parlour - what used to be your drawing-room, yo know - th' blind wor nobbut hoaf drawn down, and it wor a cotton un. I could see inside quite plain, and there they wor, and her a.sitting on his knee. As luck would have it, I wur just i' the nick o' time, for ayther I med a noise on th' gravel or they yerd summut i' th' house. Leastways, I had not been looking two minutes when up jumps Miss Fell, quite sudden like, and runs out o' th' room, and soon after Mr. Frank goes too.

"I wouldn't ha' meddled," continued Tommy, after a short pause, which did not elicit any observation from his master - " I wouldn't ha' meddled if it ha' been one o' th' factory lasses as Mr. Frank wor fooling wi'. Young chaps will be young chaps. I've bin one mysel', but yon Miss Fell is a bad lot, that's plain to be sin'; hoo's above owt but wedding, hoo is; and unless yo' do summut, hoo'l be a-hookin' on him in."

"Nay, she will not, I'll take care of that,' said Adam, with sudden energy, and a big thump of his fist on the table. "You've done quite right, Tommy, and I'm much obliged to you. How long has this been going on, do you think?"

"That's more than I can tell. Ten to one from the fost on 'em coming here. Yo' remember when th' young mayster went off huntin' last winter, Miss Fell were off too. Now I've been thinken - "

"I know what you mean, but that could not be; he was in Cheshire, and she went to see a sick aunt at Plumpton."

"Hoo said so, happen, but I expect if th' truth wor known, hoo worn't so much farther fro' him than hoo is now,"

"I think you are mistaken there, Tommy. But tell me, is this known to anybody but yourself ?"

"To nobody but our Betty and me so far as I know, and hoo's a lass as can keep her mouth shut. But if there had been a buzz I should have heard. But there soon will be if they carry on i' that way, and th' blind not drawn. By gum, I never seed owt like it. Yorkshire Joe or any o' th' chaps about th' stable mut as weel have sin' 'em as me."

"So they might, Tommy. I couldn't have believed the lad would have been so foolish. And now, I'm sure, you'll be wanting your dinner; it's nearly half-past twelve. Just keep a sharp look-out, like you have been doing, till I think what's best to be done."

So Tommy went away and left Adam to his own reflections, which, as may be supposed, were none of the pleasantest. He cursed his own folly for having engaged a young woman as housekeeper, and for not having given more heed to his wife's misgivings in reference thereto. Then he cursed his son's folly for rushing so headlong into the snare the Fells had laid for him; for that they were endeavouring, as Tommy said, "to hook him in," he had not the slightest doubt. But curses do not often lead to practical results, and Adam, after having relieved his mind by a few vigorous expletives, proceeded to think how the evil he feared could be prevented - for he was quite of the Twirler's opinion that Lydia Fell was "above anything but wedding;" and even a scandal might interfere with the success of his schemes. Should he talk the matter over with his wife? No, he said, women are always soft with their sons, however hard they may be with their daughters. Frank would talk to her, get round her, and win her over to his side, and then there would be two against him. No, he must just keep his own counsel and manage the thing himself – persuade, if necessary force, Frank to give Lydia up, and send the Fells about their business - if needful, pay them to go far enough.

As Adam was not in the habit of letting the grass grow under his feet, he resolved to enter on the matter the following day, when his son would be back from Liverpool.

CHAPTER XXIX.

FATHER AND SON.

"And now, Frank," said Adam the next day, after his son had given an account of his journey to Liverpool and what he had done in the way of cotton buying, "I have a very serious matter to discuss with you."

"Yes, father," replied Frank, with a puzzled, though unconscious look; "what is it? there's nothing wrong in the business, is there?"

"Not much, I think. It's not business I'm thinking about - it's these Fells."

This time, albeit he tried to put on an indifferent air, Frank did look conscious.

"Well, father, what about them?"

"They must go."

"What for? I thought you liked Stephen."

"So I did; but I don't like my son being too thick with Stephen Fell's sister; he must fly at higher game than that."

"Who says - ?

"There's no use denying it, Frank; it will only waste time. I can see it in your face, my lad. And let me give you a bit of advice: the next time you do any courting just see as the blind is drawn."

Frank muttered what sounded very like a curse, but made no answer.

"How long has this been going on, or, what's of more consequence, how far has it gone?"

"I can hardly tell - two or three months, perhaps."

"Do you care for Lydia?"

"I do. I love her dearly, father."

"And she?"

"She loves me with all her heart."

"Stuff! Have you promised her marriage?

"I have."

"Why, lad, you are mad - stark, staring mad. Do you want to ruin yourself?"

"Why should that ruin me? She's as good as I am - yes, better, and I mean to marry her."

  "I say you shall not."

"I say I will."

These were brave words; but this was the first time in his life Frank had braved his father, and his manner belied them. They were spoken feebly and irresolutely. The perspiration stood in thick beads upon his brow and rolled down his face, and his hands trembled with excitement.

"Frank, these people have entrapped you. This girl is an adventuress; it's your money - mine rather - not you, that she's after."

"I don't believe it, father; she's a good girl and as true as steel."

Adam laughed sarcastically.

"True or not, I'll take good care she gets none of my money - whether she gets you or not. You know me, Frank, and you know that what I say I mean. Now listen: As sure as you are sitting here, if you are so mad as to marry Lydia Fell I'll neither leave nor give you a single penny; and you will have to quit both this ground and my house, and get your living the best way you can. You must choose between her and me."

I have given my word, father, and I cannot go back from it," said Frank doggedly.

"Wait a bit, I have not done yet; I see I must tell you more of my plans than I had thought of doing. It is only right as you should know everything before you make up your mind. I was going to make you a partner after next stocktaking - give you a third of the profits, and raise your salary to a thousand a year. That would make a man of you at once. But there is more behind. I had made up my mind, if you married to suit me, to settle Brandwood Hall on you and your children. Another thing - there a no reason, when you are five or six years older; why you should not put up for Redburn and get into Parliament, and before you are my age be one of the first men in the country."

"How do you mean marrying to suit you?"

"Marrying Valérie Basel. Years ago Basel and me agreed that our families should be united - that you should marry Valerie, and Mabel Fritz. Basel's a rich man now - he is getting richer every year - and can give his daughter a handsome fortune. And that is not all. In eighteen months our partnership expires by effluxion of time. He can do without me, but I cannot do without him; and if so be as you was to put such a slight upon him as to prefer this Lydia Fell - this money-hunting pauper, for she's nowt else - to his daughter, we should have to dissolve partnership - there's no doubt about that - and I should be worse off by ten thousand a year."

"But how do you know," said Frank, as he was beginning to think that, after all, he had possibly not acted the part of a wise man in engaging himself to Lydia Fell - "how do you know that Valérie Basel would have me? I do not think she would know me if she met me, and I am sure I should not know her. She went to London just before I came back from Lausanne, and she has been there, and at Paris, ever since. She was a girl when I saw her four years since; she is a woman now."

She'll obey her parents; French children always do, they tell me. I wish English children were more like 'em. I don't want to force her on you if she is not likely to make you a good wife; but them as knows her says as she's as nice a young woman as ever stepped in shoe leather. As a lass she was good-looking; I don't suppose she has grown ugly since, and there is not one in ten thousand - nay, in twenty thousand - as has had half as good an education as Valérie Basel has had. Anyhow, this Lydia Fell's not fit to be named in the same day with her, look at it which way you will."

"That's a matter of opinion, father. But in any case, I have given my word to Lydia Fell, and even if I did not love her, I do not see how I could be untrue to her."

"I wish the devil had Lydia Fell!" exclaimed Adam passionately. "Love her! not you, it is only a bad case of calf love. In six months' time you'll laugh at yourself for ever having been such a fool as to waste a single thought on her. But look here - suppose I can prove to you, beyond any possibility of doubt, that she does not care a button top for you, that whether you give her up or not she will give you up for a sufficient consideration - will you fall in with my views then?"

"Certainly, father, I promise that," said Frank eagerly, for he had the most implicit confidence in Lydia's constancy, "but I am quite sure – "

"Never mind that - you'll see. But you must also give me your word that, until after to-morrow, you will neither see nor hold any communication with either of them - either Stephen or his sister, I mean."

"I don't see how that can be done," said Frank hesitatingly, after a moment's thought (he had agreed to spend the evening with Lydia). "Stephen is here in the office; not to speak to him would appear very strange and give rise to remark."

"That's easy got over. You are tired after your journey - you cannot miss being. You must go home and rest. Rip Van Winkle's in the stable; Yorkshire Joe shall put the saddle on him, and you can set off at once. Stop all to-morrow at Brandwood, Frank. Fritz Basel would like a day's partridge shooting, I know. I'll send him word that you'll expect him. Now the sooner you are gone the better."

Frank did not much like being bundled off in this unceremonious manner, yet he did not deem it expedient to enter into another contest with his father, and full of misgiving as to what might happen on the morrow, he set out for Brandwood Hall.

He felt that he had been sadly lacking in moral courage, and bitterly reproached himself for having allowed his father to conceive hopes which could never be realised, and which would only make his anger greater when he found out, as find out he must, how impossible it was for him to renounce Lydia and marry Miss Basel. Then the suggestion that he had been entrapped, that Lydia loved him, not for what he was but for what he had or might have, though he indignantly repudiated it, added to his uneasiness. It could not be true – and yet - and then there occurred to him several circumstances which, it was impossible to deny, seemed to lend some support to his father's theory.

So absorbed was he in his thoughts that he did not notice a robed figure before him on the road; neither, it might appear, did Rip Van Winkle; for he gave a sudden side-way jump that almost unhorsed his master, who at the same time heard a voice he well knew speaking his name.

"Frank."

"Lydia, you here! What is it?" exclaimed the young man, who seemed more surprised than pleased. "We must not be seen talking here, you know?"

"Why?"

"As if you did not know. My father might hear of it; and I fear he suspects already."

"You fear?" she replied, with a toss of her head. "If you fear, I don't - why should I? Are you coming to-night?"

"I don't think so; they want me at home."

"To-morrow night, then?"

"I will do my best; but I am not sure."

"Very well. I dare say I shall not break my heart if you don't come. And now, as we stand in such awe of our father, I won't keep you longer. Good-bye."

"Good-bye," said Frank, and, as if glad to escape, he gave Rip Van Winkle a kick with his heel and cantered quickly away out of sight.

Lydia stood for a few minutes watching the vanishing horse and its rider.

"What a coward he is," she murmured; "I've a good mind to speak to his father myself. But no, that would be to lose our power over him, and perhaps prevent him doing anything for Stephen. I must be guided by Stephen, and Stephen always says keep quiet."

Meanwhile black care rode behind the horseman, and Frank journeyed towards Brandwood in a less enviable frame of mind than ever. Lydia's manner had been anything but soothing to his feelings. He could not help acknowledging to himself that her love was far from being what it had once been or seemed to be. She would not break her heart if he did not go tomorrow night. This piqued him, and he vowed that he would go neither tomorrow night, nor the next night, nor the next after that.

Thus spoke impulse, but wisdom comes with afterthought, and as Frank grew cooler he remembered that he could hardly afford to quarrel with the Fells; and then he wondered, with an anxiety which he had never known before, what the morrow would bring forth. For he felt certain that his father intended to have an interview with Stephen, and on that interview hung his fate.

CHAPTER XXX.

THE FELLS AGREE TO GO.

Well as Frank thought he knew his father, he under-estimated the energy of the old man's character and the promptitude of his proceedings. Within an hour of his son's departure for Brandwood, Adam called Stephen Fell into his private office - ostensibly to ask for some information about his department of the business.

"I suppose you did not see much of cotton growing when you were in America, Fell (they had been discussing cotton invoices); you were too far south for that?"

"No, sir; my knowledge of America is confined to the north-eastern States, and they don't grow much cotton there."

"Is America a good country for a man to get on in - a man with a little money, I mean?

"It is that. I only wish - "

"You mean you only wish that you had a little capital - you would try your fortune there," interrupted Mr. Blackthorne. "I suppose it was shortness of capital made you come back?"

"Not quite, sir. I came back because I was befooled."

"How? Who befooled you?"

"A woman, to be sure. I don't think I'm easily befooled by a man. I came back to marry a girl, sir, and when I got here I found she had married somebody else. I would have gone straight back, but I did not like to leave Lydia; and I did not quite see my way to take her back, and provide for her and myself, too, out there."

"So you are only staying here till you have saved enough money to return to the States?"

"I don't mean that, sir," put in Stephen eagerly: "I am very well satisfied as I am. It was before I got my present situation that I thought of going back. I don't think of it now. We don't want to move, neither my sister nor me."

"I am afraid you will have to do, though, Fell."

"Why, Mr. Blackthorne? Are you not satisfied with us - have I not done my duty?"

"People have such different ideas about duty. You consider it your duty, I suppose, to encourage an intimacy between my son and your sister?"

"How, Mr. Blackthorne - who has been telling you such a lie?"

"It's no lie, Fell, as you well know. Do you consider it right, I ask, to have permitted this courtship to go on without my knowledge? I treated you with confidence - with generosity even, and you have repaid me with baseness."

"I deny it, Mr. Blackthorne, I have permitted nothing. If it be as you say, it is not of my seeking," said Stephen. (What he thought was, "How much does the old beggar know, I wonder? Can Frank have split?")

"It's only a waste of time to talk in that way, Fell; and, to cut the matter short, I may as well tell you that I had a wind yesterday of what was going on, and this morning, when I questioned Frank, he admitted having promised marriage to your sister, a circumstance of which you cannot possibly be ignorant. It will save trouble, and perhaps be to your personal advantage, to discuss the matter in a straightforward way, and without concealments, which do not deceive me. I know all, I think; indeed, I may say I'm sure."

"Suppose I do admit that I am aware of this," answered Stephen, with a curious smile, "what then?"

"What then? Why, I will not suffer this to go on. Frank shall not marry your sister."

"Why are you so hard, Mr. Blackthorne? Our family is respectable - quite as respectable as yours - and Lydia is a good girl, and would make your son a good wife."

"I refuse to go into that. It is quite sufficient that I will not let him make her his wife."

"But suppose that Mr. Frank insists on making her his wife? You seem to forget, sir, that he is of age, and his own master."

"Oh, as far as that goes, he has a perfect right to please himself. Only I want you fully to understand that if he does make your sister his wife you will have to keep him as well as her; for not another shilling would he get from me, either in my lifetime or afterwards. And, if I read you right, Fell, you would hardly like to take him on those terms."

"You surely don't mean, Mr. Blackthorne - "

"I mean that if Frank does not drop your sister, or she him - I don't care which - I shall cast him off for ever, and send you to keep him company."

Fell seemed to be revolving something in his mind.

"I think I understand what you are driving at," he said, after a moment's pause. "How much will you give?"

"Now you are talking like a sensible man. If you will leave quietly - you and your sister, I mean - and without any bother, and go to America, I will give you - let me see - three hundred pounds."

Stephen laughed scornfully.

"No, Mr. Blackthorne, that is not enough - not by a long way - why, we should get five times as much, at least, by an action for breach."

"A verdict you might get, I daresay, and judgment; but how would you recover? Frank has nothing except what I choose to give him."

"And do you mean to tell me, sir, that a gentleman in your position would let his son be sent to Lancaster Castle for non-payment of a liability which he had incurred at your own request? You are a hard man, I know, but you would not do that, Mr. Blackthorne."

Adam felt that in Stephen Fell he had a foeman worthy of his steel, and that, as he said to himself, he would have to "pay through the nose."

". How much do you ask, then?"

"Two thousand pounds," answered Fell coolly, as he picked his teeth with a new goose quill, "a thousand for Lydia and a thousand for me."

"I'll see you --- first," roared Adam, completely losing his temper at this astounding demand. "I'll give you a month's salary, that's all I'll give you, and you will just clear out at once."

"As you like, Mr. Blackthorne," said Stephen quietly, "only you will please to remember that you admitted just now that we could recover fifteen hundred, at least, by an action for breach; and as you would have to pay both your expenses and ours, it would stand you in much more than I ask. We have Mr. Frank in a pretty tight fix - tighter than you think - as you will find if we go to law."

"I daresay there is some truth in what you say," rejoined Adam, who saw that there was nothing to be gained by losing his temper. "And although I do not think your sister is entitled, morally, to as much as six-pence, yet to avoid trouble and scandal I will pay her, or you and her jointly, fifteen hundred pounds, on condition that you abandon all claim for damages, and go forthwith to America."

"No, Mr. Blackthorne," replied Stephen, as quietly as before, "I'll have two thousand or nothing, and after to-day, my price will be two thousand five hundred. You will save money by closing at once."

"Well, make it two thousand then, you infernal - "

"Don't call hard names, Mr. Blackthorne, it does no good, and wastes time"," interrupted Fell, quoting Adam's own words against him.

"Upon my word, Fell, you are a cool customer."

"I try to be, Mr. Blackthorne. And now, sir, when will the money be ready and when shall we start?"

"You shall have a cheque for a thousand to-morrow morning when you are ready to start; a second thousand when you are on hoard the packet in Liverpool, the moment before sailing, or a draft on New York, payable to you personally."

"That will be quite in order, Mr. Blackthorne. You are generally at the office soon after eight, I think. I will be here with my sister at nine, sharp, to draw the cheque and sign the receipt, which I will draw up. And if you can arrange to let me have the balance on Saturday, we will sail for New York by that day's packet."

"It's a bargain," said Adam. "Now get me those balances out I mentioned yesterday, and let Spangler write the daybook up."

"All right, sir. The books are well written up, and Spangler will have no trouble. And would you mind giving me a character, Mr. Blackthorne? It might be useful across yonder."

"No, I won't; that is not in the bargain."

"Oh, I don't make a point of it. I shall have ten thousand dollars, and that will be better than any character you can give me. I am quite content, sir."

"It's more than I am," muttered Adam, as the door closed behind the bookkeeper. "Confound the fellow, I thought I should have got off for five hundred at the outside. What a fool that lad has been, to be sure; but he is free now, and that's worth all the money - ay, ten times as much."

When he met Frank at dinner in the evening (since the removal of the Blackthornes to Brandwood they had changed their dinner hour from one o'clock to seven) neither of them made any mention of the matter of which the thoughts of both were full - Adam because he did not desire to do so until the Fells were gone, and Frank because he felt that, until his father again broached the subject, it was not for him to say anything.

Fritz Basel came the next morning to Brandwood, and the two young fellows went out for a day's shooting. Birds were pretty plentiful, and far from being wild; yet Frank, who had the reputation of being a good shot, killed scarcely any. He believed that his fate was being decided at Moorwell, and was nervous and preoccupied - feeling much as a prisoner who is awaiting the verdict of a jury of his countrymen may be supposed to feel. What could be the proposals his father was making to Stephen Fell, he was constantly asking himself, and how would Stephen receive them? And Lydia - what would she say? Would she behave in such a way as to compel him to give up for her sake his father and mother and all his fair prospects; or would she, as his father had hinted, abandon him for a consideration? He could not believe it - and yet, somehow, the possibility that she might do so kept continually recurring to him for Stephen had great influence over her, and Stephen was very fond of money. No wonder Frank fired at random, to the surprise of Fritz and the indignant wonder of the gamekeeper, who did not like to see his master outshot by "that theer Frenchman," as he called young Basel.

Fritz remained for dinner. The conversation was, therefore, necessarily general, and Frank was constrained to nurse his suspense and try to read his fate in his father's countenance. There was not much to be learnt from that; only, as it bore no traces of anger, and his father joined freely in the conversation, he tried to think that nothing very disagreeable had happened, or was about to happen.

When dinner was over, and the ladies had withdrawn, Adam took something from his pocket.

"Pray excuse me, Mr. Fritz," he said, "but here is a piece of paper I daresay Frank would like to read. It refers to a little business I've arranged to-day in which he takes a particular interest."

"Certainly, Mr. Blackthorne," said Fritz.

Frank took the document, which was written throughout in the hand of Lydia Fell, and ran as follows:

"I acknowledge the receipt from Adam Blackthorn", Esq., of one thousand pounds (on account of a sum of two thousand), in consideration of which I hereby renounce all claim for damages for breach of promise of marriage I may have against his son, Francis Adam Blackthorne; and on receiving the second thousand pounds I undertake to leave Liverpool by Saturday's packet for New York, and promise not to return to England for at least ten years. "LYDIA FELL."

As he read his eye brightened, and when he returned the document to his father he gave a sigh of relief. A few days ago he fancied he had loved Lydia to distraction, and now he actually felt pleased that she had literally sold him for two thousand pounds, and that he would probably never see her again!

"My father is right," he thought, "it was only calf love. It is quite true what he says - I have been a fool. I wonder if she and Stephen will keep their word about not coming back."

As to that, whatever may have been the case with Frank, his father cherished no illusion. He believed that the paper signed by Lydia would bar any action for breach of promise; but there was nothing in it to prevent her coming back from America whenever it might suit her. He hoped, however, she might find it to her interest to remain there; or at least that she would stay abroad until Frank was safely married to Valérie Basel.

CHAPTER XXXI.

RIDING RECOLLECTIONS.

It was one of those rare November days suggestive rather of early spring, or lingering autumn, than of impending winter and a waning year.

Every trace of the morning frost which had whitened the grass and hardened the ground had long since disappeared. Golden-hued leaves, albeit their number daily grew less, still clung feebly to their parent stems, and the hedgerows, though soon to be stripped bare by the biting blasts of December, had not yet lost their livery of the fall. Not a zephyr stirred the willows by the brook side: cattle were browsing gently in broad pastures, and the air was full of a soft stillness, as if nature were taking a breathing space before encountering the rude shocks of winter.

The sun was near his downgoing; and though the body of the luminary could not well be seen, being veiled by a silvery mist which rose from river and vale, the slowly gathering gloom showed that night was not far off.

Along a wide, white road, winding through a richly-timbered, park-like country, between tall hedgerows which in summer are gay with hawthorn, rides, in contemplative attitude, a solitary horseman. He wears a broad-brimmed hat and a red coat, the latter, as well as his brown-topped boots, smirched with mud. His steed is a big, well-bred chestnut, with three white legs, a star on his forehead, and no tail to speak of. The name of him is Rip Van Winkle, and his master is Frank Blackthorne.

Frank has been a-hunting with the Orrington harriers, and he is now thinking of the excellent day's sport he has had. His satisfaction is enhanced by the recollection of a brilliant feat of old Rip's, who had carried him over a five-foot stone wall, with a ditch on the taking off side, in a style which won him the warm applause of his comrrades of the chase. From time to time he indulges in a hearty laugh; for some of the incidents of the day were highly amusing; above all, a queer disaster that befell his father's pet aversion, Paul Dogget III.

Paul went a-hunting, not at all because he liked it, but because he considered it the right thing for a gentleman in his position, and with his prospects, to do. He always came out very spick and span in the way of costume and equipment; and his mounts, being bought regardless of expense, were generally good until he had spoiled them by his timidity and the badness of his hands. He would never go over a fence when he could get through a gap, nor go first when he could go second; and he was so constantly pulling and sawing at his horses' mouths that he never failed in the end to ruin both their mouths and their tempers.

On this particular day, as several of the field were trotting by the side of a broad drain, filled with slimy water, the hounds not being in chase at the time, young Dogget's horse, either irritated beyond endurance by his master's nervousness, or alarmed by some strange object, suddenly stopped, turned half-round, and then, without more ado, plunged into the drain. It was not very deep, but as Paul III. parted company with his steed it was quite deep enough to take him over the head; and his appearance when he emerged from his in-voluntary bath showed that he must have been deposited full length at the bottom; for he was covered with black slime and beautifully ornamented with green weeds, and one of his eyes was bunged up with a lump of mud. The onlookers, as they helped him to land, had much ado to keep from laughing in his face. Poor Paul, however, looked serious enough, and after giving himself a shake, pouring the water out of his boots, and wiping his face with a pocket-handkerchief, lent to him by one of the hunters, remounted his horse, which had been caught by one of the footpeople. But no sooner had the cavalcade made a fresh start than the creature popped into the drain a second time, and the unfortunate young Dogget, who, as before, lost his seat, made a second involuntary dive. He was again fished out, and set on his legs; but he resolutely refused to be set on his horse. Not for any earthly consideration, he said, would he ride the brute again. There was no telling what he might do. So at the suggestion of one of his friends, he led the animal to a small inn, about a mile away, put it in the stable, and himself to bed, where he remained until a carriage and a suit of clothes could be brought from Redburn.

It was a long time before Paul III went a-hunting again, and when he did he took care to give drains and ditches a very wide berth.

From thinking about young Dogget and his misfortunes Frank passed by a natural transition to Dogget senior. From Dogget senior to Blackthorne senior was only a step; and, albeit the subject was not a paticularly pleasant one, his thoughts - going rather haphazard - reverted to the Fells, and the remarkable energy which his father had shown in getting rid of them. They had been, gone now six months and more, and, barring a brief letter notifying their arrival in New York, and the receipt of the second thousand pounds, nothing had been heard of them since their departure.

"Don't be a fool again, Frank; see what it costs," was Adam's remark to his son when he handed him this letter and from that time forth the matter was no more referred to by either of them.

"I was a fool, too," said Frank to himself, as he pulled Van Winkle up while he lit a cigar. "There's no mistake about that - a bigger fool than the governor knows. But it has done me good. I shall never care for a woman again. Hallo! what's that?"

It was a travelling carriage which whirled past at such a speed as almost to make Rip jump over the hedge, tired as he was. A little farther on the road made a sudden dip and took a sharp turn. "That's a deal too fast for safety," thought Frank. "He hasn't the brake on either, and if he does not mind - gad, he has done it - just what I expected "and the youth, giving his horse a touch of the spur, cantered off to the scene of the disaster.

One of the horses had slipped down, and was trying hard to get up, while the other, restive and frightened, was in immediate peril of having his legs broken by his companion's frantic struggles to rise. The driver, who seemed to have lost his head, sat on the box, jerking violently at the reins by way of helping the prostrate horse to regain his footing.

"Down from your box this instant and loose the traces," exclaimed Frank, as he sprang from the saddle, and seizing the fallen horse's head, stopped his struggles. "That's right. Now unhook the pole chain; pull the carriage out of the way, and stand clear while the horse gets up."

This was no sooner said than done, and the next moment the horse was on his legs again.

"Is the poor creature much hurt, do you think, sir?" said a sweet, slightly tremulous voice at Frank's elbow. How very kind of you to come so promptly to our help."

Frank turned round, doffed his broad-brimmed hat, and made a low bow; for he was in the presence of two ladies.

One of them was elderly, gray and wrinkled. A very passing glance sufficed for her. But the other - she with the sweet voice - had a face to match; and it seemed to Frank as if he could never see enough of it. A rather long oval face it was, but exquisitely moulded - the nose slightly aquiline, eyes dark and sparkling, hair black, complexion richly olive, lips ripe and ruddy, and teeth of a dazzling whiteness. As touching stature, she was neither tall nor short; her figure was sylph-like, and all her movements were graceful and animated.

"God bless me! this is the most charming girl I ever saw in my life. Who is she, I wonder?

This was Frank's thought; what he said was: "Don't mention it, I beg of you. It is a very slight service to render to anybody; above all to ladies in distress. I could really hardly have done less, and if I can do anything more, I am sure I shall only be too happy."

"We thank you very much," was her answer, as she dropped her eyes before his ardent gaze. "But I don't think there is. If the poor horse is not hurt and can go on, perhaps - "

"I do not suppose he has taken much harm beyond a few scratches; but (lowering his voice) I do not think the driver is particularly capable; and if you have any fear, I should be very glad - in fact, if you will permit me, I will drive you myself."

The young lady smiled, as Frank thought, rather roguishly, and whispered a few words in the ear of her companion, who seemed hardly to understand what was going on.

"We are very much obliged for your kind offer, sir, but we could not think of giving you so much trouble," said the beautiful brunette, still with lowered eyes. "My aunt is very anxious for us to continue our journey, for it will soon be dark; but if you would add to your kindness by seeing us to the bottom of the hill, and telling the post-boy to drive a little more cautiously, we should be very grateful."

"With the greatest possible pleasure," replied Frank warmly, as seeing the ladies desired to re-enter the carriage, he opened the door and handed them to their seats.

He next saw that the harness was all in proper order, told the post-boy if he did not mind what he was doing he would report him to his master (hoping thereby to find out who his passengers were, in which, however, he did not succeed). Then mounting Rip Van Winkle, he escorted the carriage not only down the hill, but to the top of the next one. Than this it was not possible to go farther, without being guilty of rudeness; and signing the post-boy to drive on, he made a low bow to the ladies and took his leave. The brunette returned his greeting with a bend of her graceful neck and a flash of her beautiful dark eyes, which Frank saw all that night in his dreams and in the short intervals during which he slept.

"Who can they be?" he asked himself for the hundredth time, as he rode home in the darkness. " She's a lady, there can be no question about that, and as she travels post she must belong to some well-to-do people. Perhaps she is one of the Dineleys; they were going in the direction of Dineley Priory."

The Dineleys of Dineley Priory were an old county family, who looked down on all trading and manufacturing people with contempt, and would probably as soon have allowed one of their daughters to marry a groom or a gamekeeper as to mate with a son of Adam Blackthorne.

If she belonged to them she was as far above him as the stars.

"But what does it matter who she is?" said Frank, pursuing his reflections. "As I never saw her before, I shall probably never meet her again. And she may be married already for aught I know. But, by George, what eyes she has - what lips - what a figure! And then, her complexion! That rich olive tint is far before the red and white folks rave so much about. I never saw much in red cheeks myself. Besides they are so confoundedly common. But an oval face, an olive complexion set off with a peach-like bloom, dark eyes and black hair, are as beautiful as they are rare. But what is the use of letting my thoughts ramble on in this way about a girl of whose very name I am ignorant? And perhaps it is as well that it should be so; for if there were no other impediment in the way I have given my word to marry Valérie Basel. I wonder what Valérie is like; she was nothing but a shy, gawky schoolgirl when she went away. I suppose they will have polished her up in London and Paris. She is coming back soon they say, and then I shall have to buckle up to her. Heigho! And I don't care a pin for the poor girl. I hope she is not very plain - well educated and a lady she is sure to be. In any case it would not be right - no, it would not be right. I wonder if the Basels know anything about Lydia Fell. The devil fly away with Lydia Fell. I wish he had done so before she came to Moorwell. No, it would not be right unless - unless I could - "

The conclusion of Frank's meditation was cut short by a neigh from Rip Van Winkle, who, the moment he caught sight of Brandwood Park gates, uttered a neigh of joy and broke into a canter, in which his master permitted him to indulge until he reached the hall door.

At dinner Frank, contrary to his wont, was silent and preoccupied - as if his mind were still busied with the mysterious brunette, or the intrusion into his thoughts of Lydia Fell and Valérie Basel had given him cause for disquiet and damped his usually high spirits. He even forgot, or lacked energy, to tell his father of young Dogget's misadventures; and, pleading fatigue, he betook himself at an unusually early hour to bed.

"What can be the matter with Frank?" said Adam, when his son had gone.

"I suppose he's tired," answered Rachel; "that hunting must be very hard work, I am sure."

"Middling - but then he's generally full of talk when he has been out; and to-night he had hardly a word to say. It's not like him. I hope to goodness he is not going to make a fool of himself again."

"What do you mean, Adam?"

"Make a fool of himself with a lass again, to be sure. When young fellows do make fools of themselves, it is mostly with lasses, I think."

"I hope not; I sincerely hope not. I do trust that his narrow escape from that Lydia Fell will be a warning to him, and that he will never do so any more. But I sometimes ask myself, Adam, if you acted quite right in that matter. Perhaps the girl loved him, after all, and was forced by her brother to take that money and go away. Frank may have done her a wrong."

"Done her a fiddlestick," interrupted Adam. "She would have done us a wrong - would yet without a doubt, if she could make anything by it. She's a good match for her brother. I am right glad they are both of 'em in America; and I'd be better pleased still if they were at Botany Bay. As for Frank, he's soft, ridiculously soft - what some folks call susceptible - and we must get him wed before any more mischief happens. It will, mayhap, not be so readily repaired the next time. It's a good thing that Valérie's coming home."

"It's a strange way of marrying, Adam. Why, they would hardly know one another if they met. I do hope they will be happy, and that she'll make him a good wife."

"Make him a good wife? Of course she will - why should not she? She's a right menseful (modest and well-mannered), clever lass, they tell me."

"Perhaps it's all for the best," sighed the anxious mother, "only if I had been ordered to marry you, Adam, I 'am sure I never should have done."

"You would have taken Bill Nudger out of pure contrariness, I suppose," said Adam with a smile. "But it's different with these French bred young women. They never look at a man till their mothers tell 'em; and then they fall in love with the right chap right off; and are ready to marry him next day."

"Well, all I can say is, that I don't know how they do it. Love comes of liking and respect, and how can a young woman like and respect a man that she's mayhap never seen hut once or twice in all her life?"

"I loved you, Rachel, when I had only seen you once."

"Yes; but it was spontaneous. If you had been told beforehand that you had to do, I question if you would have done."

"I don't think love is as necessary in marriage as some folks fancy."

"You did not say so once, Adam Blackthorne," interrupted his wife with heightened colour. "If you had done I should never have been your wife, and that you know. If these young people have no love for each other it will be a wrong thing to let them marry, and the sin will lie at your door."

"Have I not told you, and Frank too, that they will not be forced? How could I force them? Frank is of age, and can please himself; and Basel loves his child too well to compel her to marry against her inclination. At the same time I have a very strong wish for them to make a match of it - so has Basel. And why should not they? They are quite suited to each other. Who knows? They will happen fall in love with each other at first sight."

"I don't think it's likely, Adam," said his wife pensively. "It would be almost against human nature, and too good to be true. We must go there to-morrow night, I suppose?"

"Of course we must. And that reminds me as I clean forgot to tell Frank. I must tell him in the morning before he sets off for Moorwell."

CHAPTER XXXII.

AT THE CHÂLET.

We are to dine at the Châlet this evening," said Adam to his son next morning, at the early breakfast of which they generally partook together before the departure of one or both of them for Moorwell. "I forgot to mention it last night. You will go of course?"

" I would rather not, if it would make no difference," replied Frank, who seemed little, if any, less preoccupied than he had been overnight; "I don't feel quite up to the mark somehow."

"But it would make a difference," observed the other dryly. "How often must I remind you that we cannot be too civil to the Basels? You seem to forget that we make ten thousand a year out of them. You should consider, too, the ties that are likely to unite our family and theirs, and - "

"Who will be there?" interrupted Frank, who did not seem quite to relish his father's concluding allusion.

"Nobody but ourselves - no other company I mean. It has to be quite a family affair. Here's Mrs. Basel's letter - that's what it means, I suppose, *en famille.?*"

"I suppose it is," said the young man listlessly, as he rose from the table.

"You seem very indifferent, Frank. Have you no curiosity to know how Valérie is, or when she is coming home, or anything about her?"

"All in good time, father," answered Frank, with a forced laugh. "I am in no hurry to get my head into the matrimonial noose, if that is what you mean."

"You don't surely mean as you are going to run off your bargain, Frank," broke in Adam angrily. "You know what you promised me when I got you out of that mess with Lydia Fell?"

"Never fear, father, I shall keep my word. I only meant that I saw no necessity for hurrying in the matter. Valérie and I are not violently in love with each other, nor likely to be; and that being the case, we can both afford to wait a while. At least give us time to make each other's acquaintance."

"By all means," said Adam, checking the angry reply he was about to make, as his conversation with Rachel of the night before occurred to him. "If we

Page 179

are agreed on the main point, you may manage the details in your own way. As you say, there is no hurry; and you should be better acquainted before you buckle to."

There then passed a few remarks on business, and shortly afterwards Frank mounted his hack and rode off to Moorwell.

The Châlet, as the reader has doubtless already surmised, was the residence of the Basels. The name was an after-thought; for though the house possessed some of the characteristics of a châlet, and was decidedly Swiss-looking, it might with more propriety have been described as a château or a villa than by a word which signifies a Swiss farmhouse.

Basel had begun by calling his place Uetliberg, after the Zurich mountain under whose shadow he first saw the light. That his friends and neighbours found the pronunciation of it a stumbling block from the first was a matter of indifference to him. When, however, his work-people began to speak of the place as "Rootlybug," his wife and son were so horrified that they insisted on another name being chosen, and after considerable discussion Uetliberg became "The Châlet" But so far as, the vulgar were concerned, the change came too late; and albeit the fact was carefully concealed from Mrs. Basel, her beautiful house was called by the country folks nine times out of ten "Rootlybug."

Frank, who had been occupied at Moorwell until the last moment, did not arrive at the Châlet until a few minutes after the hour fixed for dinner.

"Have my father and mother come?" he asked of the servant who admitted him.

"Yes, sir; they came twenty minutes since, and are now in the drawing-room with Mr. and Mrs. Basel and the young ladies."

When Frank entered the drawing-room his host and hostess rose to greet him, and for the moment he had eyes for nobody else.

"I think you will find somebody here you did not expect to meet," said Basel, with a smile, after the exchange of salutations, at the same time waving his hand towards a sofa on which were seated two young ladies.

One of those young ladies was Mabel Blackthorne; the other, the lovely brunette whom he had met the night before, and of whom he had since hardly for a moment ceased to think.

Frank stood stock-still, looking little less bewildered than a man who fancies himself in the presence of a ghost might be expected to do.

"Why, he does not know her!" exclaimed Mrs. Basel, with a merry laugh. "Don't you remember Valérie?"

"I did not know - I was not aware - nobody told me - " stammered Frank. And then, remembering that he must be looking very stupid, he pulled himself together, and, approaching Valérie, who had already recovered from the surprise which his appearance had occasioned her, offered her his hand.

"I was little aware when we parted company last night," he said, "that I should so soon have the pleasure of seeing you again. It never occurred to me for an instant that we had ever met before. Why, you are no more like the old Valérie than - "

"You are like the old Frank," she put in, with a merry smile. "If I had recognised you I should certainly have accepted your offer to drive us home. I am sure the post-boy was either tipsy or very stupid, for we were in constant terror - my aunt Frieda and I - after you left us, of being overturned or run away with."

"You and Valérie met last night," exclaimed Mrs. Blackthorne, with great surprise, "and you never told us?"

"So you were the red-coated cavalier who came so gallantly to the rescue of my daughter and sister," said Basel. "We have all been wondering who it could be, and now that we know we must thank you, Mr. Frank, for being so very friendly. And as for Valérie, she has been talking about you all day. I think she took you for a Prince.

Nonsense, papa; I never thought anything of the kind," rejoined Valérie, with a bright blush; "and if I had thought so I should have been very much mistaken, for I am sure he is not the least like a prince. All the same, my aunt and I were very much obliged to Mr. Frank, and so I told him last night"

"It was a very trifling service, Miss Basel, and has already been more than sufficiently acknowledged," replied Frank, who thought Valérie's remark was just a little sharp. "If I had known you were returning so soon, and that you were likely to come alone, I might have suspected who you were."

"Fritz was to have met us in Manchester; but we arrived two days sooner than we expected, and so we had to come on alone; yet I think your father knew that I had come."

"Did you know, father, that Valérie had come, and did not tell me?"

"Well, I cannot deny that I had heard of something of the sort. But when you remember the little interest you have always taken in Valérie you cannot be surprised as I did not think it worth while to tell you of her return."

This was cruel, as calculated policy is apt to he, and Frank closely watched Valérie to see what effect his father's bluntness might produce. But beyond a fleeting glance, that might be construed as bespeaking either reproach or indignation, followed by a slight drooping of eyelids, she made no sign; and before Frank could think what to say, dinner was announced.

"Will you give your arm to my daughter, Frank?" said Basel, as he offered his to Mrs. Blackthorne.

They sat next to each other, between aunt Frieda, who was rather deaf, and spoke next to no English, and Basel, who gave all his attention to Mrs. and Mr. Blackthorne, with the latter of whom he was soon deep in a discussion on business and politics. The two young people were thus almost as favourably situated for intimate conversation as if they had been *en tête-á-tête.*

At first Valérie was very shy; and Frank was sorely puzzled to account for the change that seemed to have come over her. He could hardly believe her to be the same self-possessed beauty whom he had encountered the evening before.

In truth Valerie had two manners and almost two natures. Her mother, a French lady with strictly French notions as to the training of children, had endeavoured to bring her daughter up as a *jeune fille.* But her father, who desired to rear her as maidens are reared in England or Switzerland, had done his best to counteract that design, and there had been many a friendly contention between the husband and wife on the subject. In the end a compromise was made. Valérie was brought up under two systems, both of which had been followed, even in her education. She had been taught by French and English governesses alternately; and after she had spent two years at a French school, her father, by way, as he said, of balancing the account, had insisted on her passing two years in an English school. The result was that she could be an English girl or a *jeune fille* at pleasure. In the one character she was frank, open, and outspoken; in the other reserved, silent, and retiring, answering only in mono-syllables, and never by any chance raising her eyes to look a man in the face.

She was in this mood when Frank found himself sitting next to her at dinner. When he tried to break through her reserve, and engage her in conversation, she looked down on her plate and answered only yea and nay. Nothing he suggested appeared to interest her. At length, almost in despair, he ventured on a bold experiment.

"You heard what my father said just now," he remarked, "that I took no interest in you?"

"Yes, I heard."

"It was rather unkind of him to say so, I think, but it is quite true."

"Indeed."

"And, if you will reflect, my lack of interest was not very unnatural. When you went away we were both very young, and before that time, as I was generally at school, we had seen very little of each other. Then, latterly, they were always talking about you and praising you, until, to tell the truth, I grew just a little tired of - "

"Hearing my praises, I presume. And who were they, may I ask, who were always talking about me?"

"Your father and mother, and my father and mother."

"I am not surprised you found it tiresome. I know I should have found it tiresome if somebody had always been sounding your praises to me."

"I am glad nobody did, then. But do you know, Valérie - may I call you Valérie? - we are old friends, you know, though lately we have been almost strangers."

"By all means. I would not like you to call me Miss Basel."

"Do you know what I think now, Valérie?"

"No. What do you think?"

"What I am sure, rather - that they did not praise you half enough."

"If you are going to talk in that way, Mr. Frank, I am afraid I shall find you as tiresome as you found your father and mother."

"Frank, if you please, Valérie. One good turn deserves another, you know."

"Well, please don't be tiresome, Frank"

"I must tell you the truth, even if it be tiresome. If you knew how I have been thinking about you since last night, and with what delight I found just now that the lady of my dreams was Valérie, you - "

"Then if I had not turned out to be the lady of your dreams, as you call her, you would have still found me tiresome, I suppose"

This was said with a glance of her dark eyes that made Frank's heart stand still for the space of half a minute, and then throb wildly another half minute.

"It is enough for me that you are the lady of my dreams. I decline to consider any other hypothesis."

"You heard my father say that I thought you were a prince in disguise?" remarked Valérie after a short pause. "Yes, I heard."

"Very absurd, was it not?"

"I suppose it was, since you say so," answered Frank rather dubiously; for though not so vain as to suppose he resembled a prince, he felt a great desire to be her prince.

"Do you know why?" she asked, with a playful smile at the young fellow's whiskers - which he happened just then to be rather nervously caressing - as if to signify that she guessed his thoughts.

"Why?" repeated Frank with a blush, for he was rather given to blushing at times.

"Because the only prince I ever saw was old, ugly, and fat, and - "

"A glass of wine with you, old fellow?" said Fritz from the other side of the table.

"Confound him and his wine," muttered Frank as he responded with a very ill grace to his friend's compliment.

Then he turned to Valérie, hoping she would finish her sentence; but destiny had decreed that it never should be finished. Whatever might be the cause - whether it was that the young lady thought she had been going too far, or she had read a fancied reproof in her mother's face (albeit Mrs. Basel was well pleased to see her engaged in a lively conversation with young Blackthorne), she became once more *a jeune fille*, and her answers, as before, were yea and nay.

It was certainly not her intention, but Valérie could not have adopted any more effectual method of piquing Frank's curiosity, and making him wildly in love with her, than this, to him, utterly unaccountable alteration of manner.

After dinner there was no opportunity for further conversation, except in the bearing of others. In the general conversation that ensued Valérie joined with intelligence and spirit, and when she was asked for a Swiss song she gave "Rufst du mein Vaterland" with a fire and pathos that melted her father to tears, and completed the conquest of Frank. Then, at the request of his father, Frank sang "The Fine Old English Gentleman." It was a song of which Adam had latterly grown particularly fond, and his son had. learnt it at his request.

Before they separated it was arranged that on the following day the young people should have a long ride together. The trysting place was the Châlet, where Frank and Mabel were to join Valérie and Fritz.

CHAPTER XXXIII.

CUPID AND DIANA

"Well, Frank, what think you of Valérie?" asked Adam of his son, a few days after the arrival of Miss Basal at the Châlet.

"That she is about the loveliest and most charming girl I ever saw, and as good as she is beautiful,"

"I am glad to hear you say so. I am quite of the same opinion, and your mother also. Would you like me to speak to Basel? It only requires a word, you know."

"I would not have you do so for the world," said Frank, with great earnestness; "not for the world, father."

"God bless me, Frank, what do you mean? I thought from your remark just now that you were almost, if not quite, in love with Valérie."

"Perhaps I am, father. Anyhow, I care so much for her that the last thing I desire is that she should be brought to accept me out of deference to the wish of any third person, even if that person be her own father. If Valérie ever becomes mine, I must win her for myself."

"As you like, lad," said Adam, who saw no reason to be dissatisfied with the turn things were taking.

Save Frank, all the young folks were as yet quite ignorant of their elders' schemes for their happiness. But there was no reason to suppose - at least, so thought the heads of the two families - that either Mabel or Fritz would demur to their wishes in the matter. Mabel, as her father said, was a very sensible girl, who had a shrewd idea of the value of money and the advantage of a good start in life. She had always, moreover, shown herself amenable to advice, and when the benefits likely to accrue from a marriage between herself and young Basel were explained to her, it could not be doubted that she would readily acquiesce in the proposed arrangement. As for Fritz, he had never failed in his duty towards his parents, and there was not the least question, the father assured Adam, that, when told what was expected of him, he would give a willing consent. For the rest, there was sufficient congruity of character and temperament between the two to ensure them a fair chance of happiness. They were not unlike even in personal appearances. Both were rather above middle height. Mabel was of shapely, if rather substantial, build; and Fritz, though somewhat slight, gave promise of developing into a man of girth as well as inches; while as to face neither could be considered as other than good-looking. They seemed, indeed, admirably adapted to each other, and nobody could say that the match would not be an eminently suitable one.

The return of Valérie naturally brought the two families into more frequent contact, and their relations, always friendly, assumed a character of closer intimacy. She and Mabel soon became fast friends, and either at the Châlet or at Brandwood they were together almost every day. Frank saw Valérie almost as often as Mabel saw her; for when his sister went to the Châlet he frequently took her home, and when Valérie came to Brandwood he generally found an excuse, whether Fritz was with her or not, to accompany her either all the way home or as far as the lodge gates.

Then they went out riding together, and, as Valérie seemed very fond of the exercise, Frank one day proposed that she and his sister should go a-hunting. This proposal was accepted with acclamation.

The appearance of Valérie and Mabel in the field caused somewhat of a sensation among the members of the hunt, for it was not often that ladies went out with the Orrington hounds, especially ladies that rode like Valérie, who, when Frank led the way, stopped at nothing. Mabel, being much less of a Diana than her friend, took her horse over a fence only when neither gate nor gap was available. Not that she was afraid of a jump when jumping was unavoidable, but she had no pleasure in it, and was too sensible to ride for display. She generally paired off with Fritz, who would often good-naturedly accompany her instead of riding forward with Valérie and Frank; and when he did not happen to be out there was always some timid, or elderly, or gallant hunter who was only too glad to bear Miss Blackthorne company, and show her the easiest way across country. It thus came to pass that at the close of the last run Valérie frequently found herself separated from her brother, on which occasions Frank, of course, felt it his duty to see her safely home. Sometimes they fell in with Mabel, or Fritz, or the groom, on the way thither, but oftener not, and nothing was more common than for Frank, after hunting, to ride with Valérie to the Châlet and remain for dinner.

All the world of Moorwell and Brandwood, and even Redburn, set them down as lovers long before any word of love had passed the lips of either. Frank's attentions to Valérie were becoming so marked that, had not their betrothal been regarded as a foregone conclusion, Mr. and Mrs. Basel would have considered it their duty to interfere. As it was, they and Mr. Blackthorne deemed it best not to meddle, albeit they were all rather at a loss to understand why Frank was so long in declaring himself; he was generally outspoken enough. They put no obstacle in the way, and there could be little doubt, they thought, that Valérie liked him. But Frank doubted - unless it were that the very excess and fervour of his feelings, or something in his own thoughts, rendered him timid and hesitating. For though the impression which Valérie at their first interview had made upon him had deepened into a passion of singular intensity, and he was greatly favoured by opportunity, several months passed away, and the hunting season was nearly over, before he summoned up courage to tell Valérie of his love, and even then it seemed as if the avowal came rather of sudden impulse than of deliberate resolve. He had been unable to infer from her bearing - satisfactorily to himself - whether she reciprocated his affection or not. Others thought she did; but then others were not aware that, whenever he grew tender, she became reserved; and that her invariable answer to his advances was to put on her *jeune fille* manner. It did not occur to him that this peculiarity was attributable to her French breeding, and afforded no proof that he was indifferent to her, or that she desired to repel his love. A bolder wooer would have seen in this seemingly inexplicable coldness a favourable sign, and pressed his suit with greater vigour than ever. But, as we have seen, Frank at this time was far from being a bold lover.

It was the beginning of March, and the Orrington hounds were out for the last time. There was a large field, and, what is not always the case on such an occasion, they had excellent sport. After several fair runs they found a hare - probably a gentleman hare who had been to see his lady love - that went so far and so straight that the few who were up at the finish were not sorry when they lost him in a plantation on the banks of the Ribble. Such a good hare, if hare it were - for the huntsman said he believed it was a fox - deserved to live. This was the last run of the day, and, as everybody agreed, a very satisfactory wind-up of the season.

They were a long way from home, and as looking or waiting for Fritz and Mabel (who, as usual had been thrown out) was out of the question, Valérie gladly accepted Frank's offer to accompany her to the Châlet.

They had not gone far when Frank perceived that Valerie's horse had cast a couple of shoes, and that It went feelingly, as if it were on the point of falling dead lame.

"That will never do," he said, as he Called Valerie's attention to the circumstance. "Gipsy will be dead lame before we get home if we don't have her put to rights. We must stop at the first forge we come to."

It was not long before they found one - a pleasant country smithery, with the front open to the road. Inside were a pair of brawny smiths and their strikers, hammering and shaping glowing iron into horse-shoes and ploughshares.

Next to the forge was a picturesque whitewashed cottage, with a porch half-hidden with ivy.

"Can you put this lady's horse to rights?" said Frank, riding up to the smithery door. "See, it has lost two shoes."

"Ay, that we can," said the master smith, "and yours too, if you like."

"What, has he cast a shoe too?"

"Ay, that he has, fro' th off hind foot there. Didn't you know?"

"No, indeed, I did not. Yes, you had better shoe him too."

"It'll take us a good part of an hour," continued the smith, "be as sharp as we will. And if the lady would like to sit down i' my house there a bit, or take a walk i' th' garden while the job's done, she is quite welcome, and you too."

"Thank you," said Frank, as he helped Miss Basel to dismount.

Would you like to sit down, Valérie?"

"Thank you; I don't care to sit down. I feel more disposed for a walk. Let us look at the garden."

They found the garden larger than they had expected. It was well kept, and extended to a considerable distance at the back of the cottage. At the end of one of the walks they came on a wicket-gate opening into a field. Frank opened it, and they sauntered down a path which led towards a grove of trees.

The winter had been mild, the day was still and almost warm, and all around them were to be seen premonitory signs of the birth of another spring. The trees were putting forth their buds, the hedgerows were unfolding their leaves, the pastures were pied with violets and daisies, and birds were billing and cooing and building their nests.

"Would you like to sit down now, Valérie?" said Frank, as they reached the grove of trees.

Yes," answered Valérie with an absent air; and she took a seat on a fallen trunk.

Frank leaned against a sycamore hard by and watched her. She hardly seemed conscious of his presence. All day long she had been unusually quiet, and now her preoccupation was so great that she scarcely appeared to notice what was going on about her.

To Frank, as she sat there on the fallen trunk, she had never seemed so beautiful and attractive. Her riding-habit showed off her sylph-like, undulating figure to the best advantage. Her low-crowned, wide-brimmed beaver hat (she could never be persuaded to don the regulation castor), looped up with scarlet cord, harmonised well with her oval features and raven hair. Her white gauntleted hands were laid listlessly on her knee; and her large, dark eyes, with their drooping lashes, were full of a sweet sadness which gave them an inexpressible charm. What were her thoughts? Whence this melancholy? Was its cause bodily fatigue and the reaction from the excitement of the chase, or had it some deeper source? - a hidden anxiety - a tender reminiscence. Could there he another - could there? –

The very idea was madness, and the blood mounted so hotly to Frank's brain that, but for the support of the tree he had fallen to the ground. All was dark, and for a few seconds he felt like a man suddenly bereft of a sense.

The next moment he was standing before Valérie. He laid his hands on her shoulders. She looked up in surprise at his face. What she saw there made her start with fear. His eyes were bloodshot, and fierce with suppressed passion. His lips writhed as if he were suffering from some acute physical pain, and he seemed too agitated to speak.

Then by a violent effort he mastered his emotion, "Valérie," he said hoarsely.

"What is it, Frank? Are you ill?"

"Valérie, do you love?"

"Frank!"

"Valérie," he repeated, "is there anybody you love?"

"What do you mean, Frank? Are you mad?" she exclaimed sharply, as if she resented this strange questioning.

"If I am it is with love for you. I love you, Valérie, with all my heart and soul - love you so much that if you return not my love I believe I shall kill myself. And just now, as I stood there looking at you, it came into my mind that there might be somebody else - that you perhaps preferred another, and the thought made me so wild that I could not control myself. But I am sure I have been very rash. I have frightened you - I who would give my life to save you a sorrow."

She did not speak. It was not needful that she should; for Frank read his fate in her eyes, and took his answer from her yielding lips.

For a few moments their happiness was too deep for words.

"You were not thinking of another, then?" said Frank.

"No, you foolish boy, I was thinking of nobody but you."

"Why, then, did you look so sad?"

"Because I had begun to fear that you did not love me."

"Why?"

"I can scarcely tell - perhaps because you did not tell me."

"And I have been holding back from telling you for fear you might not love me."

"How long have you loved me, Frank?"

"Nearly four months. Ever since I met you that night in the Manchester Road. And you, how long have you loved me, dearest Valérie?"

"Always, I think."

"How always, my Valérie?"

"I mean that years ago, before I went to school, I used to say to myself in my girlish fashion that I should never marry anybody but Frank Blackthorne. All the time I was at school there was not a day I did not think about you. And now, Frank, now - "

And she laid her sweet face on his shoulder, and her eyes looked lovingly into his; and he with gladsome heart pressed his lips to hers and folded her fondly in his arms.

Then she started suddenly backward, bent her head, and covered her face with her hands.

"I am forgetting myself," she exclaimed with a half-sob, "what will you think of me, Frank, and - and what will mamma say?"

"What do I think of you?" said Frank, taking both her hands in his, and kissing away the pearly tears that were trembling on her cheeks. "I think that you are the best, the dearest, the loveliest girl in the world, that you are my fairy, my princess, my queen. Have no anxiety, Valérie, about your mother. Her consent, the consent of your father and of my father and mother, are assured beforehand."

"Papa is always good," she murmured, as if still doubting; "but mamma is sometimes strict. She may think I have not behaved as a *jeune fille* ought - that I should not have allowed you to speak to me until you had first spoken to her."

"Bother a *jeune fille*," exclaimed Frank impetuously. We are in England, and you are an English maiden. So far from your mamma finding fault with you, she will be pleased. I will tell her myself to-night. Have no fear, darling; it is what they have been planning for years."

"What! That you and I - "

"And Fritz and Mabel. But that is a secret you must on no account -- "

"Oh, how charming!" exclaimed Valérie, clapping her hands. "And shall we - do you think - shall we all - ?"

"Be married on the same day? I hope so, Fritz and Mabel being willing."

"I think they will be," said Valérie demurely. Fritz I know likes her, and I am sure she would not be so unkind as to make us all miserable by refusing him."

And thus they talked on under the shadow of the trees, sometimes sitting on the fallen trunk, sometimes walking to and fro hand in hand; talked of themselves, their plans, and their future with all the egoism and confidence of young love. They gave no heed to the fleeting minutes; they did not see even that the sun had gone down behind Longride Fell, nor note that a crescent moon was showing herself above the shoulder of old Pendle. How long - when they were rudely recalled to the realities, as well as the fitness of things - they had wandered in this idyllic trance, they had only the very vaguest idea.

"Listen! What is that?" exclaimed Valérie suddenly.

"It is somebody shouting, I think."

Frank was right. It was the blacksmith shouting, "Mayster, mayster," at the top of his voice.

"We must go," said Frank. "The horses are ready."

"Dear me," said Valérie, "I had no idea they could be shod so quickly."

"I thowt yo' wor lost," observed the blacksmith with a grin, as they neared the forge. "I have been shouting on yo', aw up and down. Th' 'osses has been ready welly an hour. I've gan 'em a pound o' meal and watter apiece. Wor that reyt?

"Quite right," replied Frank. "I am much obliged to you for being so thoughtful. And now the sooner we are off the better. Here, Valérie, let me help you to mount."

"Good neet," said the blacksmith, "and much happiness to yo'."

Valérie blushed, and turned Gipsy's head towards home.

"Here," said Frank, "this is for the shoeing and the meal and water, and this - this is something for you and your mates to drink our healths with. Good-night."

"By gum!" exclaimed the smith, as he looked at his dusty palm, in which glittered a silver crown and a piece of gold. "He desarves to be happy, yon chap does. I'll be dratted if he has not gan me a sovereign. Come on' lads! We'll hav a rare do to-neet at Th' Cow with the Crumpled Horn."

CHAPTER XXXIV.

A MOONLIGHT RIDE.

Let us have a canter," exclaimed Frank. "The horses have had a rest, and the road hereabouts is like a bit of turf."

"With all my heart, dear Frank," answered Valérie with a joyous laugh. "Now, Gipsy."

Gipsy, responding to the Call, put her best foot foremost, and, as if instinctively sympathising with her fair rider, she drew close to Rip Van Winkle, Frank's favourite hunter, and the two steeds cantered gaily homewards, their steps keeping time to the hearts of their riders. They kept so near together that the lovers rode hand-in-hand, and when their horses slackened pace they drew nearer still. And then, when the young moon shed her golden beams through the sylvan screen that bordered the way, they bent over to each other and whispered vows of eternal constancy, and sounds of soft kisses and happy laughter were borne on the balmy air.

It was a glorious ride. The lovers wished nothing better than that it might last for ever. But only too soon the lights of the Châlet loomed in sight, and the clasped hands had to be unloosed, the honeyed whisperings to cease, and earthly things to be thought of once more.

"Will you tell papa to-night, Frank?" asked Valérie, as they rode up the avenue.

"The very moment I see him. It is only right that I should; and I am so very happy that I absolutely must tell somebody."

"I feel the same, but I shall wait until you have told them, and then I shall talk to them all day about you."

"And I shall think all day about you."

By this time they were at the Châlet. Frank took Valérie in his arms and lifted her from her horse.

"At last," exclaimed Mr. Basel, as they entered the hall. "We were afraid something had happened, and were beginning to grow quite uneasy. Fritz has been at home two hours and more."

"Something has happened, my dear sir," said Frank, drawing Mr. Basel aside, while Valérie rapidly disappeared. "Let us go into your room a moment."

"What is it, Frank? Nothing very serious I hope," replied Mr. Basel, pretending not to notice the joy which shone in the young man's face.

It is indeed very serious. Valérie and I love each other."

"Oh, that is all, is it? Come, let us go in to dinner. I am very hungry, and the dinner is spoiling."

This was too exasperating. All the world might have been hungry, and all the dinners in it utterly ruined, for anything Frank cared just then.

"But what am I to understand?" he said. "I thought it my duty to tell you at once, and I hope - "

"It required no telling, my boy," rejoined Basel, with a merry twinkle in his eye.

"Do you mean to say that you knew - that you had seen?"

"Had we seen? *Gotte im Himmel* bless the boy! Does he think we are blind and deaf? Of course we had seen, and it is what we wished, and we are all very glad, and I give you great joy. Will that do for you? And now do let us go to dinner - never mind your hunting coat - the others have begun; they are tired of waiting, and no wonder."

"It is as I said," exclaimed Mr. Basel, in German, as they entered the dining-room. "Frank and Valérie are *verlobt.*"

Then Mrs. Basel, who had been very hungry, and was trying to make up for lost time, rose from her seat, and gave Frank a kiss on each cheek, saying at the same time how delighted she would be to have him for a son-in-law; and Fritz, warmly grasping both his hands, assured him that he had the best wishes of every member of the family, and that he was "the only fellow he knew" whom he considered worthy of becoming his sister's husband.

A few minutes afterwards came in Valérie with rosy cheeks and happy eyes; and she blushed even more deeply, though her eyes shone none the less brightly, when she saw that her chair had been placed next to Frank's. In honour of the occasion Mr. Basel ordered some of the best champagne which his cellar contained, and, speaking in German, as he almost always did when his feelings were touched, he proposed the health of the *Braut* and *Brautigem,* to which Valérie responded by throwing her arms round the old man's neck and half smothering him with kisses, and Frank spoke a few words of suitable acknowledgement.

It was already somewhat late, and soon after dinner Frank was obliged to take his leave; for his mother, who was never very content when he was out hunting, might be uneasy about him; and he wanted to lose no time in telling her and his father of what had come to pass.

Valérie went with him to the door, and saw him off; first exacting a promise that he would come again the next day; and he rode into the darkness with the perfume of more than one kiss on his lips, while a sense of elation such as he had never known before pervaded his whole being.

When Rachel heard the news she was deeply moved - almost more so, it seemed to Frank, than the occasion warranted.

"Oh, Frank, how thankful I am?" she said. "Valérie is a dear good girl. If she does not make you happy it will be your own fault. And it is what your father has wished and looked forward to for years; and it all comes in so well that it seems almost too good to be real. We are indeed abundantly blessed. God has been very good to us."

As for Adam, his satisfaction was unbounded, and just a little boisterous. He ordered punch, and in more than one glass drank to the health of his daughter that was to be. Rachel said he had become a young man again. Frank had never before seen his father in so jovial a mood, and long after his mother had gone to bed, they sat up talking over their plans. For the first time Adam told his son exactly how much he was worth. By the time Frank's son was twenty-one - he was to have one, of course, there could be no question about that - the Brandwood rent-roll, he calculated, would be over twenty thousand a year. If the new railway that was being talked about came that way it would be worth more. The estate was to be settled on Frank and his heirs male, and if he and his father continued in business, and retained their interest in the turkey-red concern (which, now that the Blackthornes and the Basels were to be so closely united, there would be no difficulty about), he might, by the time he reached middle age, be one of the richest men in the county. Wealth would open the door of Parliament to him, and before many years were over Adam might see his son MP for Redburn.

Frank had never before been taken so fully into his father's confidence, and, prompted by gratitude and ambition, he entered heartily into his schemes. Nor had he ever before felt so great an affection for him; for was it not to his father that he owed his present happiness and the brilliant prospects which he had just foreshadowed?

"There, lad," said Adam, clapping his son on the back, just as they were about to separate for the night, wasn't I right? Is not Valérie Basel better than Lydia Fell? If you had married that hussy, you would have ruined yourself for life and broken my heart."

The allusion, though perhaps in the circumstances natural, was unfortunate. The coupling of the two names seemed to Frank almost a desecration. It evoked misgivings and self-reproaches which he would fain - but could not - have suppressed. Was it quite certain, he asked himself, that he had heard the last of Lydia Fell? What would Valérie say if she knew the folly of which he had been guilty?

Thoughts like these kept him long awake, and when at length he slept his rest was disturbed by portentous dreams. He saw Valérie on a cliff by the sea, beckoning to him. He ran to her with all the eagerness of love, but when he tried to embrace her he found himself in the arms of Lydia Fell. He felt as if paralysed in every limb, and while he struggled in vain to free himself from her grasp, she dragged him to the edge of the cliff and plunged with him into the foaming waters beneath.

Then it was his wedding day. All was bright and joyous. Brandwood Hall, and the Châlet, and the Old Factory were gay with bunting. Music was playing, hundreds of voices were shouting his name and Valérie's, and the names of Fritz and Mabel. They were in church, with his father and mother, the Basels, and troops of friends. A strange clergyman performed the marriage ceremony. When it was over Frank raised Valérie's veil; he approached his lips to hers. With a cry of rage and terror he started backward. The face was the face of Lydia. He looked round at the clergyman, and recognised the sardonic and triumphant features of Stephen Fell. He tried to speak, but his lips refused to move, and, awaking with the effort, he found himself trembling in every limb, and thanked God that it was only a dream.

CHAPTER XXXV.

MATRIMONIAL PROJECTS.

THE day after Frank's declaration there was a meeting of the fathers and mothers of the two families; for although matters were taking the course which they had expected and desired, it had become necessary, in view of the present position of things, to discuss several important points of detail that had not yet been considered. Chief among these were the fixing a time for the marriage, and the expediency of informing Fritz and Mabel of the happiness in store for them.

In the discussion which ensued Mrs. Basel took a leading part; for in everything that concerned the welfare of her children her husband almost invariably deferred to her opinion. Yet she was no more a domineering woman than Basel was an exceptionally submissive man. She simply followed the custom of her country, where the equality of the wife with the husband in domestic matters is, perhaps, more generally recognised than elsewhere in Europe, and where, as often as not, she takes something more than a passive interest in his affairs. Mrs. Basel, moreover, was an acute woman of the world, and, albeit she did not meddle with his business arrangements, her husband often paid her the compliment of asking her advice, and he not rarely acted upon it. She had been the first to suggest the union of the two families by the marriage of their children. It would assure, she thought, not alone the domestic happiness, but the material prosperity, of Valérie and Fritz; for the arrangement offered the inestimable advantage that the settlement made on Valérie would be balanced by a settlement of at least equal amount on Mabel; and, Blackthorne being a rich man, his daughter would doubtless receive a considerable accession of fortune at his death.

Nevertheless, the immediate, or, indeed, the speedy, consummation of those plans did not appear to her altogether expedient. Valérie had only just come home after an absence of four years; it would be hard to lose her before she had been with her mother one. And Frank - and the remark applied equally to Fritz - was almost too young to marry, she thought. In France men do not think of marrying until they are thirty, and Mrs. Basel's ideas were essentially French. The force of this objection was, however, rather weakened by the dislike - equally French - which she entertained for long engagements. Altogether, Mrs. Basel did not see her way quite so clearly as she generally did.

Adam Blackthorne, on the other hand, wanted Frank to be settled, as he put it, as soon as possible. He had no fear that he would prove unfaithful to Valérie, or untrue to his promise, or that the Fells could possibly give any further trouble. Still, there was no telling what might happen, and it was best to be on the safe side. Then, the sooner the lad was married, he thought, the sooner would the great scheme to which the marriage was only subsidiary be in course of realisation. Pending that event, Frank would probably give his attention chiefly to courting, and have little mind for anything else. That was only to be expected. Another motive which weighed much with Adam was the approaching expiration of his partnership with Basel; for nothing could be more certain than that the union of their families would greatly facilitate its renewal on the old basis.

When Mrs. Basel said it would be quite soon enough if the young people were married in two or three years, he artfully appealed to the lady's well-known objection to long engagements. When she urged Frank's youth as a reason for delay, he reminded her that, albeit Frenchmen did not often marry until they were thirty or thirty-five, French girls generally became wives before they were twenty, and if they waited until Frank was old enough Valérie would be too old. And Frank would not wait, he was sure he would not; he was that headstrong and hot in love, said Adam, that if they did not consent to an early marriage he would be carrying Valérie off and getting the knot tied at Gretna Green.

At this suggestion Mrs. Basel, holding up her hands in horror, declared that it was quite impossible for any properly brought-up girl to be guilty of so great an enormity.

Nevertheless, the argument had its weight, and after many *pros* and *cons* it was agreed that the marriages should take place in the following year – marriages, because Mrs. Basel expressed a rather decided wish that both her children should be married on the same day.

Adam would have stipulated for an earlier day, but Mrs. Basel said it was quite out of the question. If the two couples were to be married at the same time, two houses would have to be built, or found, and furnished, to say nothing of other preparations; and she felt quite certain that for all these things ten or twelve months would be quite little enough.

This was also Mrs. Blackthorne's opinion. "I do not think we can marry them before next year, Adam - about February or March," she said. "Where would you put them? There are no houses ready."

"Let them live with us. We have room for a dozen families."

But this proposition was voted down by an overwhelming majority, and Adam had to give way.

"How about Fritz and Mabel? " inquired somebody. "Who will tell them?"

"I will tell Fritz," observed Mrs. Basel. "He is a good boy, and will do what I want him."

"Will you tell Mabel, or shall I?" asked Adam of his wife.

"Don't you think Fritz had better tell her himself?" rejoined Rachel. "She is both docile and sensible, and I do not think you need fear any difficulty with her; yet, whatever may be the case with French girls, English maidens expect to be wooed - even the most matter-of-fact of them - just a little. Perhaps Valérie or Frank might give her a little inkling of what is going on, but the proposal should certainly come from Fritz himself."

"You ought to know best, Mrs. Blackthorne," replied Mrs. Basel, "but in France we arrange these matters differently; and I am sure our way is best."

Naturally," said her husband with a smile; "but, being in England, we must necessarily conform ourselves to English customs."

"It is true, Hermann. All the same, one must admit that English ideas are very loose. It is far too easy in this country for young people to marry themselves. The parents, they count for nothing. They may go from home for three weeks - for a month - and when they come back they may find that their daughter has run away with the master of music, and that their son has married himself to the cook."

"You are right Mrs. Basel," said Adam, whom this remark reminded of the narrow escape of his son from the wiles of Lydia Fell. "It should not be possible for lads and lasses to marry without the consent of their parents; and I should be glad to see the law altered. But we must take things as they are, you know; and, seeing how easy it is for young folks to make imprudent matches, the best thing is to marry them well before they do worse."

"Ah, I see what you mean, Mr. Blackthorne. You bring another reason for hastening the marriage of our children, and I must admit that it is a very good one. But next year will soon be here. Frank and Valérie are already betrothed, and Mabel and Fritz soon will be. They will not make any stupidities in that time, I think. At any rate, I can answer for my children."

"I am not quite sure about that," muttered Adam, who was never quite satisfied unless he got his own way in everything. "There is many a slip between the cup and the lip, you know."

When Adam returned to his office he found his son there, and told him what had been decided. Frank, without making any remark, took from his pocket a newspaper.

"Read that," he said, pointing to a marked passage. The paper was an *Albany Tomahawk* of rather ancient date, and the indicated paragraph gave an account of an accident on the Hudson near Albany. A small boat had been run down by a steamer, and of the six persons contained in it three were drowned. One of them was Miss Lydia Fell, "from Redburn, Lancashire," added the report.

"Well," said Adam, handing the paper back to his son, "are you sorry?"

""No" replied Frank, gravely. "I suppose one ought not to rejoice over anybody's death, yet I cannot truly say that I grieve for Lydia Fell. But it is very strange."

"If she had only got herself drowned a bit sooner," muttered his father, "it would have saved me two thousand pounds and a deal of trouble"

CHAPTER XXXVI

FRITZ'S WOOING.

Fritz and Mabel behaved with all the propriety that was expected of them.

Though neither had ever thought seriously of matrimony, it had probably occurred to both of them that there might be a certain fitness in a double union of the two families.

"I am willing," said Fritz, when his mother had told him his fate. "I rather like Mabel; she is not a bad sort, and then she will have a nice *dot,* and you and father want it; and Valérie and Frank will be pleased, and it will be rather jolly for us all to be turned off at the same time. Taking it altogether, mother, I do not think I could do better. Does Mabel know?"

"No; you will have to tell her yourself."

"That's rather awkward, isn't it?" said Fritz, with a look of dismay. "I never did anything of the sort before, you know. Could not you speak to her for me, mother - some day when she comes here, you know?"

"It is not my place, Fritz. It would not be *comme il faut* for a mother to ask a young lady to marry herself to her son. In my opinion it is Mabel's own mother who ought to regulate the affair; but she would not hear of it. As you say, it is very awkward; but what can we do? It is one of their absurd English customs for the *prétendent* to propose to his *future* in person. I am afraid you will have to speak to *la bell* Mabel yourself."

"Could not a fellow write? Yes, by Jove, I'll write."

"That, I imagine, would not be *comme il faut* either. If Mabel lived at a distance, you could, perhaps, do so; but when you see the young lady several times a week, such a proceeding might be attributed to *mauvaise honte,* and would make you look foolish."

"You are right, mother, as you always are. But what ought One to say - what is the right thing? You know I never - "

"I am quite aware, my son, that you never before offered yourself to a lady - at least, I hope you never did. It is not the habit, even in England, I believe, for men to propose more than two or three times in the course of their lives - and you are yet very young. As for me, I regret that I cannot give you much help. I am not experienced in English ways of love. I was bred in another school. My mamma told me one day that Hermann Basel desired to make me his wife. I said, 'Yes mamma." When he came to see me, he said he hoped to make my happiness, and I said I hoped to make his happiness. Then he kissed my hand. A month later we were married; and until we were married we were never alone together for one moment. But what would you? We have made each other's happiness, and that, after all, is everything. They manage things differently here, and I cannot tell you what you should say to Mabel. Ask Frank. He would not let anybody speak to Valérie but himself. He will give you a lesson. And then, are there not novels? And these English novels are so *convenable*, so highly moral, often, indeed, of an exemplary piety, and the characters of them are almost invariably *comme il faut.* You will find in most of them how a gallant young gentleman proposes to a peerless young lady, and how they make each other's happiness for all their lives."

"Thank you, mother," exclaimed Fritz, apparently much relieved. "It is a splendid idea. I will do as you say - I will consult Frank, and I will read some novels."

Frank did not help him much, however.

"Tell her you love her," he said, when his friend had stated the case to him," that's all you have to do."

"Exactly. But how would you advise me to put it? I cannot go to Mabel and say to her, *a propos* of nothing at all, 'I love you.' That would be too – what do you call it – too matter-of-fact you know. It is a thing that must be done delicately, and with just a touch of romance, you know. How did you propose to Valérie?"

"Really, Fritz, I cannot tell you. There are some, things men cannot tell, even if they would, and this is one of them. It happened: that is all I can say."

So Fritz was thrown back on his novels, and after studying the most sentimental he could meet with, he found a form of proposal which, with a few slight alterations he thought would answer his purpose admirably, It began, "Adorable Mabel, loadstar of my life, fairest of women," and ended, "the devotion of a heart wholly yours should not go unrewarded; deign; dearest, to become the sharer of my existence, and make me the happiest of men."

This he wrote out and committed to memory, resolving on the first opportunity to repeat it with appropriate action to the loadstar of his life.

The opportunity soon came. Frank and Valérie, and Mabel and he, went one evening for a stroll in Brandwood Park. As was natural in the circumstances, the lovers lagged behind, and Fritz and Mabel were left to themselves. "Now's the time," thought Fritz, as they reached a shady path where they were well hidden from view.

"Mabel!" he said.

"Yes, Fritz!" replied the young lady quietly.

Then there was a pause; for, though Fritz was not much given to nervousness, and there was no particular reason why he should be nervous, he felt that his beautiful speech was slipping from his memory. However, he began:

"Adorable Mabel, loadstar of my life - loadstar of my life - adorable Mabel – loadstar loadstar - loadstar of - loadstar of my life -. Hang it Mabel, will you marry a fellow? - that's what I want to say."

"If I do marry anyone, I suppose it will be a fellow!" said Mabel, with a smile. "Had you any particular fellow in your mind, Fritz?"

"Don't chaff a fellow, Mabel. It's too serious. Will you marry ME? Now, is that plain?"

"It does not leave much room for misunderstanding, I think, if that is what you mean."

"But will you, Mabel? They all want us to marry, you know - your father and mother, and my father and mother, and everybody else."

"Well, as they all want it, and everybody else, I suppose I must say - yes. I shall have to marry sometime, I presume, and I may as well marry you as any other body."

"Exactly; that is what I thought myself. And I am very fond of you, Mabel; we always did like each other, you know."

Saying which he kissed her, and the young lady received his salute with as much self-possession as she had heard his declaration.

Then they wandered away in search of Valérie and Frank, whom they shortly succeeded in finding. As both had been aware of what was coming, Valérie, indeed, having given Mabel a hint thereof - there was not much room for surprise. Congratulations were, of course, offered; and Valérie seemed beyond measure delighted with the turn things were taking.

"I am so glad," she remarked to Mabel; "we shall be doubly sisters now. Fritz is not very clever, perhaps, but he is as good as gold, and I am sure he will make you happy."

"I don't care much about your very clever men, Valérie; give me plain common sense. Yes, I daresay we shall pull pretty well together. I know what I am about, and Fritz will do what he is told, I think."

Page 203

The young people having now consented to all their elders' requirements, it remained only for the latter to make certain pecuniary arrangements and provide them with suitable habitations, in order that their great scheme for the union of the two families might be consummated. As these arrangements, especially the building part of them, could not be carried out in much less than a twelve-month, it was decided to wait till the end of the year, before fixing a day for the double event, which, however, it was generally understood should come off early in the following spring.

Meanwhile, the affianced couples were allowed to have their fling. No restraint was placed on their enjoyment. When Valérie and Fritz were not at Brandwood, Mabel and Frank were at the Châlet. They went out riding together several times a week. There were excursions to Whalley, Whitewell, to Blackpool, and to Bolton Abbey. They took carriages, and drove to Leamington, Mrs. Basel acting as chaperon. The Châlet gave a ball and Brandwood a garden party, and all went merry as a marriage bell.

It was not very good for business, perhaps, all this gaiety and gadding about. Nevertheless, Adam made no complaint. The young folks were taking a brief holiday, he thought, which, as his plans were prospering, he could well afford to let them enjoy. Serious work would come soon enough.

"Frank!" he would say, with a laugh, when people wanted to see his son, "Frank is off. He'll happen be back to-morrow or the day after, but I am not quite sure. He's very throng just now, Frank is. This house as I'm building for him will be finished soon, and he'll maybe then have less to look after, and more time for business. If he gets his bird in a cage, she'll not want so much watching, you know."

CHAPTER XXXVII

AN EVENING AT HOME.

The room at Brandwood Hall which its master liked best and most generally used was the morning-room. It was smaller and more homely than the drawing and the dining-rooms, or the library. He felt more at his ease there, and it had the additional advantage of opening directly into the back garden, through which he could pass unperceived by the servants, into any part of the grounds, or gain access to the stables. In this room he generally received his more intimate friends, and passed much of his time with Rachel when they had no company. There was a great easy-chair on each side of the fireplace, and a rocking-chair for Mrs. Blackthorne. There were nearly always two or three long pipes on the mantelpiece, and the cupboard at the right-hand corner contained an ample store of wine and spirits.

A few months after the events related in the last chapter - to be precise, in the January following - about five o'clock in the afternoon, Adam was sitting in this room, his companions being his wife and Mr. Hartwell.

The minister, who was now considerably past three-score and ten, had a few years before given up the pastorate of Moorside Chapel, albeit he still preached occasionally. He possessed a trifling income of his own, which, with an annuity allowed him by Mr. Blackthorne, made him about a hundred and twenty pounds a year-amply sufficient for his modest wants.

"You spoke a good word for me to Nanny Cooper when I was courting Rachel," said Adam when he proposed this arrangement, "and I have never forgotten it. One way and another my marriage has been the making of me; and now, when you are old and past work, and I have plenty, it is only right that I should do something towards making your declining years easy."

The Blackthornes had long since ceased attending, except occasionally, Orrington Chapel. They went generally to Moorside, where, with the help of Nanny Cooper's bequest and a lift from the family, a handsome new meeting house had been built; and of late they had gone very frequently to Clayland's Church, where Brandwood Hall possessed several pews, and the advowson of which had passed to Adam with the property. In these circumstances Adam felt that he could not do less than show a friendly feeling by appearing occasionally at church, particularly as Mr. Allthings, the rector, was a pleasant spoken gentleman - neither high in doctrine nor intolerant in practice - and withal a very fair preacher. He liked a pipe, too; could drink a glass of whisky - sometimes two or three - and was always a welcome visitor at the hall. Rachel thought him too worldly for a minister of the gospel.

"Well, he happen is," observed Adam one day, when his wife expressed this opinion. "But what can you expect better in a church person? That's the way they are brought up. Yet there's many a worse chap than Timothy Allthings."

Increased prosperity, in fact, was relaxing the rigour of Adam's Nonconformist principles; and if he had told the truth he would probably have confessed that he looked upon it as being only in accordance with the fitness of things that a man of his position and means should occasionally be seen at his parish church. He encouraged Frank to go too; for it was well that a young fellow with parliamentary aspirations should cultivate betimes the good opinion of his neighbours; and as Mr. Allthings possessed many friends and some influence at Redburn, his friendship might be valuable. Adam had indeed begun latterly to think that it might not be amiss if his son were to go over to the Church, bag and baggage; but this idea he had not as yet ventured to broach to his wife, who, though much less strict than she had been in her early days, was still a sincere Baptist and a regular attendant at Moorside Chapel. Rachel had a strong feeling that, as a family, they were far too worldly, and, to use her own expression, lamentably careless about better things. She sometimes dropped hints to this effect to her husband, but they fell on barren ground, and were no more heeded than if they had been spoken to the air; for Adam had hardly a thought that was not connected with his business or his ambition. So far as concerned her own conduct, it was as gentle and Christian-like as it had ever been. Her kindness to the poor, especially to the poor among the mill hands, was unbounded, and now that she had the means her benefactions were large almost to lavishness. Adam sometimes winced a little under the calls she made upon his purse for charitable purposes, but he consoled himself with the reflection that the outlay was rather in the nature of an investment than of an addition to his regular expenditure. It gave him a sort of reflected popularity with his hands, of which he had decided need; and it might, he thought, make things pleasanter for him in the next world; for, not-withstanding his constant endeavour to lay up treasure on earth, Adam had always the intention of making some sort of provision in heaven - when he could spare the time. Meanwhile his wife's charities, in which he considered he had, at least a joint interest, were so much to the good; for good works, he had been told, were as necessary to salvation as faith itself. He had been told, too, that the good deeds of unregenerate persons were counted as evil - a doctrine, however, which seemed to him to be equally repugnant to reason and unwarranted by Scripture, and one that a plain man might well refuse to accept without damage to his orthodoxy. In this opinion he was upheld by Mr. Allthings, who was very clever at making clear the dark things of theology, and whose views had a happy knack of tallying with those of persons whom it was his interest to humour or his pleasure to gratify.

"Building's a bother," said Adam, who had just come in from the park, as he took a pipe from the mantelpiece. "I don't care how soon this job is over. You are well off, Mr. Hartwell, in being out of bricks and mortar."

"I have no doubt I am, Master Blackthorne; yet methinks there are some of your neighbours who would have no objection to exchange places with you."

"Ah! ah! you have me there. They would take the bother if they might have the property, I suppose you mean. Well, folks may think what they like, but property does give a vast deal of trouble. I sometimes wish we were back at Walloper Hillock - eh, Rachel?"

"I wish it often, Adam. Those were our happiest days."

"It is a wish very easy of realisation," observed the minister with a smile. "Walloper Hillock belongs to you yet, I believe?"

"Nay, nay, Mr. Hartwell; it would not be so easily realised as you think. We could go back to th' Hillock, true enough; but we could not get back our youth, make our children young again, and restore to life them as is dead and gone, any more than we could lay aside our present habits and give up what we are looking forward to. I should have to give up estate and factories, and Rachel would have to give up her poor and stop her subscriptions; and I don't think she would like that. We are like to grumble a bit sometimes - it is an Englishman's privilege you know - but I think we are best as we are. We will not go backwards road if we can help it"

"Perhaps you are right, Master Blackthorne. Wealth is a great privilege, and, rightly used, may be the means of effecting great good. When do you expect Master Frank's house to be ready?"

"He's to be wed in March – 15th isn't it, Rachel? Yes, the 15th - and it should be ready then, or soon after, but it's not shaping for being just now. Nearly all the joiners are off drinking this week, and the plasterers were on the spree half last week. Since Christmas they have done next to nothing. I never saw such a lot of thirsty beggars in my life - never."

"I hope you'll have it dry for them, Adam," interposed Rachel anxiously. " do not think Valérie is very strong.”

"I am doing my best. We have made a deep drain all round; the cellars are big enough for a barracks, and fires are burning all day in every room. It's costing a bonny penny in coals alone, it is that. However if it is not quite ready for 'em to go into when they come back from their honeymoon they can live with us a bit. We have plenty of room.”

"It was a happy idea of yours, Master Blackthorne, to build a house for your son in the park," observed Mr. Hartwell. "It will be a great convenience, as well as a great pleasure, to have him and his wife near you."

"So it will, Mr. Hartwell; and it will be convenient in another way. When I'm gone, you know, Rachel can live there and let th' young folks come here. They'll be a houseful by that time, I reckon."

"Oh, Adam, don't talk in that way. I could never bide in that house all by myself. Besides, how do you know that you will be the first to go? You are not much older than I am, and the young are sometimes called before the old -- "

"Eh! what's that?" interrupted Adam.

"It sounds like a horse galloping in the coach-road," said Rachel.

"So it is; but whose is it?"

"Frank's, maybe."

"Nay; Frank took Rip Van Winkle this morning. There's been no hunting these ten days or more, and he said it would do the horse good to stretch his legs a bit; but he is not the lad to gallop his best hunter on a limestone road in a frost like this."

"Somebody's groom, perhaps."

"If a groom of mine galloped a horse in that way, he should go the next minute, whoever it was - unless it was a case of life and death. I'll ring and ask who it is."

A servant in livery answered the summons.

"Go and ask what horse it is that's just galloped up the coach-road, and seems to have gone round to the stable," ordered his master.

The man had hardly been gone a minute when he reappeared.

"If you please, Mr. Blackthorne, Yorkshire Joe is here and would like to speak to you," he said.

"Let Yorkshire Joe come in," was the prompt answer.

"What can it be I wonder?" remarked Adam, turning to his wife. "If it's an errand, I think Frank might have sent some one easier spared than Joe. But here he comes; we shall soon know what it is."

CHAPTER XXXVIII

YORKSHIRE JOE BRINGS BAD NEWS.

Joe's appearance, as he entered the room, made all its inmates start with surprise.

His face, save where darkened with soot and grime, was deadly pale; his clothes were wet torn, and dirty; his hands blood-stained; and, albeit the day was cold, his rugged throat was bare and his hairy breast uncovered.

Adam's first idea was that Joe had been drinking.

"What is it, Joe?" he asked sharply.

I've browt yo' bad news, mayster," said the man in a husky voice, and then he hesitated.

"Well, out with it," urged his master; anxiously, yet not unkindly, for there was no drunkenness in Joe's manner.

"Th' Owd Factory's bornt down."

"Oh, Adam!" exclaimed Rachel "what a terrible misfortune!"

"Don't fret Rachel, if that is all" rejoined Adam, calmly, though it was quite evident he felt the blow keenly. "It might have been worse; it's well insured. I don't think there will be any loss except what comes of the stoppage."

"But it is not all; there is something else," said Rachel, fearfully. "Look at Joe."

Adam, following the direction of his wife's glance, saw that the grime on the poor fellow's cheeks was furrowed with tears, and then he knew that some grave misfortune had befallen; for it was no light thing that could make Yorkshire Joe weep.

"You have not told all, Joe," he exclaimed. "What is it? - has somebody been burnt or? - "

Joe tried to speak, but a lump seemed to stick in his throat, and after a few inarticulate words he quite broke down.

"Sit down, Joe," said Adam, struggling to control his impatience, "and tell us quietly how it all happened. We shall come to it best in that way, I think."

Joe sat down, and mastering his emotion by a strong effort, proceeded to tell his sorrowful tale.

"I wor down at th' gashouse this afternoon, a bit afore bagging time (four o'clock)," he said, "stirring my fires up, and seeing as aw' were reyt for lighting up, when little Jem - Pee o' Dickey's lad - coom running in. 'Joe, Joe,' he says, 'th' Owd Factory's afire.' That's aw' as he said, but it wor quite enough. I run up to th' factory as fast as my legs could carry me. Afore I geet theer I could see smook rowling through th' middle room window; and th' hands wor that feared as they had run out without their jackets and waistcoats, cowd as it wor, and most o' th' lasses wor i' their barefoot feet They said as th' big spor wheels i' th' middle room begun stricking fire, and then as th' sparks set th' fluff on th' gaspipes in a blaze. Then th' rovings geet afire, and in a two thry minutes aw' th' room wor in a blaze. It couldn't miss, for every bit of woodwork i' th' hoyle wor as dry as shavings, and chokeful o' grease. Well, when I seed what wor up I run reyt to th' fire engine place, and towd some o' th' chaps to go to th' lodge, and break th' ice in, so as we could get watter. Just then yo're Frank coom up and took th' ordering, and gradely well he did it. It wor plain fro' th' fost (first) as there wor very little chance o' saving th' Owd Factory, but we dud wer best; and Frank sent to Mr. Basel for printers' blankets, and ordered 'em to be damped and put on th' tother buildings to keep sparks fro' setting them afire too.

"We had just gotten th' engine to work and wor sending a good heyd o' water in th' middle room, when I yerd a gret shout and everybody pointed to one o' th' top room windows. It wor one o' th' lasses as had not gotten out and now as th' staircase wor aw in a blaze there seemed very little chance o' saving her. Hoo wor crying and wringing her hands and begging on 'em to save her.

" 'It's Fair Alice,' somebody said; and then a woman coom rushing out o' th' crowd - for welly aw th' hands wor theer.

"It wor Fair Alice's mother.

"'It's my child,' hoo skryked (screamed); 'it's Alice. Oh, save her! Will nobody save my little lass? Hoo's th' only child as I have, and hoo's nobbut twelve year owd. Oh, Mr. Frank, Mr. Frank, save my child! Hoo wor allus a favourite o' yours.'

"'Make yourself easy,' says Frank; "we'll save her. Here, Joe, you and Ned o' Daniels and Pee o' Dickey's, fetch the long ladder as sharp as you can."

"I' less than five minutes we'd fetched it and reared it forenenst the window wheer th' lass wor standing, shryking and wringing her hands. There wor no time to loise, for smoke wor rowling out o' th' windows and corling through th' staves o' th' ladder.

"Now,' says Frank, 'which of you chaps will go up for her?"

"Nobody answered."

"Then I com forrud and said as I'd go up.

"No, no, Joe," says Mr, Frank, "this is not a job for men with families. Well, if none of th' young fellows will go up I'll go myself. I won't ask a man to do a thing I'm afraid of doing myself."

"I tried to stop him, but it wor no use; and the next minute he wor running up th' ladder like a lampleeter – a rope o'er his shoulder and an axe in his hand. When he got to the top he motioned Fair Alice to stand back, and wi' two or three blows of his axe smashed the window frame in. Then he gets inside and fastens th' rope round th' lass's body, just under her armhoiles.

"Stand under with a sheet," he shouts, 'in case the rope is too short."

"And then he lowers away.

"It wor lucky for Alice as he'd thought about a sheet; for hoo'd hardly getten past th' middle room window when flames brast out fro' one end o' th' factory to th' tother; th' rope bornt like papper, and Alice dropped into th' sheet like a stone.

'Then it wor time for Frank to look to hissel'.

But just as he war baun (going) to put his foot on top stave o' th' ladder a great lick o' flame shot out of the middle room window and lapped round it like a fiery serpent. No mon could pass through that fire and live; and he hadn't even that chance long, for i' less nor three minutes th' ladder broke reyt in two, and coom crashing to th' ground. A gret puff o' smook flared fro' th' window where Frank wor standing, and when it cleared away - "

"What then, Joe?"

"Oh, Joe, what then?"

"He wor no moor to be sin," said Joe solemnly, after a long pause.

"But you searched, Joe - you fetched another ladder - you got ropes – you "

It was Adam who spoke; Rachel sat with white face and wide-open eyes, like one turned into stone, never uttering a word. She had read Frank's fate in Joe's face before even he began his story.

"It worn't possible, mayster. Two minutes after all wor in a blaze. In quarter of an hour th' roof fell in, and there wor nowt left o' th' Owd Factory but tottering walls and reeking ruins."

Then followed a deep silence, broken only by the ticking of the mantelpiece clock and the wail of the rising wind as it twisted about the gables and soughed among the trees in the avenue.

Rachel seemed past speaking. Mr. Hartwell felt that the time had not yet come for him to offer consolation. Words at such a moment had been a mockery. And Adam was asking himself if what he had just heard could be true - if he really never should see his boy again - if it were not all an ugly dream or a waking illusion.

"Is it not all a lie you have been telling me?" he exclaimed suddenly, turning fiercely to Joe. "By G -, if it be, I'll - "

"The Lord above us forbid, mayster. I should desarve hanging if it wor."

"I don't believe it, Joe - I don't believe it. Th' Old Factory is burnt down, I daresay - that's nowt. But Frank is not killed - that cannot be. They'll find him - he's somewhere about. When they pull away the stones they'll find him. I'll go and see to it myself. Tell Kenyon to bring the carriage round first thing, Joe, and help him to put th' horses in."

Joe, without answering, left the room.

"I'll go too, Adam," said Rachel, rising from her chair.

"You'd better stop here; you can do no good yonder; and I daressay Mr. Hartwell will stop with you.

"I will go, Adam; and if you won't let me go with you I shall walk."

"Very well. Will you go too, Mr. Hartwell?"

"If you think I call be of use - if I can do any good."

"Ay, come. It will happen be a bit of comfort to Rachel to have you with us."

"Do the Basels know?" asked Adam of Joe, as they stepped out of the house to enter the carriage.

"They cannot miss. All th' country-side knows by this time. And I yerd somebody say as both th' owd chap and Fritz wor there, but I did not see 'em mysel'."

"Get on the box, Joe; and, Kenyon, drive as fast as you can."

The horses flew over the frosty road, and in less than half an hour Adam, looking in the direction of Moorwell, could see a thick cloud of smoke rising towards the stars.

"That poor girl, that poor girl! Poor Valérie!" murmured Rachel, as they passed the Châlet.

Nearly all the work-people were gathered before the factory gates. They made way respectfully for the carriage.

"It's th' owd mayster and th' missis. God help 'em," they said to each other in hushed voices.

Adam alighted; Rachel took his arm, and they went towards what was once the Old Factory, Mr. Hartwell following them.

It was a weird scene.

The four floors had all fallen in, the roof with them. Two of the walls had collapsed, and from the inner side of the two left standing projected broken beams of timber, some blackened with fire, others still glowing. Below was a mass of broken ruins - a conglomerate of stones, slates, huge wheels, twisted shafts, and shattered machinery. This was all that was left of the Old Factory.

The fire engine was still playing on the wreck.

Adam spoke a few words to one of his principal men, who seemed to be directing the operations for the complete extinction of the fire. For if a high wind arose, of which there were signs, the sparks from the yet incandescent ruins might cause a conflagration in one of the other mills.

The man shook his head.

"I am afraid there is no possibility of that, sir," he said; "but as soon as the stones and things have cooled a bit we can set a gang of men to work to sift 'em; and if we don't find him we shall maybe find summut as belonged to him."

Adam groaned. The sight of the wreck cut him to the heart, and he was beginning to realise for the first time that Frank was indeed no more.

Just then a distracted-looking woman rushed up to them. Her shawl was thrown back from her head, and her eyes were streaming with tears.

It was Fair Alice's mother.

"Oh, mayster and missis, is not this terrible? Th' young mayster is gone dead, and aw' along o' me. I asked him to save my Alice - nobody else would face the fire - but I did not think as I wor asking him for his life - I didn't know. And now th' child's welly (nearly) crazy. Hoo says as hoo'd liefer ha' deed for him than as he should ha' deed for hor. For he wor allus good to hor - he wor good to us aw' - and Alice liked him reyt weel. Oh, missis! what must yo' feel, what must yo' feel! Yo're only lad, and him just gooin' to be wed! And Miss Basel - what must hoo feel! Poor lass! Poor mother! God help yo' both!"

For the first time since this terrible stroke had fallen on her Rachel wept.

"It is not your fault, poor woman," she cried. "It is the Lord's doing. It is God who has spared your child and taken ours. Oh, Adam, we have been too worldly! We have been too much lifted up, and have not given Him the glory. And now we are punished, and our lives are darkened for ever. Oh, my son, my son, would that I had died for thee!"

"Will you take her home, Mr. Hartwell?" said Adam in a broken voice. I don't mean to stir away from here until we have either found our poor lad or some trace of him."

As the minister led the stricken lady away, Adam turned to Fair Alice's mother.

"Curse you" he said through his set teeth. "I wish your child had never been born."

CHAPTER XXXIX.

AFTER THE FIRE.

"To the Châlet" was the order given to the coachman by Mr. Hartwell at Mr. Blackthorne's request.

"I must say a word of comfort to that poor child if I can," remarked the latter. "But what can I say - what can I say? It's a judgement, a terrible judgement - don't you think it is, Mr. Hartwell, - to punish us for our worldliness. I have felt it for a long time. I have felt that we were forgetting Him, and I have been weak and sinful. I should have protested; I should have set myself more against the worldly ways we have fallen into. And now I am punished - I am rightly punished. God help me!"

"Do not say so, Mistress Blackthorne. God's dispensations are sometimes dark, but He is always a just God and a merciful. He does not punish the innocent for the sins of the guilty, neither does He punish vindictively. You, at least, have not been worldly, and you have made a noble use of the wealth with which Heaven has blessed you; for wealth, albeit sometimes a danger and a temptation, is nevertheless a great blessing. And why should the Almighty, who, if His rule be not based on justice, is not worthy of our worship, punish you and this poor young lady whom we are going to see, and your son, for sins that neither they nor you committed? Rather think that those whom God loveth He chasteneth, and that for some mysterious reason, which one day may be revealed to us, it was better for your son - better for you and his father even, and for Miss Basel - that he should die young; and we, my dear Mistress Blackthorne, we who believe in the immortality of the soul have the ineffable consolation of knowing that they who die in the Lord, are not dead, but gone before.

"Oh, but I'm afraid, Mr. Hartwell, that poor Frank was very worldly. Many's the time I have spoken to him, but could never get him to think of better things. If I could only be sure - if I could only think that he was in a state of grace - oh, what a relief it would be! Do you think he was, Mr. Hartwell?"

"It is not given to one poor erring mortal to read the heart of a fellow-man, Mistress Blackthorne. I knew little of your son's theological opinions; perhaps, like most young people, he had thought little about such things. But this we do know, that he died a noble death. He sacrificed his life in saving that of another; and I do most truly believe that he who perishes in the performance of a deed of unselfish devotion dies in a state of grace, let his creed be what it may. God has taken Frank to Himself, Mistress Blackthorne, and he awaits you up yonder in the land of the blessed."

Rachel pressed the minister's hand. She was too full for words.

They found Mrs. Basel full of demonstrative grief. She was an excitable woman, and the shock of the calamity had made her almost hysterical. In appearance, at least, her emotion was greater than that of Mrs. Blackthorne, and she threw her arms round the latter's neck in an agony of convulsive sorrow.

"This is terrible," she exclaimed, "terrible! Whatever shall we do? I never knew of such a thing in my life - such a terrible calamity. And only to think that their house is nearly finished, and the *corbeille de mariage* only arrived this morning."

"I have called to see Valérie," said Rachel, whom these allusions did not help much to console, as she disengaged herself from her friend's embrace.

"She is in her room. I will take you to her. I cannot tell what to make of her," continued Mrs. Basel in a low voice, as they went upstairs. "She neither weeps nor speaks. Perhaps seeing you may make her shed some tears."

Valérie was sitting in a low chair before her dressing-room fire. She had on a white *peignoir,* and her black hair hung loosely about her shoulders. Her face, save for a little hectic spot on each cheek, was colourless. Her dark eyes were tearless, and her general expression was one rather of defiance than of sorrow.

"Dear Mrs. Blackthorne," she said, rising to greet Rachel as the latter entered the room. "I know why you are here. You have come to tell me that Frank is dead; and you want to console me. If he were dead I should require no consolation, for I should die too. But he is not dead. I know he is not dead - he cannot be dead."

"But, my poor Valérie - "

"I know what you would say. My father, and my mother, and Fritz have said it already. You would say that there is no hope - that my Frank is gone for ever. It is no use, for I should not believe you. Show me his body - let me see him dead, and then I will believe; but until you can do this, ask me not - never, never ask me to believe that my darling is dead."

"You know that is impossible," said Rachel, almost terrified at the girl's vehemence. "His poor body (the words seemed to stick in her throat) was burnt. He died to save another, and his happy spirit is now looking down on us from on high."

"It is not true, it is not true! " cried Valérie, with an angry stamp of her foot "He cannot be happy without me, and wherever he is he will come back to me. I know it - I feel it. Only yesterday he asked me if I would always be true to him, whatever happened, and I said that in life and in death I was his, and he said he was mine. And he took some of my hair to have it worked with his into a true lover's knot, and put in that locket with 'Forget me not' on he bought for me when we were at Leamington. No, dear Mrs. Blackthorne, he is not dead. If he were my heart would tell me. That I am living is a proof that he is living. Do not fear, he will come back - he will come back - he will come--." Here the poor girl's excitement became more than her frame could bear, and she sank, not weeping but fainting, on the floor.

"She has eaten nothing all day," whispered Mrs. Basel, as she raised Valérie in her arms "I am afraid she will he ill unless we can get her to take something."

"You must humour her," answered Mrs. Blackthorne. "Do not contradict her when she says Frank will come back. Let her think so, poor child - and try to make her eat something, and get her to sleep, even if you have to give her an anodyne."

"Perhaps you are right. Valérie," she said, as the latter opened her eyes, "we may possibly see Frank again."

"I am sure we shall," interrupted Valérie eagerly. "I know his heart; he loves me so much that he could not help coming back to me even if he would."

"Well, then, my dear child, you must try to live for him. You must eat or you will not be here when he returns. Promise me now, you will try to eat something - and to sleep a little for his sake - for all our sakes."

"Dear Mrs. Blackthorne, I will do anything if you will not say that Frank is dead."

Rachel remained with her until nearly midnight, and when she went away Valérie was in a peaceful slumber.

The next day brought no change in her condition. She still refused to believe that Frank was dead, and when her father, alarmed for her reason, tried gently to convince her that she was mistaken, she grew strangely excited, accused him of unkindness, and said that he wanted to kill her.

After this had gone on for several days Mr. Basel brought a physician from Manchester, who at his own suggestion was introduced to the family as an ordinary guest, in order not to alarm Valérie, or put her on her guard; for her father greatly feared that she was suffering from incipient insanity. The physician, who was both wise and clever, introduced, as it were casually, the subject of the fire and Frank's death, and watched the effect on his unsuspecting patient.

Valérie immediately rose.

"He is not dead," she exclaimed, with an angry gesture, and quitted the room.

The doctor was of the same opinion as Mrs. Blackthorne.

"You must humour her," he said. "Do not irritate her by saying that young Mr. Blackthorne is dead. Let her indulge in the illusion - it might be worse for her if she were to realise the truth too soon. Perhaps after a while, when he does not return and she hears no news of him, her mind, which I must tell you frankly is a little disordered by the terrible shock of her lover's death, may be restored to its normal condition. Meanwhile, you cannot be too gentle with her. The only curative agents likely to be effectual are time and patience. It would be well, however, to give her a complete change of scene and surrounding. A trip to the Continent could, at least, do no harm, and might do much good."

But when this idea was broached to Valérie she positively refused to hear of it. How could they ask her to go away, she said, when Frank might come back at any moment? What would he think if he returned and found her gone? As it was not possible to argue with her, and compulsion might have been dangerous, there was nothing for it but to yield, and so Valérie remained at the Châlet. She spent most of her time indoors, and when she went out insisted on having no other companion than Broc, a huge St. Bernard mastiff, a gift from Frank.

CHAPTER XL.

FORGET ME NOT.

For some time after the fire Adam was utterly prostrated. He passed the greater part of the day in silence, and seemed equally indifferent to business and incapable of consecutive thought. So far from finding Frank alive among the ruins of the Old Factory, he had not even the sorry satisfaction of finding his charred remains, nor anything that belonged to him. A funeral was, therefore, out of the question, and, there being nobody to bury, all that could be done was to put up commemorative tablets in Claylands Church and Moorside chapel.

People thought Adam felt the blow more than his wife. In this they were mistaken; for while his depression arose as much from disappointed hopes and thwarted ambition as from natural grief for the death of his son, Rachel's sorrow was unsoiled with a single thought of self. With a glad heart she would have scattered all their wealth to the winds, and ended her days in a cottage, - if by so doing her boy could have been restored to her.

But had such an alternative been put to Adam it is doubtful if he could have accepted it in the same spirit.

He was roused from his despondency by two inquiries which were almost simultaneously addressed to him. One related to the Old Factory - should it be rebuilt or left as it was?

"Let it be rebuilt," he answered hastily. This resolution rendered it necessary for him to give orders, consider plans, make bargains. The exertion did him good, and he found in hard work, as many another has found, the best solace for trouble and disappointment.

The second inquiry was put to him by Basel, and related to a matter in which they had a common interest.

"My wife wanted me to ask you," said his partner one day, "what your ideas are about Mabel and Fritz - would you like the match to be broken off; or are they still to consider themselves engaged?"

"By all means," answered Adam, "why should not they? If poor Frank is dead and gone, that is no reason why they should not be married. But it will be a sorrowful wedding, Basel, for you and me."

"And for Valérie," said the other, in a troubled voice. "Poor child, I much fear she will never be herself again. It was a terrible stroke for all of us; hut most of all for her. But let us drop the subject for the present - it seems rather out of place yet - and I have other matters to talk to you about. Another time, and when you are so disposed, we can resume it; we understand each other, and that is sufficient for the moment."

This conversation dwelt in Adam's mind, and, after his partner had left him, there grew out of it an idea that made him for a time almost oblivious to his sorrow. Before the day drew to a close the idea had become a resolve. Frank's death, and the marring of his plans for the founding of a family, had so completely crushed him that, until Basel mooted the subject, he had forgotten all about Mabel and Fritz - almost forgotten, in fact, that he possessed a daughter. In his dreary musings as to how, in the altered circumstances, he should dispose of his property, Adam had hardly given her a thought. It now occurred to him, as if for the first time, that Mabel was as much his child as Frank had been, that her children, as much as his might have been, would be his grandchildren.

"They shall be wed," he said to himself? striking his fist on the table before him, "and soon; and I'll leave everything, except forty or fifty thousand for Mabel, to their eldest lad; and, failing him, to the next, and he shall be called Frank Blackthorne. Brandwood shall be entailed on him. I shall, maybe, live till he's grown up; I have fifteen or twenty years of life and work in me yet - I know I have. I wonder I never thought of it before. It would have saved me some trouble if I had. Poor Frank, poor lad, if he had only been spared!"

When he went home he told Rachel what had passed between Basel and himself, and, without disclosing his new plan, concluded by saying that he should like the marriage to take place soon. Though rather surprised, she offered no objection.

"Perhaps it might be for the best," she remarked. Life was uncertain; they were getting into years, and whichever of them might be taken first it was well that Mabel should be settled while they were both there to look after her.

The only conditions she made were that the wedding should be very, very quiet, and delayed by a month or two beyond the time originally fixed for the double ceremony.

Adam next spoke to the Basels, and as they desired nothing better than to fall in with his wishes, it was arranged that Fritz and Mabel should be married early in April, which would be rather more than four months after Frank's death, and that in order to ensure complete privacy, a special licence should be obtained from the Bishop and the ceremony performed at Brandwood Hall, nobody being present save the officiating clergyman, the members of the two families, and Mr. Hartwell. The young couple were to live in the house which Adam had built in Brandwood Park for Frank and Valerie; and in order to leave no doubt of his intentions, a deed was drawn up settling all his real estate on the first son born of the marriage, on condition that he should bear the name of Francis Adam Blackthorne, the rent and interest to accumulate until he was twenty-five (in the event of his grandfather dying before the child attained that age), subject to a charge in favour of Mrs. Blackthorne. The contingency of Fritz and Mabel being sonless was also provided for. In the event of no male child of the marriage being in existence fifteen years after Adam s death, the property, subject to any charges which he might meanwhile make upon it, was to pass absolutely to his daughter for her separate use.

In effect this was Adam's will, so far as concerned his estate, and inasmuch as the instrument did not partake of the nature of a contract - no consideration having passed - it was revocable; but as it formulated a deliberate, and even a solemn, declaration of his intentions, the arrangement was regarded as final. It seemed, therefore, in the highest degree probable that Fritz Basel's wife and children would inherit the whole of Adam Blackthorne's vast wealth (it went without saying that Mabel would take all the personality), a prospect which so greatly pleased Mrs. Basel that she began in her secret thoughts to look upon Frank's death as being not altogether an unmitigated misfortune. True, it was bad for Valérie, but time would cure her of her delusion, and with the settlements that Hermann could make (now that Fritz was being so amply provided for), a very fine marriage might be arranged for her.

Meanwhile it was necessary that Valérie should be informed of the approaching marriage, of which, out of a natural desire to spare her pain, she had been kept as long as possible ignorant; and, as her mother did not feel equal to the task, it was entrusted to Mabel, whose quiet common sense had latterly brought her rather frequently to the front. Even her father was beginning to find out that Mabel was a sensible lass, and since Frank's death he had taken her much into his confidence.

In truth she had more sense than sentiment, and when she was requested to break the news of the coming event to her friend she saw no impropriety in the arrangement, nor any reason why she should not make the communication at once and without circumlocution. Valérie, she felt persuaded, would not feel hurt or aggrieved because Fritz and herself, in deference to the wishes of their parents, were going to be married. Her brother's sad death had deeply affected her, and she still mourned and often wept for him; but his untimely end was, after all, no reason why she should not marry, and her remaining single a few months longer - even if she could do so without disobeying her father - would neither restore Frank to life nor do him any good where he was.

"You will find her at the farther end of the garden, in the Lady's Walk," said Mrs. Basel to Mabel, when the latter called to make the announcement. "She likes it, I think, because Frank and she used often to walk there together. But do not mention his name, please, if you can possibly help it, and if she says - as she is sure to say - that Frank will come back, you must not contradict her. The doctor told us on no account to contradict or irritate her, and that if we avoided doing so she would recover in time. We had him here again last week. Valérie, poor child, had no idea that he was not a business friend of Hermann's. He does not think she is any worse, or that your marriage is likely to do her any harm. On the contrary, it may rouse her, and help to cure her of her illusion. When you and Fritz are married, and Frank does not return to her - as she keeps hoping and thinking that he will - and time goes on, she must believe at last, you know, that he has gone to a place, poor young man, that one never returns from; and that in this world she never, never can see him again. It is very touching, my dear, this attachment to your brother, and her refusal to believe that he has died; but it is a great misfortune for us all."

Mabel found Valérie, as she expected, pacing to and fro in the Lady's Walk, followed by her faithful companion, the mastiff Broc. Although the bereaved girl's face wore an expression of melancholy which it had never displayed in her happier days, and her cheeks were wan, her friend remarked that her eyes were brighter, and her manner more animated, than they had been lately wont to be. This Mabel looked upon as a good sign, and after a few words of greeting went on to tell her news.

"Can you guess why I have come this morning, Valérie, dear?" she said, putting her arm around her friend's waist, as she walked by her side.

"To see mamma and me, I suppose. Fritz is at the works, you know, or I should perhaps suspect that an incidental object of your visit was to see him."

"Don't he absurd, Valérie. He was at Brandwood only the day before yesterday, and I am not so soft as to want to see him every day. Besides, if I did, I should certainly not come to see him, I would make him come to see me. Still it is about him that I have come today - about him and me, I should say."

"Poor Fritz, what has he done - has he vexed you?"

"Oh dear, no, he knows better than that. He is very good, and as he always does what I tell him, I have rarely occasion to find fault with him. It is nothing of that sort. But papa and the others want us to get married, and - "

"Yes," said Valérie attentively, as Mabel seemed rather to hesitate.

"And we are going to be."

"Soon?"

"On the twenty-fifth. It is rather soon after – after - I mean it is rather sooner than we thought; but papa has taken it into his head that we must be married next month, and when he decides a thing, you know, there is no saying nay."

"Oh, Mabel, dear," said Valérie reproachfully, as she placed her hands on her friend's shoulder, "could you not have waited until poor Frank came back?"

"I could wait, certainly. I am not in a hurry. But you see it does not rest with me. Papa will have it so, and you know he's not a man that one can lightly disobey."

"And Frank will be hack soon," said Valérie in an excited whisper, without appearing to notice her friend's remark. "Look here, Mabel, I have something to show you. Do you know this locket?"

It was an old-fashioned gold locket, with the words "FORGET ME NOT," in blue enamel on the back, and "HOPE" on the front.

Mabel regarded it wonderingly. It seemed to her that she had seen it somewhere before.

"Don't you recognise it?" continued the girl in the same excited whisper. "It is the locket Frank bought for me at Leamington, and he took it away with him the - the day before the fire, to have some of my hair and his hair, woven into a true lover's knot, put into it - and see (opening the locket), here it is; that is his hair and that is mine. And he has sent it to me. It could be nobody else."

"But how'" asked Mabel uneasily, for she was greatly disturbed at this new manifestation of her friend's hallucination.

"I will tell you. We were walking yesterday afternoon, Broc and I, in Throstle Nest Wood, and when we reached the most solitary part of it, near the grove of beech trees, you know, the dog started forward, and I noticed an old woman in the path before me. As there was nothing to fear from an old woman, I called Broc in and went forward. The old body, who was very dark-complexioned and queerly dressed, and evidently a stranger in these parts, seemed to want to speak to me; so when we met I stopped and made some commonplace remark about the weather.

" 'Yes,' she answered, looking at me strangely with her black eyes, 'it is very nice weather for people who have to sleep in the woods and are always afoot. I am a very old woman, but I have never slept in a house in my life, and every year I walk from one end of England to the other. But will you not let me tell you your fortune, my pretty lady? I can read the stars; give me a piece of silver and you shall know something that will make you happy."

"'No, thank you, my good woman,' I said, 'I don't believe in fortune telling. God alone knows what will befall us in the future, but here is a piece of silver for you, all the same,' and I gave her a shilling.

"'You are a kind lady, Miss Valérie Basel," she answered, "and whether I can tell your fortune or not, I will tell you something before we part that will make you cross my palm with gold."

"'How do you know my name, woman?" I asked, very much surprised, as you may well suppose, Mabel.

"'I know more than your name, pretty lady. You love a brave gentleman, and everybody but you thinks he is dead; and because you will not have it that he is dead all your friends think you are mad."

"Again I was surprised, almost bewildered, indeed, until I remembered that the old gipsy was only repeating what was probably the talk of the neighbourhood; and feeling indignant at what I thought was an attempt to impose upon me, I spoke a few sharp words and tried to pass on. Then she put her hand on my arm.

"Not so fast, my pretty lady," she answered, "I have not yet told you all I have to say. You are right and the others are wrong. Your lover is not dead;

he is true to you, and before many days you will see him again. Behold the proof."

"And then she showed me the locket. I knew it at once - knew it before I read the words on the back and the front, and saw Frank's hair inside. For a few minutes I forgot everything. I think I must have fainted; for when I recovered my senses the old woman was supporting me in her arms.

'Give me the locket,' I exclaimed; 'oh, give it me, and I snatched it from her hand. I asked her where she had got it; where Frank was. I offered her money to tell me - twenty pounds, a hundred pounds, anything - but she would not.

"'I cannot, my pretty lady. Not all the money in the world would buy the secret. One day you will know all, but you must wait. Read what is written on the golden locket and be of good courage. That is my message; and now I must go. Mayhap, before long you may see me again."

"And then?" asked Mabel, after waiting a minute or two for Valérie to continue her story.

"That is all; she went away."

"Not before you had crossed her hand with a piece of gold, I suppose," observed Mabel with a slight touch of sarcasm in her voice.

"I gave her a sovereign," said Valérie, whose excitement seemed to be merging into listlessness. "Could I have done less when she brought me news of poor Frank?"

"And will bring you plenty more at the same price, and equally true," would have been Mabel's answer, if, remembering Mrs. Basel's caution, she had not checked herself; saying instead, "I hope she told the truth."

"I am sure she did," rejoined Valérie, whose excitement this remark appeared again to kindle. "Have we not the locket in evidence? She must have told the truth; there can be no mistake. But I do not ask anyone to believe if they do not want to believe - and I can see mamma and papa do not - so I would not tell them, and I have only told you because you are Frank's sister."

As Mabel felt that she could not answer Valérie without contradicting her, she did not answer at all; and they walked in silence towards the Châlet, where the friends separated, Miss Blackthorne declaring that she had so much to do at home that she could not possibly remain to luncheon.

When her pony-carriage reached the lodge gates, however, she ordered the coachman to drive on to Moorwell; for albeit she did not believe the gipsy's tale as related by Valérie, she determined to lose no time in communicating it to Valérie's father.

Mr. Basel received her very kindly, and though he was very busy, laid aside his work and listened to his future daughter-in-law with great attention.

"Poor child!" he said, with a sigh, when she had finished her story," it is easy to see how it is. Some wretched creature has been taking advantage of her weakness - unless it is the coinage of her brain, and she has dreamt or imagined it all."

"I do not think so, Mr. Basel; she told the tale too clearly and circumstantially for it to be purely imaginary. And there is the locket. How do you account for the existence of the locket? Besides, we can easily ascertain if any gipsies have been seen in the neighbourhood lately."

"True. I will cause inquiries to be made, and if I can lay my hands on that miserable old woman I will have her prosecuted as a vagrant, if not for obtaining money under false pretences."

Still, Mr. Basel, where did the locket come from? It seems to be of gold; it is very like the one my brother bought at Leamington; it bears exactly the same devices, and the hair, to all appearance, is his and Valérie's worked into a true lover's knot. I quite agree with you that the gipsy is a rank impostor; but how can you account for her acquaintance with so many circumstances known only to our two families?"

"How can you be sure they are known only to our two families? Servants listen and servants talk. It has been said that no man is a hero to his valet, and I imagine that few of us have secrets from our servants. And then about the locket. You know it was one of the things sought for in the ruins. I heard your father myself describe it to the searchers. All the neighbourhood knows the history of that locket. And, as I understand, it was not a unique article - not made specially to order, I mean. There are, no doubt, hundreds in existence exactly like it. I daresay you might get duplicates of it in every jeweller's shop in Manchester and Redburn. This gipsy, or one of her tribe, has chanced to come across one - stolen it, I should rather say, for these people are not much given to buying. The hair and the true lover's knot would present no greater difficulty than the concoction of the story she told Valérie, and for which she got a sovereign, possibly two. I care nothing for the money, though I do most deeply regret the probable effect of the occurrence on the poor girl's mind. She will be more confirmed in her illusion than ever."

"I think if she could he reasoned with she would see how impossible - "

"No doubt. But you see the misfortune is that she refuses to listen to reason. She does not pretend to listen.

She listens only, as she says, to what her own heart tells her. Notwithstanding the doctor's orders, I tried a few days ago the effect of a little quiet remonstrance. But it was no use; she grew excited, and I had to stop. How could she, do you suppose, give one moment's heed to this preposterous gipsy's story if she were in her right mind? To begin with, how could your poor brother possibly have survived that terrible fire - by what miracle have escaped destruction? And, supposing him to have escaped, how was he spirited away? Why does he remain away? Why does he not return to his home, his family, and his betrothed? And, in the name of all that is absurd, why does he send a keepsake and a message to Valérie by an old gipsy woman? But we cannot, unfortunately, say all this to her - or rather if we did it would have no effect. We must wait in patience until her reason is fully restored, as the doctor says in time it will be, and I think he is right."

"Still, she is sensible in everything else, Mr. Basel. When I am with her she seems as sane as I am myself; and I declare that for a minute or two this afternoon she almost made me believe there really was something in the gipsy's story, preposterous as it is."

You are quite right, Mabel. Her mind generally is as sound as ever it was, and therein lies our hope of her ultimate recovery. She is suffering from temporary monomania, for which the best medicine is patience and gentleness. Only one word more, Mabel - for I see you want to go - and I am rather busy to-day. Let us keep this matter to ourselves. It will profit nothing to repeat it, and if the story gets abroad it will grow in absurdity every time it is told."

"You would not have me mention it at home, then, nor even to Mrs. Basel?"

"That is what I mean, my dear Mabel - nor even to Fritz."

"Of course not," answered the young lady, with a slight toss of her head; "that goes without saying.

"Donner Wetter!" said Mr. Basel to himself, as he returned from handing his visitor to her carriage, "what a woman of business she would make. I

should do best, I think, to make her my partner instead of Fritz, and let him stay at home to look after the house and the babies! Poor Fritz! he will have to play second fiddle; but there is one consolation - he will never know it, and it is well he should have a wife able to look after him and take care of his interests."

CHAPTER XLI.

THE LADY IN BLACK

A Month later Mabel and Fritz were married by special licence at Brandwood Hall. The strictest privacy was observed, and immediately after the ceremony the bride and bridegroom, who were already equipped for the journey, left for London, where, and at Paris, they proposed to spend a short honeymoon.

The only persons present at the wedding, besides the members of the two families, were Mr. Hartwell and Mr. Allthings, by the latter of whom the knot was of course tied. Until almost the last moment it was uncertain whether Valérie would be present or not. A few days after Mabel had informed her of the approaching event she had written to say that, so long as poor Frank was away (as she was sure, against his own will and unhappy), she did not think it would be meet for her to be present at a wedding, even that of her brother and her friend; but she would be present in spirit, and she wished them with all her heart every happiness.

The day before the wedding Mabel received a second letter, in which Valérie said she had been thinking that, if Frank could be consulted, he would probably wish her to be present at his sister's wedding, and keep his mother company after her daughter's departure; that she had therefore resolved to he present, and would come next day with her father and mother.

Notwithstanding this intimation of her intention, Valérie's appearance in the drawing-room of Brandwood Hall was somewhat of a surprise, for nobody felt sure that she might not at the last moment again change her mind and stay away; and certainly nobody expected that she would make, by her costume, a silent, yet effective, protest against the assumption that her lover was dead. While everyone else appeared in black - the bride even being arrayed in half mourning - Valérie wore a gown of pearl-gray silk, trimmed with pale blue. A white rose, Frank's favourite flower, shone in her dark hair, and suspended from a heavy gold chain was the locket given to her by the gipsy - the "Forget me not" resting on her bosom, the "Hope" turned outwards - that all might see she did not despair of her lover's return. Her face, though pale, was composed, but her eyes at times looked unutterably sad. She was thinking of what might have been; that if Frank had not been spirited away - how or by whom she could not tell - there would have been that day two weddings, one of them her own. "Oh, Frank, dear, why don't you come back?" she murmured. "If you only knew how my heart is breaking!"

Rachel read Valérie thoughts, and her heart bled for her. She took the poor girl's hand lovingly in hers, and remained by her side during the ceremony; and, as the result of a long colloquy they afterwards had together, Valérie consented to make a stay of some duration at Brandwood Hall.

Before she returned home the girl's unwavering belief, which it was still beyond the power of argument to shake, made so deep an impression on Rachel that, despite her conviction of its wild absurdity, she began to entertain a vague hope that she might, after all, see her boy again in the flesh. The idea, baseless as she could only deem it, gave her some slight comfort, and by changing the current of her thoughts enabled her the better to sustain the burden of her sorrow.

Though there was no wedding breakfast, the master of Brandwood entertained his guests at luncheon, which, to suit his convenience and that of Mr. Basel, was served shortly after the departure of the bride and bridegroom. He ordered up some of his oldest port wine, of a vintage highly appreciated by Mr. Allthings, and drank in a quiet way the health of the newly-married pair.

"Much happiness to 'em," he said, and a murmur that was supposed to be an echo of his words ran round the table; but there was nothing like speechmaking.

Altogether, Adam seemed to be in fair spirits, and more like himself, his guests thought, than he had been any time since his son's death. Though this might be due, in some degree, to the excitement of the occasion and to the effect of the old port, of which he drank rather freely, he did feel more like himself; hope was springing anew in his breast, and he saw in the marriage of his daughter a step toward, at least, a part fulfilment of the scheme which had become the chief object of his existence. True, he could no longer hope to see his son member for Redburn; but he might easily witness the birth of a grandson, the destined inheritor of his wealth and the bearer of his name; and, whether he lived to see it or not, the lad would be one of the richest men in the county, and if he "shaped right," one of the most important.

Meanwhile Adam had much to do, and though he felt his son's death less than he had done, he sorely missed his help in the business. The burning of the Old Factory, the fight with the insurance people - for after a fire generally comes a fight - and the rebuilding, had thrown immense additional weight on his shoulders. But he bore the burden bravely, and made a point of showing those about him that he was fully equal to the task. He looked into everything of importance for himself and was more exacting with his people than he had been in his son's lifetime. Not a day went by that more than one of them did not wish the young master was back again.

Luncheon over, the gentlemen adjourned to Adam's room, and after a smoke, to the accompaniment, of course, of brandy-and-water, he and Basel were driven in the Tatter's carriage to Moorwell. To a suggestion of Rachel's that he should take a holiday, he answered that he had pressing work to do which could not possibly be put off. He little suspected that work of a sort he had never had before, work which would tax his energies to the utmost, was awaiting him.

He found, as he expected, several people waiting to see him - an architect, a master builder, a commercial traveller, and one or two others. After despatching his business with these, he turned to his desk, and was soon immersed in plans and specifications, and proposals for filling the Old Factory - or, rather, the Old Factory's successor with machinery. He had been thus occupied about half an hour, when there came a knock at the door, which he answered, as usual, by a curt "Come in." Whereupon a clerk entered, and announced that a lady in the outer office desired to see him.

"Who is she?" asked his master.

"1 don't know, sir. Never saw her before, so far as I know; and if I had it would not make much difference, for she is thickly veiled and dressed in black."

"Say I am very busy, and ask her name and business. But stay - I don't know as it matters. It'll come to the same thing in the end. Show her in.

The lady came in. As the clerk had said, she was veiled and wore mourning as deep as it was possible to make it.

"Sit down. What can I do for you?" said Adam, who, thinking from the look of his visitor that he had to deal with a beggar, did not feel disposed to waste time on superfluous courtesies.

"You don't remember me, I think, Mr. Blackthorne?"

"No, I cannot say as I do, though it seems to me somehow as I have heard your voice before."

"It must be my veil, I suppose," observed the lady, at the same time drawing that impediment aside.

Adam bounded from his chair. The woman before him, dressed in widow's weeds, was Lydia Fell.

"God bless me!" he exclaimed, "I thought you were dead"

"Who said so?"

"It was in a newspaper as somebody - we thought your brother - sent us from America. You had been drowned at some place - Albany, I think - by the overturning of a boat."

"That was a mistake. There was a boat accident, and I was among the passengers, but not among the drowned."

"In any case," said Adam sternly, for he had now recovered his composure, "you have no business here. I paid you to go away and stop away. What do you want of me?"

"I want an account of the money my husband left."

"Your husband, woman! What have I to do with him. Who is he?"

"Your son, Frank, was my husband, Mr. Blackthorne, and the father of ---"

"It's a lie," exclaimed Adam fiercely, not waiting for the completion of the sentence.

"And the father of my child," continued Lydia, with outward calm, although she was trembling with suppressed anger.

"That's another lie. Have you any more to tell? You'd better out with 'em while you are at it."

"They are no lies, Mr. Blackthorne, as you will find. Frank and I were married at Manchester Old Church (here she named a date), as you will see by this paper."

"D -- your papers. I want none of 'em. Will you just tell me, then, if you were married to Frank, why you took money from me to go away, and engaged to give no further trouble, and signed your name as Lydia Fell?"

"That was Stephen's doing. I was always against it, and wanted all along to tell you the truth; but he would not let me. He said if I did we should all be sent away without a shilling."

"So you expect me to believe that Frank helped you to deceive me? For if what you say be true, he must have been an accomplice."

"I am not answerable for Frank," rejoined Lydia, sullenly. "I only know that he begged of me and my brother, and better begged, not to tell you we were married."

"Anyhow, you are answerable for yourself; and you admit that you were a party to the deceit. You either lied when you signed that paper and took my money, or you are lying now. I believe you are lying now. Now just look here, Lydia Fell - or whatever you may please to call yourself - I have been victimised once, but I don't mean to be victimised again. While Frank lived it was worth my while to keep you at a distance - at any rate, until he was safely married - but now I have nothing either to fear or hope from you; and I won't bleed another pound - no, nor a single penny piece - not if it would save your life - and the sooner you get out of this office the better."

"But, Mr. Blackthorne, just listen. I can prove --"

"Not another word, woman; not another word. And if you don't get out while I can control myself, by heaven I shall do you a mischief."

As he spoke Adam half rose from his chair; and he looked so dangerous that Lydia beat a hasty retreat to the door.

"You will repent this violence, Mr. Blackthorne," she exclaimed in an agitated voice, as she reached the threshold. "It is now war between us."

"War let it be, then," said Adam, sinking back into his seat.

Curse the hussy!" he muttered as the door closed behind Lydia; "is it possible there can be any truth in what she says? She seems very confident. But, no; Frank would never have deceived me in that way. Besides, why did they not proclaim the marriage before, if there was one? It must be a dodge; and I'll see Lydia and her clever brother hanged before I'll be done a second time."

Should he take any steps? he asked himself - see his lawyer or consult with Basel? But what steps could be taken? What facts had he to lay before Bruff, and what could the latter do in the matter? As yet there was clearly no necessity for taking legal advice, albeit the necessity might arise. True, he might consult Basel, but that was a course he felt very reluctant to adopt; for it would compel him to relate the history of Frank's entanglement with Lydia Fell, and his friend might possibly think he ought to have been told of it before the engagement. Still, Basal had a long head, and if the thing went any farther he would certainly take him into his confidence.

On the whole, concluded Adam, the best thing he could do was to be quiet and keep his own counsel. If the Fells were in earnest, and Lydia could get anybody to believe her story, and take up her case, he would hear more of it quite soon enough. If not, the least said the better.

CHAPTER XLII.

TOMMY TWIRLER HEARS A BUZZ.

Adam was right in his surmise that he might possibly hear something more of Lydia Fell and her story. A few days after that lady's visit to his office, our old friend, Tommy Twirler, sought an interview with his master, choosing, as usual, the dinner hour, as the time when they were most likely to be free from interruption.

"Oh! it's you, Tommy, is it?" said Adam, as his faithful servant walked into his room, as he generally did, without knocking. "Got something to tell me?"

"Ay, it's me," answered Tommy, taking a chair without waiting for an invitation. "I have getten a bit o' buzz (rumour) to tell you. That's what I've come for. But yo've happen yerd."

"I don't think I have. At least I have heard nowt particular. What is it?"

"It's about that theer Lydia Fell. Hoo's come back, it seems."

"Yes, I am aware of that."

"Are yo' aweer what hoo says?"

"No; what does she say?"

"Hoo says as yo're Frank and hoo wor wed, and as hoo has getten a child as he's father to - a little lad."

"The deuce she does! And does anybody believe her?"

"Ay, dun they - lots o' folk. And they sayin as Torney Oke at Orrington has agreed to take her case up - no profit no pay."

"And what think you, Tommy? Do you think as there's owt in it?"

"Well, it looks vary quare, but I can hardly believe as your Frank would be such a foo' as to go and fasten himself to th' likes of her. Yet I mon (must) say as my mind misgav me when he went off a-hunting theer, and hoo went off at th' same time to see her aunt as wor ill – hoo wornt ill, not hoo."

'It isn't true, Tommy; it cannot be true. If they wed why did she agree to go away and stop away, and sign her name to a paper I have there (pointing to his safe) as Lydia Fell? It was just like swearing as she was single."

"Hoo happen geet summut for going away?"

"She did, and a good deal too."

Mutn't (might not) that account for it, thinken you, mayster? Some folks will do owt for brass."

Adam made a grimace. The same idea had occurred to him; but he was not the man to abandon a theory which he had deliberately formed, merely because it happened to conflict with a fact or two.

"Well, it might, Tommy," he rejoined, "but I don't think it does. Depend upon it, it's all a dodge, and that Stephen is at the bottom of it - you see if he isn't. He's as deep as a well. They've heard of Frank's death, and she has come over here to try and get some more brass out of me. They've made up this tale about him and Lydia being wed. They think that sooner than have a scandal I'll pay; but they'll find out their mistake before they've done. And about this pretended child - don't you think if there had been anything of that sort we should have heard of it before now?"

"Well, it does look quare; there's no denying that. I seed no signs of owt o' th' soort afoor Lydia went; and I watched - and so did our Betty too."

"Nor anybody else. It's all a lie, like the rest. Just a lie from beginning to end."

"It may be so," answered Tommy, "and I hope so, but --" and he shook his head.

"But what, Tommy? Out with it."

"I wor nobbut (only) thinking as if there wor nowt in it 'Torney Oke would not be having owt to do wi' it. He's getten his heyd reyt screwed on, he has, and he's gradely sharp too."

"A low fellow!" exclaimed Adam angrily; "the most unscrupulous practitioner in the neighbourhood. He'll take up any dirty case if he can make six-and-eightpence by it."

"I durned know nowt about unscrupulus, but he is th' craftiest lawyer i' these 'ere parts, and maks a bonny lot o' brass they sayin' - and that's th' main point, I reckon. It's what we're all after, brass is."

"It is what Lydia Fell is after, anyway. Now look here, Tommy. I expect this thing will make some stir - be a good deal talked about, you know - and when anybody says anything about it in your hearing, you must just say as there isn't a word of truth in it, and as I've got a paper under Lydia Fell's own hand-written just before she went to America - declining that she was never wed to Frank, and has no claim on him."

This was rather a highly-coloured description of Lydia's receipt for the two thousand pounds, but Adam did not stick at trifles when his blood was up.

"I'll tell 'em reyt enough, you may be sure o' that," said Tommy. "I never did like them theer Fells, fro' th' fost (first), as I towd yo'; and I do hope as it will not torn out as Frank made a foo' of hissel wi' that Lydia. But hoo's a gradely bad lot, hoo is, yo' can see it in her een (eyes)."

After which sage reflection Tommy rose from his chair and moved towards the door.

"You'll come in now and then, Tommy, and let me know what folks say?" said his master.

"Ay, when there's owt fresh," replied Tommy, who, as he had only half an hour left in which to get his dinner, and see to the punctual pulling of the factory bell, evidently desired to bring the conversation to a close.

"Now, at any rate, I must see Basel," thought Adam, when he was left alone. "If I don't tell him somebody else will."

A few minutes afterwards he was on his way to the dyeworks, which were about a mile distant from the factory. They were a nondescript collection of buildings of all shapes and sizes, scattered about as if they had been dropped haphazard from the sky, or sprung at random from the ground. For the place had grown from small beginnings, bit by bit, and almost year by year, to be a concern of great magnitude. Symmetry in these circumstances was out of the question, and Basel had been constrained to put up new workshops as he wanted them, and where he wanted them. From an aesthetic point of view Moorwell dyeworks were about as unattractive as it is possible to imagine. Some of the buildings were of brick - old, ugly, slabsided and weatherworn; others were of sandstone - new, vast, and with some slight pretensions of shapeliness. From some of them issued clouds of steam, which shrouded the place in perpetual gloom. Two hideous chimneys vomited forth pillars of dense smoke. The roads were black, and Moorwell brook, where it flowed through the works, was foul with unspeakable abominations. The stenches beggared description, especially when, as sometimes befell, a cask of blood (which unsavoury material before the introduction of the alizarine process was largely used in turkey-red dyeing) got started in the course of conveyance from the canal wharf. Then people for miles round got a whiff that almost choked them. But no serious harm was ever known to come of these evil odours, a piece of good fortune that was generally ascribed to the existence in the neighbourhood of several chemical works, whose pungent, if not fragrant fumes acted as a sort of antidote to the scent of "Basel's blood barrels," as they were commonly called. But none of these things troubled Adam Blackthorne, as he wended his way towards his partner's office. For even if he had not been used to them he was just then in too serious a mood to be critical or censorious. After threading his way among a number of carts, some laden with coals, some with calico pieces - red, white, and gray, some with madder and other dyestuffs, some with carboys of chemicals, and passing several groups of dyers, with bare arms and enormous iron-bound clogs, their legs swathed in blanketing, bending under heavy burdens of damp cloth, he reached Basel's office. It was, however, rather a laboratory than a place for bookkeeping and correspondence. One side of it was entirely taken up by a long bench, terminating in a large slopstone. On the bench were ranged numerous stoppered bottles, test tubes, an electric machine, blowpipes, chemical weigh scales under glass shades, and other scientific instruments. On the opposite side was a large bookcase; near it a small writing-table; and by the fireside, in a wooden uncushioned armchair, sat the master of the establishment, smoking a huge porcelain pipe, and deep in the perusal of a new work on chemistry.

"Welcome, friend Blackthorne," he exclaimed, as his visitor entered. "I am glad to see you. It is not often, these days, that you come to see how we are going on."

"No, I have not time for that now, and I do not suppose you would have seen me to-day if my business had not been pressing. I am threatened with a new trouble, Basel."

"Indeed, my friend, I am sorry to hear that - nothing serious, I hope. Whatever it is, you may always count on me, as you well know."

And then Adam told him the story the reader already knows, of Frank's entanglement with Lydia Fell, of the money given her to compound her claim and to go away, of her return, and of her pretension to be his son's widow. He excused himself for not having mentioned the circumstance to his partner before, on the ground that when the Fells left England he looked upon the matter as settled, that it did not appear to him any useful purpose would be served by talking about it; and the less it was talked about, he thought, the better.

"I do not blame you for not having told me of poor Frank's intrigue with this Lydia Fell," said Basel, when Adam had concluded his story; "it was your affair and his, not mine, and you had a perfect right to keep it to yourselves. It is always best to wash one's dirty linen at home. And if it had only been an ordinary intrigue, an affair of calf-love, it would not have mattered much. But this marriage, friend Blackthorne - I fear this marriage is a bad business."

"You surely don't think that Frank could be such a fool - that it is possible --

"Alas, friend Blackthorne," interrupted Basel, shaking his head, "human folly, especially the folly of a young man, is almost as boundless as the possible itself. I know nothing of the marriage - whether there has been a marriage or not, nor whether, if there has been, it was legal. Yet it hardly seems in the nature of things that this woman should come all the way from America, and that Lawyer Hawke, who, rogue as he is, knows what he is about, should take the case up, unless they have some grounds to go upon. And do you think you acted quite wisely when Miss Fell came to your office the other day?"

"I did all I could," answered Adam grimly. "I could not very well kick her downstairs, or throw her into the cold-water lodge, but if it had been her brother I would have done both."

"And you would have done a very foolish thing, friend Blackthorne. There are times when violence answers, perhaps, though I doubt it, but it is worse than useless in a case of this sort. Here we want coolness, tact, skilful management, *finesse*. My meaning was something quite different. I meant that you would have done more wisely to have heard her story quietly to the end, examined her proofs, and, perhaps, have made it worth her while to go back quietly to America."

"What! pay her a second time? Never while her heart beats. Why, she would be here again next year, with another lying story."

"Softly, friend Blackthorne, softly. I said examine her proofs. If her proofs are wanting I would not advise you to give her a farthing. But if the evidence she can offer is of a nature likely to satisfy a reasonable man, would it not be better to pay her the sum she can claim as Frank's widow, and let her go quietly about her business, than have all the trouble, turmoil, and scandal of a trial? How much can a widow claim in this country?"

"A third of the personalty."

"And had Frank any personalty?"

"Yes, six thousand pounds. I administered."

"Then all she can claim is two thousand pounds. Better pay it twice over, friend Blackthorne, than have the worry of a lawsuit."

"As far as that goes I am quite of your opinion. But if I gave two thousand pounds to everyone as threatened me with law I should soon have nothing left. And as for Lydia Fell, I don't believe a word she says. I don't believe there has been any marriage; and unless I make a stand now this will not be the last dodge she and her brother will try. I begin to think now as I did wrong in paying them to go to America. I should just have sent them about their business, and told them to do their worst. I think I must put my foot down this time, Basel. Anyhow, before we talk about compromise, the fact of the marriage must be conclusively proved. Frank was weak and foolish, I know; but he cannot have been so soft as to fasten himself to Lydia Fell."

"I hope you are right, friend Blackthorne, but I very much fear that you are wrong, and that Frank did commit this folly. There is nothing to be gained by shutting our eyes to facts. Don't you see that the theory of such a marriage explains much of his conduct? Don't you remember how, when he was evidently in love with poor Valérie, he held back from declaring himself; how we all remarked his hesitation, and were at a loss to understand it? Now we have the explanation; for if he was married to Miss Fell his hesitation was natural, and, as I understand, he spoke to Valérie the very day, or the day after, he heard of Miss Fell's supposed death."

Adam nodded assent. It was really, as he well remembered, the day before; but, as he mentally remarked, there was no use making things to the worst.

"I think I can understand too," continued Basel, "how Frank was inveigled into a marriage. You see he was thrown into the company of the Fells nearly every day. He often stayed at Moorwell all night. He was young and impressionable, and it would not be difficult for a clever, good-looking, unscrupulous woman like Lydia to captivate him. Her superior age, instead of being a drawback, was an advantage - it was a preservative against her falling in love herself, and perhaps worse. She had her brother to help her. He, doubtless, left them often alone together, and one day Frank, artfully angled by the lady, offered her marriage. From that moment his fate was sealed. The Fells, knowing that an open marriage would certainly be opposed, and probably prevented, suggested a secret one, with the intention, doubtless, of subsequently avowing it and turning it to Stephen's advantage. When, however, they found that they would not be able to propitiate you, that if the marriage were made known you would probably cast Frank off; they grasped eagerly at the chance of receiving a handsome sum of money to compromise a claim which Lydia had forfeited by making Frank marry her. As for Frank, he remained silent out of fear of you and the consequences to himself. When he saw that Lydia was willing to abandon him for a sufficient consideration, be was cured of his illusion, and ceased to care for her; and he may have thought that if she went to America be would be rid of her for ever. At any rate, that is my reading of the riddle, always assuming, of course, that there actually has been a marriage."

Basel, on the principle, probably, of not speaking ill of the dead, did not suggest that Frank had been to blame for winning Valérie's love while he was, or thought he was, the husband of another woman.

Adam, if not convinced, was at least silenced by his partner's arguments. Struggle against the conviction as he might, he could no longer deny the possibility of a marriage.

"This is only my opinion, you know," resumed Basel, "and I would not advise you to act on it, or even accept it as in any way conclusive, without taking further advice. Why not see Bruff? He would advise you as to the legal bearings of the business."

"It is what I thought of doing. Will you go with me? Two heads are better than one sometimes.

"Certainly. When do you propose to go?"

"To-morrow. I will call for you at the Châlet - or here - and we will drive over together. Would nine o'clock suit you?"

"Exactly. And, if it makes no difference, I would rather start from here."

Very well, we will start from here then. Another thing: will you say anything at home - will you tell Mrs. Basel? - and Valérie?"

"Poor Valérie," said the other with a sigh. "If she knew it might kill her outright. But no, she would not believe it. Nevertheless, we must keep it from her. I shall tell my wife just enough, and no more, to put her on her guard and make sure that nothing of this is told to Valérie, for we shall have all sorts of rumours flying about."

"I shall say nothing to Rachel for the moment," observed Adam, as he rose to take leave. "It will be a sore trouble to her anyway; and we may as well keep it from her as long as possible."

"Perhaps you are right. Spare her as much as you can. She deserves all the consideration it is possible to give her. I think sometimes that the two best women in the world are your wife and my daughter. But you want to be going. I will walk with you up the road. I want to speak to you about one or two matters of business. I see our stock of seventy-two reeds is running very low. When can you let us have a delivery?"

The two walked and talked together until they were within sight of the factory gates, when Basel, perceiving that a man was waiting to speak to Adam, bade him adieu, and returned to his own place.

The man in question was smartly dressed, wore a shiny hat set very much on one side, and carried himself in a jaunty, and, as Adam thought, an impudent fashion.

"Mr. Blackthorne, I believe?" said the stranger.

"I believe so."

"Adam?" queried the stranger further.

"Yes."

"Then I have a couple of documents for you, Mr. Blackthorne, from Mr. Hawke, of Orrington," remarked the man, handing him at the same time two thick, oblong pieces of paper.

"What are they?"

"One is notice of an action that has been commenced against you in the Palatinate Court of Chancery, by Mrs. Lydia Blackthorne, to set aside the letters of administration granted to you as Francis Adam Blackthorne's next of kin, and to substitute her for you as administrator of his estate. The other is an order from the Palatinate Court – a bill of discovery it is generally called - for the production of all documents bearing thereupon - such as contracts of copartnership, deeds of settlement, and so forth all of which will, doubtless, be fully explained to you by your solicitor."

"Thank you," answered Adam, pocketing the papers; for despite the man's jaunty manner, he spoke civilly enough. "I will see my solicitor to-morrow and give him these things."

"Tommy Twirler was right," he muttered, as he walked slowly up the factory yard. "Hawke has taken the case up, and this is the first shot - a double one - it seems. Well, we'll see what Bruff says about it."

"And that's old Blackthorne," mentally observed the lawyer's clerk. "He looks like fighting a stiffish battle, and as he has any amount of tin, and we are cocksure to win, why we'll make him pay, that's all. Charley Hawke is the boy to run up costs - is not he just? And now I'll go and wet my whistle somewhere; it's all in the day's work."

CHAPTER XLIII.

A QUARREL.

Mr. Bruff, Adam's lawyer, was not the same shrewd old gentleman that helped Nanny Cooper to invest her savings and him to buy the Old Factory, but his son Leonard, who had succeeded to his practice and inherited half his fortune, which amounted, one way and another, people said, to nigh a hundred thousand pounds. But though the young man - if a man of thirty may still be called young - was thus rendered independent of his profession, he had an hereditary liking for the law; and having, moreover, a great respect for the office, which was established by his grandfather in the middle of the last century, and a still greater respect for the handsome income it produced, he wrought almost as assiduously at his calling as either of his predecessors had done. He was, however, considered to be less clever than his father; and, though his clients had the most implicit confidence in his integrity, they had sometimes reason to regret that he was not a little quicker of apprehension and a little more fertile in resource. His practice lay principally among people having money to invest, property to purchase, conveyances to make, and wills to draw. He had several fat agencies withal, cared little for contentious cases, and would not take up a police affair at any price. He said he could afford to pick his business, and if anything requiring sharp practice were proposed to him he would quietly refer the offerer to one of his less scrupulous brethren.

This was the man upon whom Adam Blackthorne and Basel waited the day after their interview at the latter's works.

"I am glad you have come," said the lawyer, as he shook hands with his client. "You have saved me the trouble of running over to Moorwell. I got a document yesterday that requires both explanation and attention - an order from the Chancery Court of the County Palatine, requiring me to produce any papers I may have in my possession relating to an action which has been commenced against you at the suit of Lydia Blackthorne. Who is Lydia Blackthorne, and what does it all mean?"

"I have got a similar document, and another also. Here they are."

"Ah, I see; they come from the office of Mr. Hawke. Just like him, to do a dirty trick like this. He knows I am your legal adviser, and would have accepted service on your behalf; and yet he must needs put you to the annoyance of being served personally. But what does it all mean? Who is Lydia Blackthorne, and on what ground does she claim to have these letters of administration set aside?"

Then Adam told the lawyer the story of Lydia Fell, of her past relations with his son, and of her present claim.

"It's very strange," remarked Bruff reflectively, taking off and wiping his spectacles (He was a spare, dim-eyed man, with sallow features and thin lips); "I never heard of such a thing in all my life before - never. And they say there is a child, do they?"

"Yes, a boy."

"Then why doesn't she get him made a ward in Chancery?"

"That I cannot tell. But what do you think – do you think there was a marriage?"

"That of course I cannot say until I have had an opportunity of inspecting the marriage certificate. But I am afraid there was, Mr. Blackthorne. It looks very like it."

"I differ from you, Bruff. I don't think it is likely. I think it is very unlikely."

"As I have said, I cannot give a final opinion until I have seen the evidence. But I should say, knowing what I do of Charley Hawke, that he would not have taken the case - if, as you have heard, he is taking it up on speculation - unless he had first satisfied himself as to the fact and the validity of the alleged marriage."

"D - Charley Hawke!" exclaimed Adam. "You all throw that fellow in my teeth. Has he all the sense, and sharpness, and skill in the world, and are we to throw up the sponge at the mere sound of his name? Is there nobody as knows law but him?"

"You asked my opinion, Mr. Blackthorne," rejoined the lawyer coldly, whom this outburst had deeply offended, "and I can only give it you honestly, based on such data as I have."

"It seems to me," interposed Basel, "as I said to my friend yesterday, that the best thing he can do, even if there be some doubt about the marriage, is just to pay the two thousand pounds, which is all the woman can claim, and have done with the business. Frank is dead.

It can make no difference to him whether this woman calls herself his widow or not and the two thousand pounds she is after, if she takes it as a settlement in full of all demands - which, of course, must he a condition *sine quâ non* -will be well spent if it only serves to prevent scandal, and the worry and excitement of a law-suit."

"But I fear two thousand will not satisfy her;" said Bruff. "And then there's the child."

"I don't much believe in the child," answered Basel.

"Anyhow if there is one let her provide for him out of the two thousand I propose to be given her, and the two thousand she has already got. Why don't you think she will be satisfied with the two thousand? It is all she can demand."

"Because Mr. Blackthorne, by a deed we have in the office here, has charged the Brandwood estate with an annuity of fifteen hundred a year in favour of his son's widow, and settled the estate itself on his son and heirs male in tail. And I don't think it is likely that this Miss Lydia Fell, or whatever may be her right name, is the sort of woman to give up fifteen hundred a year for a lump sum of two thousand."

"Man, what do you mean?" exclaimed Adam so roughly and vehemently that he offended Mr. Bruff a second time.

"I mean exactly what I say, Mr. Blackthorne. You surely cannot have forgotten the arrangement of December last, when, in anticipation of your son's approaching marriage, you had a new deed of copartnership drawn, and the Brandwood estate settled on him for his life (after your death), and in remainder on his eldest son?"

"That was in anticipation of his marriage with Miss Valérie Basel, and not with a hussy like this Lydia Fell"

"But the deed is general, and applies to any marriage; not specifically to his marriage with Miss Valérie."

"Well, then, I'll revoke it. What I did I can undo."

"It's very unfortunate, Mr. Blackthorne; but I am afraid that it is not within your power."

"Why not?"

"Because the settlement is in the nature of a contract. You will remember that the original deed of copartnership with your son gave him a third of the profits; but when you proposed to settle on him the Brandwood estate, and assure his widow an annuity of fifteen hundred a year, you thought it was only fair to reduce the proportion of profit falling to his share to one-fifth. We discussed the matter in the office here at the time - I and my managing clerk - and we came to the conclusion that it was expedient to record this fact in the settlement. The deed therefore recites that, in consideration of Frank Blackthorne surrendering a portion of his interest in the business at Moorwell, you settle upon him your estate at Brandwood. It is consequently a contract, and can only be rescinded by the consent of both the parties.

Whatever possessed you to make such a fool of a settlement as that, Bruff?"

Really, Mr. Blackthorne, if you cannot use more courteous language I shall be obliged to terminate the interview. How could I know your son had contracted a secret marriage, of which there was issue, or might be issue? If I acted in ignorance so did you. I read the deed over to you, explained its effect, and answered all your questions concerning it. What could I do more? In what respect am I to blame?"

Where is this deed?"

In my strong room, in your deed chest"

Would you be good enough to send for it or fetch it?"

Certainly; and I will read it over to you."

"I am not going to hear it read over. I know more about it than I want already. I'm just going to stick it in the fire."

"Then I cannot let you have it, Mr. Blackthorne," replied the lawyer with great deliberation, yet with great firmness.

"What for?" demanded Adam, his face flushing red, and his hands trembling with suppressed passion. "Is it not mine - have I not paid you for it - cannot I do what I like with my own?"

"Not in this case, Mr. Blackthorne. I have received notice of a bill of discovery having been filed in the Palatinate Court, calling on me to produce all papers connected with the case in my possession. If I were to surrender this deed, now that you have expressed your intention of destroying it, I should be guilty of contempt of court"

"What then?"

"What then? Why I should be liable to imprisonment, besides injuring my professional reputation. No, Mr. Blackthorne, you must not ask me to connive at the destruction of this, or any other instrument, that I may be required to produce."

"But nobody would be the wiser. Hawke does not know of the existence of this deed, or he would have said something about it."

"That does not follow, Mr. Blackthorne. Things ooze out, you know. This deed has never been looked upon as a secret. Your son, or yourself or one of my clerks, may have casually mentioned it to somebody. It is hardly possible that all knowledge of it should be confined to us three. Hawke is sure to ferret it out sooner or later, and a nice mess we should be in if it were found that we had destroyed such a document. Besides, I may be put on my oath, and you would surely not have me perjure myself. No, Mr. Blackthorne, I am sorry to disoblige you, but I cannot, after what you have said, let this deed go out of my hands."

"But you would not need to know anything about my destroying it. In fact, I have changed my mind. I want to take it home and look it over. That deed is my property; what I do with it is my business, and nobody else's.

"I cannot do it, Mr. Blackthorne; the order from the court is peremptory. I am responsible for the safe-keeping of this and all other documents in my custody that I may be called upon to produce; and I must refuse to give them up. Copies you may have, but the originals I shall certainly keep."

"If that be your resolution, Mr. Bruff, you have lost me for a client. I mean to fight this case to the end. I will carry it to the Court of Queen's Bench; I will carry it to the Chancery Court in London; I will carry it to the House of Lords. I'll do owt – owt - rather than let Lydia Fell and her bastard have Brandwood. Have not I willed it to Mabel's children? And I'll try to find a lawyer, Mr. Bruff; as has more brains and fewer scruples than you have."

Be it so, Mr. Blackthorne," returned Bruff, who was now in as great a rage as Adam himself. "I would rather lose every client I have than connive at the absurd and dangerous act which you desire to commit. I hope you'll find a lawyer as unscrupulous as yourself, that's all - somebody who will be a match for Charley Hawke. I don't profess to compete with such men. I never did. Yes, you had better find another lawyer; I am too honest for you. But you will lose your case all the same - that I am sure of. Your papers are, of course, always at your disposal, except those connected with the Chancery proceedings instituted by your daughter-in-law; and of them you may have copies. Good-morning, gentlemen; I have the honour to bid you good-morning."

"My daughter-in-law!" muttered Adam, as he stepped into the street. "D-- the fellow!"

CHAPTER XLIV.

LAWYER KEAN

"I am sorry, friend Blackthorne," observed Basel, as he and Adam waited in the bar parlour of The Bull's Head while their carriage was being got ready

- "I am sorry you quarrelled with Bruff. He was a friend, and now I much fear you have made an enemy of him."

"But don't you see, Basel, that he is not the man for a job like this? Why, he decided the case offhand, without a fair consideration of the facts. He yields at the first summons. What is the good of a lawyer like that?"

"There I am disposed to agree with you. While it was thought to be a matter of two thousand pounds I counselled compromise. Now I counsel resistance until, at any rate, it is quite clear we have not even the ghost of a chance; and we are certainly not at that point yet. You must have a lawyer with more fight and resource in him than Mr. Bruff. Nevertheless, I am sorry you quarrelled with him."

"Well, perhaps I was a little hasty. But I could not help it. He aggravated me past bearing. And you may say what you like, Basel, he managed desperate badly about that deed. I never told him to make it irrevocable, and I swear I never knew before to-day as it was irrevocable. But there is no use talking about that now. The question is what to do next? We must see another lawyer, and that soon. Do you know of any as you can recommend?"

"I think so. I made the acquaintance, a few months ago, of a Mr. Kean - the firm is Cutbill and Kean, though Cutbill has retired, I am told. He is just the man for you."

"At Manchester?"

"Yes, it is a Manchester firm. He was solicitor for Fairfield's failure. I was one of the trustees, you remember. That is how I came to know him. I liked his ways, and I have given him several little jobs since. Yes, Kean is the man for you, and being young and aspiring, and eager for business, he will do his best, especially as you will be a new client."

"I'll go and see him to-morrow."

"I think you had better. I shall not be able to go with you, though; but you will do very well yourself. I will write a note from here and say you are going to call upon him on important business. What time shall we fix?"

"Let me see. I won't go by coach. I shall drive right through - say half past one."

Basel called for paper and pen and began to write.

"Stay," interrupted Adam. "How would it be to ask him to have the register of the Old Church searched, to see if any marriage between Frank and Lydia Fell was celebrated there? Tell him to begin twelve months since, and search backwards - it will not be much of a job."

"A very excellent idea, friend Blackthorne. I need not go into any particulars, you can do that to-morrow - merely tell him to make the search."

A letter to this effect was written and posted before the partners left Redburn; and the next day at the time named Adam presented himself at the office of Messrs. Cutbill and Kean. It was at the top of a gloomy flight of stairs, in a dark entry in King Street; and Adam had almost as much difficulty in finding the entry as in mounting the stairs, which, like the law wherein he was to plunge, had traps for the unwary in the shape of unsuspected holes and untrustworthy steps. Cutbill and Kean's outer office, which would have been none the worse for a good scrubbing and sweeping, was occupied a small boy and a stout clerk. The boy, who sat on a high stool, was bending so low over a sheet of foolscap that he seemed to be writing with the tip of his nose. The clerk was warming himself before the fire and picking his teeth with a quill pen.

"Is Mr. Kean in?" asked Adam of the stout clerk.

"He is. Are you Mr. Blackthorne? You have an appointment, I think?"

"I am Mr. Blackthorne, and my friend, Mr. Basel, sent word yesterday that I would be here about this time, I believe."

"Will you please sit down a moment, and I'll see if he's at liberty?"

The clerk disappeared up a dark lobby, out of which, in a few seconds, he again emerged.

"Mr. Kean is engaged just now," he said, "but he will see you in one minute. Will you please sit down," for Adam still remained standing.

He was an impatient man, and if there was one thing more than another that he disliked it was waiting. A minute, however, was not long, so he accepted the clerk's invitation and took a seat. But when he had waited, not one minute only, but five, ten - nearly fifteen indeed - and nothing came of it, he began to feel slightly exasperated. They never treated him in that way at Bruff's office.

"Look here, young man," he said at length, rising from his chair, "you told me Mr. Kean would see me in one minute, and here I have been waiting twenty, and for aught I know I may go on waiting twenty more."

"No, not twenty, Mr. Blackthorne; not quite fifteen."

"It seems more like half an hour. It is a vast sight more than one minute, and that is what you said. Did you tell him that I was here waiting?"

"We never speak to Mr. Kean when he is engaged with a client. I wrote on a piece of paper that a gentleman was waiting to see him by appointment, and he said, 'In one minute.'"

"That's what he always says, I expect, is it not?"

"Well, he says it very often," said the clerk with a grin. "If he said quarter of an hour or half an hour, clients might not wait sometimes, you know."

"They might go somewhere else," suggested Adam.

"Exactly; and that is what we don't want," rejoined the clerk frankly.

"Well, if you don't want me to go somewhere else, just put on one of your pieces of paper that Mr. Blackthorne, of Moorwell, has been waiting half an hour to see Mr. Kean, and as he does not feel like waiting any longer - and anything else you like."

This message, which was forthwith written out and sent into Mr. Kean, acted as an open sesame, and Adam, not in the sweetest of tempers, was ushered into the lawyer's private office. It was a large, gloomy, dusty room, and matched well with the blind alley, the staircase, and the outer office. One side of it was filled with shelves crowded with ponderous law books. A large table and the floor were littered with papers and parchments black with dust; and the single window, grim with dirt, looked into a little court filled with old barrels, bottles, and packing cases, the property of a spirit merchant who occupied the ground floor. The only bright thing in this limbo of the law was its occupant, Solicitor Kean, a dapper little man with a full, almost round, vivacious face, sharp white teeth, dark expressive eyes, and a forehead both broad and high.

"Ah, Mr. Blackthorne," he exclaimed, as Adam entered, "I am so sorry to have kept you waiting. But the fact is I had a client whose appointment preceded yours, and I could net get rid of him a minute sooner."

His manner was so pleasant, and he seemed so genuinely sorry to have made Adam wait, that the latter's anger was completely appeased, and he proceeded in his usual straightforward way to explain his business.

Kean listened attentively, asked a few questions, and, in a marvellously short time, as Adam thought, he knew the inns and outs of the case as well as his client.

"I think I understand," he said "you want us to resist Miss Lydia and her claim to the last extremity?"

"Yes. Would not you advise me to do so?"

"Certainly. Always fight when you have nothing to gain by compromising; and you may be sure we will do our best for you. I am bound to say, however, that at the first blush - so far as appears to me at the moment the case will be a very difficult one."

"You think the chances are against us, then?"

"At present they are - rather. But do not be discouraged. I have not seen all the papers yet, remember, nor had time fully to consider the matter. But I have won many a more unpromising suit. Something may happen. I may find a fatal flaw in Mr. Hawke's case. In any event we will put a bold face on and make a hard struggle for victory. Meanwhile I have got that marriage certificate. Here it is."

The document which the lawyer handed to Adam was to this effect.

Adam read and re-read this certificate, or rather extract, at least a dozen times, dwelling on every word and date, before be returned it to Mr. Kean. When he did so, his face was blanched and his hands trembled.

"There was a marriage, then?" he said, in a husky voice.

"Undoubtedly, for there is no question as to the genuineness of the extract. I sent my own clerk for it, and, as you see, sir, it is vouched for by the chaplain. No loophole here, I fear."

"But it says what is not true. Frank never lived at Warrington in his life, and she never lived at Lower Broughton - any way she was not living at Lower Broughton then - and I am not sure he was of age on the 13th of February. I think he did not come of age till the 1st of March."

184-.—Marriage solemnised at the Collegiate and Parish Church, in the Parish of Manchester, in the County of Lancaster.

No.	When Married.	Name and Surname.	Age.	Condition.	Rank or Profession.	Residence at time of Marriage.	Father's Name and Surname.	Rank or Profession of Father.
20	February 13	Frank Blackthorne	Full	Bachelor	Cotton Spinner	Warrington	Adam Blackthorne	Cotton Spinner
		Lydia Fell	Full	Spinster		Lower Broughton	Timothy Fell	Farmer

Married in the above Church according to the Rites and Ceremonies of the Established Church, after license, by me,

EDWARD HARVEY, M.A., Chaplain.

This marriage { FRANK BLACKTHORNE   in the { MARK BINYON.
was   presence
solemnised { LYDIA FELL   of us { STEPHEN FELL.
between us

I do hereby certify that the above extract is a true copy, taken from the original entry, made in the Marriage Register Book of the Collegiate and Parish Church of Manchester. As witness my hand this 20th day of May, 184-.

JOHN M. JONES, Officiating Minister.

Page 251

That is not material, Mr. Blackthorne. If your son has made a false statement he may be liable to prosecution, but the marriage remains good. As to his living at Warrington, it is sufficient if he were staying there at the time of the marriage. Was he?"

He might be. I know he went off into Cheshire hunting about that time; and Lydia went to see her aunt, as she said was ill."

"That explains it. They evidently went away for the purpose of getting married, and, as you are aware, the law allows considerable latitude in the matter of residence; indeed I fancy the requirement is one generally honoured rather in the breach than the observance. But, as I just said, something may turn up. Don't lose your courage, and the next time you are in Manchester, give me a call. Meanwhile, I will ask Mr. Bruff to send me all your papers, or copies of them. You know I have seen nothing yet. Perhaps, if we cannot upset the marriage, we can prevent Miss Lydia from coming into her fifteen hundred a year, and her son, if there be a son, from inheriting your entailed estate."

"Oh, there is one more matter I must mention. I have a paper, signed by this Lydia, agreeing for a payment of two thousand pounds, to release Frank from any claim she might have upon him and go to America. I have mentioned it already, I think; but, in the hurry of starting, I forgot to put the document in my pocket. Shall I send it you?"

"By all means. It may not be worth much, but send it all the same. Let me have every document bearing on the case, however insignificant it may seem. So far as I can see at present, the best game we can play is a waiting one. Time may help, and cannot well injure us. I can, and, if necessary, will, protract the proceedings almost *ad infinitum.* Meanwhile, I shall make a rigid inquiry into the antecedents of Miss Lydia Fell. Gad, who knows? she may have committed bigamy - such things have happened. If anything further occurs, you will, of course, let me know; and when I want to see you I will apprise you by post."

"That's right, Mr. Kean; spare no expense in making enquiries. I should not at all wonder if that woman had committed bigamy - or murder either, for that matter - she would do either as soon as look, if it suited her purpose. And see here, I know law is an expensive game, and you will have to spend a lot of money. Take this hundred-pound note to be going on with; and when you want more you have only to speak."

"Thank you, Mr. Blackthorne," replied Kean, as he accompanied his client to the outer door; "you are very kind; rest assured we shall do our best for you. I will tell our cash-keeper to send you a receipt by post. You need not take the trouble to wait. Waiting is evidently not your forte, Mr. Blackthorne - ah, ah! Good-day - ah, ah!" After the utterance of which little joke, the man of law retreated briskly into his dusky den, while Adam carefully felt his way down the rickety staircase.

CHAPTER XLV.

DISCOURAGEMENT.

Never since the death of his son and the destruction of the Old Factory had the master of Moorwell felt so desolate, disappointed, and discouraged as when he emerged from the gloomy portal of Cutbill and Kean's office into the light of King Street - such light as there was; for the air was thick with smoke and dark clouds hung low in the sky.

Leaving for another day several business calls which he had intended to make, he went straight to the inn where he had left his horse and gig. On his way thither he was warmly greeted by several old acquaintances, and respectfully saluted by sundry persons whom he hardly knew even by sight; for Adam was now a wealthy man, and candidates for the notice of the wealthy are never wanting. His appearance, moreover, was sufficient to attract some observation. Despite his nearly sixty winters and his white hair, his back was as straight, his step was firm, as when, thirty years before, he had thrashed Bill Nudger and wooed Rachel Orme; and although time had left its imprint on his features, his face was as ruddy as of yore, and showed no sign either of failing health or waning powers. He held his head high, smiled when people saluted him, and spoke cheerfully to the few with whom he stopped to exchange greetings. Yet his heart was heavy within him, and it was a sense of relief that he found himself alone in his room at The White Bear. Ordering a glass of whisky, he sat down before the fire, lighted a pipe, and fell into a deep reverie.

"And this is all that it has come to," he thought; "this is the end of my strivings, my schemes, my almost life-long work. My only son dead - dead that a poor little factory girl might live - the fine estate, and all the money I have spent upon it, the very house I live in, destined, in all probability, to become the property of Lydia Fell's child, and myself; maybe, compelled to pay her while I live fifteen hundred a year! Rachel a bereaved mother, Valérie a broken-hearted girl with a clouded mind, and I a rich man whom everybody envies, whose best-laid plans have failed, and at present tenant for life of his own house and lands, without power either to sell or bequeath them."

For Adam could no longer resist the conviction that Frank and Lydia had actually been married, and that the knot was properly tied. He was a stubborn man, hard to persuade, and slow to change his belief; but facts are stubborn things, and the marriage certificate, backed by Kean's opinion, not even he could gainsay. He did not derive much encouragement from the crumb of comfort held out to him by the lawyer - the possibility of finding a flaw in the marriage or an informality in the settlement - whereby the claims of Lydia and her son might be barred. The possibility was almost wildly remote, and it was plain to see that Kean had only suggested it by way of putting the best face on the matter and keeping up his client's spirits. It was something like a doctor's sentence on a moribund patient, that while there is life there is hope; and if the lawyer did succeed in hunting out a flaw, no one, probably, would be more surprised than himself. Yet, notwithstanding these misgivings, Adam never for a moment faltered in his resolve to fight the case to the end. His hatred of Lydia Fell as the cause of all his troubles (he almost persuaded himself that, but for her, his son would not have died) was boundless, and he vowed that if she did win, her victory should cost her dear. Had Frank been alive, he would doubtless have been angry with him too, almost angry enough to disown him. But it is even more difficult to be angry with a non-existent individual than with the wind, the stars, or the sun. All Adam's rage was concentrated upon the woman who called herself his daughter-in-law, and he rather pitied Frank as the victim of her wiles than blamed him for his folly.

After drinking another glass of whisky without any perceptible effect on his spirits, he summoned his servant and started for home. Three hours later he arrived at Brandwood. How different was its aspect from that of the gloomy and smoke polluted town he had so lately left! Spring was bursting forth in all its glory. The park was covered with verdure, and pied with violets and daisies; the chestnuts in the avenue were donning their livery of green; hundreds of swallows were darting hither and thither in chase of invisible flies; a skylark was singing its sweet carol aloft; the rooks in the lime-trees were cawing a lusty chorus; and, as the rays of the setting sun fell on the old hall, with its dormer windows, its quaint gargoyles, its gray, lichen-grown roof, and its ivy-mantled walls, it seemed to Adam that he had never seen anything so beautiful, and his heart filled with exultation and pride; for he was as fond of the place as if he had inherited it from a long line of acred ancestors. But the feeling was only momentary, and when be remembered that Brandwood could not long be his, would never be his son's, and might pass to one whom he regarded as an alien and an impostor, he bowed his head and his eyes filled with tears.

When Rachel, as was her habit, met her husband in the hall, she saw that something was wrong, and led him into the morning-room, where she bad been sitting alone.

"What is it, Adam?" she said anxiously. "No more had news, I hope."

"It's not very good, Rachel, my poor lass; almost as bad, it seems to me, as losing Frank."

And then he told her the miserable story he had already told to Basel, to Bruff, and to Kean. He kept nothing back; and for the first time he imparted to her his scheme for founding a family, and the hope he had entertained of one day seeing Frank member for Redburn.

Rachel heard him quietly to the end. When he had finished she gave a sigh of relief. She had feared some-thing much more calamitous. Her husband's words and manner had made her apprehensive that some terrible misfortune might have befallen Mabel and Fritz, or that Valérie, whom she had not seen for several days, had become hopelessly insane.

It is very bad, Adam," she said, "and I am very sorry that poor Frank should have been so led away, and, what is worse, deceived us; but we ought to be thankful it is no worse."

"Why, how could it be worse, Rachel?"

"It would have been worse if this had come to light after he and Valérie were married. Oh, Adam, what should we have done?"

This was a new idea to Adam. He had been so pre-occupied with his own peculiar trouble that he had given little thought to the troubles - actual or potential - of others.

"It is bad enough," he replied, after a pause. "Just think: I may have to pay this hussy fifteen hundred a year, and, as likely as not, her child will get Brandwood."

"Why, I thought you wanted Frank's child to have it."

"But not Lydia Fell's; and who knows whether it is his child or not? It is as like as not one as she has picked up over yon."

"There are ways of finding that out, I suppose. But if it can be proved to be Frank's lawful child I don't see why the prospect of its coming into Brandwood should disturb you so much. We cannot take the estate with us. It will have to go to somebody. I don't like Lydia Fell any more than you do. But we could have the lad here - I daresay the mother would be willing enough to part with him - and bring him up as our own. The house would be brighter with a child in it, and we should soon forget that it was anybody's but Frank's." As Rachel spoke her voice trembled, and her loving eyes were wet with tears.

Nay, we will have none of Lydia Fell's brats in this house," rejoined Adam, but in a much less resolute tone than Rachel had expected. A few days previously such a suggestion would have put him in a rage, and been indignantly rejected.

"She is a right bad one," he continued. "I wonder how she managed so to befool Frank, Rachel?"

"Poor Frank! He was very weak, I'm afraid, and she very designing. But don't you think, Adam, that we have been more to blame than Frank?"

"What way - what could we have done different?"

"We should not have left Moorwell; or, if we had, we should not have come so far away as this. We ought to have kept him more with us. Instead of that we threw him into Lydia Fell's way - a girl that we knew next to nothing about - at an age when young men are most flighty and foolish. It was not wise; it was exposing them both to temptation. She thought Frank a great catch, and it was only natural, perhaps, that she should try to entrap him. But the person most to blame is that brother of her's. The moment he saw anything going on between them he should have stopped it, or told you. Instead of that he helped it on - maybe planned it from the first."

"He did; there is no doubt about that, and he is prompting Lydia now. That is what vexes me. I hate being deceived, and I cannot abide being beat. It may come to what you say in the end, Rachel, but Stephen Fell has not got the better of me yet. We will see what this Kean can do before we talk of throwing up the sponge. He's sharp; he'll happen find out something as will put a spoke in their wheel."

Rachel sighed. She abhorred all strife, and could not think that any good would come of the contest in which her husband had engaged.

CHAPTER XLVI

THE SUSPECTED FLAW

Adam did not forget his promise to Kean. He sent him, the very next day, Lydia Fell's receipt for the two thousand pounds, in consideration of which she undertook to quit England and release Frank from his engagement to marry her.

By return of post he received a letter to the following effect:

BLACKTHORNE v BLACKTHORNE.

"Dear Sir,

"Unless I am greatly mistaken, the document I have received from you to-day points to the possibility of a serious flaw in the plaintiff's case. I cannot, however, pronounce positively until I have some further information, and to this end I shall feel obliged if you will favour me with a call at your earliest convenience.

I am, dear sir, yours faithfully,

CHRISTOPHER KEAN.

Adam Blackthorne, Esq., Moorwell."

Half an hour after receiving this missive the master of Moorwell was speeding towards Manchester as fast as a pair of his fleetest horses could take him. With the exception of a short halt at Bury, the coachman did not draw rein until he pulled up opposite the seedy-looking entrance to Cutbill and Kean's office in King Street.

Adam had no tedious waiting this time. Mr. Kean was at liberty, and a minute after his name had been sent in he was requested to step forward.

"Ah, Mr. Blackthorne - glad to see you!" exclaimed the lawyer, smiling cheerily above the barricade of foolscap and parchment of which his writing-table seemed to be chiefly composed. "I thought you would come. Take a seat, please. You have brought a fine morning with you. I hope you left Mrs. Blackthorne quite well. I need hardly ask how you are, you look so rosy. Ah! I wish I could live in the country - there is nothing I would like better - but it is quite out of the question; I have not the time. I live as far out as I can, though. Near Cheetham Hill - you know Cheetham Hill, of course?"

"Yes, I know Cheetham Hill," answered Adam with just a shade of impatience in his voice. "I passed it this morning. As soon as ever I got your letter I set off, and I have driven through in little more than two hours."

Have you, really. Why, that beats the coach! You must have capital horses. And, now, about your case. You would see by my letter that I think I have found a flaw - only think mind - for all I can say at present is that I see the possibility of a flaw. Whether there really is one or not depends on circumstances of which I am as yet not fully informed, and as to which precise information may not easily be obtained. I gather from the document I received yesterday - Miss Fell's receipt and release to your son - that his name was Francis Adam?"

Adam nodded assent.

"He was christened Francis Adam, I suppose?"

"Not christened - we are Baptists, and don't christen - he was only named."

"No matter, it's all the same - legally at least, whatever it may be theologically. But, according to this extract from the marriage book of the Collegiate Church, he was married - or somebody else - in the name of Frank Blackthorne."

"Does that make any difference?"

"It may make a great deal of difference. Was Miss Fell aware, do you suppose, that your son's correct designation was Francis Adam?"

"Of course she was; she could not miss."

"But can we prove it? Moral certainty is not legal proof."

"Isn't that paper you have there sufficient proof? It is in Lydia Fell's handwriting, and signed by her, and she describes him as Francis Adam."

"I am afraid not. You see it was written after the marriage; and what we want is evidence that she knew before the marriage. The fact that she spontaneously thus described him might possibly serve to corroborate more positive evidence; alone it is nothing. You say she could not miss knowing. Could you swear she knew - that you have, for instance, heard her address him as Francis Adam, or your son so addressed by others in her presence?"

"I could not justly say at this moment," rejoined Adam, after a pause. "I shall have to think. Is it important?"

"So important that, if we can prove that Lydia Fell at the time of the marriage knew that your son's name was Francis Adam, it is null and void - in short, no marriage at all. If she did not know, and was no party to the deception, then the marriage stands good, provided, of course, the other side can prove the identity of your son with the Frank Blackthorne who went through a form of marriage with Lydia Fell at the Collegiate Church."

"They'll do that easy enough."

"Not so easily as you think. Your son is dead, and cannot be produced. A man calling himself Frank Blackthorne, of Warrington, was married to Lydia Fell - that we allow. But it remains to be proved that this man and your son, Francis Adam Blackthorne, are one and the same person. Don't you see?"

"But will not the witnesses and the parson be able to swear to him."

"That depends whether or not they knew him as your son - as Francis Adam Blackthorne, in fact. I don't say, mind you, that they will not be able to prove the marriage in the end; but they will not find it very easy, and I shall admit nothing."

"If they get hold of Stephen Fell he will prove it fast enough."

"Ah! he was one of the witnesses. He knew your son well, I suppose?"

He was our head bookkeeper, and lived at Moorwell. It was him as planned it all."

"Did he know your son's full name, do you suppose?"

"Of course he did - as well as I know it myself"

"But is it susceptible of legal proof?"

"I should think so. Frank always signed his name 'F. A. Blackthorne ' - sometimes 'Francis A' – never Frank in a business letter. He had my procuration, and signed cheques in the same way. These were always coming under Stephen's notice. Letters used to come to him addressed in full. Stephen could not miss but see them. I think, too, his name always appears in the books as 'Francis' or 'F. A.'"

"In the books of account kept by Stephen Fell?"

"Yes, in the ledger and cashbook and that. As soon as ever I get back I will look."

"Those entries you speak of would be in Stephen Fell's handwriting, I suppose?"

"Of course, that is what I mean."

"Capital, capital!" said Kean, rubbing his hands, and showing his sharp white teeth. "We shall win yet, I do believe. We have strong presumptive proof already. Stephen Fell knew your son's name. He was a witness to the marriage, and, therefore, a party to the fraud. If he says his sister did not know also - his sister who lived in the same house with him, and whom he was in the habit of seeing every day - he won't find many people to believe him. And the other side will be obliged to call him, for without his evidence they cannot prove the marriage. The second witness, Mark Binyon, as I have ascertained, is one of the pew openers of the Collegiate Church. I don't think he knew your son; nor that Mr. Harvey, the chaplain, knew him either."

"I am sure they did not," put in Adam.

"Then they must call Stephen Fell - very fortunately for us - for I imagine we should have some difficulty in finding him."

"Difficulty! It's much if we could find him at all, and if we did he would not come. He is somewhere in America."

"Hawke will find him. You may be sure of that; and it will go hard if we do not prove out of his mouth that his sister was a consenting party to the fraud. I shall retain Serjeant Pumpemdry forthwith. He will drag the truth out of him if anybody can. All the same, we must leave no stone unturned to find corroborative evidence. Anything of a documentary character would be simply invaluable. A letter, for instance, addressed to Lydia to your son as 'Francis A.' would settle the matter at once. Perhaps you may discover something of the sort amongst his papers. Failing that, you must try to ascertain if anybody remembers hearing Miss Fell speak of him as 'Francis Adam,' or addressed by that name in her hearing."

"I will do my best When will the trial come off, do you think? I thought it was a Chancery case."

"So it is. But it must end in a trial at the Assizes. Lydia Fell - Lydia Blackthorne she calls herself - has instituted proceedings in Chancery to procure a revocation of the grant of administration, which you obtained as your son's next of kin. We answer by denying the marriage. The next step will be for the Court of Chancery to send down the main issue - the proof of marriage - to be tried by a jury at the Assizes, so as to enable the Chancery Judge to come to a right decision in the matter. When Hawke gets wind of the settlement as by means of the bill of discovery he is sure to do, he may file a bill for specific performance of your engagement to charge the Brandwood estate with an annuity of fifteen hundred a year in favour of your son's widow. But that also will depend on the verdict."

"And the child?"

"They are evidently keeping the child in the back-ground for the present. Perhaps, as it is supposed to have been born in America, there may be some difficulty in proving its birth. For, as you are doubtless aware, unless it can be established that it came into the world within a certain time after your son's death, it will not be deemed either his next of kin or heir-at-law. Or Hawke, in order to swell his costs, may intend to make the child's claim the subject of another and subsequent action. But that is a matter of secondary importance. It will be time enough to consider it when the marriage is proved or disproved."

"Altogether, then, Mr. Kean, you think we have a good case?"

"Say, rather, hopeful. If you can find conclusive proof of Lydia Fell's complicity in the fraud I shall call it a good one."

"Well, I'll do my best. But fraud is rather a strong word, is it not?"

"Nevertheless, it was a fraud if done intentionally, albeit your son and the Fells may have looked upon it as nothing more than an innocent deception. Indeed, you may be sure that, if Miss Lydia and her brother had been aware of the consequences, they would never have allowed your son to describe himself as Frank Blackthorne, or suggested that he should do so; for the idea is as likely to have originated with them as with him."

I see. But you don't say when the case is likely to be tried - at the next Assizes?"

"Probably. At the next Lancaster Assizes. But that will give us plenty of time to hunt up evidence. They will not come off until after the long vacation - three or four months hence. All the same, you would do well to look through your papers, and your son's, and make searching inquiry of all who came in contact with them for further proofs of the Fells' complicity."

CHAPTER XLVII

SEARCHING FOR EVIDENCE.

Adam Blackthorne's worst enemies could not accuse him of lack of promptitude in matters of business, and even if he had been an indolent man his anxiety to upset Frank's marriage would have caused him to use all possible diligence in acting on his lawyer's advice. The day after his visit to Manchester he made careful search through all the papers likely to contain the proof so much desired by Mr. Kean.

Of Stephen Fell's knowledge of Frank's surname the most ample evidence was forthcoming. Every time the former had written the name in the cashbook and elsewhere - and he had written it some scores of times - it appeared as "F.A." - never as "Frank Blackthorne " - while in one instance, the heading of Frank's account in the private ledger, he had put it down in full, "Francis Adam Blackthorne." There would be no difficulty in proving that these entries were made by Stephen - the fact could be sworn to by Adam himself and by every clerk in the office.

So far as the brother went it was a clear case, but as touching the sister the most minute and repeated quests brought to light only one scrap of evidence from which might be inferred her knowledge of the fact in question. The inference, moreover, was far from being an inevitable one. Frank had evidently destroyed every written record of his connection with Lydia - if he had ever possessed any - for the only piece of paper found in his desk in any way relating to her was the back of a letter addressed to "F. A. Blackthorne, Esq.," and bearing the Manchester postmark of a date a few days prior to the alleged marriage. From a comparison of the handwriting with that of the receipt there could be little doubt that this address had been penned by Lydia; and the postmark and date pointed to the conclusion that the letter of which it had once formed a part was posted in Manchester shortly after her departure from Moorwell on her pretended visit to her aunt.

As for oral evidence, the only person who could testify to anything of importance was Mabel. She said that one evening, shortly after they left

Moorwell for Brandwood, she took tea with Frank at the old house. She and her brother were teasing each other, as they often did - quite good-humouredly of course-and she remembered saying (in reply to a chaffing observation about her growing fat, she believed it was): "If you go on in that way, Francis Adam, I shall not take tea with you again." She often called him Francis Adam when they were teasing. This seemed to surprise Lydia. " I was not aware Mr. Frank had two names," she said. "I like Frank much better than Francis Adam. It is such a pretty name; don't you think it is, Miss Blackthorne?"

Mabel had a vivid recollection of this conversation, and was ready to swear to it. It had impressed itself particularly on her mind because she considered Lydia rather forward in making the observation, and, to show her displeasure, had not deigned to reply.

Adam regarded his daughter's testimony as weighty and conclusive. He thought it rendered victory certain. Not so Mr. Kean.

"I do not for a moment question Mrs. Fritz Basel's statement," he said, when his client had acquainted him with its purport. "To my mind, indeed, it is, as you deem it, conclusive. But you must remember that we have to consider its effect on the minds of a jury, minimised as it will be by the sophistications of a clever advocate. It is more than a year since the conversation took place. When the action is tried it will be a year and a half. Your daughter made no record of the conversation at the time of its occurrence - she keeps no diary, I presume?"

Adam gave a negative shake of his head.

"It is therefore purely an affair of memory. The memory is proverbially treacherous. If it be treacherous as regards incidents, as regards spoken words it is utterly untrustworthy. Then, too, Mrs. Fritz Basel has a strong personal interest in the result of the trial, not merely a sentimental interest such as your daughter could not fail to have, but as your heiress. It depends upon the issue of the case whether her child - if she has one - or Lydia Fell's inherits the Brandwood estate. It is scarcely possible in these circumstances that her evidence can be impartial. It will be more or less warped by the feeling of hostility to the plaintiff and her cause, which she would be something more than human not to entertain. Mrs. Fritz's testimony, therefore, must be taken rather as the expression of a strong belief than as proof of a fact. This will be the line of argument adopted by the other side, and it is so plausible that it can hardly fail to tell with the jury. Nevertheless I shall call your daughter as a witness. If we cannot win a verdict by one overwhelming piece of evidence - a single powerful stroke as it were - we must try the effect of a multitude of feebler strokes - make up by numbers what we lack in strength."

As for the letter back, Kean had already informed Adam that, while not without value, it was less valuable than might at first appear. Everything would depend upon the opinion of the experts in handwriting who would have to be consulted and called; and the evidence of experts in caligraphy was very much like that of mad doctors - what one of them affirms another could be got to deny. Altogether, as could easily be seen, the lawyer was far from sanguine as to the result, and it seemed to Adam that his confidence grew less as the hour of trial drew near. The case was following precisely the course which Kean in the first instance had anticipated. After his answer traversing the bill filed in the Palatine Court of Chancery, the Judge had ordered certain issues to be tried at the Assizes. Hence the case, though beginning in Equity, would be virtually decided by a jury and a Common Law Judge. For if the plaintiff succeeded in proving the marriage, Adam could prolong the fight only by raising legal quibbles, which would not affect the ultimate issue, and profit only the lawyers.

CHAPTER XLVIII.

ADAM ORDERS A LOCK-OUT.

Meanwhile the approaching trial, and the strange circumstances out of which it had arisen, were the talk of all the country-side. The merits of it were debated almost nightly in every public-house between Redburn and Orrington. People took sides on the question. Some were for Adam, others for Mrs. Frank Blackthorne, as she called herself and was generally spoken of. The factory operatives of the neighbourhood were among her warmest partisans. If her claims could have been put to the vote she would have won by an overwhelming majority. Working people looked upon her as almost one of themselves. True, she had never been a weaver or a winder, but her brother had been bookkeeper at Moorwell, and she had occupied an almost menial position in the Blackthorne household. Adam's repudiation of his son's marriage was ascribed to pure pride and malevolence. He was a tyrant and an oppressor, people said, using his position and his vast wealth to crush a beautiful and virtuous girl, whose only offence had been falling in love with his own son. The women were, of course, nearly all for Lydia.

Lydia and her adviser, Charley Hawke, were not slow to take advantage of this popular enthusiasm for her cause. She showed herself everywhere. Hawke drove her about in his phaeton. One day they carried the war into the enemy's camp by driving past Moorwell just as the factories were "loosing." Lydia was, of course, dressed in her widow's weeds, and she looked so sad, so pretty, and so interesting, that some of the hands gave her a hearty cheer.

When Adam heard of this he pretended to treat the incident with indifference; yet, as will speedily be seen, he did not forget it. Then, at the suggestion of a friend of Charley Hawke, a subscription was started towards Mrs. Frank Blackthorne's legal expenses, and in the course of two or three weeks as many hundred pounds were either paid or promised - to the lawyer's great delight for he began to perceive that lose who might, he was in a fair way to gain. Among the subscribers to the fund were many persons of condition, more than one of whom, it was rumoured, had called upon Lydia for the purpose of personally tendering their sympathy and expressing their best wishes for her success.

The newspapers were, of course, constrained to take some notice of the matter; though, as it was *sub judice,* they could do little more than mention the fact of the approaching trial, and the circumstances, so far as they were known, out of which it had arisen. The *Redburn Rooster,* however, ventured to go farther than this. It was the Tory organ of the town, and, Adam Blackthorne being both a Radical and a Dissenter, it could not resist the temptation of gibbeting an opponent. In an article entitled "A Radical at Home," it held the master of Moorwell up to public odium, stigmatised him as a tyrant at home and a hypocrite abroad, and called upon its readers to give a generous support to the cause of truth and justice, meaning thereby the cause of Mrs. Frank Blackthorne.

Adam showed this production to his lawyer, who was extremely anxious to indict the writer of the article and the proprietor of the paper for slander, and to move the Chancery Court to punish their audacity in commenting on a case *sub judice* by committing them for contempt. But Adam, thinking one lawsuit at a time was enough, would only permit Kean to write to the *Rooster* people demanding an apology, and threatening them with all sorts of pains and penalties if the offence should be repeated. The apology, as indicated by Kean - and which was as abject as the provocation had been wanton and illegal - was made, and the *Rooster* was careful thereafter to give no further cause for complaint.

These manifestations were a revelation to Adam. As he observed to Basel, he never knew before how many enemies he had, nor what it was to be well hated.

"Ah, friend Blackthorne," observed his partner sententiously, "all rich men have their enemies, and every prosperous man is hated by his neighbours. You are both rich and prosperous, and all who covet your wealth and are jealous of your rise - and have nothing to hope from you - have now an opportunity of safely gratifying their feelings by siding with Lydia Fell. Then, we must not forget that hers is the popular cause. I daresay, if the truth were known, many, if not most, of your own hands would throw up their hats for her tomorrow, if they dared."

"I know they would," rejoined Adam dryly. "They did as much the other day; they cheered her as she went by - her and Charley Hawke's wife. All the same, Basel, it is not right. Don't I pay 'em their wages? There's fifteen hundred here, to say nothing of those at your place; and for one as comes to the factory there's three as stops at home. That makes more than five thousand mouths as I find food for every week of their lives. What would become of them, think you, if I were to stop the tap - shut the place up? They would not be so prodigal then."

"Probably not; but then you know, friend Blackthorne, there are always two ways of looking at a question. Your work-people may possibly think that their labour has made you what you are. If you could get at their real opinion, it might even be found that they believe the obligation to be on your side rather than on theirs."

"Happen. But their belief would not make it so. It stands to reason that the man as provides work for folks, and pays money, confers an obligation on them as receives it. There is no getting over that. Am I not under an obligation to my customers? I will take my hat off any time to a man as gives me a good order."

"By the same rule, you would take off your hat to a tenant who pays you a good rent?"

"And glad to do it, if it would be any satisfaction to him. I look on a farmer as does his duty by the land, and is always up to time with his rent, as a good customer, and I always try to treat him accordingly. As for the hands, I only expect them to treat me with the respect as is due to him as pay. If they don't, it will be worse for 'em - that's all."

A few days after this conversation, Adam learnt, in a rather unpleasant way, that his theory of the relations that ought to subsist between employer and employed did not obtain general acceptance - or, at any rate, was not always acted upon - among those whom it most nearly concerned - his own work-people.

He happened to be leaving Moorwell one evening at "loosing" time. As the hands were beginning to pour through the factory gates he was stepping into the gig which was to convey him to Brandwood Hall. At the same moment and as appeared at a given signal, there arose from the sea of shawled heads and paper caps a loud, prolonged, and unmistakable hiss. There were even cries of "Shame!" and "Tyrant!" Adam looked sharply round with glittering eyes, and there was a portentous tremor on his lips and a hot flush on his cheeks.

"Tell Pearson I want him," he exclaimed to his groom, who stood at the horse's head.

In three minutes Pearson, the manager, was on the spot.

"We won't start to-morrow, Pearson. You can make a holiday of it"

"What! None of the engines?"

"None of. 'em."

"When shall I tell the hands to come, then?"

"When I give orders, and not before."

Whereupon Adam gave his mare a sharp cut with the whip, and, being a high-spirited creature, she went off in the direction of Brandwood at her fastest trot.

"You hear," shouted Pearson to the work-people, most of whom had been waiting to see the upshot of the incident, "you have not to come to-morrow. And I don't know when we are to start again nayther - not till th' mayster gives orders, he says."

The lads and lasses laughed - the prospect of lakeing (playing) a day or two being by no means disagreeable to them - but the older people - fathers and mothers with many little mouths to feed - looked far from pleased, and they went home full of misgivings touching the next week's supply of porridge.

For three days the Moorwell engines did not turn round. Every morning when Pearson applied to the "old master " (as he was still called, albeit there was no more a young one) for instructions he received the same answer - " Not yet." On the third morning, instead of Pearson, there came a deputation. It consisted of three women - Betty Twirler, Jane o' Jonathan's, and Mally-fro'-th'-Green - all "old hands," good weaver - two of them mothers of families and great favourites with their master.

Mally-fro'-th'-Green opened the conversation.

"We've come to ax yo', mayster," she said, "when we can start ageean."

"I don't know, Mally; not just yet."

"But what will become on us? We shall aw be clemming (starving) soon."

"Dunnot you think, mayster," put in Betty Twirler, "as it is rather hard to clem us aw just because some o' th' young 'uns has been foolish? It worn't reyt to hiss yo'; we dunnot howd wi' it a bit - dun we, Jane?"

"No, we dunnot; nor nobody else wi' ony sense nayther. And there worn't mony on 'em as dud hiss - nobbut a two thry o' th' young 'uns.

"A two thry hundred, you mean, Jane," said Adam.

"Well, we dudn't," exclaimed Betty Twirler.

"I am sure you did not, Betty."

"Well, what do yo' lock us out for then?"

"I was like to make an example, you know;" was Adam's rather weak answer to this home-thrust.

"Well," said Mally-fro'-th'-Green, "lass and woman I've wrought here gooin' i' thirty year. I worked for yo' when yo' started th' Owd Factory, and this is th' fost time as I've bin locked out; and torn out I never would. And aw up o' account o' that theer Lydia Fell - wi' her stuck-up ways and her white eebraes (eyebrows) as I never could abide."

"Nor me nayther," affirmed Betty Twirler.

"Nor me nayther," echoed Jane o' Jonathan's.

"Hoo's a besom," put in Mally.

"Hoo's a hussy," exclaimed Jane.

"Hoo's a gradely good-for-nowt, and no moor wed to the young mayster than I am mysel'," said Betty Twirler, by way of bringing matters to a climax.

"And now, mayster," asked Mally-fro'-th'-Green, putting her arms akimbo with an air rather of command than entreaty, "when con we start - me, as has been here gooin' i' thirty year; Jane theer, as has been working for yo' nearly as long; and Betty, as has never wrought nowheer else? And we have sixteen childer between us - Jane and me - and not aboon hoaf on 'em as addles (earns) owt - and th' badge (grocer) to pay, and th' rent and coils, and th' clogger. And there's a Scotchman (travelling draper) coming to our house next week as wants fifteen shilling on me, and he says if he does not get it he'll sell us up. And, bithmon, I believe he's i' arnest."

"Very well," said Adam, who was really glad of an excuse to recommence work, "send Pearson here, and I'll give him orders to start to-morrow."

"Couldn't yo' say one o'clock to-day, mayster, and let us work till eight to-neet? It 'ud mak a difference of seven hours, and we shall hev fearfu' little brass to draw o' Saturday, strive as we will."

"If they can get the steam up in time I have no objection; but I would not have done it for anybody else, lasses."

"They're getting it up awready," observed Jane o" Jonathan's with a smile. "They set agate (began) when we agreed to come and see yo',"

"Ay, I daresay," rejoined Adam. "They know I am always soft when I'm tackled by a woman; and three together is more than either me or any man else could cope wi'."

And then there was a hearty laugh all round, and the three weavers ran off to announce the good news to their friends, who were waiting outside. Two hours later Moorwell Mills were once more in full swing.

"They will not hiss me any more, I think," muttered Adam, as the door closed behind his visitors.

He was right; his hands never hissed him again.

CHAPTER XLIX.

THE DRY COMPANY.

Although The Bay Mare was not quite the first of Redburn inns - that position being by general consent assigned to The Bull's Head - it was nevertheless a highly respectable and well-accustomed house, and one of the oldest in the town. Its liquors were of the best; the snugness of its bar parlour left nothing to be desired; and the hostess, Mrs. Poker, who, albeit forty, was neither fat nor fair, enjoyed a deserved popularity among her customers.

For many years Adam Blackthorne had put up at The Bay Mare on his weekly visits to Redburn market; nor would he ever have put up anywhere else had not Mrs. Poker refused, on two several occasions, to give a vote to the candidates whose success he had at heart.

It must not be inferred from this circumstance that at the time in question the ladies of Redburn possessed the parliamentary franchise. But if Mrs. Poker was not herself an elector she owned one, which amounts to pretty much the same thing. She had a husband whose name was on the electoral roll of the borough - a husband who belonged to her, body and soul. He was a quiet little man; with a bald head, straw-coloured whiskers, and a subdued manner. He acted as butler to the establishment, went errands when he was sober (which was not often), and made himself generally useful. The frequenters of the house always called him "Tom." He was never by any chance addressed as "Mr. Poker." Except in one particular, he obeyed his wife with the promptness and docility of a trained spaniel - he would not refrain from drink. Not that he refused verbal obedience; nobody could be more profuse in promises. The misfortune was that he never kept them. Do what she would, Mrs. Poker could not keep Tom sober, and he rarely went to bed less than half drunk. In all other things, however, he rendered faithful service, and invariably voted as his wife bade him - often despite strong temptations to the contrary. At every election attempts were made to bottle him. But as Will Dayman, one of the most faithful customers of The Bay Mare, remarked, you might as well try to bottle a brewery; for Tom Poker, let him be as tipsy as he would, never lost control of his legs. He might not be able to see, perhaps, but he could always contrive to walk, and did walk when his would-be bottlers were lying under the table or rolling in the gutter.

It is hardly necessary to say that nobody in Redburn ever committed the absurdity of asking Tom how he proposed to vote. His wife, on the other hand, was always assiduously canvassed by the representatives of both political parties; and though, on one or two occasions, when very hard pressed by the Liberals, she bestowed upon them one vote, she had latterly given her undivided support to their opponents.

Now, it was the custom at Redburn, when an election was in prospect, for the leading Liberals and Conservatives to call upon their principal supporters, especially those of them who were large employers of labour, to do all they could for the cause which they respectively favoured. This meant securing, by every means in their power, the votes of such of their work-people as possessed the franchise, and of the tradesmen with whom they had dealings - a proceeding which in local parlance was known as "putting on the screw."

Moorwell being outside the borough, Adam Blackthorne had no voters in his employ, nor was he an elector himself. Nevertheless, he did his best for his party; and, as he was at the head of a large concern, his influence was considerable. He had large accounts with sundry Redburn tradesmen. Being a good paymaster, his custom was highly esteemed; but no shop-keeper or mill-furnisher who did not vote for at least one of the Liberal candidates had much chance of getting an order at Moorwell. Adam saw no wrong in this. The other side did the same; and did not landowners always control the votes of their tenants? He even went so far as to change his doctor because that gentleman's political principles, or rather his votes, were not to his liking.

"Let him sell his physic to the Tories," he said; "I'll have none of it."

When Mrs. Poker gave both of her votes to the Tory candidates, instead of giving one to each side, as she had formerly done, he signified his displeasure by dropping one of the two or three glasses of whisky he had been wont to consume on market days. When she committed the offence the second time he left The Bay Mare altogether, and betook himself thenceforth to The Bull's Head.

The landlady of The Bay Mare, like most of her sex, was not much of a politician. She had many prejudices, but few principles. She knew, however, on which side her bread was buttered; and the proceeding that lost her the custom of Adam Blackthorne secured her the much more valuable custom of the Dry Company. The Dry Company - presumably so called because the members of it were generally thirsty - consisted of a number of Redburn tradesmen, who met every night of the week in the bar-parlour of The Bay Mare to discuss the affairs of the nation - from a strictly Conservative point of view - and retail the gossip of the neighbourhood. There might be a dozen of them, all told. The most regular attendants et the symposium were the Will Dayman already mentioned, who lived on his means and a few commissions he earned as agent in heald yarn and gold thread, which he sold exclusively to Tory manufacturers; Peter Pigskin, a political saddler and harness- maker; Paul Purge, a constitutional apothecary; George Pincop, a cotton spinner of correct principles; and Richard Roe, managing clerk to Garlick, Onions, and Sage, the mustiest and most orthodox firm of legal practitioners in the town. The most important and highly-esteemed frequenter of Mrs. Poker's bar-parlour, however, was Isaac Grains, a wealthy brewer, and the owner of The Bay Mare. As he owned, besides, many other public-houses in the borough, his influence was invaluable to his party, and his utterances were always treated with profound respect by his cronies of the Dry Company. Grains was strictly orthodox, his loyalty to the Crown being only exceeded by his devotion to the Church and his reverence for the Bible. If his education had not unfortunately been neglected in early youth he would probably have been one of the borough members. Not that the free-and-easy electors of Redburn were particularly exacting in the matter of literary qualifications. Mere faults of orthography they could pardon, and the misuse of the aspirate in a community by whom the letter "H" was either generally ignored or deliberately despised was rather a recommendation than a cause of offence. But the line must be drawn somewhere, and even the most ardent admirer of ancient institutions might hesitate to vote for a man who wrote "i" when he meant "I," spoke of his opponents as "them theer rascally Radicals," and of the liquor he brewed as "that theer beer," Nevertheless, Grains had his hopes. Wealth and the will to spend it, together with sufficient sense to vote straight, are sometimes preferred by constituencies to intellect and learning; and before the brewer died he had the proud satisfaction of writing after his name the magic letters "M.P.," which he probably esteemed all the more highly that he had paid for them at the rate of five thousand pounds apiece.

On a certain evening, some two or three months after the events related in the last chapter, several of the members of the Dry Company were assembled in Mrs. Poker's bar-parlour, and a very pleasant bar-parlour it was. A bright fire burnt merrily in a wide old-fashioned grate, on the hob end whereof was planted a huge highly-polished copper kettle, the steam from the curved spout of it curling gracefully up the chimney. On either side of the fireplace was a capacious comfortably cushioned arm-chair. In one of these chairs sat slender Will Dayman; in the other reposed the portly form of Grains the brewer. The remainder of the company present were seated on benches ranged round the wall. The side of the room opposite the fireplace was occupied by a rack filled with glittering crystal from the midst of which stood out half-a-dozen copper-bound spirit barrels, like a brigade of field guns escorted by a regiment of light cavalry. On a large mahogany table in the centre of the room lay a multitude of long clay pipes, interspersed with many toddy tumblers, wherefrom rose a savoury odour of rum, whisky, nutmeg, and lemon, for the mixing of the ingredients - without due consumption of which a right discussion of the affairs of the nation had been impossible - was in active operation.

"I don't think as this 'ere whisky," observed the saddler, as he watched carefully the effect of commingling water with spirit, "is as good as Mrs. Poker used to give us. Seems to me as there is more o' that what-d'-you--call it - that fuzleum ile in it"

"Fusil hoil, not fuzleum ile, Pigskin," said Purge, with a smile of superiority.

"Fusil, then. Drat it, there's so many words nowadays as one can hardly mind 'em all, much less pronounce 'em right I don't know what folks wants with so many words. What do they say fusil for? - why cannot they say whisky ile - hoil, I mean - I wonder? Everybody would know what they meant then. But don't you think, Purge, as this whisky is just rather new? I only drank six glasses last night, and - you will hardly believe it - but I was really a bit unfine this morning."

"You are losing your head, Pigskin, that's what it is," put in Dayman; "the whisky's right enough. It does not make my head ache, and I knock plenty of it into me."

"I always stick to rum," remarked the brewer, who, having mixed his liquor, was proceeding to fill his pipe. "Do you know why?"

Whereupon the company promptly said no, albeit Grains had asked and answered the same question times without number, and everybody knew what was coming.

"Because - because after the battle of Trafalgar - "

At this moment the brewer lost for a moment the attention of his auditors. They were all looking at a newcomer who had just entered the room; for although the bar-parlour of The Bay Mare was occupied at nights chiefly by the Dry Company, it was open as well to the general public. Yet it rarely happened for an entire stranger to be seen therein; and the individual who had just put in an appearance was unknown to any member of the company, and seemingly not a townsman. He might be about twenty-five or thirty years old, had a very yellow face, huge sandy whiskers, long curly hair, wore green spectacles, and his clothes were clearly not of the Redburn cut.

"Good-evening, gentlemen," he said, and then taking a seat ordered a glass of rum and lighted a pipe.

"As I was saying," remarked Grains, when his friends had done staring at the newcomer, "I always drinks rum, because, after the battle of Trafalgar, Lord Nelson's body was brought home in a puncheon of it. I honours the memory of Lord Nelson, therefore I drinks rum. And I think too, gentlemen, as what was good for his outside cannot miss being good for my inside."

"And quite right you are too, Mr. Grains," observed Pincop. "I look upon rum as the national spirit; it has made us what we are. Look at our sailors, how they carried all afore 'em in the last war! Do you think they could have done what they did without rum - roast beef and rum? Where would they have been, and where would the country have been, if they had had nowt to eat and drink but frogs and sour wine, like them French?"

"Ah, those were glorious times!" said Dayman, who posed as the literary character of the company; "no Reform Bills then, no Chartists, no Corn-law League, no teetotalers, no infernal railways cutting up the country and marring the beauty of the scenery - "

"And none of them theer Radical beggars going up and down making speeches and disturbing folks' minds. As for that Corn-law League, I look upon it as a d -- dissenting do. It is Corn Laws now; it will be the Church next. There's Bright, one of th' leaders, he is a Quaker; there's Fox, he is a hinfidel; and there's Cobden, he's a - he's a -"

"Churchman," suggested the stranger with the sandy whiskers.

"Then he's a d-- bad Churchman. I don't believe i' Churchmen as mixes with Radicals, Cornlaw Leaguers, and sich like riff-raff."

"Talking of the Corn-law League," said Dayman, "have you heard that Adam Blackthorne has subscribed a thousand pounds to the Repeal Fund?"

"Ay, he's another of 'em. Better keep his brass for that lawsuit of his with his daughter-in-law. It will cost a bonny penny, they tell me; and he is sure to lose - isn't he, Mr. Roe?"

"Sure," answered the lawyer's clerk, with an air of quiet confidence which was very impressive. "They have not a leg to stand on. They want to prove that Mrs. Francis Blackthorne - for she is as much Mrs. Francis Blackthorne as my wife is Mrs. Richard Roe - was party to a fraudulent marriage; that she let young Blackthorne call himself Frank only, when she knew all along that his name was Francis Adam."

If they could prove that, the marriage would be no good, I suppose?"

"Of course not. But, Lord bless you! they cannot. We know, because we are Mr. Hawke's agents. They have only got a bit of presumptive evidence, that Serjeant Buster will knock to pieces in no time; and Mrs. Francis and her brother Stephen will swear that she never knew her husband's full name before the marriage - whatever she may have known after."

"When does the trial come off?"

"Directly. The commission will be opened on Monday, and the case of Blackthorne against Blackthorne is pretty sure to be called the day after, or, at any rate, the next day."

"What has become of the child, Roe? There is one, they say; but nobody seems to have seen it," observed apothecary Purge.

"Oh yes; and all the Brandwood estate is settled on it. Mrs. Francis was obliged to leave it in America - the boy, for it is a boy, was born there, you know. He is very delicate, and the docters thought a sea voyage might be dangerous, or even fatal, until he gets a little older. But when the trial is over Mrs. Francis will go back and bring him herself; and then he will probably be made a ward in Chancery."

"I am glad to hear you say as Blackthorne will be beat, Mr. Poe," said Pigskin. "What business has he to have any family pride, I should like to know? Are not the Fells quite as good as him? Why, I've seen Adam Blackthorne - Squire of Brandwood, they call him now - carrying a pack of pieces up this 'ere street! But from what I hear he quite counts on winning. Mr. Basel's coachman was in my shop yesterday, and he says as Mr. Blackthorne's coachman told him as they are cocksure to win."

"Mr. Blackthorne's groom?" rejoined the brewer with much scorn. "What does Mr. Blackthorne's groom know about it? Look here, Pigskin, I'll bet you any thing you like; I'll lay you ten pounds to one - twenty to one - ay, fifty to one - you or anybody else - as Adam Blackthorne loses his case."

Pigskin was silent. To have accepted the brewer's offer might have seemed like differing from him; and no member of the Dry Company had ever yet had the audacity to differ openly from Mr. Grains.

"I beg your pardon, sir," said the stranger, who could not be expected to know the unwritten law of the place, "if nobody else cares to take the bet I will. Fifty to one I think you said, that Mr. Blackthorne loses his case."

"You have the advantage of me, sir; I have not the pleasure of knowing you," answered Grains, rather rudely.

"That does not matter in the least. One man's money is as good as another's, I suppose. Here is a sovereign, which I will put into the hands of any gentleman present - or perhaps the landlady would kindly take charge of it"

"Yes, yes; give it to the landlady," exclaimed-several members of the company.

"Oh, I'll stand to my offer," said Grains, who saw that if he tried to back out of it he might lose credit with his companions. "I am a man of my word. But you are a stranger. You perhaps will not be here when the result of the trial is known."

"When do you think it will be known?" looking at the lawyer's clerk.

"Let me see - this is Thursday. The Assizes begin on Monday. The result should be known here on next Thursday, or the day after - say to-morrow week."

Well then," said the stranger, handing a sovereign to Mrs. Poker, "I will try to be here on the evening of to-morrow week. If I lose the landlady will of course give you the sovereign."

The landlady nodded assent.

"So if I lose I need not come. If; on the other hand, I win, and do not come, you will perhaps do me the favour to pay the fifty pounds to Mrs. Poker on my behalf."

"If I lose, certainly. But I am sure to win"

"But what must I do with it?" exclaimed the land-lady. "Take care of it until you do come?"

"No, you shall give it on my behalf to some charity, or otherwise dispose of it for the public good. Can any gentleman suggest anything?"

"The restoration of the Parish Church," said Dayman.

"The Church Missionary Society," exclaimed Grains.

"The Dispensary," said Purge.

"The Soup Kitchens," said Pincop.

"The Blind Asylum," said Pigskin.

"No, I have it," exclaimed the stranger briskly. "Mr. Grains seems very fond of the Anti-corn-law League. If I win, Mrs. Poker, you shall hand over my winnings to the Anti-corn-law League, in the name of John Robinson, please."

"It will be your money, sir, and I shall of course follow your instructions," said the landlady.

"Thank you, Mrs. Poker. Good-evening, gentlemen."

And before the members of the Dry Company could bethink themselves what to say, Mr. John Robinson had disappeared.

"Who is he?" asked every man of his neighbour, and though nobody could answer the question, all agreed that a person who had ventured to treat Mr. Grains with such open disrespect must of necessity be an entire stranger in Redburn.

"Who he is I cannot tell," remarked the brewer, "but what he is it is plain to see. He's a himpudent fellow and unless I'm much mistaken, one of them theer rascally Radicals."

CHAPTER L.

THE STRANGER IN NUMBER FOURTEEN.

ON the morning after this conversation, as Mr. Basel sat in his office at Moorwell, a letter, brought by special messenger from Redburn, was put into his hand. It ran as follows

"If Mr. Basel would render a great service to the Blackthorne family, he is urgently requested to call this afternoon, between two and three o'clock, at The Bull's Head, Redburn, for the purpose of receiving important information in reference to the approaching trial. If he inquires for the gentleman in No.14, he will obtain an interview with the writer of this note. Meanwhile Mr. Basel is earnestly besought to keep this communication and the object of his visit to Redburn a profound secret. If he fails herein danger will befall."

"Donner Wetter!" muttered Basel, after he had read and re-read this missive, *"was ist los"* (what is up) now, I wonder? It might be a summons from the Holy Vehm. If I fail herein danger may befall! Danger to whom or

what? Shall I be hanged at midnight in a forest, or stabbed in my bed while asleep? But I will go. I shall be glad to render a service to friend Blackthorne, and I feel very curious to know what this mystery means. One has heard before now of traps being laid in this way to rob and murder people. But no-nobody would be so mad as to attempt such a deed at a house like The Bull's Head, and by broad daylight too."

He ordered the messenger to be called in.

"Tell the gentleman who gave you this note," he said - "the gentleman in No.14 - that Mr. Basel will come. You can remember?"

Yes, sir; I shall not forget."

"But you might. Everything is possible. See, give him this card - that will be surer."

The card bore the words "Mr. Basel will come."

Four hours later, as the clock of Redburn parish church chimed three, Mr. Basel's carriage stopped opposite The Bull's Head.

It was a much larger house than The Bay Mare. A broad flight of steps led up to the great outer door, which, save for a few hours in the early morning, was always open. It was a busy place, and people were perpetually going in and out, for The Bull's Head was virtually the exchange and newsroom of the town. The corridor was littered with the boxes of arriving and departing bagmen; and as Basel mounted the steps he met a group of parcel-laden and red-faced commercial travellers, who, having eaten their dinners and taken their allowance of port, sherry, and brandy-and-water, were sallying forth to call on their customers.

He went into the bar.

"Is there a gentleman staying in the house who occupies No.14, Mrs. Broadbeam?" he asked of the landlady, a portly dame of commanding presence, decided manner, and most unfeminine curtness of speech, who was engaged in pumping beer into a big jug.

"There is, Mr. Basel"

"Do you know his name?"

"I do not, Mr. Basel. All that I know is that he came here the day before yesterday by the Manchester coach, takes his meals in his own room, and, so far as I know, has never been out except for an hour or two last night."

"Confound the fellow!" thought Basel, "it is only a clerk from Kean's office, after all. What does he mean by sending such an absurd note, and making all this mystery?"

"Can I see this gentleman, Mrs. Broadbeam? I have business with him."

"Certainly. Here, Thomas" (raising her voice).

Whereupon Thomas, a stout little fellow, with a red face, a red waistcoat, and a game eye - the boots and odd man of the establishment - promptly appeared.

"Take Mr. Basel to No.14, Thomas."

"Will you come this way, sir?" said the boots, who, having much to do, was always in a hurry.

Basel went that way accordingly, and after ascending a wide stone staircase, and traversing a variety of passages, they arrived at No.14, which, as Thomas informed him, consisted of a sitting-room and a bedroom *en suite.*

"Come in," exclaimed a deep voice, in answer to Basel's knock.

As Basel entered, his anonymous correspondent rose from an arm-chair in which he had been sitting, and – as appeared from a newspaper lying on the floor – reading. He was a tall, spectacled man, with long red whiskers and hair of similar hue - the same, in fact, who had laid the bet the night before with Grains the brewer, in The Bay Mare, and given the name of John Robinson.

"Ah, Mr. Basel," he exclaimed, seizing the surprised dyer's hand, and warmly shaking it, "I am glad to see you. It is very kind of you to comply so promptly with my request. I suppose you thought it very strange."

"Very," said Basel, staring very hard at his host's red whiskers. "But really, sir, you have the advantage of me. You seem to know me very well; but I cannot call to mind that I ever met you before."

"What! Is it possible - don't you really know me, Mr. Basel?"

"No," replied the dyer, after a pause, as he put on his spectacles, the better to examine the stranger's enigmatical countenance. "I cannot make you out. I thought at first you might he somebody from Kean's office, but don't remember ever to have seen you there."

"Who is Kean?"

"You don't know who Kean is, and yet profess to have an important communication to make in reference to the approaching trial. Why, Kean is Mr. Blackthorne's lawyer.

"I thought - I thought - " rejoined the stranger. Then, as if moved by a sudden impulse, he plucked off his green spectacles.

"Do you know me now, Mr. Basel?" he exclaimed.

As Basel looked into the man's eyes they seemed strangely familiar to him, and. a suspicion crossed his mind which made him tremble and grow pale. But it went as quickly as it came. A moment's reflection sufficed to show its absurdity.

"No," he replied, after another long look at his questioner's orange-coloured face, "I do not know you even yet. You had better tell me who you are. This is only trifling, and I came here, as I supposed, for a business purpose."

"Well then, do you know me now?" said the stranger, stripping himself by two rapid movements of his red whiskers and sandy hair.

"Frank Blackthorne?" gasped Basel, who was so overcome that he had to lean against the wall for support "It is either Frank Blackthorne or the devil."

"Yes, it is Frank Blackthorne."

"In the body?" gasped Basel, still leaning against the wall; for though he was a philosopher and a firm disbeliever in the supernatural, there are occasions in life when the best of us lack the courage of our principles.

"In the body, as you see," replied Frank, quietly and sadly.

"But it is not possible. You were burnt in the fire. Everybody said you were. I saw you fall into the flames myself. And if you were not, how did you escape? - where have you been? - why did you not tell us? - what does it all mean?"

"You will soon learn, Mr. Basel. I asked you to come here in order that I might tell you. But first of all I want you to tell me something. How are they all? - my father and mother and Mabel - Mrs. Basel and Fritz?"

"They are all in good health, I think, but much harassed - your father especially - by this most unhappy trial."

"And Valérie," said Frank, anxiously yet hesitatingly - " is she also well? I dare not ask if she is happy?"

"It is very little you care about Valérie, I think, or you would not have behaved as you have done. She is pretty well in health, poor girl, but sorely troubled in spirit. We feared at times for her sanity. She has proved right in one thing, however. She refused to believe you were dead, and has always insisted, that you would come back."

"Dear Valérie! Then she never forgot me or lost hope."

"Forgot me – hope -" repeated Basel. And then he remembered the incident of the locket, and a dark thought rose in his mind. "Tell me, Frank - tell me truly - is it possible that Valérie has known all the time that you were alive? Has she been privy to this mystery, this concealment? No, it is not possible; I will not believe it."

"You wrong your daughter deeply, Mr. Basel, to suggest even the bare possibility of such a thing. If she thought I still lived it was because our love is so deep that her heart told her the truth. She knew I lived, as I should have known if she had died, by sympathy. As for my conduct, you shall judge when you have heard what I am about to tell you."

"I am afraid you are talking nonsense, Frank. I should rather say that Valérie refused to believe you were dead because she did not want to believe, and because, as no vestige of your body could be found, there was some slight ground for hoping you might still be alive; partly, too, because of that locket which she rightly regarded as being sent by you. But that is neither here nor there. I am impatient for an explanation of the mystery. Pray go on."

CHAPTER LI

A STRANGE STORY.

"My story," said Frank, "begins with the coming of the Fells to Moorwell. As you know, they were put in to take care of the old house, and, as I lunched there four or five times every week, and sometimes supped and stayed there all night, I speedily became very intimate with them. Stephen is very sharp and clever. He has no scruples, and he was not long in acquiring over me that ascendancy which a designing man of pleasant manners, who has seen the world, so easily obtains over one several years his junior, and so inexperienced as I then was. I don't want to lay on others the blame of my own folly. I have been weak - almost criminally weak - that there is no use denying; but looking back and passing all the circumstances in review, I can come to no other conclusion than that, from the very moment of their arrival at Moorwell, the Fells laid the train which ended in my marriage with Lydia. You know how soft and silly young fellows can be, and it was not long before I fell in love - or fancied I did - with Lydia. She can be very pleasant when she likes - though she has a queer temper of her own - and she flattered me and won my regard by those subtle little attentions to which few men of my age could be insensible. I did not fall in love with her all at once; and I am sure of this: that if I had not been thrown so much in her way I should have cared for her no more than I cared for any other girl about the place, and that the idea of marrying would never have entered my head. I was in for it before I knew what I was doing, or had given the slightest thought to the consequences. One evening on going in to supper - I was staying that night at Moorwell - I found Lydia in tears. I inquired what was the matter. She replied something about my not caring for her, and that of late I had been less kind to her than usual. This exhibition of emotion both touched and flattered me. What I said I do not remember, but a few minutes later my arms were around her and I was kissing away her tears. While we were in this interesting position who should come in but Stephen! He naturally demanded an explanation - wanted to know if I really loved his sister, and asked if my intentions were honourable. As I had only just vowed -probably in his hearing - that I did love her, I could only repeat to him what I had said to Lydia; and as my mind up to that moment, so far as my intentions were concerned, had been a blank, I was able to say with a good conscience that they were not dishonourable.

"Very well," said Stephen, "then we will consider you engaged."

"On this it occurred to me, for the first time, that this was an arrangement to which my father might possibly object, and I mentioned my misgivings to the two Fells.

"'Why should he object?" answered Stephen.

"'1 am so young,' I replied. For I did not like to hurt their feelings by suggesting that which I thought, and saying, "Because of Lydia's comparatively humble condition in life."

"It was a weak answer, as Stephen soon let me know.

"That is easily got over," he rejoined. "We will keep the thing quiet until you get a bit older. You will be twenty-one in a few months, and then we will tell your father. If you and Lydia are prudent nobody need suspect anything, and I am sure I shall say nothing."

"I was not at all sure that my father's objections to the match would diminish with time - or rather I was sure - they would not. But it was something to put off the evil day; and I eagerly assented to Stephen's proposal.

"You may imagine how green I was when I tell you that I actually felt grateful to Stephen for agreeing to keep the engagement secret. I did not see that he had made the proposal entirely in his own interest and that of his sister. He knew even better than I did that my father would leave no stone unturned to prevent my marrying Lydia, and that the day he heard of our engagement might be the last of their sojourn at Moorwell.

"From that time I was in their power. Lydia begged of me to write to her when I could not come. I agreed, and though I did not write often, or at great length, I wrote quite enough to confirm, ten times over; the promise of marriage I had verbally made. This was another link in the chain which the Fells were forging about me.

"All went on smoothly for two or three months. If I was not much enamoured of Lydia I was at least fond of her, and I had the most unlimited confidence in Stephen. It never once occurred to me that his friendship, any more than Lydia's love, was otherwise than disinterested. About the time I came of age he began to hint at the expediency of a secret marriage. His idea, I suppose, being that, whereas my father, if asked beforehand, might refuse his consent, he would easily be reconciled to a *fait accompli*. But I could not make up my mind to take so serious a step without the consent - the knowledge even - of my father and mother, and I met the suggestion with a direct negative. Then he took another line - pointed out that, when it became known I had been all this time engaged to his sister - seeing her every day, and almost living in a house in which the only other person of her own sex was a young servant-of-all-work, her character would be seriously compromised.

"I admitted the force of this argument, without, how-ever, accepting its logical conclusion - a secret marriage; and I proposed to get over the difficulty by coming less frequently to the house, and never remaining there over night.

"That will not do," observed Stephen. 'The mischief is done. For the last two or three months you have been coming nearly every day, sometimes twice a day, and sleeping here at least twice a week. Moreover, to make a sudden change like that would be just the thing to rouse suspicion. Everybody would be asking what was the matter.'

"Then he put before me two alternatives: either to marry Lydia or tell my father of our engagement. If I did not he said he would. He regretted being forced to take this course, yet he felt if he were to do otherwise he would be wronging his sister. His first duty was to her, and whatever were the consequences to me or himself he could not let Lydia's reputation suffer. As for the marriage it would be the easiest thing in the world to keep it quiet; he would pledge his honour not to divulge it without my consent, and Lydia, of course, in that, as in everything else, would be guided by my wishes.

"I consented. The threat of telling my father was an argument I could not resist. Of course it was very wrong - and stupid at that, as an American would say - for my father was sure to get to know sometime. But as a lad I had always stood much in awe of him - you know his high temper, and his old-fashioned ideas about the bringing up of children; and though he had latterly begun to treat me very differently, almost as an equal, in fact, I could not shake off the old feeling. I simply dared not tell him of the engagement I had been so foolish as to contract with Lydia, and I would have consented to even more than Stephen demanded-had that been possible-to put off the evil day.

"We were married at Manchester, as you doubtless know. Stephen arranged it all - got the licence, took lodgings for Lydia, who was supposed to be away seeing a sick aunt somewhere in the Fylde, saw the parson, gave his sister away, and signed the register."

"Was it he that proposed you should be married as Frank Blackthorne?" asked Basel.

"That was the name in which he got the licence. He arranged everything, I tell you. I was simply passive. All that I did was to present myself at the Collegiate Church, and go through a form of marriage with Lydia"

"All!" exclaimed Mr. Basel. "*Gott im Himmel!* what would the man have? It is that 'all' that has done all the mischief, Frank. But tell me, was Lydia privy to the fraud - did she know your full name?"

"Of course she did."

"Can that be proved?"

"Fully. But I will come to that point presently. Let me go on with my story. It is not a very pleasant one, and I want to get it finished."

"I am burning to know how you escaped from the fire."

"You shall soon know. I need not tell you how my father discovered my intimacy with Lydia. I daresay he has told you himself"

Basel nodded.

"But he could not tell you, because he did not know, how near I was to making a clean breast of it, and confessing all the foolishness of which I had been guilty. The words were on my lips. I had gone so far as to say I would not give Lydia up - I was just going to say I could not give her up - when he told me roughly that if I did not he would disinherit me, turn me out of the house, and exclude me from the business. Worse than this could not befall me in any case, so I just remained silent and let things take their course. I did not care enough for Lydia to sacrifice everything for her, and I thought I could trust Stephen not to divulge the marriage without my consent. Even if my father should fulfil his threat of sending them away the secret might still be kept; for I believed as much as ever in Stephen's loyalty and Lydia's love. I believed in them until my father put into my hands Lydia's undertaking to go to America, and her 'virtual repudiation of our marriage, for a consideration of two thousand pounds. Then I was disenchanted with a vengeance. I saw it all then - saw how I had been led on, played with, used, deceived, and befooled. All my love was turned to hate - if ever I really did love Lydia, which is now hard to believe; but my contempt for myself, for my weakness and folly, was greater than my hatred for her and Stephen. I had, however, one consolation - they were gone, and not likely to return.

"I come now to the most painful part of my story - my relations with Valérie. I know I have been greatly to blame, yet there are extenuating circumstances which may, I hope, obtain for me your indulgence, and, perhaps, forgiveness.

"I saw Valérie, and I loved her. Loved her, did I say? I love her now, as I think man has rarely loved woman. I love her so much that if she were to say, 'Go and kill yourself' I would go and kill myself. If she were to say, 'Go away, and never come back', I should go away and never come back."

"You all wondered - she wondered too - why I was so slack at declaring the love which you could hardly doubt that I felt. You know now. I was restrained by the ties that still bound me to Lydia Fell. She was far away, and I hoped and believed she would never come back. All the same I felt that it would be wrong to speak of love to Valérie so long as Lydia was alive and my wife before the law; and though it was a hard struggle, and I had to keep a constant watch over myself, I remained true to this resolution for a time that seemed to me cruelly long. But one day, when we were coming home from hunting, Valérie dropped a remark which, in my then mood, made me fancy I might have, a rival. There was madness in the very thought. I forgot everything; and before I knew what I did, I had told her of my love and drawn from her a confession of hers.

"It may seem very strange, Mr. Basel, but from that moment, until after I had parted from Valérie and informed you and my father and mother of what had come to pass, I was as oblivious of the existence of any impediment to our marriage as if Lydia Fell had never been born. I could think only of my happiness. It was not until my father made a chance allusion to Lydia, and I found myself alone in my own room, and my excitement began to subside, that I bethought me of what I had done - of the cruel wrong I had inflicted on Valérie, and of the sea of trouble into which I had plunged. I passed a wretched night, and morning brought me little relief. I could see no way out of the difficulties that surrounded me - no way, at least, that I had the courage to adopt. To give up Valérie and to let the engagement go on seemed equally impossible. I could make up my mind to neither course. I was in this miserable state of indecision and mental torture when the post came. Among the papers I received was one from America. I tore off the cover, which was addressed in Stephen Fell's handwriting, with a certitude that anything sent by him could bode me no good. Imagine, then, my feelings, when I found in the paper a marked paragraph giving an account of the death of Lydia Fell. She had been drowned by the overturning of a boat on the Hudson, near Albany. I could hardly believe my eyes. I read the paragraph a hundred times. I felt like a man who has escaped from a mortal danger. I was raised at once from the depths of despair to a state of happiness greater even than I had felt the evening before, when Valérie gave me the assurance of her love.

I showed the paragraph to my father. He attributed my emotion to the shock caused by news so startling and unexpected, and to some lingering affection that he supposed I still entertained for Lydia. It did not occur to either of us that the news might be false - the more especially as it was reported a few days later in the *Redburn Rooster* - and I consequently took no steps to obtain confirmation of it. It was too good not to be true.

"I need not tell you about our courtship - how happy we were, how the time was fixed for our marriage and that of Mabel and Fritz; and how the days flew past on golden wings.

"It proved to be a fool's paradise I was living in, and a rude awakening was in store for me. A week before the Old Factory was burnt down I received a second communication from America - this time in the shape of a letter from Stephen Fell. They had heard, he wrote, he and his sister, that I was either married, or about to be married to Miss Basel. 1 must remember, however, that Lydia was still my lawful wife, and that they could stop the marriage if they thought fit. Not that they desired to do so; far from it. They were comfortably settled, doing well, and had no wish to return to England. If I were willing to pay Lydia ten thousand pounds she would remain where she was, and enter into an engagement never to trouble me. If; on the other hand, they did not have a satisfactory answer in a reasonable time - say with, in three months of the date of the letter - Lydia would come over and claim me as her husband, and, if I were already married, prosecute me for bigamy. They did not demand the ten thousand pounds all at once, Stephen was good enough to add. Lydia was willing to accept two thousand pounds down - the balance on my acceptances at three, six, and twelve months.

"If Lydia had appeared in person it could hardly have given me a greater shock than this letter gave me. It was like a bolt from the blue. All my happiness was gone in a moment. I fell into deeper despondency than that from which the news of her death had raised me. As for accepting Stephen's offer, I never thought of it for a moment. I loved Valérie too well to marry her only in name; and I hope I respected you too much to repay your kindness by so base a wrong. But how to act - what to do - was the pressing question. Valérie was of a nature so sensitive, she loved me so deeply, that I feared she would hardly survive the knowledge that I was the husband of another woman and might never be hers. As for myself; I felt that life without her would be so little worth having that I had serious thoughts of solving the difficulty by blowing out my brains. Then it occurred to me that the first story might be true - that Lydia might be dead, after all. The letter was not written by her, and I knew that to get hold of ten thousand pounds, or even a much smaller sum, there was nothing short of murder that Stephen would stick at. If I could have contrived any plausible excuse, I would have gone to America at once and found out the truth for myself. I even thought of going secretly. My mind was in a whirl, and I conceived and rejected a new scheme almost every hour.

"This was the state of things when the fire took place, as I mentioned, a few days after the receipt of Stephen Fell's letter. I need not relate the history of the fire; you are sure to know what happened."

"I was there," observed Basel; "I came up just as you lowered Fair Alice from the window."

"Then you would see that, after the flames seized on the ladder, rendering escape that way impossible, I fell back from the window?"

"We could not see anything distinctly - the view was obscured by smoke; but that was certainly our impression.

"Well, I did fall back, and, in order to get as far away from the smoke as possible, I ran to the other end of the room. I knew that a horrible death stared me in the face - that hardly anything short of a miracle could save me; yet somehow the very extremity of the peril seemed to sharpen my faculties and increase my presence of mind.

"In the part of the room to which I ran was a hoist used for bringing up bobbins from the cardroom in the bottom storey - or, rather a hole in the floor through which the box containing the bobbins went up and down. As it happened, the box was below. Without a moment's hesitation I grasped the hoist-ropes and let myself down hand under hand. The next room was all in a blaze, and in going through it I ran the risk of being either stifled or burnt. However, I managed to reach the lower storey without much damage.

"By this time it also was burning. Part of the ceiling had fallen in, and every way of egress was closed.

"I was hemmed in between a blank wall and a mass of moving fire. The flames crept over the floor; they leaped from one carding engine to another; they curled round the steam-pipes. The heat became almost insupportable; the place was full of smoke. I thought my last hour was come, and, more in desperation than in the hope of prolonging my life by getting a breath of pure air, I threw myself on the floor. As I fell, my hand struck against an iron ring fastened in a flag, and then I remembered that, underneath the floor, and right through the foundations of the Old Factory, ran the culvert - a vaulted passage - which conducted the waste water from the big wheel race to Moorwell Brook. The flag covered the entrance to a manhole opening into the culvert.

"The next moment I was on my feet, tugging at the ring with all the energy of despair.

"But the flag had not been moved for years, and, tug as I would, it refused to yield. I rushed, heedless of the smoke and heat, to the nearest drawing frame, tore away one of the rods, and used it as a lever. It broke in my hand, yet not before I had stirred the flag so that, by exerting all my strength, I succeeded in moving it from the orifice. I then threw down the hole a bag of sweepings which chanced to be by - for a fall on the paved bottom of the culvert might have broken my limbs - and, with a muttered prayer, dropped down into the darkness.

" I fell on the bag of sweepings, which probably saved my life. Five minutes later, as I lay there, partially stunned, and utterly exhausted, I heard a great crash. It was the roof of the Old Factory falling in."

CHAPTER LII

AFTERTHOUGHTS.

"For an hour or more," Frank went on, "I could not move, probably from the effects of the smoke; for towards the last I had been nearly suffocated. But I could think, and my thoughts naturally went back to Lydia Fell, and the terrible difficulty in which Stephen's letter had placed me. Why should I not, I asked myself, after a long cogitation - why should I not make use of the present opportunity to carry out my idea of - going to America - go there without letting it be known that I had escaped from the fire? It would be believed by this time that I had perished, the first bitterness of the shock would be over, and the unhappiness resulting from my supposed death could hardly be greater than the unhappiness that would be caused by the revelation of my marriage with Lydia. If I found that Lydia was dead I could come back, make a frank explanation of my motives, and trust to your friendship and Valérie's love for forgiveness. If she were still alive I would remain away forever. I would be as one dead. For, rightly or wrongly, it seemed to me then that it were better almost to die than be tied all my life to Lydia. It was a desperate expedient, but I was in desperate straits; and before I began to grope my way out of the culvert I had resolved to carry it out and laid my plans.

"I anticipated little or no difficulty in getting away unperceived. It was considerably after sunset, and as my clothes were torn, my face blackened, and I had no hat, it was little likely that I should be recognised. Anybody that chanced to meet me would take me for a man who had been helping to put out the fire.

"When I reached the outlet of the culvert, which, owing to the water-wheel being stopped, was almost dry, I looked carefully round, and, seeing nobody about, I waded over Moorwell Brook, and struck across the fields in the direction of Black Dyke, which, as I daresay you know, is at the far end of the Brandwood property, and some six miles from Moorwell. I could not well carry out my plan without help, and my object in going thither was to see a gipsy woman, of the name of Myra Lee, who was under a slight obligation to me for having prevailed on my father to let her and her people stay at Black Dyke after he had ordered them to quit. She professed great gratitude at the time, and said that, after what I had done for them, the gipsies would go through fire and water for me. I had almost forgotten the incident, but it seemed to me now that as I was almost forced to trust somebody, the best thing I could do was to go to the encampment and ask Myra to assist me in getting unobserved out of the country.

"It was late when I reached Black Dyke, and I had to rouse Myra from her sleep, or rather the dogs which guarded the tents made such a noise at my approach as to rouse the entire encampment. When old Mother Lee appeared I told her what I wanted of her, and in doing so I was necessarily compelled to take her, under a strict pledge of secrecy, a good deal into my confidence. I did not, however, trust altogether to promises. I made her understand that it would be worth her while, in more ways than one, to do my bidding and keep my secret. She agreed to everything I proposed, and before I laid down on a truss of straw in one of the covered carts all our arrangements were made.

"At daybreak next morning I donned a suit of gipsy clothes, stained my face and hands to the gipsy tint with a decoction prepared by Mother Lee, and set out, accompanied by one of her young men, for Liverpool. We followed by-paths and unfrequented roads, carefully avoiding places where I should run any risk of being recognised. On the evening of the second day we reached the great seaport. We passed the night in a small inn in the outskirts of the town, where my companion was known. The next day I bought a portmanteau, laid in a stock of clothing, and bespoke a passage in a ship appointed to sail within the next twenty-four hours."

"How did you manage that?" asked Basel. "Where did the money come from?"

"Oh, I was pretty well provided in that respect. A waste dealer paid me an account - very nearly three hundred pounds, I think it was - only an hour or two before the fire, and I had the amount in my pocket, mostly in bank notes. Then I had my diamond ring and watch, worth between them at least two hundred more."

"And you took your passage, you were saying?"

"Yes, I took my passage and dismissed my companion, and the ship - the *Maiden Queen* she was called - dropped down the river only two days after the time fixed for her sailing. Nothing worth telling happened in the early part of the voyage. Until we were halfway across the Atlantic we had calm seas and cloudless skies, and every day was exactly like its predecessor. But after that the weather became frightful. One storm followed another. Sails were blown away. Once the vessel got on her beam-ends, and before she could be righted the fore and main masts had to be cut away. Then the rudder top broke, and for several days the wreck was at the mercy of the winds and waves. We were blown and drifted hundreds of miles out of our course. Fortunately the ship was staunch, and the captain a first-rate seaman, or we should assuredly have gone to the bottom. As it was we had all, both passengers and crew, to be put on short allowance. After knocking about the Atlantic for weeks we finally reached the island of St. Thomas, in the West Indies, where we were almost as far from New York as we had been at Liverpool. As the *Maiden Queen* could not be refitted and made seaworthy under three or four weeks, the captain advised me to go on to New Orleans by a vessel that was just on the point of leaving for that port. I could easily, he said, get from New Orleans to New York. I acted on this advice without hesitation, and after a stay at St. Thomas of little more than two days I was on my way to the Gulf of Mexico.

"We made a quick passage. It might have been a pleasant one, if I could have forgotten. But I could not. I had always before me two sad and reproachful, forgiving, faces - my mother's and Valérie's. The two beings in all the world I most loved I had plunged into the bitterest grief. I knew they were sorrowing for me as those sorrow who are without hope, and my heart was very heavy, Mr. Basel. I began to have serious doubts as to the expediency of the course I had adopted. A proceeding which caused so much pain to all who loved me would be hard to justify. Then I felt so lonely, so utterly bereft of sympathy, so entirely cut off from all companionship. I could speak to nobody of my past. My future was dark and uncertain. I was a waif, a homeless, nameless wanderer, whom men thought dead, and to those I cared for, if I carried out my plan, I might always remain dead. But my resolution not to return to England in the event of Lydia Fell being alive was beginning to be seriously shaken. The more I thought of it the more impossible did it seem for me, if I lived, never to look on Val□rie's face again, never again to see my mother or my father, who, in spite of the sternness of his character, had latterly treated me not unkindly.

"At New Orleans another misfortune befell me. The day after my arrival, just as I was preparing to start for New York, I was struck down by yellow fever, which laid me up for a long time. Though unaware of it myself - for after the first attack I lapsed into a state of semi-unconsciousness - I believe I very nearly went under. The doctor, as he told me afterwards, at one time gave me up altogether. However, he managed to pull me through, and as soon as I was fit for travel I made my way first to New York, and then to Albany, where, without of course disclosing my real name, I made inquiry about the Fells. I had no need to disguise myself. I am yellow now, I was the colour of a guinea then. I had let my hair and beard grow long, and my own mother, let alone Lydia or Stephen, would not have known me. What the latter had told me in his letter was so far true that they were comfortably settled and believed to be doing well. Lydia was not dead. There had been an accident like that mentioned in the *Albany Tomahawk,* and she was reported to be one of the victims, though, as it turned out, she was one of the rescued. As to this, then, Stephen had told no lie; but he had carefully omitted to tell me that his sister was married, and the mother of a little boy. She was married shortly after the boat accident (which took place some time before we heard of it) to an individual of the name of Freebody, with whom Stephen was in partnership in a commission business. This was startling news; but what startled me more - alarmed me even - was to hear that both sister and brother were in England. Lydia had been gone several months, but Stephen had left only a few days before my arrival. I feared they were after no good, and resolved at once to follow them.

"After obtaining certified proof of Lydia's marriage with Mr. Freebody I returned to New York, and took the first steamer for England. I landed in Liverpool last week, and saw there in one of the papers a mention of the approaching trial of Blackthorne versus Blackthorne. Then I went to Manchester by railway, and came on here the day before yesterday by coach. Last night I spent an hour in the bar-parlour of The Bay Mare, where I thought I might hear what was going on without asking many questions. Nor was I disappointed. I think I learnt the main facts of the case of Blackthorne versus Blackthorne. Then I sent for you. I thought it would be well to keep my presence here as quiet as possible until after the trial, and for that reason I have as yet made myself known only to you. But as to this and my proceedings generally I need hardly say, Mr. Basel, that I am willing - nay, more than willing, anxious - to be guided by your advice."

CHAPTER LIII.

AT THE KING'S ARMS.

Basel was unfeignedly glad to find that Frank had not perished in the Old Factory fire, as all had believed. Being, moreover, a tolerant, generous-minded man, he was not given to impute evil motives, preferring rather to judge others, if he judged them at all, leniently, and put the most charitable construction on their doings. Hence, albeit there was much in Frank's conduct of which he could not approve, he spoke no words of blame. Except when he was very angry, he found it difficult to censure even his own workmen; and Frank's appearance just then would have softened the heart of a much harder man than Hermann Basel. His body was gaunt, his skin yellow, his cheeks were drawn, his eyes hollow, and their lids dark. When he spoke his voice trembled, and his whole manner and bearing betokened impaired health, severe nervous prostration, and deep mental distress.

"Well, I am heartily glad you are risen from the dead, dear boy, though you did give me such a terrible shock," said Basel cheerfully, after a short pause. "I am glad for all our sakes - you were always one of my favourites you know - but especially for the sake of your father and mother and poor Val▢rie; for I am sure she would rather you were alive than dead, even if it should turn out, after all, that you are Lydia Fell's husband. As for your conduct generally, we had better, I think, leave that for discussion another day. I must have time for further consideration before I deliver my verdict. I will, however, say this - if you had not gone away as you did after the fire we might not have discovered the flaw in this unfortunate marriage of yours."

"About the name, you mean?"

"Exactly."

"That is not the only flaw."

"Indeed! What is the other?"

"Lydia's marriage with Freebody. I consulted a solicitor as I came through Liverpool, and this, he assured me, would be sufficient to procure a decree of separation from the Court of Arches, and afterwards a divorce from the House of Lords - by Act of Parliament, you know."

"Then you have two strings to your bow. Failing the flaw, you can fall back on the divorce. But the name is the best - getting a divorce would be a very tedious business. You said just now that Lydia knew your right name at the time you were married - went through the form of marriage, rather, How can this be proved?"

"By herself; by her own handwriting."

"You have letters, then?"

"I have nothing; but more conclusive proof than any likely to be contained in letters exists, and can easily be procured."

"In what shape?"

"In the shape of a transfer of railway scrip. I used to dabble a little in shares, you know. Well, a month or two before I committed the folly of marrying Lydia, I received some transfers of Leeds and Manchester stock to sign. They had to be returned the same evening. As it fell out, I went that day to dine with Stephen and Lydia. My father was not at home. After dinner I mentioned having some transfers to sign, and asked Stephen to remind me of them when we got back to the counting-house, so that the matter might not be forgotten.

"'Nothing like time present,' said Stephen; 'sign them now. I daresay Lydia will witness them for you.'

"Then I had to explain to Lydia what a transfer was, and, as the suggestion seemed to please her, I signed the three documents in her presence as 'Francis Adam Blackthorne,' and she witnessed them every one."

"Capital. And where can we find these transfers?"

"In the offices of the railway company at Manchester. I am sure, the business being explained to him, the secretary will let us have the tranfers for a few days, against your or my father's undertaking to return them."

"Well, I will tell you what I will do, Frank. I will go to Manchester to-morrow, get these transfers, if they are to be got; see Kean, the lawyer who has charge of the suit, you know, tell him of your resurrection and return, and ask him what is best to be done in the altered circumstances of the case. I shall return here to-morrow night, and tell you how I have sped. If I am prevented from coming I will send you word. Meanwhile, I shall tell nobody else, not even your father, of your reappearance; and you will, of course, maintain your incognito."

Frank expressed his approval of these proposals, and gave his friend all the particulars he could remember concerning the three railway transfers.

"I shall tell Mrs. Broadbeam you are an old acquaintance of mine," observed Basel, as he rose to go, "just by way of allaying her curiosity, you know. But what name shall I say?"

"John Robinson is the name I gave last night at The Bay Mare."

"Good. Mr. Robinson let it be then. And now, friend Frank, I must say *Auf wiedersehen.*"

"Just one question more, before you go," said Frank timidly. "Is Valérie at home?"

"No. She is at Lytham with your mother. We thought they were better out of the way until the trial is over, of which, as I told you, Valérie knows nothing. Your mother and she have taken very much to each other since Fritz and Mabel were married."

"God bless me!" exclaimed Frank, "are Fritz and Mabel married?"

"That they are," laughed Basel; "and, what is more, your sister has just made Fritz the father of a bouncing boy, who has to he called 'Francis Adam Blackthorne.'"

He did not tell Frank that Mabel and Fritz were living in the house which had been built for Valérie and himself.

Late on the following evening, Basel, in fulfilment of his promise, came a second time to The Bull's Head. He had succeeded in getting possession of the three transfers which, as Frank had said, bore his signature in full, attested by Lydia Fell. But he had not seen Kean. The lawyer had left that very morning for Lancaster. He would stay all night in Preston, and arrive, his clerk thought, in the county town on Saturday evening, so as to have an opportunity of conferring with counsel on Sunday, and be in readiness for the opening of the Assizes on the following day.

"That is very unfortunate, is it not?" said Frank, when he heard the news. "What do you propose to do now?"

Well, we must see Kean, and the sooner the better. It is of the utmost importance that he should know of your reappearance on the scene and the finding of the transfers. What I propose to do is this: You remain here to-morrow - although I daresay you are growing rather weary of Redburn and The Bull's Head - as you have done to-day. On Sunday morning at eight o'clock I shall call for you here; we will drive to Preston in my carriage, and post thence to Lancaster. We shall get there before one o'clock, and can, if necessary, have all the afternoon with Kean. What do you say?"

"I am quite agreeable to do whatever you think best, and I do not think I can suggest any improvement on your plan. As you say, it is slow work staying here, but (smiling) I have undergone many worse hardships than a dull day at Redburn since the Old Factory fire, Mr. Basel."

This programme was carried out to the letter. At one o'clock on the Sunday afternoon Basel and Frank arrived at the King's Arms Hotel, Lancaster, where Kean was staying, and where they also proposed to put up.

After taking some refreshment, Basel sent his card to the lawyer's room, and received, in reply, a message to the effect that Mr. Kean would be glad to see him at once.

"Shall I go with you?" asked Frank.

"By all means; you are indispensable; but I shall not tell Kean in the first instance who you are."

"Good-morning, Mr. Basel. How do you do?" said the lawyer, as the two men entered his room, which was almost as much littered with papers as his office in Manchester. "I hardly expected to see anybody from Moorwell to-day. Pray take a seat. I hope you bring good news."

"I think so. Look at these papers (handing him the transfers), and tell me if they have not an important bearing on the case. We are entirely indebted to this gentleman (pointing to Frank) for their discovery."

The lawyer bowed, took the documents, and glanced them hastily over.

"Transfer of fifty shares Leeds and Manchester stock from Francis Adam Blackthorne to Jabez Johnstone. signed by the aforesaid Francis Adam Blackthorne in the presence of Lydia Fell. By Jove (striking his fist on the table) this is exactly what we want. These transfers will win us the case. How did you come by them, Mr. Basel?"

"As I just now told you, by the help of this gentleman."

"I am sure we are all greatly obliged to him," said Kean, with a polite bow to Frank; "but I do not remember - I am afraid I have not the honour of knowing him."

"He is, nevertheless, deeply interested in the case," observed Basel. "More than anybody else, I may say. "

"More than Mr. Blackthorne?"

"More even than Mr. Blackthorne, for he is Mr. Blackthorne's son."

"Indeed! I was not aware Mr. Blackthorne had a second son."

"Nor has he; this is his only son and heir."

"Are you serious, Mr. Basel?" said Kean, with a puzzled look. "Why, this son you speak of is dead; he was burnt alive."

"He was supposed to be, but he has come to life again, or, rather, he never died."

And then Basel briefly related the main facts connected with Frank's disappearance and reappearance.

"What an extraordinary story!" exclaimed Kean, when Basel had finished his narrative. "I never heard such a thing in all my life - never met with anything like it in all my experience."

And then the lawyer leaned back in his chair with a sigh, the look of astonishment which his face had just worn giving place to one of mingled disappointment and disgust, - like that of a lover whose sweetheart fails in her tryst, of an author whose manuscript is returned by a hard-hearted publisher, or of a Manchester calico printer when requested to step over to a customer's warehouse "to look at a lot of jobs."

"What is the matter?" said Mr. Basel, alarmed at this portentous symptom.

"Matter!" rejoined the lawyer "Why, don't you see? the game is up. We shall have no trial now."

"But why not?" exclaimed Basel, more alarmed than ever. "I thought these transfers - and Lydia Fell's signature and all - made us cocksure of winning."

"So they would, my dear sir, if there was anything to win. But since this gentleman has thought fit to return to life there are no longer any grounds for a trial - there is nothing to try. The issue set down for trial is really whether Lydia Fell is Francis Adam Blackthorne's widow or not. But if he is not dead, it is quite clear she cannot be his widow, and her claim on the estate vanishes into thin air. Don't you perceive."

"Yes, I perceive," answered Basel, albeit he still looked somewhat puzzled. "But in that case is Lydia Frank's wife or not? That is what we want to get at, is it not, Frank?"

"It is everything for me," replied Frank, in a despondent voice. "I thought Mr. Kean said those transfers--"

"Stay," interrupted the lawyer, drawing himself up in his chair, and speaking with all his wonted vivacity. "I have an idea. You would like to have this marriage pronounced -authoritatively pronounced, I mean - null and void, would you not?"

Basel and Frank responded eagerly in the affirmative.

"Until it is, you know, there will always be a doubt. In the face of those documents I have no hesitation in saying the marriage is void. It is impossible that a judge and a jury should take any other view of the case and a verdict for the defendant in this suit of Blackthorne *versus* Blackthorne would settle the matter once for all. And I really think, after all, the trial might be allowed to go on. The Court of Chancery, at whose instance these proceedings are being taken, knows nothing of Mr. Frank Blackthorne's return, and, in point of fact, neither do I. You, Mr. Basel, may believe that this gentleman is Mr. Blackthorne's son; but your belief may not be my belief, and I am bound to say that, until he has been recognised and acknowledged by his family, I cannot share in your belief. You may be mistaken, you know."

"Of course I may," said Basel, with a smile; "and I think you are quite right in suspending your judgement until you have had an opportunity of consulting Mr. Blackthorne. By all means let the trial go on. I believe I did not tell you that Frank, that this gentleman's name - his travelling name, I should say - is Robinson. Allow me to introduce you to each other - Mr. Kean, Mr. Robinson; Mr. Robinson, Mr. Kean."

"Glad to make your acquaintance, Mr. Robinson," said the lawyer. "You have done us an inestimable service in bringing under our notice these railway transfers, a service for which we cannot be sufficiently grateful. You will remain here until the trial is over, I suppose, Mr. Robinson?"

"I came here with that intention," said Frank gravely.

"Glad to hear it. I hope to have the Opportunity of making your better acquaintance. You will, of course (addressing Basel), say nothing of this to Mr. Blackthorne until after the trial. What has passed here among us three is, for the present at least, a profound secret."

"Certainly," said Basel.

"Certainly," repeated Frank.

"And now, gentlemen," the lawyer went on, looking at his watch, "I am afraid I must terminate our interview; but the fact is I have an appointment in three minutes with Serjeant Pumpendry, and he is the most punctual of men. If you are not otherwise engaged, will you do me the honour to dine with me this evening, here, in this room, at half-past six? - if that time would be convenient."

The invitation was cordially accepted, and the two friends withdrew.

"Capital," said Kean, rubbing his hands briskly together as the door closed behind the visitors. "I am glad that idea occurred to me. Mr. John Robinson - ah, ah! Gad, when I come to think of it, he does look very like a resuscitated corpse. To have missed such a beautiful trial would have been nothing less than a calamity. It will be a leading case, and give us a capital advertisement - to say nothing of the nice addition it will make to my bill of costs. I have had nothing so good for a long time. Miss coming off! Not if I know it."

CHAPTER LIV.

THE TRIAL.

The cause list was not heavy. A considerable amount of business was got through on the Monday and Tuesday, and on the evening of the latter day Kean informed Basel and Adam (who had arrived on the previous afternoon) that the special jury cases would begin on Wednesday, and that the first down for trial was that of Blackthorne against Blackthorne. Later in the evening Basel communicated this news to Frank, who, in anticipation of his father's arrival, had left The King's Arms for another lodging. It was hardly possible that Adam would have penetrated his son's disguise, but Kean thought it better to avoid all chance of such a contingency by keeping them apart.

There was no reason, however, why Frank should not be present at the trial, and, entering the court-house shortly after the judge had mounted his dais, he took a seat among the spectators. His father, Basel, and Kean were already there. They had been accommodated with seats behind the bar, as had also Lydia and her brother, so that the parties to the suit and their legal champions were almost within earshot of each other.

The plaintiff's case was opened by Serjeant Buster, a pudgy little man, with small dark eyes, very black eyebrows, a coarse red face, and a huge mouth, but possessed of a voice at once sonorous and flexible, and gifted with marvellous readiness of speech. After explaining very fairly and clearly the legal bearings of the case - how it had originated in the Palatinate Court of Chancery, and had been sent down for trial at the present Assizes, and the issues to be tried - he proceeded to tell, in florid and picturesque language, of the loves of Lydia and Frank. He described Lydia as a young, beautiful, lovely, and accomplished woman, who had seen better days, and been forced by stress of fortune to earn her living by plying her needle. He spoke of her brother in terms hardly less laudatory: as a fine fellow who had never failed in affection for his parents, in devotion to his sister, or in his duty to his employers. His conduct, in short, had been exemplary in every relation of life, and his character was little less than perfect. The learned serjeant next described their meeting with the elder Blackthorne, their engagement, the one as bookkeeper, the other as lady housekeeper (he laid particular emphasis on the "lady"), and their removal to Moorwell. Then Frank was brought on the scene. If Buster's sketch of the brother and sister had been glowing, his portrayal of Lydia's lover was nothing less than gushing. As for his physical endowments, he was tall, stalwart and handsome; as touching his moral and mental qualities, he was high-principled, pure-minded, and sublimely disinterested. And though a ripe scholar and a master of many language; he was an energetic and successful man of business, and positively adored by his work-people.

As Frank listened to this enumeration of his virtues he shifted uneasily in his seat, and his face became so red that Basel, who happened to look round at the same moment was surprised and almost alarmed to observe how like he was to his old self.

Then Serjeant Buster, in language equally brilliant adorned with many poetic quotations, told how this noble youth and maiden met and loved; how their love grew day by day until Frank, unable longer to conceal the passion that consumed him, and listening only to the promptings of his heart, avowed his attachment and demanded Lydia's hand in marriage, and she, feeling herself not unworthy to become his wife, accepted his offer. But the lovers had to reckon with a formidable obstacle to the consummation of their hopes - a hard-hearted father. And then Buster went on to sketch Adam Blackthorne's character and conduct in terms so little flattering, that the object of his censures restrained himself with difficulty from reaching over and knocking his calumniator's wig off. The serjeant described him as purse-proud, arrogant, and ambitious; as a tyrannical father, and an exacting master, and as despising the class from which he had sprung. He had begun life as a farmer's boy, yet thought a farmer's daughter not good enough to mate with his son.

After casting unmeasured opprobrium on the defendant, and prejudicing him to the utmost possible extent in the minds of the jury, the eloquent advocate related how, for the fear of the opposition of this cruel father, the young people were constrained to contract a secret marriage at the Collegiate Church of Manchester. It was in every respect a legal marriage, said the serjeant, and he would prove beyond a shadow of doubt that, at the time it was solemnised, his client had not the most remote idea that her husband possessed any other name than Frank. He ascribed Lydia's departure for America to her romantic devotion to her husband, and her desire to shield him from the anger of his father, who, having accidentally discovered their attachment - albeit he did not know of their marriage - had threatened, if the Fells did not leave Moorwell, not alone to disinherit his son, but to turn him out of house and home. Then he drew a moving picture of the burning of the Old Factory, of the rescue of Fair Alice, of Frank's heroic death, of Lydia's unutterable grief and desolation when she knew that her young husband "had perished in his splendid adolescence," and concluded with a peroration that melted into tears all the ladies who heard it, and visibly and deeply affected every member of the jury.

"Exactly what I expected," whispered Kean to Basel. "He has taken the jury on their blind side. Without these transfers we should not have had a ghost of a chance."

The witnesses first examined were Mr. Harvey, the Chaplain of the Collegiate Church, who had performed the ceremony, and Mark Binyon, who, together with Stephen Fell, had witnessed the marriage. Their evidence was very brief. They testified to the fact of the marriage described in the registry having taken place. They identified the *soi-disant* Lydia Blackthorne as the woman who was married to Frank Blackthorne; but whether Frank Blackthorne and Francis Adam Blackthorne were one and the same person they were unable to say.

Stephen Fell was then called. He entered the witness-box with an air of great assurance, and was as cool and self-possessed throughout his examination, and answered Buster's questions and Pumpemdry's cross-questions with as much readiness and assurance as if he had been supplied with copies of them beforehand, and rehearsed his part in private. He gave the same evidence about the marriage as the previous witnesses, with the addition of swearing to the identity of the Frank Blackthorne in question with Francis Adam, son of Adam Blackthorne, of Moorwell and Brandwood.

"Were you aware that his legal appellation was Francis Adam?" asked Serjeant Buster.

"I was."

"Why then did you permit him to marry your sister as Frank?"

"I did not know there was any wrong in it. Frank was the name he always went by, and it never occurred to me that it was not as good for the purpose as any other."

"I presume if you had thought that the use of young Mr. Blackthorne's colloquial name in place of his legal one might give rise to doubts as to the legality of the marriage, you would have insisted on his full name being used?"

"Certainly."

"Did your sister know his full name?"

"To the best of my belief she did not. I never told her, nor, so far as I am aware, did anybody else ever tell her."

When Buster had done with Stephen, Pumpemdry took him in hand;

"Will you swear," he asked, "that your sister did not know that young Mr. Blackthorne was called Francis Adam?"

"How can I swear as to what another person knows? You had better put that question to my sister, Mr. Pumpemdry."

"Who procured the licence?"

"I did."

"Now, did you not deliberately procure it in the name of Frank, with a view to conceal Mr. Blackthorne's identity, and throw possible inquirers off the scent?"

"No, I did not. It was pure inadvertence I tell you. If I erred at all it was from ignorance."

"In any case you connived at a clandestine marriage. Do you think you acted honourably, being at the time In Mr. Blackthorne's employment, in helping his son clandestinely to marry your sister?"

"Well, I see no dishonour in it. My sister was as good as him. He was my friend, and I helped him as I would have helped any other friend in the same circumstances. If old Mr. Blackthorne had not been the man he was it might have been different."

"What do you mean by that? Why was it right to deceive Mr. Blackthorne when it would have been wrong to deceive any other body?"

"Because he was so unreasonable and tyrannical."

"So you deceived Mr. Blackthorne because he was tyrannical. How was he tyrannical?"

"Why, he thinks nothing of kicking a man that does not please him downstairs, or throwing him into the lodge."

"Did you ever know him do any of those things?

"No, but I have heard of him doing them."

Page 303

"Why did you go to America?"

"Because Mr. Blackthorne sent us away from Moorwell."

"Any other reason?"

"Yes, he gave us - my sister, perhaps I ought to say - two thousand pounds to take ourselves away."

"'Was there no other consideration for this two thousand pounds? It seems a large sum to pay for so little."

"Yes, my sister agreed to abandon all claim in respect of Mr. Frank's promises to her."

"Promises of marriage, I suppose you mean?"

"That is what I mean."

"Do you think that was very honest?"

"In which way?"

"Why, taking the two thousand pounds to compromise a supposed claim for breach of promise, when you knew, or believed, that your sister and young Mr. Blackthorne were already married?"

"Well, frankly, if you put it in that way, I do not. But you see, the old gentleman was so unreasonable, and two thousand pounds is a large sum, and--"

"You may step down," interrupted Pumpemdry sternly. "I have no further questions to ask you."

"Not a bad witness," whispered Kean to Basel; "though I am not quite sure that his evidence will go down well with the jury. That admission about the two thousand was damaging - just a little too brutally frank."

The next witness, and, as it proved, the last was the plaintiff. Her widow's weeds, which she still wore, became her well. Her fair eyebrows and lashes were in keeping with the snowy whiteness of her cap, and seemed to deepen by contrast the melancholy blackness of her crape. She looked pale, pretty, and interesting. As she stepped into the box a little thrill of excitement ran through the court, and all eyes were bent upon her, an ordeal which she sustained with a modest confidence, as if conscious of the justice of her cause.

Serjeant Buster conducted the examination-in-chief with great tact. He sank his sonorous voice to a soft whisper, took every occasion to address his witness ostentatiously as "Mrs. Blackthorne," with an air that seemed to imply supreme contempt for the theory that she had no right to the name, and he treated her with marked deference and respect.

After a few unimportant questions, relating principally to the fact of the marriage, he inquired if the witness knew at the time of the ceremony that her husband's name was other than Frank.

"Never," she replied, clasping her hands, a gesture which she accompanied with an upward glancing of her eyes, as if calling heaven to witness the truth of her denial. "Never, until the day before we left Moorwell, did I know that my dear husband had any other name than Frank."

When asked about her journey to America, she was so overcome by emotion that Buster had to wait a few minutes until she could recover herself. She had been prevailed upon to leave England, she said, sorely against her wishes, by her brother's advice and the pressing entreaties of her dear husband. Had she insisted on remaining in England and avowing her marriage Frank would have been ruined; his father would have disowned and disinherited him. It was represented to her, moreover, that their separation would be only for a year or two - that so soon as Frank could reconcile his father to their marriage, or make himself pecuniarily independent of him, she should return and be openly acknowledged as his wife. As for the two thousand pounds, she took it not for herself; but for her brother, who, through his devotion to her interests, had lost his situation.

"Thank you, Mrs. Blackthorne," said Serjeant. Buster, when she had concluded her evidence, "that will do very well, I think. Perhaps my brother Pumpemdry would now like to ask you a few questions, which I am sure you will answer with the same transparent candour that has characterised your replies to mine."

"Yes," rejoined Serjeant Pumpemdry, a burly north countryman, with a shrewd face, and a strong border accent. "I think I would like to ask this lady a question or two. Now, madam (handing her the receipt for the two thousand pounds), will you be good enough to look at that and tell me if the signature there, 'Lydia Fell,' be in your handwriting?"

"Yes, sir.

"It is all in your handwriting, I think?"

"Yes, sir, it is."

"When you wrote and signed that undertaking to leave England in consideration of a sum of two thousand pounds, you were already the wife, you say, of Francis Blackthorne?"

"I was."

"You signed a lie then, and obtained this money from Mr. Blackthorne under false pretences. I hope you are going to tell the truth now."

"This is a gross outrage," interrupted Serjeant Buster, with some heat "What right have you to suggest that the witness will not tell the truth? - I protest against the insinuation."

"Brother Pumpemdry's observation was certainly just a little strong," remarked the judge. "Still you must remember that the witness admits having signed a document in a name not her own, for the purpose of obtaining a sum of money which, had the truth been known, would certainly not have been paid to her. It may not, therefore, be amiss to warn her to adhere strictly to the truth in the answers she is about to give. I think, however, the warning would have been none the less effective had it been a little less bluntly expressed."

This little episode over, Serjeant Pumpemdry proceeded with his cross-examination.

"You said just now that you first became aware that your husband's name was Francis Adam on the eve of your departure for America. Under what circumstances did you arrive at this knowledge?"

"My brother drafted the agreement with Mr. Blackthorne, and I wrote it out fair. He told me then for the first time what my husband's name really was."

"Ah, that was the way, was it? Were you surprised?"

"Very much. It seemed so strange that I had never known it before."

"I quite agree with you; it was strange. Now, are you quite sure that you had never, before the time you speak of - when you were on the eve of sailing for America, you know - seen any other document in which your husband, as you call him, was described as 'Francis Adam?' No letter, envelope, or deed, for instance? Just try to recollect now."

"Never; I am quite sure that I never did," answered Lydia very positively.

"How were his letters generally addressed?"

"That I am unable to say. They never came to the house; they were always sent to the Old Factory."

"How did he sign his letters?"

"His letters to me were always signed 'Frank.' How those he sent to other people were signed I cannot tell you."

"So far as your knowledge goes, then, he always wrote himself as 'Frank,' and 'Frank' only?"

"Always."

"Very good." (Here the serjeant paused to take a pinch of snuff.) Now, will you kindly look at this paper, and tell me if this is not your signature?"

Here the serjeant showed her one of the transfers, the upper part of which, perhaps by accident, was doubled down. Lydia, who had probably forgotten having witnessed the signing of the transfer, and noticing only her own autograph, acknowledged without hesitation the signature to be hers.

"Yes," she said, "I believe that is my signature."

"And yet you say that at the time of your supposed marriage you were not aware that young Mr. Blackthorne had any other name but Frank?"

"No more I was."

"Wait until I have read the document to which your signature is appended, and then I will ask you again. It runs thus: 'I, Francis Adam Blackthorne, in consideration of the sum of five hundred pounds raid by Jabez Johnstone, hereinafter called the said transferee, do hereby bargain, sell, and assign to the said transferee ...... And the said transferee doth hereby agree to accept and take the said shares subject to the conditions aforesaid. As witness our hands this - day of -, one thousand eight hundred and forty --. Francis Adam Blackthorne. Signed, sealed, and delivered by the above-named Francis Adam Blackthorne, in the presence of Lydia Fell.'"

"What do you say now?" demanded the advocate sternly.

"I had forgotten all about those transfers - quite forgotten," replied Lydia hardily, albeit she was evidently a good deal disturbed.

"That is very probable, I think. But do you admit that at the time of your marriage you knew your husband's correct name? You see the date of this transfer precedes by a month the date of your marriage?"

"No, I do not."

"How! You witnessed his signature three times on the same day, and yet a month afterwards did not know Mr. Francis Blackthorne's name. Is that what you ask the court to believe?

"I did not read the transfers. I did not look at them. Frank said, 'Put your name down here, Lydia,' and I put my name down there."

"You shut your eyes while he signed, I suppose, and then put your name down as having witnessed what you had never seen?"

"I did not know what it was about. I had forgotten all about it," said Lydia doggedly.

"So you forgot what you never knew. Very remarkable, I must say. I have done with you now, Mrs. Freebody; you may step down."

On hearing herself thus addressed, Lydia gave a little scream and turned very pale.

"You seem surprised," continued the serjeant. "You were probably not aware that I had here the certificate of your marriage with Jeremiah Freebody, celebrated at Albany on - let me see - "

Here Serjeant Buster rose to protest. The document mentioned by Pumpemdry was not evidence. Reference to it was altogether irregular. He protested, too, against the share transfers being received as evidence. This led to a rather prolonged wrangle, the dispute being finally settled by the judge, who decided that the transfers were evidence, but that the marriage certificate was not.

On this Serjeant Pumpemdry announced that he was not going to call any more witnesses, and proceeded to address the jury. His speech was very short. He contended that his case was proved by Lydia Fell's evidence alone, whose name, he said, was neither Fell nor Blackthorne, but Freebody. If she knew that young Blackthorne's name was not Frank, but something else, then she was privy to a fraud, and her marriage with him was void. And that she did know was abundantly proved by the transfers; for it was an insult to the understanding of the jury to suppose that she could have witnessed the three signatures of Francis Adam Blackthorne

Page 308

without seeing them. In short, the plaintiff's case had completely broken down, and he asked with the fullest confidence their verdict for his client.

The judge summed up almost in the same sense. If the jury believed, he said, that at the time of the marriage the plaintiff knew that the man to whom she was being married was wrongly described in the licence - that, in fact, he was not Frank Blackthorne at all, but Francis Adam Blackthorne - they would find for the defendant on the main issue. If, on the other hand, they considered, in spite of her admission of the genuineness of her signature as witness to the transfers, she did not know his name was other than Frank, they would give their verdict for the plaintiff.

After a short consultation the jury returned a verdict for the defendant on all the issues.

"If you like," said Kean to Adam, as they walked together to the outer gate of the Castle, "we will have these Fells arrested and prosecuted for perjury; they richly deserve it. I rather fancy they are apprehensive of something of the sort, for I saw them slip quietly out of court just as Pumpemdry began his speech."

"Nay, I think we had better not," replied Adam pensively; it has not been a very creditable business to any of us, as far as I can see, and the sooner we let it drop the better. Let 'em go back to America. I don't suppose they'll ever trouble us again. They have had a lesson as they will not soon forget. And there's another I'd like to give a lesson to - that Serjeant Buster. Confound the fellow. If he ever comes near Moorwell I'll have him put in a sowlin (size) tub, wig and all."

"I don't think you are likely to catch him at Moorwell," said Kean, with a laugh. "He certainly was rather rough on you, hut it was all in the way of business, you know. I have no doubt he has forgotten all about it by this time."

"Happen; but I haven't, and I don't think I ever shall."

Just then they were joined by Basel. Before leaving the court-house he whispered to Frank that, if Kean saw no objection, he would break the news of his return to his father, and named a time for him to come to The King's Arms.

CHAPTER LV.

KILLING THE FATTED CALF.

Frank looked forward to seeing his father with considerable misgiving. He would much rather have first seen his mother, from whom he knew he might count on full forgiveness and a loving welcome. She would have smoothed the way for the interview. Her gentle influence might have mollified his father's anger, and been the means of sparing him the reproaches which, though he felt he had in a great measure deserved, he would have preferred to avoid.

But it was not now possible to defer the ordeal, and after stripping off his disguise, and making himself look as much like his old self as possible, he went to The King's Arms at the hour named by Basel. With a full heart he knocked at the door of the latter's room.

"Come in," said a well-known voice.

He obeyed the summons and entered the room. His father was there alone, standing near the fireplace and looking eagerly towards the door.

"Oh Frank, my lad," he exclaimed, as he came forward to meet him, "how ill you look!"

Then Frank knew that there was neither anger to mollify nor reproach to fear.

Adam put his arms round his son's neck and regarded him with a look in which sadness and satisfaction seemed to be struggling for the mastery. Frank perceived that his father's eyes were filled with tears. He had never in all his life before seen him so deeply moved.

"Can you forgive me, father?" he said, in a voice trembling with emotion.

"Forgive thee? I have not been thinking of that. Is it not enough that my son, as I thought was dead, is alive? If there is owt to forgive it is forgiven and forgotten from this moment, my lad. And now that we have got rid of Lydia Fell I'd forgive anything. But I don't understand rightly how it has all come about. Since Basel told me you were not dead I have been that dazed as I feel almost as if I were in a dream. Come and sit down here, close to me, and tell me all about it."

Then Frank told his story a second time.

"You asked me a while since," said Adam, after the narrative was concluded, and several questions had been asked and answered, "if I could forgive you. I suppose you mean for marrying Lydia Fell and going away after the fire, so as we all thought you were dead?"

"Yes; I was very foolish, and - "

"Well, if there were nothing else," the father went on, "it would be hard to refuse forgiveness to my own lad as had suffered so much and been twice at the point of death. But that is not all. I am not free from blame myself. As Basel has just been saying, I did wrong in throwing you and those Fells so much together. It's nothing but what I might have expected. And if that fellow Buster is right, I have a good deal more to answer for."

You must not mind what he said, father. He talked to suit his own purpose."

"But other folks will mind if I don't. And I am not quite sure as there is not just a hit of truth in what he said. I happen have been too hard, though I am sure I have meant no ill."

"I am sure you have not, father, and the less you think of what Sergeant Buster said the better. But you do not say anything about my mother. When do you think I. may see her?"

"Ay, poor Rachel; she will be right fain when she knows; so will Valérie. If you like we will go together to-morrow to Lytham and see them."

"If I like! Why, I would go to-night if it were possible."

"We could not well go to-night, and it would not he well if we could. We must contrive to warn them, or at any rate give them a hint beforehand, what to expect. Stay, I will drop a line to your mother by to-night's post."

So, pens and paper being on the table, a note was there and then written to Rachel. It was very short, and ran thus:

"We have won. I am coming to-morrow, and will give you all particulars. I shall bring SOMEBODY with me that you little expect. Prepare for a GREAT SURPRISE."

"There," observed Adam, as he folded the letter, "she will show it to Valérie, and as Valérie has always believed you would come back, and has half-persuaded your mother to believe so too, they will be partly prepared for your coming; but they will not be prepared for your sallow skin and yellow eyes."

At this moment Basel entered the room.

It is all right, Basel," said Adam cheerily; " we are going to Lytham to-morrow, Frank and me, and I have just written to Rachel to tell her to expect something extraordinary. We are not going by coach; we shall take a post-chaise - I have a good deal to talk over with Frank - and you can go with us as far as Preston, you know."

"Thank you, friend Blackthorne, it will give me much pleasure to have your company. By-the-bye, when do you propose to dine? I am beginning to feel very hungry."

"Soon; and what is more, we'll have a right good dinner - as good as the house can give us. If you will just touch that bell there, we'll have the head-waiter or the landlord up, and give the order."

The head-waiter was summoned accordingly, and Adam gave his instructions. The viands were to be of the very best, and the wines the finest and oldest The King's Arms could produce. An ancient and very crusty port of a famous vintage was ordered for the special benefit of Frank, who seemed to be greatly lacking in strength, and whose general appearance, as his father remarked, suggested a want of reddening up. Adam had a profound belief in the restorative qualities and medicinal virtues of port-wine, and during the dinner he plied his son so assiduously with the "old crusty" that Frank had much ado to keep sober.

At Basel's suggestion Kean was invited to dine with them, and altogether they had a very good time. The principal subject of conversation was, of course, the trial. The lawyer again expressed the opinion that, but for the production of the railway transfers, the Fells would have gained their case; and had not Frank returned, their next proceeding would have been to bring Mrs. Freebody's son from America, swear he was Frank's child, support the claim with forged documents, make him a ward in Chancery, and otherwise prepare the way for asserting his supposed rights under the Brandwood settlement.

"How would Mr. Freebody have gone on in that case?" asked Basel.

"Oh, Freebody would have been all right. Mr. Frank once dead, Lydia could of course marry again. They would have post-dated their marriage by a year; that's all."

"A risky game that, though."

"I suppose they thought it worth the candle. Anyhow, their first move came within an ace of succeeding; and to have won that would have been half the battle."

Before they separated for the night, every preparation was made for an early start the next morning.

Rachel, when she received her husband's note, acted precisely as he had anticipated. She showed it to Valérie.

"You know who it is," said the girl, as she looked at Rachel with flushed face and flashing eyes.

"You don't mean - it is impossible - it cannot be! And yet - and yet there is something that tells me. Oh Valérie? Can it be true - can my boy be alive?"

"It is Frank that is coming. I am sure it is. Mr. Blackthorne would never write in this way if it were not. He says he is bringing somebody with him, and we are to prepare for a great surprise. It is Frank. Frank is alive. Frank's coming. Who else could he bring that would give us a great surprise? For the arrival of what other person would he think it necessary to prepare us?"

"God grant that you are right! Oh that it may be true! But it is impossible. How can it be true!"

"How, I know not, but I am sure he is coming."

They passed the next few hours in a state of feverish suspense. They could neither eat nor rest, and their suspense was so great that they could hardly speak. They met the coach from Preston, and when they saw nobody alight from it whom they knew, they returned to their lodgings in bitter disappointment.

"They are perhaps posting," murmured Valérie. I will look out of the window."

As for Rachel, her excitement and emotion were so great that she was obliged to lie down on the sofa.

An hour later a carriage with four horses was drawn up at the door.

"They are come," said Valérie, rising from her chair.

"Frank?" gasped Rachel.

Valérie nodded; she was past speaking.

Then there were hurried footsteps on the stairs, the door opened, and the next moment Valérie was clasped in her lover's arms.

He led her to the sofa where his mother, utterly unable to rise, still reclined. He kissed her, and, taking both her hands in his, asked her the same question he had asked his father - if she could forgive him.

"Oh Frank," she exclaimed passionately, "why do you ask me such a question? Yes, a thousand times yes. I don't know why you went away. I don't know where you have been. I don't know what there is to forgive. But whatever it is, I forgive you, Frank, with all my heart. Am I not your mother? God has restored you to me. Is not that enough?"

"And to me," murmured Valérie. "Oh Frank, who stole you from me? Where have you been this long weary time? They all said you were dead; but I knew you were not; I knew you would come back to us. How thin you are, and how ill you look! How you must have suffered, my poor Frank!"

And then Frank had to tell his tale a third time. He was treading on delicate ground, for Valérie as yet knew nothing of Lydia Fell, and Lydia was the alpha and omega of the story - his connection with her the head and front of his offending. When a man is defending his own cause in the hearing of the woman he loves, he would be either more or less human were he not to do his utmost to put his conduct - if it should be open to two constructions - in the most favourable light. He touched as briefly as possible on his entanglement with the Fells, and his unfortunate marriage with Lydia. He allowed it to be inferred, rather than positively affirmed, that he was the innocent and unsuspecting victim of an odious plot; and so well did he plead his cause, that both Valérie and his mother firmly believed that he had been inveigled into marrying Lydia almost without knowing it, as people in olden times are said to have been unwittingly entrapped into unhallowed compacts with the enemy of mankind. When he related his escape from the fire, Valérie's excitement was intense, and Rachel trembled and turned deadly pale. When he told of his illness and sufferings at New Orleans, and how narrowly he escaped death a second time, they pitied him and wept; and when he had wound up his narrative with an account of the trial at Lancaster, it would have been hard to say which of the two women was the more vehement in her denunciations of the Fells, or showed the greater compassion for their victim.

"And you left England and crossed the Atlantic, and underwent all the troubles and hardships out of love for me, dear Frank," said Valérie softly.

"If I had known the truth I could have borne your absence better. But you were quite right. You did well not to tell me; for if I had known you were in the power of that wicked woman, that for anything you knew you were married to her, I do really believe I should have died or gone mad.

"That was it," rejoined Frank eagerly; "that was why I went away."

Happy as Rachel was, she sighed. It is hard for a mother to conceive that she has only a second place in a child's love. Frank had left her without a word, had allowed her to believe he had perished, in order to keep Valérie in ignorance of his marriage with Lydia Fell. It almost seemed as if to save his mistress a pang, he was ready to break his mother's heart. And yet Frank did not think himself an undutiful or unloving son, nor did she think him one. If she had consulted Basel on the subject, he would probably have told her that, as love is the most engrossing of passions, so lovers are the most selfish of mankind. As it was, she consoled herself with mentally repeating the text "For this cause shall a man leave his father and mother and cling to his wife, and they twain shall be one flesh," and remembering that Frank and Valérie, in preferring each other to all the world, even to their own mothers, were only doing what their fathers and mothers had done before them, and what their children would do after them.

When the excitement caused by Frank's appearance and the telling of his story had sufficiently subsided to admit of some attention being given to the more humdrum matters, Adam mentioned that he had pressing business at Moorwell, and must leave them early on the following morning; but Kean being of opinion that his son's return had better not be made generally known for a few days, it might be well for Frank to remain at Lytham a week or so before presenting himself at Brandwood.

As may be supposed, this proposal was warmly welcomed by Frank, and, as Rachel and Valérie were delighted with the idea of having him all to themselves for a while, the proposed arrangement gave general satisfaction. They stayed at Lytham until the end of the following week, and then all returned home together.

CHAPTER LVI.

AN UNEXPECTED DIFFICULTY.

"You may say what you like, Hermann; Frank Blackthorne has behaved very badly. I cannot pretend to forgive him, whatever you may do, and I will not give my consent to his marriage with Valérie. Did he not conceal his marriage with that Lydia Fell, and pay his court to Valérie, when, for aught he knew, he was that woman's husband? It is an insult to the whole family. You say he thought she was dead. I am not sure that he thought anything of the sort. A man who deceives his parents will deceive anybody. He is bad, thoroughly bad, that is my opinion, and no fit husband for a good girl like Valérie."

"You are altogether too uncharitable, my dear. I know that in some respects Frank has behaved very badly; nobody would admit it more freely than himself. But in some things he has acted well - nobly, one might say. A man who risks his life, as Frank did, to save a poor girl from a horrible death, cannot be wholly bad. And you should bear in mind that, when he had reason to suspect Lydia was still living, he did all he could - sacrificed himself one may say - in order to find out the truth. I have never said so before - and I know there are two ways of regarding any subject - but I look upon his going to America after the fire as positively heroic. He preferred to efface himself to abandon all rather than marry Valérie, so long as a doubt remained of his right to do so. If he had been the villain you make him out to be, he would have married her and said nothing; and bribed the Fells to say nothing."

"As you say," replied Mrs. Basel scornfully, "there are two ways of looking at his conduct. He ran away because he was afraid, that is my opinion; afraid of the truth being known. Why, when he had reason to believe that woman was still alive, did he not tell his father like a man, and go to America openly, and not sneak off like a coward?"

"You forget Valérie; it would have killed her."

"I doubt it. Girls are not so easily killed as some people think."

"At any rate the event proves him to have been right. It was well he did go. And before you blame him so severely, just think how young he was when that marriage took place - that he was simply victimised - more sinned against than sinning, any reasonable person would say."

"That means I am not a reasonable person, I suppose," said Mrs. Basel, with an angry toss of her head. "You can marry your daughter how you please, Hermann; you are the head of the family, you know. But I will not give my consent; I will not be present at the marriage; and if Frank Blackthorne comes here I will not speak to him."

This was not the first conversation of the sort that had taken place between Mr. and Mrs. Basel since the return of the former from Lancaster; and do all that he could he had not been able to persuade his wife to let bygones be bygones, receive Frank into favour, and sanction his engagement with Valérie. The fact was, albeit she took care not to avow it, that his reappearance had caused her a bitter disappointment. She wished him no ill, but being away she would have been glad had he remained away. Fritz was her favourite child, and it had been a great gratification to her to think that Fritz and Mabel would be the inheritors of Adam Blackthorne's wealth, and their firstborn the heir of Brandwood. Frank's return had frustrated these hopes, and she felt as much annoyed as if he had done her a personal injury. Another grievance was, that when Valérie and Frank married - if they did marry - her son and his wife would have to leave the house in Brandwood Park, where they were now comfortably settled.

Mrs. Basel carried out the resolution she had announced to her husband. When Frank called at the Châlet the day after his return from Lytham, and they met in the hall, she cut him dead. Greatly disconcerted at this unexpected reception, if reception it could be called, he turned to Valérie for an explanation. As she had shortly before had a long talk with her mother, in the course of which the latter had expressed her views about Frank with as little reserve as she had expressed them to her husband, Valerie had no difficulty in enlightening her lover as to the true state of the case, although, out of regard for his feelings, she spared him the most bitter of the bitter remarks Mrs. Basel had made about him.

"I am very sorry, Frank dear," said the girl apologetically. "I did all I could, and papa helped me, to persuade her to speak to you, if it were only a word. And that is not the worst. She has withdrawn her consent to our engagement, and says, if we are married, she will not be at the wedding. And she is my mother, you know. Oh Frank, I will never give you up; but I could not be married if mamma were not there. She has always been kind, you know - always until now - and papa thinks she will relent in a few days. She is never angry long. We can wait, and you can come as usual, Frank dear. If she does not speak to you for a short time - for a week or two - you will not mind much. I know it is hard. It is hard for me too; but you will bear it for my sake, won't you, darling?"

"I will bear anything for your sake, my own Valérie. Have you not borne a thousand times more for my sake? Yes, we will wait until she is less angry, and more just. It cannot be long."

Frank was mistaken. They had much longer to wait than they thought for. A month passed, and Mrs. Basel was just as resolute as ever not to recognise him, nor to sanction his marriage with her daughter. At the end of the second month it was just the same. The more her husband and Valérie tried to reconcile her, the more submissive Frank showed himself, the more she seemed to harden her heart. It was bad for them all. Valérie began to droop, Frank was wretched, Basel miserable. The latter, albeit far from being a weak man, was highly sensitive. He liked above all things to have peace at home. When, as sometimes happened, his wife showed temper, he would withdraw quietly to his room, and read and smoke quietly by himself until the storm was overpast. A divided household, such as his had been since Frank's return, was simply intolerable to him, and he almost wished at times that Frank had carried out his intention of remaining away altogether.

One evening about this time, when Frank presented himself at the Châlet, and Mrs. Basel, as she had latterly been wont to do, left the drawing-room by one door as he entered it by another, Basel drew him aside.

"I cannot stand this sort of thing any longer, Frank," he said. "I will make a change. We are going abroad for a few months."

"Going abroad!" replied Frank, greatly surprised. "What good will that do? And the winter is far from being over yet. You will not find it pleasant travelling, I am afraid."

"I don't care for that. At any rate it will be pleasanter than living in this way. And Mrs. Basel likes the Continent. The mere announcement of the intended trip will put her in a better humour. The bustle of travel, new scenes, and absence from home will give quite another turn to her thoughts. Our friends in France, with whom we shall spend a few weeks, will certainly not countenance her in this foolishness, and it may be well, too, to separate her for a while from Mabel."

"What on earth for? - what has Mabel done?"

"Oh blind young man, do you not see that by returning to life you have put Adam Blackthorne Basel's nose out of joint; and are you not aware that the little fellow is an immense favourite with his mother, and, if possible, a still greater one with his grandmother? And is it not more than probable that the two often talk the matter over, and are quite agreed that it is a very hard case for the deposed heir of Brandwood?"

"God bless me! and do you really think that Mrs. Basel's opposition arises from motives so unworthy? I certainly never looked at the matter in that light before; and yet, when I think of it, Mabel's manner is far from being what it used to be - less sisterly and more reserved; but I attributed the peculiarity to her marriage, and her absorption in her matronly duties."

The best of us is apt to be influenced by unworthy motives," replied Basel dryly, "often, too, without knowing it. There are unknown lights and shades in the character of everyone. We all develop as we grow older - either develop or deteriorate. You think Valérie an angel now. How do you know that in twenty years hence she may not be a shrew and you a henpecked husband or domestic tyrant?"

"Heaven forbid?" exclaimed Frank.

"Well, I do not think such a Consummation is likely," rejoined Basel, with a smile. "But everything is possible. If it be true that few people know themselves, how much fewer must those be who know what they will become? Talking of development, have you noticed how greatly your father has changed of late? He is not like the same man. Your disappearance and supposed death, and, above all, your so unexpected return, made a profound impression on him, and that speech of Serjeant Buster's, unjust and exaggerated as it was, opened his eyes as nothing else could have done."

"Yes, my father is much more genial and yielding than he used to be. Still, I think, if he were to come across the serjeant in a convenient place, it would be a bad job for the lawyer. You know, I suppose, how anxious my father is for Valérie and me to be married?"

"Yes, he was speaking to me about it the other day. But it cannot be just yet. You know what importance French-bred people attach to their parents' consent in these matters, and it would break Valérie's heart, I think, to be married without her mother's blessing. You must possess your soul in patience a little while longer, my boy. It will be all right in the end, you'll see. You and Valérie will correspond, of course, and so soon as Mrs. Basel is in a more placable mood I shall not fail to let you know."

"How long do you suppose you will be away?"

"That depends altogether on circumstances. Three or four months probably. I daresay we shall return in the spring or summer."

What could Frank say? The indefinite postponement of his marriage, and the prospect of a six months' separation from Valérie - for he foresaw that it might be so long - were far from pleasing to him; yet he had to remember that the trouble was of his own making, and that Mrs Basel, whatever might be her motives, was quite within her right in withholding her sanction from the engagement and in refusing to be present at the wedding. There was nothing for it but, as Basel said, to possess his soul in patience, and acquiesce as cheerfully in the proposed arrangement as he might. He accompanied the travellers to Manchester, and bade a sorrowful farewell to Valérie at the station; but Mrs. Basel, obdurate to the last, did not acknowledge his presence by so much as a glance.

CHAPTER LVII.

ON THE BANKS OF LAKE LEMAN.

After lingering awhile in Paris, whither they journeyed by easy stages, the Basels went on to the east of France, made there a stay of some weeks with Mrs. Basel's relatives, and then proceeded to Zurich, on a visit to her husband's kinsfolk. From Zurich they travelled by Thun, Interlaken, Lucerne, and Lausanne, to Geneva; and the spring being by this time well advanced, Mr. Basel took a villa on the bank of the lake, about two miles north of the city.

It was a delightful spot. The house was situated on the brow of a gentle acclivity. In front of it ran a long wide verandah, its red granite pillars festooned with trailing rose-trees and the climbing clematis. A flight of broad steps led to the garden, which sloped down to the water's edge. The walks were bordered with acacia trees; the vines were in full leaf, the fruit-trees bursting into bloom. The flower-beds were gay with the graceful anemone and the beautiful blue scilla. The miniature grass-plot was gemmed with violets, primroses, and marguerites. And under the shadow of a magnificent lilac tree, whose fragrance filled the air, a fountain sprang from a marble basin, in which water-lilies floated. The garden terminated in a vine-covered terrace, bounded by a low ivy-mantled wall. At one end of the terrace the branches of a gigantic chestnut tree in full bloom, stooping over the wall, kissed the blue waters of the lake; at the other rose a rustic bower, begirt with woodbine and eglantine.

In this bower, on an evening in May, sat Valérie Basel. Not a zephyr ruffled the emerald surface of the lake. The gentle hills of Faucigny were bright with verdure, while far away to the south-east towered the dazzling summits of the Pennine Alps. A veil of fleecy cloud hung about the flanks of Mont Blanc, but the imposing mass of the Col du Dromédaire, white with the gathered winter of a thousand years, loomed large in the darkening sky. As the sun sank behind the forest - crowned and empurpled Jura the mountain-top grew blood-red, the fleecy clouds became suffused with crimson, and the rocky gorges and rugged peaks of the Valley of Sixt glowed as if lit up by volcanic fires. Then, as the sun went lower, the erst-while rose-tinted snows took the hue of death, Mont Blanc showed huge and pallid like a shrouded giant on his bier, the ruddy glare of the rocks faded into utter gloom, and night hid the scene from view.

A few minutes later a red streak appeared in the sky over the Môle, and a crescent moon, floating from behind the mountain, cast her yellow beams across the lake, and bathed in golden light the bower in which Valérie, with clasped hands and uplifted head, sat like one entranced.

"Oh," she murmured, "how beautiful God has made everything in this glorious land! How I wish Frank were here to enjoy it with me!"

"Valérie," exclaimed a voice, as if in answer to her thought, and turning her head she saw a shadowy form at the entrance of the bower.

"It is - no, it cannot be - yes, it is - it is - it is - "

"Yes, Valérie, it is I - Frank," said her lover softly, as he folded her in his arms.

"But where have you sprung from - how have you come? I heard nothing. How strange that you should appear just when I was thinking about you, and wishing so much you were with me."

"I came in answer to your thoughts. You wished to see me, and I appeared."

"Ah, Frank, if you were always where I wished you to be you would never be away from me. But tell me the sober truth - how did you come?"

"From Moorwell I have come by railroad and steamship. I arrived at Geneva a little more than an hour ago, and have come hither in a small boat. As the moon lit up the bower I saw in it a form I thought I knew. When I heard the sweetest voice in all the world murmur my name my surmise became a certainty, and I uttered aloud the word which is ever present in my thoughts, and which I do not forget even in my dreams - Valérie."

"Dear Frank!" said the girl softly, as she laid her head on his shoulder and looked lovingly into his eyes. "But why, when you last wrote, did you not tell me you were coming?"

"Because, until six days ago, I had no idea of coming, and I left so suddenly, and have travelled so swiftly, that I must have outstripped the post by at least twelve hours. I had a letter from your father. Did he not tell you?"

"No; what was it about?"

"Then he wanted to surprise you. He left it to me - dear good man that he is! - to tell you the news - to tell you that your mother has received me once more into favour, agreed to sanction our engagement, and be present at our marriage. In two hours after I received that letter I was on my way to Geneva."

"I thought so. I thought mamma was relenting. She has been so much kinder lately - so much more like her old self. But she never mentioned your name, neither did we; papa and I had agreed that we would not. He thought it was the best way of bringing her round, as he said. How good it was of you, Frank, to come so soon, and how very very tired you must be!"

Frank declared he was never less tired in his life, and proved the truth of his assertion in a most lover-like fashion.

"Listen!" exclaimed Valérie, as she disengaged herself from her lover's embrace, "that is the supper-bell. Let us go up to the house before I am missed and sought for."

As they approached the house, Frank perceived under the verandah a table covered with crystal and silver, in the midst of which stood several bottles of elegant shape and refreshing aspect. At this table were seated Mr. and Mrs. Basel.

"Frank Blackthorne! Frank Blackthorne!" shouted the former, as soon as he caught sight of him. "Where have you sprung from? I quite expected you to answer my letter in person, but I did not expect you quite so soon. You must have travelled night and day."

"I have," answered Frank, as his friend rose to greet him. "I don't think the journey from Manchester to Geneva was ever before done in so short a time."

Then Mrs. Basel came forward, just as if there had never been any estrangement between them, offered her cheek for the young man's salute, in the manner of her country, inquired after his father and mother, and asked him to make their house his home during his stay at Geneva.

"Sit down and have some supper, my boy," said Basel. "I am sure you will want it. We live quite in the Swiss fashion, you see - dinner in the middle of the day, bagging - they call it *goûter* here - at five, and supper at nine - and not a bad fashion either. What wine will you take? If you take my advice you will try this Yvorne. Perhaps it will taste better if Valérie pours it out for you."

"If she tastes it first it will," answered Frank gallantly. Whereupon Valérie, with a happy smile and a deep blush, after pouring out a glass of the limpid Yvorne, touched it with her lips and handed it to Frank.

They sat over the supper so long, that when it came to an end the ladies declared it was time to retire, and Frank, accepting the hint, rose to take his leave.

"Go!" exclaimed Basel. "*Donner Wetter!* you will do nothing of the sort. You will stay here all night. We can find him a bed, can we not, mamma?"

"Certainly," replied Mrs. Basel; "it shall be prepared at once."

"But my things are at the hotel," said Frank.

"Never mind your things. I can find you what you want. We can send for them in the morning. Besides, the gates are shut by this time, and you could not go to your hotel if you would. Come, let us have a smoke and a talk while your bed is being got ready."

"I told you," he continued, as he produced two enormous porcelain pipes, one of which he handed to Frank, "I told you I would win her over. The very moment she breathed the air of France she began to relent. I could read it in her eye, see it in her manner. But I took no notice. She talked the matter over with some of her friends in Elsass, and I can assure you she got no encouragement from them. The only thing I did was to suggest the other day that, as your father was so anxious for you to be settled, it might be politic, in the interests of Fritz's family, not to throw any impediment in the way. She took the hint, said she did not want to throw any impediment in the way - never had done, in fact - and, so far as she was concerned, the sooner you and Valérie were made one the better she would be pleased. This was certainly rather startling, but I did not deem it expedient to make any remark. The meaning of it all I take to be, that she does not want to have the subject discussed."

"And I am sure I do not care to discuss the subject. I am quite satisfied with the result. Now, don't you think, Mr. Basel, seeing that Mrs. Basel is in so amiable a humour, and we have had to wait so long, that we might be married here?"

"God bless me, Frank, that would be very sudden, would it not? What would your father say?"

"My father suggested it just as I was coming away. He said he would like much to be present at my wedding if it were possible. But in the circumstances, considering what a sensation the trial made, and how often we have figured in the papers lately, it would be well if we could be married quietly here at Geneva."

"Well, there is sense in that," said Basel reflectively, as he relit his pipe, which, in his surprise, he had allowed to go out. "And I really do not see why it should not be as you wish. If my wife does not object I shall not. You will probably not find it very difficult to persuade Valérie. But I am by no means sure that she will consent; women always want so much time for preparation, you know, and some of them would rather have no wedding at all than a quiet one."

This anticipation was so far realised that Mrs. Basel, when the matter was first mooted to her, declared that she could not possibly think of letting her daughter be married without a proper trousseau. But after a little reflection it occurred to her that Valérie's trousseau had been partly prepared before Frank's supposed death, and when her husband suggested that what was lacking could be purchased at London or Paris as they went back, and that it would be ready on the return home of the bride and bridegroom, whose arrival theirs would precede, she thought the difficulty might, perhaps, be overcome in that way, and finally gave her consent.

As for Valérie, Frank did not find the task of procuring her assent to his proposal a very onerous one. She would rather be married in England, she said; but as Frank wished the ceremony to take place where they were, and her father and mother were willing, she was willing too. Within a month of his appearance at Geneva they were married, and so quietly that the event was hardly known to anyone but the chaplain and the consul, and to those concerned.

After their marriage, Frank and Valérie went up the Valley of the Rhone, crossed the Simplon, and spent their honeymoon on the shores of Maggiore and Como; while Mr. and Mrs. Basel returned to England by the shortest route, in order to prepare for the arrival of the newly-wedded pair.

CHAPTER LVIII

GRATITUDE AND HOPE

A few weeks later five of the principal characters of our story (Adam Blackthorne and Rachel, Valérie and Frank and Valérie's father) were assembled in the morning room at Brandwood. The bride and bridegroom had returned the day before, and, pending the completion of the house which was being prepared for Fritz and Mabel, were staying at the Hall.

"And now, my lad," Adam was saying, as he laid his hand on his son's shoulder, "you will have to buckle to. I have had all the weight of the business and the property on my back long enough, and now I want you to take your share of the burden. I don't feel quite as young as I once did."

"I know, father, I know. It was too bad of me to leave you in the lurch. You have been sorely tried, and it is my duty to make all the amends in my power. I am ready and willing, not only to take a share of the burden, as you say, but to relieve you entirely - to take all care and work off your hands."

"Softly, lad, softly. The lion's share you may have, and welcome, but not all. As long as I am sound in wind, limb, and eyesight, I don't mean to be idle. Too much work is better than none. I would liefer wear than rust. And now there is another thing I have to say. I have learnt a lesson or two lately. All here know, I think, that I settled Brandwood on Frank and his heirs, and you know how near it went to being somebody's as was neither his heir nor mine. I don't suppose such a thing is likely to occur again; but, all the same, I have made up my mind to undo this settlement. I never looked at it in that light before; yet, when you come to think closely, it is about as stupid a thing as a man could well do to leave a large property, the possession of which carries with it serious responsibilities, to one as is unborn. Who can tell how the unborn will turn out -whether he will not be a wastrel, and so utterly unworthy of the trust? Why should I make my grand-son or my great-grandson, that I have never seen and cannot know, better off than my own son? It would be a fine thing if Brandwood could belong to our children and our children's children to the third and fourth generation, and even longer, and I hope it may be so; but if they cannot keep it by their own virtues and their own strength - cannot hold what I have won - let it go to somebody as can. That is the conclusion I have come to. All the same, I shall leave Brandwood to Frank, and ask him in my will, as I ask him now, to leave it in turn, not to his eldest or his youngest, or any other son, but to the worthiest and most able of them. If he does that, the family will last, and what is more, it will deserve to last. Another thing as I have been thinking - and I have had several talks with Basel about it since he came back - is that we should do a bit of something for them as has helped us to rise in the world - the hands, I mean. Frank here shall have his fling at building some new cottages fit for folks to live in. There is not a decent school in the neighbourhood. We will build one, and get a good teacher. Only one thing, no parson shall have owt to do with it, and then we shall happen keep clear of bother. There is talk of a new church at Moorwell, and as a good many of our hands are churchfolks, and there is no church nearer than Orrington, I have promised to give land, find stones and timber, and be a thousand pounds towards the endowment fund. That is all, I think, at present. No, there is one thing more. I am going to create a special fund for the support of old hands as have served us long and faithfully and are past work, such as Tommy Twirler and Yorkshire Joe."

"Oh Adam," said Rachel, taking her husband's band in both hers, "how thankful I am to hear you say so! I don't think I have felt so glad since the time you took me home to Walloper Hillock, thirty years since."

"It is worth more than all it will cost to hear you say that, Rachel," replied Adam, with a look that reminded her of days long gone by. "And now I am going to ask Valérie to do us a favour - the concern, I mean - Adam Blackthorne and Son, you know."

"I shall be delighted, father. There is nothing in the world - nothing in my power - that I would not do for Adam Blackthorne and Son."

"Particularly for the junior partner, I suppose," answered Adam, with a smile. "I am not going to call on you to do anything very great. It is only to christen our new engines - a pair of sixties."   -

"What, those in the new factory?"

"Yes; they should start next week. But I don't mean to call it a new factory. I have had some of the stones of the old one built into it."

"So it is rather a continuation than a fresh edition," suggested Basel.

"Exactly; that is it. It is new, and yet old."

"What names have you decided to give the engines?" asked Rachel.

"I have decided nothing. I want to know what you think."

"Suppose we call one after my mother, the other Valérie," said Frank.

"Nay, I was not thinking of giving them folk's names. I want something – something - "

"Emblematic?"

"Yes, that's it; something emblematic."

"How would Industry and Perseverance do?" suggested Frank.

"Not so well, I think. It would look too much like self-praise, that would. Come now, Rachel. Rachel shall suggest a name for one, Valérie for the other. You first Rachel - what 'shall it be?"

"I say Gratitude," replied Rachel, in answer to this appeal.

"And I, Hope," said Valérie.

"So let it be, then," said Adam. "Grateful and hopeful we may all be; yet gratitude seems better suited to a generation that is passing away, hope more befitting those who are following in our footsteps, and with whom the real business of life is only just beginning. Is it not so, Basel?"

"It is so, friend Blackthorne. Yet would I rather say, let the two be linked together; and as you, by building a new mill with stones taken from that which served you so well, and without which we should never have been partners nor our families united, have shown your respect for the Old Factory, so let our children, while full of faith in the future, never fail in reverence for the past. And they will best manifest their gratitude, both in the sense which is doubtless meant by Mrs. Blackthorne and to those whose labours have made life easier and brighter for them, by continuing and improving the work they have begun, by striving to leave the world better than they found it, and a happier abode for the generations to come.

THE END.